THE MAMMOTH BOOK OF

Fantasy

THE MAMMOTH BOOK OF

Fantasy

Edited by Mike Ashley

CARROLL & GRAF PUBLISHERS
New York

Carroll & Graf Publishers
An imprint of Avalon Publishing Group, Inc.
161 William Street
16th Floor
New York
NY 10038–2607
www.carrollandgraf.com

First published in the UK by Robinson,
an imprint of Constable & Robinson Ltd 2001

First Carroll & Graf edition 2001

Reprinted 2001

Collection and editorial material
copyright © Mike Ashley 2001

ISBN 0–7867–0917–0

Printed and bound in the EU

Contents

Copyright and Acknowledgments

Introduction: A Voyage of Wonder

There are those who think that fantasy fiction first appeared with J. R. R. Tolkien and *Lord of the Rings*, and that's the only type of fantasy there is. Others think it all began with Terry Pratchett's Discworld novels, and I suspect yet others may think there was nothing before J. K. Rowling's brilliant Harry Potter books.

I know when I first discovered the wonders of fantasy fiction (and this was with a retelling of the Greek legends, so I'm going back a while) I searched around for anything else like it. At that time it was not easy to find anything. So much of the older material had gone out of print and we had not yet entered the boom period that came with the paperback publication of *Lord of the Rings* in the mid-sixties.

Then I discovered the magazines, especially *Fantastic* and *Science Fantasy*, and these opened up whole new worlds to me. Suddenly I discovered Michael Moorcock and Robert E. Howard and Roger Zelazny and Mervyn Peake and plenty more.

I also began to appreciate just what a huge world fantasy fiction was. It wasn't just retellings of myths, or adventure stories set in magical worlds, or stories of goblins and elves. It covered almost everything where something unusual happens, something magical, something that makes you realize that the world is rather more special than you thought.

In a fantasy world anything can happen – *anything*. But a good fantasy story doesn't rely on the extreme. It takes you from the ordinary to the extra-ordinary and en route it opens your mind, stimulates your imagination and awakens your senses of awe and wonder. That's what I want this anthology to do. To take you on a voyage of wonder. And to do that I've selected stories that show the range and development of fantasy fiction and how much more there is to it than simply Tolkien, Pratchett or Rowling, no matter how wonderful they all are.

Mike Ashley

𝕿𝖍𝖊 𝖂𝖆𝖑𝖑 𝕬𝖗𝖔𝖚𝖓𝖉 𝖙𝖍𝖊 𝖂𝖔𝖗𝖑𝖉

Theodore R. Cogswell

When I read the first of the Harry Potter books parts of it reminded me of the following story. I doubt that J. K. Rowling has read this story, so I can't imagine it served as any inspiration, but it goes to show how great minds think alike. Except that in the case of Ted Cogswell it was fifty years ago. Cogswell (1918–87) was an American author and academic, who was refreshingly challenging. His fiction, of which there is all too little, was always original, clever and ingenious. His best work will be found in the story collections The Wall Around the World *(1962) and* The Third Eye *(1968).*

THE WALL THAT WENT ALL THE WAY AROUND the world had always been there, so nobody paid much attention to it – except Porgie.

Porgie was going to find out what was on the other side of it – assuming there was another side – or break his neck trying. He was going on fourteen, an age that tends to view the word *impossible* as a meaningless term invented by adults for their own peculiar purposes. But he recognized that there were certain practical difficulties involved in scaling a glassy-smooth surface that rose over 1,000 feet straight up. That's why he spent a lot of time watching the eagles.

This morning, as usual, he was late for school. He lost time finding a spot for his broomstick in the crowded rack in the school yard, and it was exactly six minutes after the hour as he slipped guiltily into the classroom.

For a moment, he thought he was safe. Old Mr Wickens had his back to him and was chalking a pentagram on the blackboard.

But just as Porgie started to slide into his seat, the schoolmaster turned and drawled, "I see Mr Mills has finally decided to join us."

The class laughed, and Porgie flushed.

"What's your excuse this time, Mr Mills?"

"I was watching an eagle," said Porgie lamely.

"How nice for the eagle. And what was he doing that was of such great interest?"

"He was riding up on the wind. His wings weren't flapping or anything. He was over the box canyon that runs into the east wall, where the wind hits the wall and goes up. The eagle just floated in circles, going higher all the time. You know, Mr Wickens, I'll bet if you caught a whole bunch of eagles and tied ropes to them, they could lift you right up to the top of the wall!"

"That," said Mr Wickens, "is possible – if you could catch the eagles. Now, if you'll excuse me, I'll continue with the lecture. When invoking Elementals of the Fifth Order, care must be taken to . . ."

Porgie glazed his eyes and began to think up ways and means to catch some eagles.

The next period, Mr Wickens gave them a problem in Practical Astrology. Porgie chewed his pencil and tried to work on it, but couldn't concentrate. Nothing came out right – and when he found he had accidentally transposed a couple of signs of the zodiac at the very beginning, he gave up and began to draw plans for eagle traps. He tried one, decided it wouldn't work, started another—

"Porgie!"

He jumped. Mr Wickens, instead of being in front of the class, was standing right beside him. The schoolmaster reached down, picked up the paper Porgie had been drawing on, and looked at it. Then he grabbed Porgie by the arm and jerked him from his seat.

"Go to my study!"

As Porgie went out the door, he heard Mr Wickens say, "The class is dismissed until I return!"

There was a sudden rush of large-, medium-, and small-sized boys out of the classroom. Down the corridor to the front door they pelted, and out into the bright sunshine. As they ran past Porgie, his cousin Homer skidded to a stop and accidentally on purpose jabbed an elbow into his ribs. Homer, usually called "Bull Pup" by the kids because of his squat build and pugnacious face, was a year older than Porgie and took his seniority seriously.

"Wait'll I tell Dad about this. You'll catch it tonight!" He gave Porgie another jab and then ran out into the schoolyard to take command of a game of Warlock.

Mr Wickens unlocked the door to his study and motioned Porgie inside. Then he shut and locked it carefully behind him. He sat down in the high-backed chair behind his desk and folded his hands.

Porgie stood silently, hanging his head, filled with that helpless guilty anger that comes from conflict with superior authority.

"What were you doing instead of your lesson?" Mr Wickens demanded.

Porgie didn't answer.

Mr Wickens narrowed his eyes. The large hazel switch that rested on top of the bookcase beside the stuffed owl lifted lightly into the air, drifted across the room, and dropped into his hand.

"Well?" he said, tapping the switch on the desk.

"Eagle traps," admitted Porgie. "I was drawing eagle traps. I couldn't help it. The wall made me do it."

"Proceed."

Porgie hesitated for a moment. The switch tapped. Porgie burst out, "I want to see what's on the other side! There's no magic that will get me over, so I've got to find something else!"

Tap, went the switch. "Something else?"

"If a magic way was in the old books, somebody would have found it already!"

Mr Wickens rose to his feet and stabbed one bony finger accusingly at Porgie. "Doubt is the mother of damnation!"

Porgie dropped his eyes to the floor and wished he was somewhere else.

"I see doubt in you. Doubt is evil, Porgie, *evil*! There are ways permitted to men and ways forbidden. You stand on the brink of the fatal choice. Beware that the Black Man does not come for you as he did for your father before you. Now, bend over!"

Porgie bent. He wished he'd worn a heavier pair of pants.

"Are you ready?"

"Yes, sir," said Porgie sadly.

Mr Wickens raised the switch over his head. Porgie waited. The switch slammed – but on the desk.

"Straighten up," Mr Wickens said wearily. He sat down again. "I've tried pounding things into your head, and I've tried pounding things on your bottom, and one end is as insensitive as the other. Porgie, can't you understand that you aren't supposed to try and find out new things? The Books contain everything there is to know. Year by year, what is written in them becomes clearer to us."

He pointed out the window at the distant towering face of the wall that went around the world. "Don't worry about what is on the other side of that! It may be a place of angels or a place of demons – the Books do not tell us. But no man will know until he is ready for that knowledge. Our broomsticks won't climb that high, our charms aren't strong enough. We need more skill at magic, more understanding of the strange unseen forces that surround us. In my grandfather's time, the best of the broomsticks wouldn't climb over 100 feet in the air. But Adepts in the Great Tower worked and worked until now, when the clouds are low, we can ride right up among them. Some day we will be able to soar all the way to the top of the wall—"

"Why not now?" Porgie asked stubbornly. "With eagles."

"Because we're not *ready*," Mr Wickens snapped. "Look at mind-talk. It was only thirty years ago that the proper incantations were worked out, and even now there are only a few who have the skill to talk across the miles by just thinking out their words. Time, Porgie – it's going to take time. We were placed here to learn the Way, and everything that might divert us from the search is evil. Man can't walk two roads at once. If he tries, he'll split himself in half.''

"Maybe so," said Porgie. "But birds get over the wall, and they don't know any spells. Look, Mr Wickens, if everything is magic, how come magic won't work on everything? Like this, for instance—"

He took a shiny quartz pebble out of his pocket and laid it on the desk.

Nudging it with his finger, he said:

> Stone fly,
> Rise on high,
> Over cloud
> And into sky.

The stone didn't move.

"You see, sir? If words work on broomsticks, they should work on stones, too."

Mr Wickens stared at the stone. Suddenly it quivered and jumped into the air.

"That's different," said Porgie. "You took hold of it with your mind. Anybody can do that with little things. What I want to know is why the words won't work by themselves."

"We just don't know enough yet," said Mr Wickens impatiently. He released the stone and it clicked on the desktop. "Every year we learn a little more. Maybe by your children's time we'll find the incantation that will make everything lift." He sniffed. "What do you want to make stones fly for, anyhow? You get into enough trouble just throwing them."

Porgie's brow furrowed. "There's a difference between *making* a thing do something, like when I lift it with my hand or mind, and putting a spell on it so it does the work by itself, like a broomstick."

There was a long silence in the study as each thought his own thoughts.

Finally Mr Wickens said, "I don't want to bring up the unpleasant past, Porgie, but it would be well to remember what happened to your father. His doubts came later than yours – for a while he was my most promising student – but they were just as strong."

He opened a desk drawer, fumbled in it for a moment, and brought out a sheaf of papers yellow with age. "This is the paper that damned him: 'An Enquiry into Non-Magical Methods of Levitation'. He wrote it to qualify for his Junior Adeptship." He threw the paper down in front of Porgie as if the touch of it defiled his fingers.

Porgie started to pick it up.

Mr Wickens roared, "Don't touch it! It contains blasphemy!"

Porgie snatched back his hand. He looked at the top paper and saw a neat sketch of something that looked like a bird – except that it had two sets of wings, one in front and one in back.

Mr Wickens put the papers back in the desk drawer. His disapproving eyes caught and held Porgie's as he said, "If you want to go the way of your father, none of *us* can stop you." His voice rose sternly, "But there is one who can . . . Remember the Black Man, Porgie, for his walk is terrible! There are fires in his eyes and no spell may defend you against him. When he came for your father, there was darkness at noon and a high screaming. When the sunlight came back, they were gone – and it is not good to think where."

Mr Wickens shook his head as if overcome at the memory and pointed towards the door. "Think before you act, Porgie. Think well!"

Porgie was thinking as he left, but more about the sketch in his father's paper than about the Black Man.

The orange crate with the two boards across it for wings had looked something like his father's drawing, but appearances had been deceiving. Porgie sat on the back steps of his house feeling sorry for himself and alternately rubbing two tender spots on his anatomy. Though they were at opposite ends, and had different immediate causes, they both grew out of the same thing. His bottom was sore as a result of a liberal application of his uncle's hand. His swollen nose came from an aerial crack-up.

He'd hoisted his laboriously contrived machine to the top of the woodshed and taken a flying leap in it. The expected soaring glide hadn't materialized. Instead, there had been a sickening fall, a splintering crash, a momentary whirling of stars as his nose banged into something hard.

He wished now he hadn't invited Bull Pup to witness his triumph, because the story'd got right back to his uncle – with the usual results.

Just to be sure the lesson was pounded home, his uncle had taken away his broomstick for a week – and just so Porgie wouldn't sneak out, he'd put a spell on it before locking it away in the closet.

"Didn't feel like flying, anyway," Porgie said sulkily to himself, but the pretence wasn't strong enough to cover up the loss. The gang was going over to Red Rocks to chase bats as soon as the sun went down, and he wanted to go along.

He shaded his eyes and looked towards the western wall as he heard a distant halloo of laughing voices. They were coming in high and fast on their broomsticks. He went back to the woodshed so they wouldn't see him. He was glad he had when they swung low and began to circle the house yelling for him and Bull Pup. They kept hooting and shouting until Homer flew out of his bedroom window to join them.

"Porgie can't come," he yelled. "He got licked and Dad took his broom away from him. Come on, gang!"

With a quick looping climb, he took the lead and they went hedge-hopping off towards Red Rocks. Bull Pup had been top dog ever since he got his big stick. He'd zoom up to 500 feet, hang from his broom by his knees and then let go. Down he'd plummet, his arms spread and body arched as if he were making a swan dive – and then, when the ground wasn't more than 100 feet away, he'd call and his broomstick would arrow down after him and slide between his legs, lifting him up in a great sweeping arc that barely cleared the treetops.

"Show-off!" muttered Porgie and shut the woodshed door on the vanishing stick-riders.

Over on the workbench sat the little model of paper and sticks that had got him into trouble in the first place. He picked it up and gave it a quick shove into the air with his hands. It dived towards the floor and then, as it picked up speed, tilted its nose towards the ceiling and made a graceful loop in the air. Levelling off, it made a sudden veer to the left and crashed against the woodshed wall. A wing splintered.

Porgie went to pick it up. Maybe what works for little things doesn't work for big ones, he thought sourly. The orange crate and the crossed boards had been as close an approximation of the model as he had been able to make. Listlessly, he put the broken glider back on his workbench and went outside. Maybe Mr Wickens and his uncle and all the rest were right. Maybe there was only one road to follow.

He did a little thinking about it and came to a conclusion that brought forth a secret grin. He'd do it their way – but there wasn't any reason why he couldn't hurry things up a bit. Waiting for his grandchildren to work things out wasn't getting *him* over the wall.

Tomorrow, after school, he'd start working on his new idea, and this time maybe he'd find the way.

In the kitchen, his uncle and aunt were arguing about him. Porgie paused in the hall that led to the front room and listened.

"Do you think I like to lick the kid? I'm not some kind of an ogre. It hurt me more than it hurt him."

"I notice you were able to sit down afterwards," said Aunt Olga dryly.

"Well, what else could I do? Mr Wickens didn't come right out and say so, but he hinted that if Porgie didn't stop mooning around, he might be dropped from school altogether. He's having an unsettling effect on the other kids. Damn it, Olga, I've done everything for that boy I've done for my own son. What do you want me to do, stand back and let him end up like your brother?"

"You leave my brother out of this! No matter what Porgie does, you don't have to beat him. He's still only a little boy."

There was a loud snort. "In case you've forgotten, dear, he had his thirteenth birthday last March. He'll be a man pretty soon."

"Then why don't you have a man-to-man talk with him?"

"Haven't I tried? You know what happens every time. He gets off with those crazy questions and ideas of his and I lose my temper and pretty soon we're back where we started." He threw up his hands. "I don't know what to do with him. Maybe that fall he had this afternoon will do some good. I think he had a scare thrown into him that he won't forget for a long time. Where's Bull Pup?"

"Can't you call him Homer? It's bad enough having his friends call him by that horrible name. He went out to Red Rocks with the other kids. They're having a bat hunt or something."

Porgie's uncle grunted and got up. "I don't see why that kid can't stay at home at night for a change. I'm going in the front room and read the paper."

Porgie was already there, flipping the pages of his schoolbooks and looking studious. His uncle settled down in his easy chair, opened his paper, and lit his pipe. He reached out to put the charred match in the ashtray, and as usual the ashtray wasn't there.

"Damn that woman," he muttered to himself and raised his voice: "Porgie."

"Yes, Uncle Veryl?"

"Bring me an ashtray from the kitchen, will you please? Your aunt has them all out there again."

"Sure thing," said Porgie and shut his eyes. He thought of the kitchen until a picture of it was crystal-clear in his mind. The beaten copper ashtray was sitting beside the sink where his aunt had left it after she had washed it out. He squinted the little eye inside his head, stared hard at the copper bowl, and whispered:

Ashtray fly,
Follow eye.

Simultaneously he lifted with his mind. The ashtray quivered and rose slowly into the air.

Keeping it firmly suspended, Porgie quickly visualized the kitchen door and the hallway and drifted it through.

"Porgie!" came his uncle's angry voice.

Porgie jumped, and there was a crash in the hallway outside as the bowl was suddenly released and crashed to the floor.

"How many times have I told you not to levitate around the house? If it's too much work to go out to the kitchen, tell me and I'll do it myself."

"I was just practising," mumbled Porgie defensively.

"Well, practise outside. You've got the walls all scratched up from banging things against them. You know you shouldn't fool around with telekinesis outside sight range until you've mastered full visualization. Now go and get me that ashtray."

Crestfallen, Porgie went out the door into the hall. When he saw where the ashtray had fallen, he gave a silent whistle. Instead of coming down the centre of the hall, it had been 3 feet off course and heading directly for the hall table when he let it fall. In another second, it would have smashed into his aunt's precious black alabaster vase.

"Here it is, Uncle," he said, taking it into the front room. "I'm sorry."

His uncle looked at his unhappy face, sighed and reached out and tousled his head affectionately.

"Buck up, Porgie. I'm sorry I had to paddle you this afternoon. It was for your own good. Your aunt and I don't want you to get into any serious trouble. You know what folks think about machines." He screwed up his face as if he'd said a dirty word. "Now, back to your books – we'll forget all about what happened today. Just remember this, Porgie: if there's anything you want to know, don't go fooling around on your own. Come and ask me, and we'll have a man-to-man talk."

Porgie brightened. "There's something I have been wondering about."

"Yes?" said his uncle encouragingly.

"How many eagles would it take to lift a fellow high enough to see what was on the other side of the wall?"

Uncle Veryl counted to ten – very slowly.

The next day Porgie went to work on his new project. As soon as school was out, he went over to the public library and climbed upstairs to the main circulation room.

"Little boys are not allowed in this section," the librarian said. "The children's division is downstairs."

"But I need a book," protested Porgie. "A book on how to fly."

"This section is only for adults."

Porgie did some fast thinking. "My uncle can take books from here, can't he?"

"I suppose so."

"And he could send me over to get something for him, couldn't he?"

The librarian nodded reluctantly.

Porgie prided himself on never lying. If the librarian chose to misconstrue his questions, it was her fault, not his.

"Well, then," he said, "do you have any books on how to make things fly in the air?"

"What kind of things?"

"Things like birds."

"Birds don't have to be made to fly. They're born that way."

"I don't mean real birds," said Porgie. "I mean birds you make."

"Oh, Animation. Just a second, let me visualize." She shut her eyes and a card catalogue across the room opened and shut one drawer after another. "Ah, that might be what he's looking for," she murmured after a moment, and concentrated again. A large brass-bound book came flying out of the stacks and came to rest on the desk in front of her. She pulled the index card out of the pocket in the back and shoved it towards Porgie. "Sign your uncle's name here."

He did and then, hugging the book to his chest, got out of the library as quickly as he could.

By the time Porgie had worked three-quarters of the way through the book, he was about ready to give up in despair. It was all grown-up magic. Each set of instructions he ran into either used words he didn't understand or called for unobtainable ingredients like powdered unicorn horns and the blood of red-headed female virgins.

He didn't know what a virgin was – all his uncle's encyclopedia had to say on the subject was that they were the only ones who could ride unicorns – but there was a redhead by the name of Dorothy Boggs who lived down the road a piece. He had a feeling, however, that neither she nor her family would take kindly to a request for 2 quarts of blood, so he kept on searching through the book. Almost at the very end he found a set of instructions he thought he could follow.

It took him two days to get the ingredients together. The only thing that gave him trouble was finding a toad; the rest of the stuff, though mostly nasty and odoriferous, was obtained with little difficulty. The date and exact time of the experiment was important and he surprised Mr Wickens by taking a sudden interest in his Practical Astrology course.

At last, after laborious computations, he decided everything was ready.

Late that night, he slipped out of bed, opened his bedroom door a crack, and listened. Except for the usual night noises and resonant snores from Uncle Veryl's room, the house was silent. He shut the door carefully and got his broomstick from the closet – Uncle Veryl had relented about that week's punishment.

Silently he drifted out through his open window and across the yard to the woodshed.

Once inside, he checked carefully to see that all the windows were covered. Then he lit a candle. He pulled a loose floorboard up and removed the book and his assembled ingredients. Quickly, he made the initial preparations.

First there was the matter of moulding the clay he had taken from the graveyard into a rough semblance of a bird. Then, after sticking several white feathers obtained from last Sunday's chicken into each side of the figure to make wings, he anointed it with a noxious mixture he had prepared in advance.

The moon was just setting behind the wall when he began the incantation. Candlelight flickered on the pages of the old book as he slowly and carefully pronounced the difficult words.

When it came time for the business with the toad, he almost didn't have the heart to go through with it; but he steeled himself and did what was necessary. Then, wincing, he jabbed his forefinger with a pin and slowly dropped the requisite three drops of blood down on the crude clay figure. He whispered:

> Clay of graveyard,
> White cock's feather,
> Eye of toad,
> Rise together!

Breathlessly he waited. He seemed to be in the middle of a circle of silence. The wind in the trees outside had stopped and there was only the sound of his own quick breathing. As the candlelight rippled, the clay figure seemed to quiver slightly as if it were hunching for flight.

Porgie bent closer, tense with anticipation. In his mind's eye, he saw himself building a giant bird with wings powerful enough to lift him over the wall around the world. Swooping low over the schoolhouse during recess, he would wave his hands in a condescending gesture of farewell, and then as the kids hopped on their sticks and tried to follow him, he would rise higher and higher until he had passed the ceiling of their brooms and left them circling impotently below him. At last he would sweep over the wall with hundreds of feet to spare, over it and then down – down into the great unknown.

The candle flame stopped flickering and stood steady and clear. Beside it, the clay bird squatted, lifeless and motionless.

Minutes ticked by and Porgie gradually saw it for what it was – a smelly clod of dirt with a few feathers tucked in it. There were tears in his eyes as he picked up the body of the dead toad and said softly, "I'm sorry."

When he came in from burying it, he grasped the image of the clay bird tightly in his mind and sent it swinging angrily around the shed. Feathers fluttered behind it as it flew faster and faster until in disgust he released it and let it smash into the rough boards of the wall. It crumbled into a pile of foul-smelling trash and fell to the floor. He stirred it with his toe, hurt, angry, confused.

His broken glider still stood where he had left it on the far end of his workbench. He went over and picked it up.

"At least you flew by yourself," he said, "and I didn't have to kill any poor little toads to make you."

Then he juggled it in his hand, feeling its weight, and began to wonder. It had occurred to him that maybe the wooden wings on his big orange-box glider had been too heavy.

Maybe if I could get some long, thin poles, he thought, and some cloth to put across the wings . . .

During the next three months, there was room in Porgie's mind for only one thing: the machine he was building in the roomy old cave at the top of the long hill on the other side of Arnett's grove. As a result, he kept slipping further and further behind at school.

Things at home weren't too pleasant, either; Bull Pup felt it was his duty to keep his parents fully informed of Porgie's shortcomings. Porgie didn't care, though. He was too busy. Every minute he could steal was spent in either collecting materials or putting them together.

The afternoon the machine was finally finished, he could hardly tear himself away from it long enough to go home for dinner. He was barely able to choke down his food, and didn't even wait for dessert.

He sat on the grass in front of the cave, waiting for darkness. Below, little twinkling lights marked the villages that stretched across the plain for a full 40 miles. Enclosing them like encircling arms stretched the dark and forbidding mass of the wall. No matter where he looked, it stood high against the night. He followed its curve with his eyes until he had turned completely around, and then he shook his fist at it.

Patting the ungainly mass of the machine that rested on the grass beside him, he whispered fiercely, "I'll get over you yet. Old *Eagle* here will take me!"

Old *Eagle* was an awkward, boxkite-like affair; but to Porgie she was a thing of beauty. She had an uncovered fuselage composed of four long poles braced together to make a rectangular frame, at each end of which was fastened a large wing.

When it was dark enough, he climbed into the open frame and reached down and grabbed hold of the two lower members. Grunting, he lifted until the two upper ones rested under his armpits. There was padding there to support his weight comfortably once he was airborne. The bottom of the machine was level with his waist and the rest of him hung free. According to his thinking, he should be able to control his flight by swinging his legs. If he swung forward, the shifting weight should tilt the nose down; if he swung back, it should go up.

There was only one way to find out if his ifs were right. The *Eagle* was a heavy contraption. He walked awkwardly to the top of the hill, the cords standing out on his neck. He was scared as he looked down the long steep slope that stretched out before him – so scared that he was having trouble breathing. He swallowed twice in a vain attempt to moisten his dry throat, and then lunged forward, fighting desperately to keep his balance as his wobbling steps gradually picked up speed.

Faster he went, and faster, his steps turning into leaps as the wing surfaces gradually took hold. His toes scraped through the long grass and then they were dangling in free air.

He was aloft.

Not daring even to move his head, he slanted his eyes down and to the left. The earth was slipping rapidly by a dozen feet below him. Slowly and cautiously, he swung his feet back. As the weight shifted, the nose of the glider rose. Up, up he went, until he felt a sudden slowing down and a clumsiness of motion. Almost instinctively, he leaned forward again, pointing the nose down in a swift dip to regain flying speed.

By the time he reached the bottom of the hill, he was 150 feet up. Experimentally, he swung his feet a little to the left. The glider dipped slightly and turned. Soaring over a clump of trees, he felt a sudden lifting as an updraught caught him.

Up he went – 10, 20, 30 feet – and then slowly began to settle again.

The landing wasn't easy. More by luck than by skill, he came down in the long grass of the meadow with no more damage than a few bruises. He sat for a moment and rested, his head spinning with excitement. He had flown like a bird, without his stick, without uttering a word. There *were* other ways than magic!

His elation suddenly faded with the realization that, while gliding down was fun, the way over the wall was *up*. Also, and of more immediate importance, he was half a mile from the cave with a contraption so heavy and unwieldy that he could never hope to haul it all the way back up the hill by himself. If he didn't get it out of sight by morning, there was going to be trouble, serious trouble. People took an unpleasant view of machines and those who built them.

Broomsticks, he decided, had certain advantages, after all. They might not fly very high, but at least you didn't have to walk home from a ride.

If I just had a great big broomstick, he thought, I could lift the *Eagle* up with it and fly her home.

He jumped to his feet. It might work!

He ran back up the hill as fast as he could and finally, very much out of breath, reached the entrance of the cave. Without waiting to get back his wind, he jumped on his stick and flew down to the stranded glider.

Five minutes later, he stepped back and said:

> Broomstick fly,
> Rise on high,
> Over cloud
> And into sky.

It didn't fly. It couldn't. Porgie had lashed it to the framework of the *Eagle*. When he grabbed hold of the machine and lifted, nine-tenths of its weight was gone, cancelled out by the broomstick's lifting power.

He towed it back up the hill and shoved it into the cave. Then he looked uneasily at the sky. It was later than he had thought. He should be home and in bed – but when he thought of the feeling of power he had had in his flight, he couldn't resist hauling the *Eagle* back out again.

After checking the broomstick to be sure it was still fastened tightly to the frame, he went swooping down the hill again. This time when he hit the thermal over the clump of trees, he was pushed up 100 feet before he lost it. He curved through the darkness until he found it again and then circled tightly within it.

Higher he went and higher, higher than any broomstick had ever gone!

When he started to head back, though, he didn't have such an easy time of it. Twice he was caught in downdraughts that almost grounded him before he was able to break loose from the tugging winds. Only the lifting power of his broomstick enabled him to stay aloft. With it bearing most of the load, the *Eagle* was so light that it took just a flutter of air to sweep her up again.

He landed the glider a stone's throw from the mouth of his cave.

Tomorrow night! he thought exultantly as he unleashed his broomstick. Tomorrow night!

There was a tomorrow night, and many nights after that. The *Eagle* was sensitive to every updraught, and with care he found he could remain aloft for hours, riding from thermal to thermal. It was hard to keep his secret, hard to keep from shouting the news, but he had to. He slipped out at night to practise, slipping back in again before sunrise to get what sleep he could.

He circled the day of his fourteenth birthday in red and waited. He had a reason for waiting.

In the world within the wall, fourteenth birthdays marked the boundary between the little and the big, between being a big child and a small man. Most important, they marked the time when one was taken to the Great Tower where the Adepts lived and given a full-sized broomstick powered by the most potent of spells, sticks that would climb to a full 600 feet, twice the height that could be reached by the smaller ones the youngsters rode.

Porgie needed a man-sized stick, needed that extra power, for he had found that only the strongest of updraughts would lift him past the 300-foot ceiling where the lifting power of his little broomstick gave out. He had to get up almost as high as the wall before he could make it across the wide expanse of flat plain that separated him from the box canyon where the great wind waited.

So he counted the slowly passing days and practised flying during the rapidly passing nights.

The afternoon of his fourteenth birthday found Porgie sitting on the front steps expectantly, dressed in his best and waiting for his uncle to come out of the house. Bull Pup came out and sat down beside him.

"The gang's having a coven up on top of old Baldy tonight," he said. "Too bad you can't come."

"I can go if I want to," said Porgie.

"How?" said Bull Pup and snickered. "You going to grow wings and fly? Old Baldy's 500 feet up and your kid stick won't lift you that high."

"Today's my birthday."

"You think you're going to get a new stick?"

Porgie nodded.

"Well, you ain't. I heard Mom and Dad talking. Dad's mad because you flunked Alchemy. He said you had to be taught a lesson."

Porgie felt sick inside, but he wouldn't let Bull Pup have the satisfaction of knowing it.

"I don't care," he said. "I'll go to the coven if I want to. You just wait and see."

Bull Pup was laughing when he hopped on his stick and took off down the street. Porgie waited an hour, but his uncle didn't come out.

He went into the house. Nobody said anything about his new broomstick until after supper. Then his uncle called him into the living room and told him he wasn't getting it.

"But, Uncle Veryl, you promised!"

"It was a conditional promise, Porgie. There was a big if attached to it. Do you remember what it was?"

Porgie looked down at the floor and scuffed one toe on the worn carpet. "I tried."

"Did you really, son?" His uncle's eyes were stern but compassionate. "Were you trying when you fell asleep in school today? I've tried talking with you and I've tried whipping you and neither seems to work. Maybe this will. Now you run upstairs and get started on your studies. When you can show me that your marks are improving, we'll talk about getting you a new broomstick. Until then, the old one will have to do."

Porgie knew that he was too big to cry, but when he got to his room, he couldn't help it. He was stretched out on his bed with his face buried in the pillows when he heard a hiss from the window. He looked up to see Bull Pup sitting on his stick, grinning malevolently at him.

"What do you want?" sniffed Porgie.

"Only little kids cry," said Bull Pup.

"I wasn't crying. I got a cold."

"I just saw Mr Wickens. He was coming out of that old cave back of Arnett's grove. He's going to get the Black Man, I'll bet."

"I don't know anything about that old cave," said Porgie, sitting bolt upright on his bed.

"Oh, yes, you do. I followed you up there one day. You got a machine in there. I told Mr Wickens and he gave me a quarter. He was real interested."

Porgie jumped from his bed and ran towards the window, his face red and his fists doubled. "I'll fix you!"

Bull Pup backed his broomstick just out of Porgie's reach, and then stuck his thumbs in his ears and waggled his fingers. When Porgie started to throw things, he gave a final taunt and swooped away towards old Baldy and the coven.

Porgie's uncle was just about to go out in the kitchen and fix himself a sandwich when the doorbell rang. Grumbling, he went out into the front hall. Mr Wickens was at the door. He came into the house and stood blinking in the light. He seemed uncertain as to just how to begin.

"I've got bad news for you," he said finally. "It's about Porgie. Is your wife still up?"

Porgie's uncle nodded anxiously.

"She'd better hear this, too."

Aunt Olga put down her knitting when they came into the living room.

"You're out late, Mr Wickens."

"It's not of my own choosing."

"Porgie's done something again," said his uncle.

Aunt Olga sighed. "What is it this time?"

Mr Wickens hesitated, cleared his throat, and finally spoke in a low, hushed voice: "Porgie's built a machine. The Black Man told me. He's coming after the boy tonight."

Uncle Veryl dashed up the stairs to find Porgie. He wasn't in his room.

Aunt Olga just sat in her chair and cried shrilly.

The moon stood high and silver-lit the whole countryside. Porgie could make out the world far below him almost as if it were day. Miles to his left, he saw the little flickering fires on top of old Baldy where the kids were holding their coven. He fought an impulse and then succumbed to it. He circled the *Eagle* over a clump of trees until the strong rising currents lifted him almost to the height of the wall. Then he twisted his body and banked over towards the distant red glowing fires.

Minutes later, he went silently over them at 800 feet, feeling out the air currents around the rocks. There was a sharp down-draught on the far side of Baldy that dropped him suddenly when he glided into it, but he made a quick turn and found untroubled air before he fell too far. On the other side, towards the box canyon, he found what he wanted, a strong, rising current that seemed to have no upward limits.

He fixed its location carefully in his mind and then began to circle down towards the coven. Soon he was close enough to make out individual forms sitting silently around their little fires.

"Hey, Bull Pup," he yelled at the top of his lungs.

A stocky figure jumped to its feet and looked wildly around for the source of the ghostly voice.

"Up here!"

Porgie reached in his pocket, pulled out a small pebble and chucked it down. It cracked against a shelf of rock 4 feet from Bull Pup. Porgie's cousin let out a howl of fear. The rest of the kids jumped up and reared back their heads at the night sky, their eyes blinded by firelight.

"I told you I could come to the coven if I wanted to," yelled

Porgie, "but now I don't. I don't have any time for kid stuff; I'm going over the wall!"

During his last pass over the plateau he wasn't more than 30 feet up. As he leaned over, his face was clearly visible in the firelight.

Placing one thumb to his nose, he waggled his fingers and chanted, "Nyah, nyah, nyah, you can't catch me!"

His feet were almost scraping the ground as he glided over the drop-off. There was an anxious second of waiting and then he felt the sure, steady thrust of the up-current against his wings.

He looked back. The gang was milling around, trying to figure out what had happened. There was an angry shout of command from Bull Pup, and after a moment of confused hesitation they all made for their brooms and swooped up into the air.

Porgie mentally gauged his altitude and then relaxed. He was almost at their ceiling and would be above it before they reached him.

He flattened out his glide and yelled, "Come on up! Only little kids play that low!"

Bull Pup's stick wouldn't rise any higher. He circled impotently, shaking his fist at the machine that rode serenely above him.

"You just wait," he yelled. "You can't stay up there all night. You got to come down some time, and when you do, we'll be waiting for you."

"Nyah, nyah, nyah," chanted Porgie and mounted higher into the moonlit night.

When the updraught gave out, he wasn't as high as he wanted to be, but there wasn't anything he could do about it. He turned and started a flat glide across the level plain towards the box canyon. He wished now that he had left Bull Pup and the other kids alone. They were following along below him. If he dropped down to their level before the canyon winds caught him, he was in trouble.

He tried to flatten his glide still more, but instead of saving altitude, he went into a stall that dropped him 100 feet before he was able to regain control. He saw now that he could never make it without dropping to Bull Pup's level.

Bull Pup saw it, too, and let out an exultant yell: "Just you wait! You're going to get it good!"

Porgie peered over the side into the darkness where his cousin rode, his pug face gleaming palely in the moonlight.

"Leave him alone, gang," Bull Pup shouted. "He's mine!"

The rest pulled back and circled slowly as the *Eagle* glided quietly down among them. Bull Pup darted in and rode right alongside Porgie.

He pointed savagely towards the ground: "Go down or I'll knock you down!"

Porgie kicked at him, almost upsetting his machine. He wasn't fast enough. Bull Pup dodged easily. He made a wide circle and came back, reaching out and grabbing the far end of the *Eagle*'s front wing. Slowly and maliciously, he began to jerk it up and down, twisting violently as he did so.

"Get down," he yelled, "or I'll break it off!"

Porgie almost lost his head as the wrenching threatened to throw him out of control.

"Let go!" he screamed, his voice cracking.

Bull Pup's face had a strange excited look on it as he gave the wing another jerk. The rest of the boys were becoming frightened as they saw what was happening.

"Quit it, Bull Pup!" somebody called. "Do you want to kill him?"

"Shut up or you'll get a dose of the same!"

Porgie fought to clear his head. His broomstick was tied to the frame of the *Eagle* so securely that he would never be able to free it in time to save himself. He stared into the darkness until he caught the picture of Bull Pup's broomstick sharply in his mind. He'd never tried to handle anything that big before, but it was that or nothing.

Tensing suddenly, he clamped his mind down on the picture and held it hard. He knew that words didn't help, but he uttered them anyway:

> Broomstick stop,
> Flip and flop!

There was a sharp tearing pain in his head. He gritted his teeth and held on, fighting desperately against the red haze that threatened to swallow him. Suddenly there was a half-startled, half-frightened squawk from his left wingtip, and Bull Pup's stick jerked to an abrupt halt, gyrating so madly that its rider could hardly hang on.

"All right, the rest of you," screamed Porgie. "Get going or I'll do the same thing to you!"

They got, arcing away in terrified disorder. Porgie watched as they formed a frightened semicircle around the blubbering Bull Pup. With a sigh of relief, he let go with his mind.

As he left them behind in the night, he turned his head back and yelled weakly, "Nyah, nyah, nyah, you can't catch me!"

He was only 50 feet off the ground when he glided into the far end of the box canyon and was suddenly caught by the strong updraught. As he soared in a tight spiral, he slumped down against the arm-rests, his whole body shaking in delayed reaction.

The lashings that held the front wing to the frame were dangerously loose from the manhandling they had received. One more tug and the whole wing might have twisted back, dumping him down on the sharp rocks below. Shudders ran through the *Eagle* as the supports shook in their loose bonds. He clamped both hands around the place where the rear wing spar crossed the frame and tried to steady it.

He felt his stick's lifting power give out at 300 feet. The *Eagle* felt clumsy and heavy, but the current was still enough to carry him slowly upwards. Foot by foot he rose towards the top of the wall, losing a precious 100 feet once when he spiralled out of the updraught and had to circle to find it. A wisp of cloud curled down from the top of the wall and he felt a moment of panic as he climbed into it.

Momentarily, there was no left or right or up or down. Only damp whiteness. He had the feeling that the *Eagle* was falling out of control; but he kept steady, relying on the feel for the air he had got during his many practice flights.

The lashings had loosened more. The full strength of his hands wasn't enough to keep the wing from shuddering and trembling.

He struggled resolutely to maintain control of ship and self against the strong temptation to lean forward and throw the *Eagle* into a shallow dive that would take him back to normalcy and safety.

He was almost at the end of his resolution when with dramatic suddenness he glided out of the cloud into the clear moon-touched night. The up-current under him seemed to have lessened. He banked in a gentle arc, trying to find the centre of it again.

As he turned, he became aware of something strange, something different, something almost frightening. For the first time in his life, there was no wall to block his vision, no vast black line stretching through the night.

He was above it!

There was no time for looking. With a loud *ping*, one of the lashings parted and the leading edge of the front wing flapped violently. The glider began to pitch and yaw, threatening to nose over into a plummeting dive. He fought for mastery, swinging his legs like desperate pendulums as he tried to correct the erratic side swings that threatened to throw him out of control. As he fought, he headed for the wall.

If he were to fall, it would be on the other side. At least he would cheat old Mr Wickens and the Black Man.

Now he was directly over the wall. It stretched like a wide road underneath him, its smooth top black and shining in the moonlight. Acting on quick impulse, he threw his body savagely forward and to the right. The ungainly machine dipped abruptly and dived towards the black surface beneath it.

Eighty feet, 70, 60, 50 – he had no room to manoeuvre, there would be no second chance – 30, 20—

He threw his weight back, jerking the nose of the *Eagle* suddenly up. For a precious second the wings held, there was a sharp breaking of his fall; then, with a loud, cracking noise, the front wing buckled back in his face. There was a moment of blind whirling fall and a splintering crash that threw him into darkness.

Slowly, groggily, Porgie pulled himself up out of the broken wreckage. The *Eagle* had made her last flight. She perched precariously, so near the outside edge of the wall that part of her rear wing stretched out over nothingness.

Porgie crawled cautiously across the slippery wet surface of the top of the wall until he reached the centre. There he crouched down to wait for morning. He was exhausted, his body so drained of energy that in spite of himself he kept slipping into an uneasy sleep.

Each time he did, he'd struggle back to consciousness trying to escape the nightmare figures that scampered through his brain. He was falling, pursued by wheeling, batlike figures with pug faces. He was in a tiny room and the walls were inching in towards him and he could hear the voice of Bull Pup in the distance chanting, "You're going to get it." And then the room turned into a long, dark corridor and he was running. Mr Wickens was close behind him, and he had long, sharp teeth and he kept yelling, "Porgie! Porgie!"

He shuddered back to wakefulness, crawled to the far edge of the wall and, hanging his head over, tried to look down at the outside world. The clouds had boiled up and there was nothing underneath him but grey blankness hiding the sheer 1,000-foot drop. He crawled back to his old spot and looked towards the east, praying for the first sign of dawn. There was only blackness there.

He started to doze off again and once more he heard the voice: "Porgie! Porgie!"

He opened his eyes and sat up. The voice was still calling, even though he was awake. It seemed to be coming from high up and far away.

It came closer, closer, and suddenly he saw it in the darkness – a black figure wheeling above the wall like a giant crow. Down it came, nearer and nearer, a man in black with arms outstretched and long fingers hooked like talons!

Porgie scrambled to his feet and ran, his feet skidding on the slippery surface. He looked back over his shoulder. The black figure was almost on top of him. Porgie dodged desperately and slipped.

He felt himselt shoot across the slippery surface towards the edge of the wall. He clawed, scrabbling for purchase. He couldn't stop. One moment he felt wet coldness slipping away under him; the next, nothingness as he shot out into the dark and empty air.

He spun slowly as he fell. First the clouds were under him and then they tipped and the star-flecked sky took their places. He felt cradled, suspended in time. There was no terror. There was nothing.

Nothing – until suddenly the sky above him was blotted out by a plummeting black figure that swooped down on him, hawk-like and horrible.

Porgie kicked wildly. One foot slammed into something solid and for an instant he was free. Then strong arms circled him from behind and he was jerked out of the nothingness into a world of falling and fear.

There was a sudden strain on his chest and then he felt himself being lifted. He was set down gently on the top of the wall.

He stood defiant, head erect, and faced the black figure.

"I won't go back. You can't make me go back."

"You don't have to go back, Porgie."

He couldn't see the hooded face, but the voice sounded strangely familiar.

"You've earned your right to see what's on the other side," it said. Then the figure laughed and threw back the hood that partially covered its face.

In the bright moonlight, Porgie saw Mr Wickens!

The schoolmaster nodded cheerfully. "Yes, Porgie, I'm the Black Man. Bit of a shock, isn't it?"

Porgie sat down suddenly.

"I'm from the Outside," said Mr Wickens, seating himself carefully on the slick black surface. "I guess you could call me a sort of observer."

Porgie's spinning mind couldn't catch up with the new ideas that were being thrown at him. "Observer?" he said uncomprehendingly. "Outside?"

"Outside. That's where you'll be spending your next few years. I don't think you'll find life better there, and I don't think you'll find it worse. It'll be different, though, I can guarantee that." He chuckled. "Do you remember what I said to you in my office that day – that man can't follow two paths at once, that mind and nature are bound to conflict? That's true, but it's also false. You can have both, but it takes two worlds to do it.

"Outside, where you're going, is the world of the machines. It's a good world, too. But the men who live there saw a long time ago that they were paying a price for it; that control over nature meant that the forces of the mind were neglected, for the machine is a thing of logic and reason, but miracles aren't. Not yet. So they built the wall and they placed people within it and gave them such books and such laws as would ensure development of the powers of the mind. At least they hoped it would work that way – and it did."

"But – but why the wall?" asked Porgie.

"Because their guess was right. There is magic." He pulled a bunch of keys from his pocket. "Lift it, Porgie."

Porgie stared at it until he had the picture in his mind and then let his mind take hold, pulling with invisible hands until the keys hung high in the air. Then he dropped them back into Mr Wickens's hand.

"What was that for?"

"Outsiders can't do that," said the schoolmaster. "And they can't do conscious telepathy – what you call mind-talk – either. They can't because they really don't believe such things can be done. The people inside the wall do, for they live in an atmosphere of magic. But once these things are worked out, and become simply a matter of training and method, then the ritual, the mumbo-jumbo, the deeply ingrained belief in the existence of supernatural forces will be no longer necessary.

"These phenomena will be only tools that anybody can be trained to use, and the crutches can be thrown away. Then the wall will come tumbling down. But until then" – he stopped and frowned in mock severity – "there will always be a Black Man around to see that the people inside don't split themselves up the middle trying to walk down two roads at once."

There was a lingering doubt in Porgie's eyes. "But you flew without a machine."

The Black Man opened his cloak and displayed a small, gleaming disc that was strapped to his chest. He tapped it. "A machine, Porgie. A machine, just like your glider, only of a different sort and much better. It's almost as good as levitation. Mind and nature . . . magic and science . . . they'll get together eventually."

He wrapped his cloak about him again. "It's cold up here. Shall we go? Tomorrow is time enough to find out what is outside the wall that goes around the world."

"Can't we wait until the clouds lift?" asked Porgie wistfully. "I'd sort of like to see it for the first time from up here."

"We could," said Mr Wickens, "but there is somebody you haven't seen for a long time waiting for you down there. If we stay up here, he'll be worried."

Porgie looked up blankly. "I don't know anybody Outside. I—" He stopped suddenly. He felt as if he were about to explode. "Not my father!"

"Who else? He came out the easy way. Come, now, let's go and show him what kind of man his son has grown up to be. Are you ready?"

"I'm ready," said Porgie.

"Then help me drag your contraption over to the other side of the wall so we can drop it inside. When the folk find the wreckage in the morning, they'll know what the Black Man does to those who build machines instead of tending to their proper business. It should have a salutary effect on Bull Pup and the others."

He walked over to the wreckage of the *Eagle* and began to tug at it.

"Wait," said Porgie. "Let me." He stared at the broken glider until his eyes began to burn. Then he gripped and pulled.

Slowly, with an increasing consciousness of mastery, he lifted until the glider floated free and was rocking gently in the slight breeze that rippled across the top of the great wall. Then, with a sudden shove, he swung it far out over the abyss and released it.

The two stood silently, side by side, watching the *Eagle* pitch downwards on broken wings. When it was lost in the darkness below, Mr Wickens took Porgie in his strong arms and stepped confidently to the edge of the wall.

"Wait a second," said Porgie, remembering a day in the schoolmaster's study and a switch that had come floating obediently down through the air. "If you're from Outside, how come you can do lifting?"

Mr Wickens grinned. "Oh, I was born Inside. I went over the Wall for the first time when I was just a little older than you are now."

"In a glider?" asked Porgie.

"No," said the Black Man, his face perfectly sober. "I went out and caught myself a half-dozen eagles."

Darkrose and Diamond

Ursula K. Le Guin

*If the last story may be seen as a forerunner to Harry Potter,
the following may loosely be seen as a child of* Lord of the
Rings. *Though let me hasten to add that Ursula Le Guin is no
slavish imitator of Tolkien. Far from it. Although her Earthsea books began to appear in the years immediately after the
success of the paperback edition of* Lord of the Rings, *Le Guin
had been considering ideas for the background and setting of
Earthsea for several years, starting with her earliest stories,
"The Word of Unbinding" and "The Rule of Names", both
published in 1964. Le Guin (b. 1929) was a fan of the work of
Lord Dunsany from her youth and also delighted in the worlds
created by Tolkien and E. R. Eddison. Elements from all of
these books may be seen entangled in the background of her
Earthsea series which began with* A Wizard of Earthsea
(1968) and was followed by The Tombs of Atuan *(1971),*
The Farthest Shore *(1972) and, more recently,* Tehanu
(1990). Although Tehanu *was subtitled "The Last Book of
Earthsea", Ms Le Guin has since written further new stories
including the following.*

A Boat-Song from West Havnor

Where my love is going
There will I go.
Where his boat is rowing
I will row.

We will laugh together,
Together we will cry.
If he lives I will live,
If he dies I die.

Where my love is going
There will I go.
Where his boat is rowing
I will row.

IN THE WEST OF HAVNOR, among hills forested with oak and chestnut, is the town of Glade. A while ago, the rich man of that town was a merchant called Golden. Golden owned the mill that cut the oak boards for the ships they built in Havnor South Port and Havnor Great Port, he owned the biggest chestnut groves; he owned the carts and hired the carters that carried the timber and the chestnuts over the hills to be sold. He did very well from trees, and when his son was born, the mother said, "We could call him Chestnut, or Oak, maybe?" But the father said, "Diamond," diamond being in his estimation the one thing more precious than gold.

So little Diamond grew up in the finest house in Glade, a fat, bright-eyed baby, a ruddy, cheerful boy. He had a sweet singing voice, a true ear, and a love of music, so that his mother, Tuly, called him Songsparrow and Skylark, among other loving names, for she never really did like Diamond. He trilled and carolled about the house, he knew any tune as soon as he heard it, and invented tunes when he heard none. His mother had the wise woman Tangle teach him *The Creation of Éa* and *The Deed of the Young King*, and at Sunreturn when he was eleven years old he sang the Winter Carol for the Lord of the Western Land, who was visiting his domain in the hills above Glade. The lord and his lady praised the boy's singing and gave him a tiny gold box with a diamond set in the lid, which seemed a kind and pretty gift to Diamond and his mother. But Golden was a bit impatient with the singing and the trinkets. "There are more important things for you to do, son," he said. "And greater prizes to be earned."

Diamond thought his father meant the business – the loggers, the sawyers, the sawmill, the chestnut groves, the pickers, the carters, the carts – all that work and talk and planning, complicated, adult matters. He never felt that it had much to do with him, so how was he to have as much to do with it as his father expected? Maybe he'd find out when he grew up.

But in fact Golden wasn't thinking only about the business. He had observed something about his son that had made him not exactly set his eyes higher than the business, but glance above it from time to time, and then shut his eyes.

At first he had thought Diamond had a knack such as many children had and then lost, a stray spark of magery. When he was a little boy, Golden himself had been able to make his own shadow shine and sparkle. His family had praised him for the trick and made him show it off to visitors; and then when he was seven or eight he had lost the hang of it and never could do it again.

When he saw Diamond come down the stairs without touching the stairs, he thought his eyes had deceived him, but a few days later, he saw the child float up the stairs, just a finger gliding along the oaken banister rail. "Can you do that coming down?" Golden asked, and Diamond said, "Oh, yes, like this," and sailed back down smooth as a cloud on the south wind.

"How did you learn to do that?"

"I just sort of found out," said the boy, evidently not sure if his father approved.

Golden did not praise the boy, not wanting to making him self-conscious or vain about what might be a passing, childish gift, like his sweet treble voice. There was too much fuss already made over that.

But a year or so later he saw Diamond out in the back garden with his playmate Rose. The children were squatting on their haunches, heads close together, laughing. Something intense or uncanny about them made him pause at the window on the stairs landing and watch them. A thing between them was leaping up and down: a frog? a toad? a big cricket? He went out into the garden and came up near them, moving so quietly, though he was a big man, that they in their absorption did not hear him. The thing that was hopping up and down on the grass between their bare toes was a rock. When Diamond raised his hand the rock jumped up in the air, and when he shook his hand a little the rock hovered in the air, and when he flipped his fingers downwards it fell to earth.

"Now you," Diamond said to Rose, and she started to do what he had done, but the rock only twitched a little. "Oh," she whispered, "there's your dad."

"That's very clever," Golden said.

"Di thought it up," Rose said.

Golden did not like the child. She was both outspoken and defensive, both rash and timid. She was a girl, and a year younger than Diamond, and a witch's daughter. He wished his son would play with boys his own age, his own sort, from the respectable families of Glade. Tuly insisted on calling the witch "the wise woman", but a witch was a witch and her daughter was no fit companion for Diamond. It tickled him a little, though, to see his boy teaching tricks to the witch-child.

"What else can you do, Diamond?" he asked.

"Play the flute," Diamond said promptly, and took out of his pocket the little fife his mother had given him for his twelfth birthday. He put it to his lips, his fingers danced, and he played a sweet, familiar tune from the western coast, "Where My Love Is Going".

"Very nice," said the father. "But anybody can play the fife, you know."

Diamond glanced at Rose. The girl turned her head away, looking down.

"I learned it really quickly," Diamond said.

Golden grunted, unimpressed.

"It can do it by itself," Diamond said, and held out the fife away from his lips. His fingers danced on the stops, and the fife played a short jig. It hit several false notes and squealed on the last high note. "I haven't got it right yet," Diamond said, vexed and embarrassed.

"Pretty good, pretty good," his father said. "Keep practising." And he went on. He was not sure what he ought to have said. He did not want to encourage the boy to spend any more time on music, or with this girl, he spent too much already, and neither of them would help him get anywhere in life. But this gift, this undeniable gift – the rock hovering, the unblown fife – well, it would be wrong to make too much of it, but probably it should not be discouraged.

In Golden's understanding, money was power, but not the only power. There were two others, one equal, one greater. There was birth. When the Lord of the Western Land came to his domain near Glade, Golden was glad to show him fealty. The lord was born to govern and to keep the peace, as Golden was born to deal with commerce and wealth, each in his place, and each, noble or common, if he served well and honestly, deserved honour and respect. But there were also lesser lords whom Golden could buy and sell, lend to or let beg, men born noble who deserved neither fealty nor honour. Power of birth and power of money were contingent, and must be earned lest they be lost.

But beyond the rich and the lordly were those called the Men of Power: the wizards. Their power, though little exercised, was absolute. In their hands lay the fate of the long-kingless kingdom of the Archipelago.

If Diamond had been born to that kind of power, if that was his gift, then all Golden's dreams and plans of training him in the business, and having him help in expanding the carting route to a regular trade with South Port, and buying up the chestnut forests above Reche – all such plans dwindled into trifles. Might Diamond go (as his mother's uncle had gone) to the School of Wizards on Roke Island? Might he (as that uncle had done) gain glory for his family and dominion over lord and commoner, becoming a Mage in the Court of the Lords Regent in the Great Port of Havnor? Golden all but floated up the stairs himself, borne on such visions.

But he said nothing to the boy and nothing to the boy's mother. He was a consciously close-mouthed man, distrustful of visions until they could be made acts; and she, though a dutiful, loving wife and mother and housekeeper, already made too much of Diamond's talents and accomplishments. Also, like all women, she was inclined to babble and gossip, and indiscriminate in her friendships. The girl Rose hung about with Diamond because Tuly encouraged Rose's mother the witch to visit, consulting her every time Diamond had a hangnail, and telling her more than she or anyone ought to know about Golden's household. His business was none of the witch's business. On the other hand, Tangle might be able to tell him if his son in fact showed promise, had a talent for magery . . . but he flinched away from the thought of asking her, asking a witch's opinion on anything, least of all a judgment on his son.

He resolved to wait and watch. Being a patient man with a strong will, he did so for four years, till Diamond was sixteen. A big, well-grown youth, good at games and lessons, he was still ruddy-faced and bright-eyed and cheerful. He had taken it hard when his voice changed, the sweet treble going all untuned and hoarse. Golden had hoped that that was the end of his singing, but the boy went on wandering about with itinerant musicians, ballad-singers and such, learning all their trash. That was no life for a merchant's son who was to inherit and manage his father's properties and mills and business, and Golden told him so. "Singing time is over, son," he said. "You must think about being a man."

Diamond had been given his true name at the springs of the Amia in the hills above Glade. The wizard Hemlock, who had known his great-uncle the Mage, came up from South Port to name him. And Hemlock was invited to his nameday party the year after, a big party, beer and food for all, and new clothes, a shirt or skirt or shift for every child, which was an old custom in the west of Havnor, and dancing on the village green in the warm autumn

evening. Diamond had many friends, all the boys his age in town
and all the girls too. The young people danced, and some of them
had a bit too much beer, but nobody misbehaved very badly, and it
was a merry and memorable night. The next morning Golden told
his son again that he must think about being a man.

"I have thought some about it," said the boy, in his husky
voice.

"And?"

"Well, I," said Diamond, and stuck.

"I'd always counted on your going into the family business,"
Golden said. His tone was neutral, and Diamond said nothing.
"Have you had any ideas of what you want to do?"

"Sometimes."

"Did you talk at all to Master Hemlock?"

Diamond hesitated and said, "No." He looked a question at his
father.

"I talked to him last night," Golden said. "He said to me that
there are certain natural gifts which it's not only difficult but
actually wrong, harmful, to suppress."

The light had come back into Diamond's dark eyes.

"The master said that such gifts or capacities, untrained, are
not only wasted, but may be dangerous. The art must be learned,
and practised, he said."

Diamond's face shone.

"But, he said, it must be learned and practised for its own
sake."

Diamond nodded eagerly.

"If it's a real gift, an unusual capacity, that's even more true. A
witch with her love potions can't do much harm, but even a
village sorcerer, he said, must take care, for if the art is used for
base ends, it becomes weak and noxious . . . Of course, even a
sorcerer gets paid. And wizards, as you know, live with lords, and
have what they wish."

Diamond was listening intently, frowning a little.

"So, to be blunt about it, if you have this gift, Diamond, it's of
no use, directly, to our business. It has to be cultivated on its own
terms, and kept under control – learned and mastered. Only then,

he said, can your teachers begin to tell you what to do with it, what good it will do you. Or others," he added conscientiously.

There was a long pause.

"I told him," Golden said, "that I had seen you, with a turn of your hand and a single word, change a wooden carving of a bird into a bird that flew up and sang. I've seen you make a light glow in thin air. You didn't know I was watching. I've watched and said nothing for a long time. I didn't want to make too much of mere childish play. But I believe you have a gift, perhaps a great gift. When I told Master Hemlock what I'd seen you do, he agreed with me. He said that you may go study with him in South Port for a year, or perhaps longer."

"Study with Master Hemlock?" said Diamond, his voice up half an octave.

"If you wish."

"I, I, I never thought about it. Can I think about it? For a while – a day?"

"Of course," Golden said, pleased with his son's caution. He had thought Diamond might leap at the offer, which would have been natural, perhaps, but painful to the father, the owl who had – perhaps – hatched out an eagle.

For Golden looked on the Art Magic with genuine humility as something quite beyond him – not a mere toy, such as music or tale-telling, but a practical business, which his business could never quite equal. And he was, though he wouldn't have put it that way, afraid of wizards. A bit contemptuous of sorcerers, with their sleights and illusions and gibble-gabble, but afraid of wizards.

"Does Mother know?" Diamond asked.

"She will when the time comes. But she has no part to play in your decision, Diamond. Women know nothing of these matters and have nothing to do with them. You must make your choice alone, as a man. Do you understand that?" Golden was earnest, seeing his chance to begin to wean the lad from his mother. She as a woman would cling, but he as a man must learn to let go. And Diamond nodded sturdily enough to satisfy his father, though he had a thoughtful look.

"Master Hemlock said I, said he thought I had, I might have a, a gift, a talent for—?"

Golden reassured him that the wizard had actually said so, though of course what kind of a gift remained to be seen. The boy's modesty was a great relief to him. He had half-consciously dreaded that Diamond would triumph over him, asserting his power right away — that mysterious, dangerous, incalculable power against which Golden's wealth and mastery and dignity shrank to impotence.

"Thank you, Father," the boy said. Golden embraced him and left, well pleased with him.

Their meeting place was in the sallows, the willow thickets down by the Amia as it ran below the smithy. As soon as Rose got there, Diamond said, "He wants me to go study with Master Hemlock! What am I going to do?"

"Study with the wizard?"

"He thinks I have this huge great talent. For magic."

"Who does?"

"Father does. He saw some of the stuff we were practising. But he says Hemlock says I should come study with him because it might be dangerous not to. Oh." And Diamond beat his head with his hands.

"But you do have a talent."

He groaned and scoured his scalp with his knuckles. He was sitting on the dirt in their old play-place, a kind of bower deep in the willows, where they could hear the stream running over the stones nearby and the clang-clang of the smithy further off. The girl sat down facing him.

"Look at all the stuff you can do," she said. "You couldn't do any of it if you didn't have a gift."

"A little gift," Diamond said indistinctly. "Enough for tricks."

"How do you know that?"

Rose was very dark-skinned, with a cloud of crinkled hair, a thin mouth, an intent, serious face. Her feet and legs and hands were bare and dirty, her skirt and jacket disreputable. Her dirty toes and fingers were delicate and elegant, and a necklace of amethysts gleamed under the torn, buttonless jacket. Her mother, Tangle, made a good living by curing and healing, bone-knitting and birth-easing, and selling spells of finding, love-potions, and sleeping-draughts. She could afford to dress herself and her daughter in new clothes, buy shoes, and keep clean, but it didn't occur to her to do so. Nor was housekeeping one of her interests. She and Rose lived mostly on boiled chicken and fried eggs, as she was often paid in poultry. The yard of their two-room house was a wilderness of cats and hens. She liked cats, toads and jewels. The amethyst necklace had been payment for the safe delivery of a son to Golden's head forester. Tangle herself wore armfuls of bracelets and bangles that flashed and crashed when she flicked out an impatient spell. At times she wore a kitten on her shoulder. She was not an attentive mother. Rose had demanded, at seven years old, "Why did you have me if you didn't want me?"

"How can you deliver babies properly if you haven't had one?" said her mother.

"So I was practice," Rose snarled.

"Everything is practice," Tangle said. She was never ill-natured. She seldom thought to do anything much for her daughter, but never hurt her, never scolded her, and gave her whatever she asked for, dinner, a toad of her own, the amethyst necklace, lessons in witchcraft. She would have provided new clothes if Rose had asked for them, but she never did. Rose had looked after herself from an early age, and this was one of the reasons Diamond loved her. With her, he knew what freedom was. Without her, he could attain it only when he was hearing and singing and playing music.

"I do have a gift," he said now, rubbing his temples and pulling his hair.

"Stop destroying your head," Rose told him.

"I know Tarry thinks I do."

"Of course you do! What does it matter what Tarry thinks? You already play the harp about nine times better than he ever did."

This was another of the reasons Diamond loved her.

"Are there any wizard musicians?" he asked, looking up.

She pondered. "I don't know."

"I don't either. Morred and Elfarran sang to each other, and he was a mage. I think there's a Master Chanter on Roke, that teaches the lays and the histories. But I never heard of a wizard being a musician."

"I don't see why one couldn't be." She never saw why something could not be. Another reason he loved her.

"It always seemed to me they're sort of alike," he said, "magic and music. Spells and tunes. For one thing, you have to get them just exactly right."

"Practice," Rose said, rather sourly. "I know." She flicked a pebble at Diamond. It turned into a butterfly in mid-air. He flicked a butterfly back at her, and the two flitted and flickered a moment before they fell back to earth as pebbles. Diamond and Rose had worked out several such variations on the old stone-hopping trick.

"You ought to go, Di," she said. "Just to find out."

"I know."

"What if you got to be a wizard! Oh! Think of the stuff you could teach me! Shapechanging – We could be anything. Horses! Bears!"

"Moles," Diamond said. "Honestly, I feel like hiding underground. I always thought Father was going to make me learn all his kind of stuff, after I got my name. But all this year he's kept sort of holding off. I guess he had this in mind all along. But what if I go down there and I'm not any better at being a wizard than I am at bookkeeping? Why can't I do what I know I *can* do?"

"Well, why can't you do it all? The magic and the music, anyhow? You can always hire a bookkeeper."

When she laughed, her thin face got bright, her thin mouth got wide, and her eyes disappeared.

"Oh, Darkrose," Diamond said, "I love you."

"Of course you do. You'd better. I'll witch you if you don't."

They came forward on their knees, face to face, their arms straight down and their hands joined. They kissed each other all over their faces. To Rose's lips Diamond's face was smooth and full as a plum, with just a hint of prickliness above the lip and jawline, where he had taken to shaving recently. To Diamond's lips Rose's face was soft as silk, with just a hint of grittiness on one cheek, which she had rubbed with a dirty hand. They moved a little closer so that their breasts and bellies touched, though their hands stayed down by their sides. They went on kissing.

"Darkrose," he breathed in her ear, his secret name for her.

She said nothing, but breathed very warm in his ear, and he moaned. His hands clenched hers. He drew back a little. She drew back.

They sat back on their ankles.

"Oh, Di," she said, "it will be awful when you go."

"I won't go," he said. "Anywhere. Ever."

But of course he went down to Havnor South Port, in one of his father's carts driven by one of his father's carters, along with Master Hemlock. As a rule, people do what wizards advise them to do. And it is no small honour to be invited by a wizard to be his student or apprentice. Hemlock, who had won his staff on Roke, was used to having boys come to him begging to be tested and, if they had the gift for it, taught. He was a little curious about this boy whose cheerful good manners hid some reluctance or self-doubt. It was the father's idea, not the boy's, that he was gifted. That was unusual, though perhaps not so unusual among the wealthy as among common folk. At any rate he came with a very good prenticing fee paid beforehand in gold and ivory. If he had the makings of a wizard Hemlock would train him, and if he had, as Hemlock suspected, a mere childish flair, then he'd be sent home with what remained of his fee. Hemlock was an honest, upright, humourless, scholarly wizard with little interest in feelings or ideas. His gift was for names. "The art begins and ends in naming," he said, which indeed is true, although there may be a good deal between the beginning and the end.

So Diamond, instead of learning spells and illusions and transformations and all such gaudy tricks, as Hemlock called them, sat in a narrow room at the back of the wizard's narrow house on a narrow back street of the old city, memorizing long,

long lists of words, words of power in the Language of the Making. Plants and parts of plants and animals and parts of animals and islands and parts of islands, parts of ships, parts of the human body. The words never made sense, never made sentences, only lists. Long, long lists.

His mind wandered. "Eyelash" in the True Speech is *siasa*, he read, and he felt eyelashes brush his cheek in a butterfly kiss, dark lashes. He looked up startled and did not know what had touched him. Later when he tried to repeat the word, he stood dumb.

"Memory, memory," Hemlock said. "Talent's no good without memory!" He was not harsh, but he was unyielding. Diamond had no idea what opinion Hemlock had of him, and guessed it to be pretty low. The wizard sometimes had him come with him to his work, mostly laying spells of safety on ships and houses, purifying wells, and sitting on the councils of the city, seldom speaking but always listening. Another wizard, not Roke-trained but with the healer's gift, looked after the sick and dying of South Port. Hemlock was glad to let him do so. His own pleasure was in studying and, as far as Diamond could see, doing no magic at all. "Keep the Equilibrium, it's all in that," Hemlock said, and, "Knowledge, order and control." Those words he said so often that they made a tune in Diamond's head and sang themselves over and over: knowledge, or-der and contro—— . . .

When Diamond put the lists of names to tunes he made up, he learned them much faster; but then the tune would come as part of the name, and he would sing out so clearly – for his voice had re-established itself as a strong, dark tenor – that Hemlock winced. Hemlock's was a very silent house.

Mostly the pupil was supposed to be with the master, or studying the lists of names in the room where the lorebooks and wordbooks were, or asleep. Hemlock was a stickler for early abed and early afoot. But now and then Diamond had an hour or two free. He always went down to the docks and sat on a pierside or a waterstair and thought about Darkrose. As soon as he was out of the house and away from Master Hemlock, he began to think about Darkrose, and went on thinking about her and very little else. It surprised him a little. He thought he ought to be homesick, to think about his mother. He did think about his mother quite often, and often was homesick, lying on his cot in his bare and narrow little room after a scanty supper of cold pea-porridge – for this wizard, at least, did not live in such luxury as Golden had imagined. Diamond never thought about Darkrose, nights. He thought of his mother, or of sunny rooms and hot food, or a tune would come into his head and he would practise it mentally on the harp in his mind, and so drift off to sleep. Darkrose would come to his mind only when he was down at the docks, staring out at the water of the harbour, the piers, the fishing boats, only when he was outdoors and away from Hemlock and his house.

So he cherished his free hours as if they were actual meetings with her. He had always loved her, but had not understood that he loved her beyond anyone and anything. When he was with her, even when he was down on the docks thinking of her, he was alive. He never felt entirely alive in Master Hemlock's house and presence. He felt a little dead. Not dead, but a little dead.

A few times, sitting on the waterstairs, the dirty harbour water sloshing at the next step down, the yells of gulls and dock workers wreathing the air with a thin, ungainly music, he shut his eyes and saw his love so clear, so close, that he reached out his hand to touch her. If he reached out his hand in his mind only, as when he played the mental harp, then indeed he touched her. He felt her hand in his, and her cheek, warm-cool, silken-gritty, lay against his mouth. In his mind he spoke to her, and in his mind she answered, her voice, her husky voice saying his name, "Diamond . . ."

But as he went back up the streets of South Port he lost her. He swore to keep her with him, to think of her, to think of her that night, but she faded away. By the time he opened the door of Master Hemlock's house he was reciting lists of names, or wondering what would be for dinner, for he was hungry most of the time. Not till he could take an hour and run back down to the docks could he think of her.

So he came to feel that those hours were true meetings with her, and he lived for them, without knowing what he lived for until his feet were on the cobbles, and his eyes on the harbour and the far line of the sea. Then he remembered what was worth remembering.

The winter passed by, and the cold early spring, and with the warm late spring came a letter from his mother, brought by a carter. Diamond read it and took it to Master Hemlock, saying, "My mother wonders if I might spend a month at home this summer."

"Probably not," the wizard said, and then, appearing to notice Diamond, put down his pen and said, "Young man, I must ask you if you wish to continue studying with me."

Diamond had no idea what to say. The idea of its being up to him had not occurred to him. "Do you think I ought to?" he asked at last.

"Probably not," the wizard said.

Diamond expected to feel relieved, released, but found he felt rejected, ashamed.

"I'm sorry," he said, with enough dignity that Hemlock glanced up at him.

"You could go to Roke," the wizard said.

"To Roke?"

The boy's drop-jawed stare irritated Hemlock, though he knew it shouldn't. Wizards are used to overweening confidence in the young of their kind. They expect modesty to come later, if at all. "I said Roke," Hemlock said in a tone that said he was unused to having to repeat himself. And then, because this boy, this soft-headed, spoiled, moony boy had endeared himself to Hemlock by his uncomplaining patience, he took pity on him and said, "You should either go to Roke or find a wizard to teach you what you need. Of course you need what I can teach you. You need the names. The art begins and ends in naming. But that's not your gift. You have a poor memory for words. You must train it diligently. However, it's clear that you do have capacities, and that they need cultivation and discipline, which another man can give you better than I can." So does modesty breed modesty, sometimes, even in unlikely places. "If you were to go to Roke, I'd send a letter with you drawing you to the particular attention of the Master Summoner."

"Ah," said Diamond, floored. The Summoner's art is perhaps the most arcane and dangerous of all the arts of magic.

"Perhaps I am wrong," said Hemlock in his dry, flat voice. "Your gift may be for Pattern. Or perhaps it's an ordinary gift for shaping and transformation. I'm not certain."

"But you are – I do actually—"

"Oh yes. You are uncommonly slow, young man, to recognize your own capacities." It was spoken harshly, and Diamond stiffened up a bit.

"I thought my gift was for music," he said.

Hemlock dismissed that with a flick of his hand. "I am talking of the True Art," he said. "Now I will be frank with you. I advise you to write your parents – I shall write them too – informing them of your decision to go to the School on Roke, if that is what you decide; or to the Great Port, if the Mage Restive will take you on, as I think he will, with my recommendation. But I advise against visiting home. The entanglement of family, friends, and so on is precisely what you need to be free of. Now, and henceforth."

"Do wizards have no family?"

Hemlock was glad to see a bit of fire in the boy. "They are one another's family," he said.

"And no friends?"

"They may be friends. Did I say it was an easy life?" A pause. Hemlock looked directly at Diamond. "There was a girl," he said.

Diamond met his gaze for a moment, looked down, and said nothing.

"Your father told me. A witch's daughter, a childhood play-mate. He believed that you had taught her spells."

"She taught me."

Hemlock nodded. "That is quite understandable, among children. And quite impossible now. Do you understand that?"

"No," Diamond said.

"Sit down," said Hemlock. After a moment Diamond took the stiff, high-backed chair facing him.

"I can protect you here, and have done so. On Roke, of course, you'll be perfectly safe. The very walls, there . . . But if you go home, you must be willing to protect yourself. It's a difficult thing for a young man, very difficult – a test of a will that has not yet been steeled, a mind that has not yet seen its true goal. I very strongly advise that you not take that risk. Write your parents, and go to the Great Port, or to Roke. Half your year's fee, which I'll return to you, will see to your first expenses."

Diamond sat upright and still. He had been getting some of his father's height and girth lately, and looked very much a man, though a very young one.

"What did you mean, Master Hemlock, in saying that you had protected me here?"

"Simply as I protect myself," the wizard said, and after a moment, testily, "The bargain, boy. The power we give for our power. The lesser state of being we forgo. Surely you know that every true man of power is celibate."

There was a pause, and Diamond said, "So you saw to it . . . that I . . ."

"Of course. It was my responsibility as your teacher."

Diamond nodded. He said, "Thank you." Presently he stood up. "Excuse me, Master," he said. "I have to think."

"Where are you going?"

"Down to the waterfront."

"Better stay here."

"I can't think, here."

Hemlock might have known then what he was up against, but having told the boy he would not be his master any longer, he could not in conscience command him. "You have a true gift, Essiri," he said, using the name he had given the boy in the springs of the Amia, a word that in the Old Speech means Willow. "I don't entirely understand it. I think you don't understand it at all. Take care! To misuse a gift, or to refuse to use it, may cause great loss, great harm."

Diamond nodded, suffering, contrite, unrebellious, unmovable.

"Go on," the wizard said, and he went.

Later he knew he should never have let the boy leave the house.

He had underestimated Diamond's willpower, or the strength of the spell the girl had laid on him. Their conversation was in the morning; Hemlock went back to the ancient cantrip he was annotating; it was not till suppertime that he thought about his pupil, and not until he had eaten supper alone that he admitted that Diamond had run away.

Hemlock was loth to practise any of the lesser arts of magic. He did not put out a finding spell, as any sorcerer might have done. Nor did he call to Diamond in any way. He was angry, perhaps he was hurt. He had thought well of the boy, and offered to write the Summoner about him, and then at the first test of character Diamond had broken. "Glass," the wizard muttered. At least this weakness proved he was not dangerous. Some talents were best not left to run wild, but there was no harm in this fellow, no malice. No ambition. "No spine," said Hemlock to the silence of the house. "Let him crawl home to his mother."

Still it rankled him that Diamond had let him down flat, without a word of thanks or apology. So much for good manners, he thought.

As she blew out the lamp and got into bed, the witch's daughter heard an owl calling, the little, liquid hu-hu-hu-hu that made people call them laughing owls. She heard it with a mournful heart. That had been their signal, summer nights, when they sneaked out to meet in the willow grove, down on the banks of the Amia, when everybody else was sleeping. She would not think of him at night. Back in the winter she had sent to him night after night. She had learned her mother's spell of sending, and knew that it was a true spell. She had sent him her touch, her voice saying his name, again and again. She had met a wall of air and silence. She touched nothing. He would not hear.

Once or twice, all of a sudden, in the daytime, there had been a moment when she had known him close in mind and could touch him if she reached out. But at night she knew only his blank absence, his refusal of her. She had stopped trying to reach him, months ago, but her heart was still very sore.

"Hu-hu-hu," said the owl, under her window, and then it said,

"Darkrose!" Startled from her misery, she leaped out of bed and opened the shutters.

"Come on out," whispered Diamond, a shadow in the starlight.

"Mother's not home. Come in!" She met him at the door.

They held each other tight, hard, silent for a long time. To Diamond it was as if he held his future, his own life, his whole life, in his arms.

At last she moved, and kissed his cheek, and whispered, "I missed you, I missed you, I missed you. How long can you stay?"

"As long as I like."

She kept his hand and led him in. He was always a little reluctant to enter the witch's house, a pungent, disorderly place thick with the mysteries of women and witchcraft, very different from his own clean comfortable home, even more different from the cold austerity of the wizard's house. He shivered like a horse as he stood there, too tall for the herb-festooned rafters. He was very highly strung, and worn out, having walked 40 miles in sixteen hours without food.

"Where's your mother?" he asked in a whisper.

"Sitting with old Ferny. She died this afternoon, Mother will be there all night. But how did you get here?"

"Walked."

"The wizard let you visit home?"

"I ran away."

"Ran away! Why?"

"To keep you."

He looked at her, that vivid, fierce, dark face in its rough cloud of hair. She wore only her shift, and he saw the infinitely delicate, tender rise of her breasts. He drew her to him again, but though she hugged him she drew away again, frowning.

"Keep me?" she repeated. "You didn't seem to worry about losing me all winter. What made you come back now?"

"He wanted me to go to Roke."

"To Roke?" She stared. "To Roke, Di? Then you really do have the gift – you could be a sorcerer?"

To find her on Hemlock's side was a blow.

"Sorcerers are nothing to him. He means I could be a wizard. Do magery. Not just witchcraft."

"Oh, I see," Rose said after a moment. "But I don't see why you ran away."

They had let go of each other's hands.

"Don't you understand?" he said, exasperated with her for not understanding, because he had not understood. "A wizard can't have anything to do with women. With witches. With all that."

"Oh, I know. It's beneath them."

"It's not just beneath them—"

"Oh, but it is. I'll bet you had to unlearn every spell I taught you. Didn't you?"

"It isn't the same kind of thing."

"No. It isn't the High Art. It isn't the True Speech. A wizard mustn't soil his lips with common words. 'Weak as women's magic, wicked as women's magic.' You think I don't know what they say? So, why did you come back here?"

"To see you!"

"What for?"

"What do you think?"

"You never sent to me, you never let me send to you, all the time you were gone. I was just supposed to wait until you got tired of playing wizard. Well, I got tired of waiting." Her voice was nearly inaudible, a rough whisper.

"Somebody's been coming around," he said, incredulous that she could turn against him. "Who's been after you?"

"None of your business if there is! You go off, you turn your back on me. Wizards can't have anything to do with what I do, what my mother does. Well, I don't want anything to do with what you do, either, ever. So go!"

Starving hungry, frustrated, misunderstood, Diamond reached out to hold her again, to make her body understand his body, repeating that first, deep embrace that had held all the years of their lives in it. He found himself standing 2 feet back, his hands stinging and his ears ringing and his eyes dazzled. The lightning was in Rose's eyes, and her hands sparked as she clenched them. "Never do that again," she whispered.

"Never fear," Diamond said, turned on his heel, and strode out. A string of dried sage caught on his head and trailed after him.

He spent the night in their old place in the sallows. Maybe he hoped she would come, but she did not come, and he soon slept in sheer weariness. He woke in the first, cold light. He sat up and thought. He looked at life in that cold light. It was a different matter from what he had believed it. He went down to the stream in which he had been named. He drank, washed his hands and face, made himself look as decent as he could, and went up through the town to the fine house at the high end, his father's house.

After the first outcries and embraces, the servants and his mother sat him right down to breakfast. So it was with warm food in his belly and a certain chill courage in his heart that he faced his father, who had been out before breakfast seeing off a string of timber-carts to the Great Port.

"Well, son!" They touched cheeks. "So Master Hemlock gave you a vacation?"

"No, sir. I left."

Golden stared, then filled his plate and sat down. "Left," he said.

"Yes, sir. I decided that I don't want to be a wizard."

"Hmf," said Golden, chewing. "Left of your own accord? Entirely? With the master's permission?"

"Of my own accord entirely, without his permission."

Golden chewed very slowly, his eyes on the table. Diamond had seen his father look like this when a forester reported an infestation in the chestnut groves, and when he found a mule-dealer had cheated him.

"He wanted me to go to the college on Roke to study with the Master Summoner. He was going to send me there. I decided not to go."

After a while Golden asked, still looking at the table, "Why?"

"It isn't the life I want."

Another pause. Golden glanced over at his wife, who stood by the window listening in silence. Then he looked at his son. Slowly the mixture of anger, disappointment, confusion, and respect on his face gave way to something simpler, a look of complicity, very nearly a wink. "I see," he said. "And what did you decide you want?"

A pause. "This," Diamond said. His voice was level. He looked neither at his father nor his mother.

"Hah!" said Golden. "Well! I will say I'm glad of it, son." He ate a small pork pie in one mouthful. "Being a wizard, going to Roke, all that, it never seemed real, not exactly. And with you off there, I didn't know what all this was for, to tell you the truth. All my business. If you're here, it adds up, you see. It adds up. Well! But listen here, did you just run off from the wizard? Did he know you were going?"

"No. I'll write him," Diamond said, in his new, level voice.

"He won't be angry? They say wizards have short tempers. Full of pride."

"He's angry," Diamond said, "but he won't do anything."

So it proved. Indeed, to Golden's amazement, Master Hemlock sent back a scrupulous two-fifths of the prenticing fee. With the packet, which was delivered by one of Golden's carters who had taken a load of spars down to South Port, was a note for Diamond. It said, "True Art requires a single heart." The direction on the outside was the Hardic rune for willow. The note was signed with Hemlock's rune, which had two meanings: the hemlock tree, and suffering.

Diamond sat in his own sunny room upstairs, on his comfortable bed, hearing his mother singing as she went about the house. He held the wizard's letter and reread the message and the two runes many times. The cold and sluggish mind that had been born in him that morning down in the sallows accepted the lesson. No magic. Never again. He had never given his heart to it. It had been a game to him, a game to play with Darkrose. Even the names of the True Speech that he had learned in the wizard's house, though he knew the beauty and the power that lay in them, he could let go, let slip, forget. That was not his language.

He could speak his language only with her. And he had lost her, let her go. The double heart has no true speech. From now on he could talk only the language of duty: the getting and the spending, the outlay and the income, the profit and the loss.

And beyond that, nothing. There had been illusions, little spells, pebbles that turned to butterflies, wooden birds that flew on living wings for a minute or two. There had never been a choice, really. There was only one way for him to go.

Golden was immensely happy and quite unconscious of it. "Old man's got his jewel back," said the carter to the forester. "Sweet as new butter, he is." Golden, unaware of being sweet, thought only how sweet life was. He had bought the Reche grove, at a very stiff price to be sure, but at least old Lowbough of Easthill hadn't got it, and now he and Diamond could develop it as it ought to be developed. In among the chestnuts there were a lot of pines, which could be felled and sold for masts and spars and small lumber, and replanted with chestnut seedlings. It would in time be a pure stand like the Big Grove, the heart of his chestnut kingdom. In time, of course. Oak and chestnut don't shoot up overnight like alder and willow. But there was time. There was time, now. The boy was barely seventeen, and he himself just forty-five. In his prime. He had been feeling old, but that was nonsense. He was in his prime. The oldest trees, past bearing, ought to come out with the pines. Some good wood for furniture could be salvaged from them.

"Well, well, well," he said to his wife, frequently, "all rosy again, eh? Got the apple of your eye back home, eh? No more moping, eh?"

And Tuly smiled and stroked his hand.

Once instead of smiling and agreeing, she said, "It's lovely to have him back, but," and Golden stopped hearing. Mothers were born to worry about their children, and women were born never to be content. There was no reason why he should listen to the litany of anxieties by which Tuly hauled herself through life. Of course she thought a merchant's life wasn't good enough for the boy. She'd have thought being king in Havnor wasn't good enough for him.

"When he gets himself a girl," Golden said, in answer to whatever it was she had been saying, "he'll be all squared away. Living with the wizards, you know, the way they are, it set him back a bit. Don't worry about Diamond. He'll know what he wants when he sees it!"

"I hope so," said Tuly.

"At least he's not seeing the witch's girl," said Golden. "That's done with." Later on it occurred to him that neither was his wife seeing the witch any more. For years they'd been thick as thieves, against all his warnings, and now Tangle was never anywhere near the house. Women's friendships never lasted. He teased her about it. Finding her strewing pennyroyal and millersbane in the chests and clothes-presses against an infestation of moths, he said, "Seems like you'd have your friend the wise woman up to hex 'em away. Or aren't you friends any more?"

"No," his wife said in her soft, level voice, "we aren't."

"And a good thing too!" Golden said roundly. "What's become of that daughter of hers, then? Went off with a juggler, I heard?"

"A musician," Tuly said. "Last summer."

"A nameday party," said Golden. "Time for a bit of play, a bit of music and dancing, boy. Nineteen years old. Celebrate it!"

"I'll be going to Easthill with Sul's mules."

"No, no, no. Sul can handle it. Stay home and have your party. You've been working hard. We'll hire a band. Who's the best in the country? Tarry and his lot?"

"Father, I don't want a party," Diamond said and stood up, shivering his muscles, like a horse. He was bigger than Golden now, and when he moved abruptly it was startling. "I'll go to Easthill," he said, and left the room.

"What's that all about?" Golden said to his wife, a rhetorical question. She looked at him and said nothing, a non-rhetorical answer.

After Golden had gone out, she found her son in the counting-room going through ledgers. She looked at the pages. Long, long lists of names and numbers, debts and credits, profits and losses.

"Di," she said, and he looked up. His face was still round and a bit peachy, though the bones were heavier and the eyes were melancholy.

"I didn't mean to hurt Father's feelings," he said.

"If he wants a party, he'll have it," she said. Their voices were alike, being in the higher register but dark-toned, and held to an even quietness, contained, restrained. She perched on a stool beside his at the high desk.

"I can't," he said, and stopped, and went on, "I really don't want to have any dancing."

"He's matchmaking," Tuly said, dry, fond.

"I don't care about that."

"I know you don't."

"The problem is . . ."

"The problem is the music," his mother said at last.

He nodded.

"My son, there is no reason," she said, suddenly passionate, "there is *no* reason why you should give up everything you love!"

He took her hand and kissed it as they sat side by side.

"Things don't mix," he said. "They ought to, but they don't. I found that out. When I left the wizard, I thought I could be everything. You know – do magic, play music, be Father's son, love Rose . . . It doesn't work that way. Things don't mix."

"They do, they do," Tuly said. "Everything is hooked together, tangled up!"

"Maybe things are, for women. But I . . . I can't be double-hearted."

"Doublehearted? You? You gave up wizardry because you knew that if you didn't, you'd betray it."

He took the word with a visible shock, but did not deny it.

"But why did you give up music?"

"I have to have a single heart. I can't play the harp while I'm bargaining with a mule-breeder. I can't sing ballads while I'm figuring what we have to pay the pickers to keep 'em from hiring out to Lowbough!" His voice shook a little now, a vibrato, and his eyes were not sad, but angry.

"So you put a spell on yourself," she said, "just as that wizard

put one on you. A spell to keep you safe. To keep you with the
mule-breeders, and the nut-pickers, and these." She struck the
ledger full of lists of names and figures, a flicking, dismissive tap.
"A spell of silence," she said.

After a long time the young man said, "What else can I do?"

"I don't know, my dear. I do want you to be safe. I do love to see
your father happy and proud of you. But I can't bear to see you
unhappy, without pride! I don't know. Maybe you're right. Maybe
for a man it's only one thing ever. But I miss hearing you sing."

She was in tears. They hugged, and she stroked his thick,
shining hair and apologized for being cruel, and he hugged her
again and said she was the kindest mother in the world, and so she
went off. But as she left she turned back a moment and said, "Let
him have the party, Di. Let yourself have it."

"I will," he said, to comfort her.

Golden ordered the beer and food and fireworks, but Diamond
saw to hiring the musicians.

"Of course I'll bring my band," Tarry said, "fat chance I'd
miss it! You'll have every tootler in the west of the world here for
one of your dad's parties."

"You can tell 'em you're the band that's getting paid."

"Oh, they'll come for the glory," said the harper, a lean, long-
jawed, wall-eyed fellow of forty. "Maybe you'll have a go with us
yourself, then? You had a hand for it, before you took to making
money. And the voice not bad, if you'd worked on it."

"I doubt it," Diamond said.

"That girl you liked, witch's Rose, she's running about with
Labby, I hear. No doubt they'll come by."

"I'll see you then," said Diamond, looking big and handsome
and indifferent, and walked off.

"Too high and mighty these days to stop and talk," said Tarry,
"though I taught him all he knows of harping. But what's that to a
rich man?"

Tarry's malice had left his nerves raw, and the thought of the
party weighed on him till he lost his appetite. He thought

hopefully for a while that he was sick and could miss the party.
But the day came, and he was there. Not so evidently, so
eminently, so flamboyantly there as his father, but present,
smiling, dancing. All his childhood friends were there too, half
of them married by now to the other half, it seemed, but there was
still plenty of flirting going on, and several pretty girls were
always near him. He drank a good deal of Gadge Brewer's
excellent beer, and found he could endure the music if he was
dancing to it and talking and laughing while he danced. So he
danced with all the pretty girls in turn, and then again with
whichever one turned up again, which all of them did.

It was Golden's grandest party yet, with a dancing floor built
on the town green down the way from Golden's house, and a tent
for the old folks to eat and drink and gossip in, and new clothes
for the children, and jugglers and puppeteers, some of them hired
and some of them coming by to pick up whatever they could in
the way of coppers and free beer. Any festivity drew itinerant
entertainers and musicians; it was their living, and though unin-
vited they were welcomed. A tale-singer with a droning voice and
a droning bagpipe was singing "The Deed of the Dragonlord" to
a group of people under the big oak on the hilltop. When Tarry's
band of harp, fife, viol and drum took time off for a breather and a
swig, a new group hopped up on to the dance floor. "Hey, there's
Labby's band!" cried the pretty girl nearest Diamond. "Come
on, they're the best!"

Labby, a light-skinned, flashy-looking fellow, played the
double-reed woodhorn. With him were a violist, a tabor-player
and Rose, who played fife. Their first tune was a stampy, fast and
brilliant, too fast for some of the dancers. Diamond and his
partner stayed in, and people cheered and clapped them when
they finished the dance, sweating and panting. "Beer!" Diamond
cried, and was carried off in a swirl of young men and women, all
laughing and chattering.

He heard behind him the next tune start up, the viol alone,
strong and sad as a tenor voice: "Where My Love Is Going".

He drank a mug of beer down in one draught, and the girls with
him watched the muscles in his strong throat as he swallowed,

and they laughed and chattered, and he shivered all over like a cart-horse stung by flies. He said, "Oh! I can't –!" He bolted off into the dusk beyond the lanterns hanging around the brewer's booth.

"Where's he going?" said one, and another, "He'll be back," and they laughed and chattered.

The tune ended. "Darkrose," he said, behind her in the dark. She turned her head and looked at him. Their heads were on a level, she sitting cross-legged up on the dance platform, he kneeling on the grass.

"Come to the sallows," he said.

She said nothing. Labby, glancing at her, set his woodhorn to his lips. The drummer struck a triple beat on his tabor, and they were off into a sailor's jig.

When she looked around again Diamond was gone.

Tarry came back with his band in an hour or so, ungrateful for the respite and much the worse for beer. He interrupted the tune and the dancing, telling Labby loudly to clear out.

"Ah, pick your nose, harp-picker," Labby said, and Tarry took offence, and people took sides, and while the dispute was at its brief height, Rose put her fife in her pocket and slipped away.

Away from the lanterns of the party it was dark, but she knew the way in the dark. He was there. The willows had grown, these two years. There was only a little space to sit among the green shoots and the long, falling leaves.

The music started up, distant, blurred by wind and the murmur of the river running.

"What did you want, Diamond?"

"To talk."

They were only voices and shadows to each other.

"So," she said.

"I wanted to ask you to go away with me," he said.

"When?"

"Then. When we quarrelled. I said it all wrong. I thought . . ." A long pause. "I thought I could go on running away. With you. And play music. Make a living. Together. I meant to say that."

"You didn't say it."

"I know, I said everything wrong. I did everything wrong. I betrayed everything. The magic. And the music. And you."

"I'm all right," she said.

"Are you?"

"I'm not really good on the fife, but I'm good enough. What you didn't teach me, I can fill in with a spell, if I have to. And the band, they're all right. Labby isn't as bad as he looks. Nobody fools with me. We make a pretty good living. Winters, I go stay with Mother and help her out. So I'm all right. What about you, Di?"

"All wrong."

She started to say something, and did not say it.

"I guess we were children," he said. "Now . . ."

"What's changed?"

"I made the wrong choice."

"Once?" she said. "Or twice?"

"Twice."

"Third time's the charm."

Neither spoke for a while. She could just make out the bulk of him in the leafy shadows. "You're bigger than you were," she said. "Can you still make a light, Di? I want to see you."

He shook his head.

"That was the one thing you could do that I never could. And you never could teach me."

"I didn't know what I was doing," he said. "Sometimes it worked, sometimes it didn't."

"And the wizard in South Port didn't teach you how to make it work?"

"He only taught me names."

"Why can't you do it now?"

"I gave it up, Darkrose. I had either to do it and nothing else, or not do it. You have to have a single heart."

"I don't see why," she said. "My mother can cure a fever and ease a childbirth and find a lost ring; maybe that's nothing compared to what the wizards and the dragonlords can do, but it's not nothing, all the same. And she didn't give up anything for it. Having me didn't stop her. She had me so that she could *learn* how to do it! Just because I learned how to play music from you, did I have to give up saying spells? I can bring a fever down now too. Why should you have to stop doing one thing so you can do the other?"

"My father," he began, and stopped, and gave a kind of laugh. "They don't go together," he said. "The money and the music."

"The father and the witchgirl," said Darkrose.

Again there was silence between them. The leaves of the willows stirred.

"Would you come back to me?" he said. "Would you go with me, live with me, marry me, Darkrose?"

"Not in your father's house, Di."

"Anywhere. Run away."

"But you can't have me without the music."

"Or the music without you."

"I would," she said.

"Does Labby want a harper?"

She hesitated, she laughed. "If he wants a fife-player," she said.

"I haven't practised ever since I left, Darkrose," he said. "But the music was always in my head, and you . . ." She reached out her hands to him. They knelt facing, the willow leaves moving across their hair. They kissed each other, timidly at first.

In the years after Diamond left home, Golden made more money than he had ever done before. All his deals were profitable. It was as if good fortune stuck to him and he could not shake it off. He grew immensely wealthy. He did not forgive his son. It would have made a happy ending, but he would not have it. To leave so, without a word, on his nameday night, to go off with the witchgirl, leaving all the honest work undone, to be a vagrant musician, a harper twanging and singing and grinning for pennies – there was nothing but shame and pain and anger in it for Golden. So he had his tragedy.

Tuly shared it with him for a long time, since she could see her son only by lying to her husband, which she found hard to do. She wept to think of Diamond hungry, sleeping hard. Cold nights

of autumn were a misery to her. But as time went on and she
heard him spoken of as Diamond the sweet singer of the west of
Havnor, Diamond who had harped and sung to the great lords in
the Tower of the Sword, her heart grew lighter. And once, when
Golden was down at South Port, she and Tangle took a donkey
cart and drove over to Easthill, where they heard Diamond sing
the "Lay of the Lost Queen," while Rose sat with them, and
Little Tuly sat on Tuly's knee. And if not a happy ending, that
was a true joy, which may be enough to ask for, after all.

The Valley of the Worm

Robert E. Howard

*At the same time that the Tolkien phenomenon was taking hold
in the mid-sixties, the Conan phenomenon was also erupting.
Although the Conan stories had been written in the early
thirties, it was only in the mid-sixties that they had all been
comprehensively available in paperback, edited and augmented
by L. Sprague de Camp. The creator of Conan was a young
Texan author, Robert E. Howard (1906–36), who became a
prolific writer of adventure, fantasy, western and sports stories
for a career of little more than ten years before he killed himself
following the death of his mother. The first Conan story to
appear was "The Phoenix on the Sword" (Weird Tales,
December 1932). Before then Howard had written similar
heroic adventure stories featuring King Kull, Bran Mak Morn
and Solomon Kane, all of which betray elements that later
came together in the Conan stories. Howard would have been
amazed at the success of Conan in later years, and the extent to
which it inspired a whole new sub-genre of fantasy, dubbed
"sword-and-sorcery". The Conan stories are regularly reprinted and I wanted to use one of Howard's lesser known
stories, but one that fits well into the theme of this anthology.
Its northern setting was one that also fascinated Tolkien and
inspired the background to Middle Earth, while the eternally
re-born hero of Howard's story, like Michael Moorcock's
Eternal Champion, is central to the whole fantasy genre which
is constantly recreating itself.*

𝕴 WILL TELL YOU OF NIORD AND THE WORM. You have heard the tale before in many guises wherein the hero was named Tyr, or Perseus, or Siegfried, or Beowulf, or St George. But it was Niord who met the loathly demoniac thing that crawled hideously up from hell, and from which meeting sprang the cycle of hero-tales that revolves down the ages until the very substance of the truth is lost and passes into the limbo of all forgotten legends. I know whereof I speak, for I was Niord.

As I lie here awaiting death, which creeps slowly upon me like a blind slug, my dreams are filled with glittering visions and the pageantry of glory. It is not of the drab, disease-racked life of James Allison I dream, but all the gleaming figures of the mighty pageantry that have passed before, and shall come after; for I have faintly glimpsed, not merely the shapes that come after, as a man in a long parade glimpses, far ahead, the line of figures that precede him winding over a distant hill, etched shadow-like against the sky. I am one and all the pageantry of shapes and guises and masks which have been, are, and shall be the visible manifestations of that illusive, intangible, but vitally existent spirit now promenading under the brief and temporary name of James Allison.

Each man on earth, each woman, is part and all of a similar caravan of shapes and beings. But they cannot remember – their minds cannot bridge the brief, awful gulfs of blackness which lie between those unstable shapes, and which the spirit, soul or ego, in spanning, shakes off its fleshy masks. I remember. Why I can remember is the strangest tale of all; but as I lie here with death's black wings slowly unfolding over me, all the dim folds of my previous lives are shaken out before my eyes, and I see myself in many forms and guises – braggart, swaggering, fearful, loving, foolish, all that men have been or will be.

I have been man in many lands and many conditions; yet – and here is another strange thing – my line of reincarnation runs straight down one unerring channel. I have never been any but a man of that restless race men once called Nordheimr and later Aryans, and today name by many names and designations. Their history is my history, from the first mewling wail of a hairless white ape cub in the wastes of the Arctic, to the death-cry of the last degenerate product of ultimate civilization, in some dim and unguessed future age.

My name has been Hialmar, Tyr, Bragi, Bran, Horsa, Eric and John. I strode red-handed through the deserted streets of Rome behind the yellow-maned Brennus; I wandered through the violated plantations with Alaric and his Goths when the flame of burning villas lit the land like day and an empire was gasping its last under our sandalled feet; I waded sword in hand through the foaming surf from Hengist's galley to lay the foundations of England in blood and pillage; when Leif the Lucky sighted the broad white beaches of an unguessed world, I stood beside him in the bows of the dragon-ship, my golden beard blowing in the wind; and when Godfrey of Bouillon led his Crusaders over the walls of Jerusalem, I was among them in steel cap and brigandine.

But it is of none of these things I would speak. I would take you back with me into an age beside which that of Brennus and Rome is as yesterday. I would take you back through, not merely centuries and millenniums, but epochs and dim ages unguessed by the wildest philosopher. Oh far, far and far will you fare into the nighted past before you win beyond the boundaries of my race, blue-eyed, yellow-haired, wanderers, slayers, lovers, mighty in rapine and wayfaring.

It is the adventure of Niord Worm's-bane of which I would speak – the rootstem of a whole cycle of herotales which has not yet reached its end, the grisly underlying reality that lurks behind time-distorted myths of dragons, fiends and monsters.

Yet it is not alone with the mouth of Niord that I will speak. I am James Allison no less than I was Niord, and as I unfold the tale, I will interpret some of his thoughts and dreams and deeds from the mouth of the modern I, so that the saga of Niord shall not be a meaningless chaos to you. His blood is your blood, who are sons of Aryan; but wide misty gulfs of aeons lie horrifically between, and the deeds and dreams of Niord seem as alien to your deeds and dreams as the primordial and lion-haunted forest seems alien to the white-walled city street.

It was a strange world in which Niord lived and loved and fought, so long ago that even my aeon-spanning memory cannot recognize landmarks. Since then the surface of the earth has changed, not once but a score of times; continents have risen and sunk, seas have changed their beds and rivers their courses, glaciers have waxed and waned, and the very stars and constellations have altered and shifted.

It was so long ago that the cradle-land of my race was still in Nordheim. But the epic drifts of my people had already begun, and blue-eyed, yellow-maned tribes flowed eastward and southward and westward, on century-long treks that carried them around the world and left their bones and their traces in strange lands and wild waste places. On one of these drifts I grew from infancy to manhood. My knowledge of that northern homeland was dim memories, like half-remembered dreams, of blinding white snow plains and ice fields, of great fires roaring in the circle of hide tents, of yellow manes flying in great winds, and a sun setting in a lurid wallow of crimson clouds, blazing on trampled snow where still dark forms lay in pools that were redder than the sunset.

That last memory stands out clearer than the others. It was the field of Jotunheim, I was told in later years, whereon had just been fought that terrible battle which was the Armageddon of the Æsir-folk, the subject of a cycle of hero-songs for long ages, and which still lives today in dim dreams of Ragnarok and Goetterdaemmerung. I looked on that battle as a mewling infant; so I must have lived about – but I will not name the age, for I would be called a madman, and historians and geologists alike would rise to refute me.

But my memories of Nordheim were few and dim, paled by memories of that long, long trek upon which I had spent my life. We had not kept to a straight course, but our trend had been for ever southward. Sometimes we had bided for a while in fertile upland valleys or rich river-traversed plains, but always we took up the trail again, and not always because of drouth or famine. Often we left countries teeming with game and wild grain to push into wastelands. On our trail we moved endlessly, driven only by our restless whim, yet blindly following a cosmic law, the workings of which we never guessed, any more than the wild geese guess in their flights around the world. So at last we came into the Country of the Worm.

I will take up the tale at the time when we came into jungle-clad hills reeking with rot and teeming with spawning life, where the tom-toms of a savage people pulsed incessantly through the hot breathless night. These people came forth to dispute our way – short, strongly built men, black-haired, painted, ferocious, but indisputably white men. We knew their breed of old. They were Picts, and of all alien races the fiercest. We had met their kind before in thick forests, and in upland valleys beside mountain lakes. But many moons had passed since those meetings.

I believe this particular tribe represented the easternmost drift of the race. They were the most primitive and ferocious of any I ever met. Already they were exhibiting hints of characteristics I have noted among black savages in jungle countries, though they had dwelled in these environs only a few generations. The abysmal jungle was engulfing them, was obliterating their pristine characteristics and shaping them in its own horrific mould. They were drifting into head-hunting, and cannibalism was but a step which I believe they must have taken before they became extinct. These things are natural adjuncts to the jungle; the Picts did not learn them from the black people, for then there were no blacks among those hills. In later years they came up from the south, and the Picts first enslaved and then were absorbed by them. But with that my saga of Niord is not concerned.

We came into that brutish hill country, with its squalling abysms of savagery and black primitiveness. We were a whole tribe marching on foot, old men, wolfish with their long beards and gaunt limbs, giant warriors in their prime, naked children running along the line of march, women with tousled yellow locks carrying babies which never cried – unless it were to scream from

pure rage. I do not remember our numbers, except that there
were some 500 fighting-men – and by fighting-men I mean all
males, from the child just strong enough to lift a bow, to the
oldest of the old men. In that madly ferocious age all were
fighters. Our women fought, when brought to bay, like tigresses,
and I have seen a babe, not yet old enough to stammer articulate
words, twist its head and sink its tiny teeth in the foot that
stamped out its life.

Oh, we were fighters! Let me speak of Niord. I am proud of
him, the more when I consider the paltry crippled body of James
Allison, the unstable mask I now wear. Niord was tall, with great
shoulders, lean hips and mighty limbs. His muscles were long and
swelling, denoting endurance and speed as well as strength. He
could run all day without tiring, and he possessed a co-ordination
that made his movements a blur of blinding speed. If I told you
his full strength, you would brand me a liar. But there is no man
on earth today strong enough to bend the bow Niord handled
with ease. The longest arrow-flight on record is that of a Turkish
archer who sent a shaft 482 yards. There was not a stripling in my
tribe who could not have bettered that flight.

As we entered the jungle country we heard the tom-toms
booming across the mysterious valleys that slumbered between
the brutish hills, and in a broad, open plateau we met our
enemies. I do not believe these Picts knew us, even by legends,
or they had never rushed so openly to the onset, though they
outnumbered us. But there was no attempt at ambush. They
swarmed out of the trees, dancing and singing their war-songs,
yelling their barbarous threats. Our heads should hang in their
idol-hut and our yellow-haired women should bear their sons.
Ho! ho! ho! By Ymir, it was Niord who laughed then, not James
Allison. Just so we of the Æsir laughed to hear their threats –
deep thunderous laughter from broad and mighty chests. Our
trail was laid in blood and embers through many lands. We were
the slayers and ravishers, striding sword in hand across the
world, and that these folk threatened us woke our rugged
humour.

We went to meet them, naked but for our wolfhides, swinging our bronze swords, and our singing was like rolling thunder in the hills. They sent their arrows among us, and we gave back their fire. They could not match us in archery. Our arrows hissed in blinding clouds among them, dropping them like autumn leaves, until they howled and frothed like mad dogs and changed to hand-grips. And we, mad with the fighting joy, dropped our bows and ran to meet them, as a lover runs to his love.

By Ymir, it was a battle to madden and make drunken with the slaughter and the fury. The Picts were as ferocious as we, but ours was the superior physique, the keener wit, the more highly developed fighting-brain. We won because we were a superior race, but it was no easy victory. Corpses littered the blood-soaked earth; but at last they broke, and we cut them down as they ran, to the very edge of the trees. I tell of that fight in a few bald words. I cannot paint the madness, the reek of sweat and blood, the panting, muscle-straining effort, the splintering of bones under mighty blows, the rending and hewing of quivering sentient flesh; above all the merciless abysmal savagery of the whole affair, in which there was neither rule nor order, each man fighting as he would or could. If I might do so, you would recoil in horror; even the modern I, cognizant of my close kinship with those times, stand aghast as I review that butchery. Mercy was yet unborn, save as some individual's whim, and rules of warfare were as yet undreamed of. It was an age in which each tribe and each human fought tooth and fang from birth to death, and neither gave nor expected mercy.

So we cut down the fleeing Picts, and our women came out on the field to brain the wounded enemies with stones, or cut their throats with copper knives. We did not torture. We were no more cruel than life demanded. The rule of life was ruthlessness, but there is more wanton cruelty today than ever we dreamed of. It was not wanton bloodthirstiness that made us butcher wounded and captive foes. It was because we knew our chances of survival increased with each enemy slain.

Yet there was occasionally a touch of individual mercy, and so it was in this fight. I had been occupied with a duel with an especially valiant enemy. His tousled thatch of black hair scarcely came above my chin, but he was a solid knot of steel-spring muscles, than which lightning scarcely moved faster. He had an iron sword and a hide-covered buckler. I had a knotty-headed bludgeon. That fight was one that glutted even my battle-lusting soul. I was bleeding from a score of flesh wounds before one of my terrible, lashing strokes smashed his shield like cardboard, and an instant later my bludgeon glanced from his unprotected head. Ymir! Even now I stop to laugh and marvel at the hardness of that Pict's skull. Men of that age were assuredly built on a rugged plan! That blow should have spattered his brains like water. It did lay his scalp open horribly, dashing him senseless to the earth, where I let him lie, supposing him to be dead, as I joined in the slaughter of the fleeing warriors.

When I returned reeking with sweat and blood, my club horridly clotted with blood and brains, I noticed that my antagonist was regaining consciousness, and that a naked tousle-headed girl was preparing to give him the finishing touch with a stone she could scarcely lift. A vagrant whim caused me to check the blow. I had enjoyed the fight, and I admired the adamantine quality of his skull.

We made camp a short distance away, burned our dead on a great pyre, and after looting the corpses of the enemy, we dragged them across the plateau and cast them down in a valley to make a feast for the hyenas, jackals and vultures which were already gathering. We kept close watch that night, but we were not attacked, though far away through the jungle we could make out the red gleam of fires, and could faintly hear, when the wind veered, the throb of tom-toms and demoniac screams and yells – keenings for the slain or mere animal squallings of fury.

Nor did they attack us in the days that followed. We bandaged our captive's wounds and quickly learned his primitive tongue, which, however, was so different from ours that I cannot conceive of the two languages having ever had a common source.

His name was Grom, and he was a great hunter and fighter, he boasted. He talked freely and held no grudge, grinning broadly and showing tusk-like teeth, his beady eyes glittering from under the tangled black mane that fell over his low forehead. His limbs were almost ape-like in their thickness.

He was vastly interested in his captors, though he could never understand why he had been spared; to the end it remained an inexplicable mystery to him. The Picts obeyed the law of survival even more rigidly than did the Æsir. They were the more practical, as shown by their more settled habits. They never roamed as far or as blindly as we. Yet in every line we were the superior race.

Grom, impressed by our intelligence and fighting qualities, volunteered to go into the hills and make peace for us with his people. It was immaterial to us, but we let him go. Slavery had not yet been dreamed of.

So Grom went back to his people, and we forgot about him, except that I went a trifle more cautiously about my hunting, expecting him to be lying in wait to put an arrow through my back. Then one day we heard a rattle of tom-toms, and Grom appeared at the edge of the jungle, his face split in his gorilla grin, with the painted, skin-clad, feather-bedecked chiefs of the clans. Our ferocity had awed them, and our sparing of Grom further impressed them. They could not understand leniency; evidently we valued them too cheaply to bother about killing one when he was in our power.

So peace was made with much pow-wow, and sworn to with many strange oaths and rituals – we swore only by Ymir, and an Æsir never broke that vow. But they swore by the elements, by the idol which sat in the fetish-hut where fires burned for ever and a withered crone slapped a leather-covered drum all night long, and by another being too terrible to be named.

Then we all sat around the fires and gnawed meat-bones, and drank a fiery concoction they brewed from wild grain, and the wonder is that the feast did not end in a general massacre; for that liquor had devils in it and made maggots writhe in our brains. But no harm came of our vast drunkenness, and thereafter we dwelled at peace with our barbarous neighbours. They taught us many things, and learned many more from us. But they taught us iron-workings, into which they had been forced by the lack of copper in those hills, and we quickly excelled them.

We went freely among their villages – mud-walled clusters of huts in hilltop clearings, overshadowed by giant trees – and we allowed them to come at will among our camps – straggling lines of hide tents on the plateau where the battle had been fought. Our young men cared not for their squat beady-eyed women, and our rangy clean-limbed girls with their tousled yellow heads were not drawn to the hairy-breasted savages. Familiarity over a period of years would have reduced the repulsion on either side, until the two races would have flowed together to form one hybrid people, but long before that time the Æsir rose and departed, vanishing into the mysterious hazes of the haunted south. But before that exodus there came to pass the horror of the Worm.

I hunted with Grom and he led me into brooding, uninhabited valleys and up into silence-haunted hills where no men had set foot before us. But there was one valley, off in the mazes of the south-west, into which he would not go. Stumps of shattered columns, relics of a forgotten civilization, stood among the trees on the valley floor. Grom showed them to me, as we stood on the cliffs that flanked the mysterious vale, but he would not go down into it, and he dissuaded me when I would have gone alone. He would not speak plainly of the danger that lurked there, but it was greater than that of serpent or tiger, or the trumpeting elephants which occasionally wandered up in devastating droves from the south.

Of all beasts, Grom told me in the gutturals of his tongue, the Picts feared only Satha, the great snake, and they shunned the jungle where he lived. But there was another thing they feared, and it was connected in some manner with the Valley of Broken Stones, as the Picts called the crumbling pillars. Long ago, when his ancestors had first come into the country, they had dared that grim vale, and a whole clan of them had perished, suddenly, horribly and unexplainably. At least Grom did not explain. The horror had come up out of the earth, somehow, and it was not good to talk of it, since it was believed that It might be summoned by speaking of It – whatever It was.

But Grom was ready to hunt with me anywhere else; for he was the greatest hunter among the Picts, and many and fearful were our adventures. Once I killed, with the iron sword I had forged with my own hands, that most terrible of all beasts – old sabre-tooth, which men today call a tiger because he was more like a tiger than anything else. In reality he was almost as much like a bear in build, save for his unmistakably feline head. Sabre-tooth was massive-limbed, with a low-hung, great, heavy body, and he vanished from the earth because he was too terrible a fighter, even for that grim age. As his muscles and ferocity grew, his brain dwindled until at last even the instinct of self-preservation vanished. Nature, who maintains her balance in such things, destroyed him because, had his super-fighting powers been allied with an intelligent brain, he would have destroyed all other forms of life on earth. He was a freak on the road of evolution – organic development gone mad and run to fangs and talons, to slaughter and destruction.

I killed sabre-tooth in a battle that would make a saga in itself, and for months afterwards I lay semi-delirious with ghastly wounds that made the toughest warriors shake their heads. The Picts said that never before had a man killed a sabre-tooth single-handed. Yet I recovered, to the wonder of all.

While I lay at the doors of death there was a secession from the tribe. It was a peaceful secession, such as continually occurred and contributed greatly to the peopling of the world by yellow-haired tribes. Forty-five of the young men took themselves mates simultaneously and wandered off to found a clan of their own. There was no revolt; it was a racial custom which bore fruit in all the later ages, when tribes sprung from the same roots met, after centuries of separation, and cut one another's throats with joyous abandon. The tendency of the Aryan and the pre-Aryan was always towards disunity, clans splitting off the main stem, and scattering.

So these young men, led by one Bragi, my brother-in-arms, took their girls and venturing to the south-west, took up their abode in the Valley of Broken Stones. The Picts expostulated, hinting vaguely of a monstrous doom that haunted the vale, but the Æsir laughed. We had left our own demons and weirds in the icy wastes of the far blue north, and the devils of other races did not much impress us.

When my full strength was returned, and the grisly wounds were only scars, I girt on my weapons and strode over the plateau to visit Bragi's clan. Grom did not accompany me. He had not been in the Æsir camp for several days. But I knew the way. I remembered well the valley, from the cliffs of which I had looked down and seen the lake at the upper end, the trees thickening into forest at the lower extremity. The sides of the valley were high sheer cliffs, and a steep broad ridge at either end cut it off from the surrounding country. It was towards the lower or south-western end that the valley floor was dotted thickly with ruined columns, some towering high among the trees, some fallen into heaps of lichen-clad stones. What race reared them none knew. But Grom had hinted fearsomely of a hairy, apish monstrosity dancing loathsomely under the moon to a demoniac piping that induced horror and madness.

I crossed the plateau whereon our camp was pitched, descended the slope, traversed a shallow vegetation-choked valley, climbed another slope, and plunged into the hills. A half-day's leisurely travel brought me to the ridge on the other side of which lay the valley of the pillars. For many miles I had seen no sign of human life. The settlements of the Picts all lay many miles to the east. I topped the ridge and looked down into the dreaming valley with its still blue lake, its brooding cliffs and its broken columns jutting among the trees. I looked for smoke. I saw none, but I saw vultures wheeling in the sky over a cluster of tents on the lake shore.

I came down the ridge warily and approached the silent camp. In it I halted, frozen with horror. I was not easily moved. I had seen death in many forms, and had fled from or taken part in red massacres that spilled blood like water and heaped the earth with corpses. But here I was confronted with an organic devastation that staggered and appalled me. Of Bragi's embryonic clan, not one remained alive, and not one corpse was whole. Some of the hide tents still stood erect. Others were mashed down and flattened out, as if crushed by some monstrous weight, so that at first I wondered if a drove of elephants had stampeded across the camp. But no elephants ever wrought such destruction as I saw strewn on the bloody ground. The camp was a shambles, littered with bits of flesh and fragments of bodies – hands, feet, heads, pieces of human debris. Weapons lay about, some of them stained with a greenish slime like that which spurts from a crushed caterpillar.

No human foe could have committed this ghastly atrocity. I looked at the lake, wondering if nameless amphibian monsters had crawled from the calm waters whose deep blue told of unfathomed depths. Then I saw a print left by the destroyer. It was a track such as a titanic worm might leave, yards broad, winding back down the valley. The grass lay flat where it ran, and bushes and small trees had been crushed down into the earth, all horribly smeared with blood and greenish slime.

With berserk fury in my soul I drew my sword and started to follow it, when a call attracted me. I wheeled, to see a stocky form approaching me from the ridge. It was Grom the Pict, and when I think of the courage it must have taken for him to have overcome all the instincts planted in him by traditional teachings and personal experience, I realize the full depths of his friendship for me.

Squatting on the lake shore, spear in his hands, his black eyes ever roving fearfully down the brooding tree-waving reaches of the valley, Grom told me of the horror that had come upon Bragi's clan under the moon. But first he told me of it, as his sires had told the tale to him.

Long ago the Picts had drifted down from the north-west on a long, long trek, finally reaching these jungle-covered hills, where, because they were weary, and because the game and fruit were plentiful and there were no hostile tribes, they halted and built their mud-walled villages.

Some of them, a whole clan of that numerous tribe, took up

their abode in the Valley of the Broken Stones. They found the columns and a great ruined temple back in the trees, and in that temple there was no shrine or altar, but the mouth of a shaft that vanished deep into the black earth, and in which there were no steps such as a human being would make and use. They built their village in the valley, and in the night, under the moon, horror came upon them and left only broken walls and bits of slime-smeared flesh.

In those days the Picts feared nothing. The warriors of the other clans gathered and sang their war-songs and danced their war-dances, and followed a broad track of blood and slime to the shaft-mouth in the temple. They howled defiance and hurled down boulders which were never heard to strike bottom. Then began a thin demoniac piping, and up from the well pranced a hideous anthropomorphic figure dancing to the weird strains of a pipe it held in its monstrous hands. The horror of its aspect froze the fierce Picts with amazement, and close behind it a vast white bulk heaved up from the subterranean darkness. Out of the shaft came a slavering mad nightmare which arrows pierced but could not check, which swords carved but could not slay. It fell slobbering upon the warriors, crushing them to crimson pulp, tearing them to bits as an octopus might tear small fishes, sucking their blood from their mangled limbs and devouring them even as they screamed and struggled. The survivors fled, pursued to the very ridge, up which, apparently, the monster could not propel its quaking mountainous bulk.

After that they did not dare the silent valley. But the dead came to their shamans and old men in dreams and told them strange and terrible secrets. They spoke of an ancient, ancient race of semi-human beings which once inhabited that valley and reared those columns for their own weird inexplicable purposes. The white monster in the pits was their god, summoned up from the nighted abysses of mid-earth uncounted fathoms below the black mould by sorcery unknown to the sons of men. The hairy anthropomorphic being was its servant, created to serve the god, a formless elemental spirit drawn up from below and cased in flesh, organic but beyond the understanding of humanity. The

Old Ones had long vanished into the limbo from whence they crawled in the black dawn of the universe, but their bestial god and his inhuman slave lived on. Yet both were organic after a fashion, and could be wounded, though no human weapon had been found potent enough to slay them.

Bragi and his clan had dwelled for weeks in the valley before the horror struck. Only the night before, Grom, hunting above the cliffs, and by that token daring greatly, had been paralyzed by a high-pitched demon piping, and then by a mad clamour of human screaming. Stretched face down in the dirt, hiding his head in a tangle of grass, he had not dared to move, even when the shrieks died away in the slobbering, repulsive sounds of a hideous feast. When dawn broke he had crept shuddering to the cliffs to look down into the valley, and the sight of the devastation, even when seen from afar, had driven him in yammering flight far into the hills. But it had occurred to him, finally, that he should warn the rest of the tribe, and returning, on his way to the camp on the plateau, he had seen me entering the valley.

So spoke Grom, while I sat and brooded darkly, my chin on my mighty fist. I cannot frame in modern words the clan feeling that in those days was a living vital part of every man and woman. In a world where talon and fang were lifted on every hand, and the hands of all men raised against an individual, except those of his own clan, tribal instinct was more than the phrase it is today. It was as much a part of a man as was his heart or his right hand. This was necessary, for only thus banded together in unbreakable groups could mankind have survived in the terrible environments of the primitive world. So now the personal grief I felt for Bragi and the clean-limbed young men and laughing white-skinned girls was drowned in a deeper sea of grief and fury that was cosmic in its depth and intensity. I sat grimly, while the Pict squatted anxiously beside me, his gaze roving from me to the menacing deeps of the valley where the accursed columns loomed like broken teeth of cackling hags among the waving leafy reaches.

I, Niord, was not one to use my brain over-much. I lived in

a physical world, and there were the old men of the tribe to do my thinking. But I was one of a race destined to become dominant mentally as well as physically, and I was no mere muscular animal. So as I sat there, there came dimly and then clearly a thought to me that brought a short fierce laugh from my lips.

Rising, I bade Grom aid me, and we built a pyre on the lake shore of dried wood, the ridge-poles of the tents, and the broken shafts of spears. Then we collected the grisly fragments that had been parts of Bragi's band, and we laid them on the pile, and struck flint and steel to it.

The thick sad smoke crawled serpent-like into the sky, and, turning to Grom, I made him guide me to the jungle where lurked that scaly horror, Satha, the great serpent. Grom gaped at me; not the greatest hunters among the Picts sought out the mighty crawling one. But my will was like a wind that swept him along my course, and at last he led the way. We left the valley by the upper end, crossing the ridge, skirting the tall cliffs, and plunged into the fastnesses of the south, which was peopled only by the grim denizens of the jungle. Deep into the jungle we went, until we came to a low-lying expanse, dank and dark beneath the great creeper-festooned trees, where our feet sank deep into the spongy silt, carpeted by rotting vegetation, and slimy moisture oozed up beneath their pressure. This, Grom told me, was the realm haunted by Satha, the great serpent.

Let me speak of Satha. There is nothing like him on earth today, nor has there been for countless ages. Like the meat-eating dinosaur, like old sabre-tooth, he was too terrible to exist. Even then he was a survival of a grimmer age when life and its forms were cruder and more hideous. There were not many of his kind then, though they may have existed in great numbers in the reeking ooze of the vast jungle-tangled swamps still further south. He was larger than any python of modern ages, and his fangs dripped with poison a thousand times more deadly than that of a king cobra.

He was never worshipped by the pure-blood Picts, though the blacks that came later deified him, and that adoration persisted in the hybrid race that sprang from the negroes and their white conquerors. But to other peoples he was the nadir of evil horror, and tales of him became twisted into demonology; so in later ages Satha became the veritable devil of the white races, and the Stygians first worshipped, and then, when they became Egyptians, abhorred him under the name of Set, the Old Serpent, while to the Semites he became Leviathan and Satan. He was terrible enough to be a god, for he was a crawling death. I had seen a bull elephant fall dead in his tracks from Satha's bite. I had seen him, had glimpsed him writhing his horrific way through the dense jungle, had seen him take his prey, but I had never hunted him. He was too grim, even for the slayer of old sabre-tooth.

But now I hunted him, plunging further and further into the hot, breathless reek of his jungle, even when friendship for me could not drive Grom further. He urged me to paint my body and sing my death-song before I advanced further, but I pushed on unheeding.

In a natural runway that wound between the shouldering trees, I set a trap. I found a large tree, soft and spongy of fibre, but thick-boled and heavy, and I hacked through its base close to the ground with my great sword, directing its fall so that when it toppled, its top crashed into the branches of a smaller tree, leaving it leaning across the runway, one end resting on the earth, the other caught in the small tree. Then I cut away the branches on the underside, and cutting a slim, tough sapling I trimmed it and stuck it upright like a prop-pole under the leaning tree. Then, cutting away the tree which supported it, I left the great trunk poised precariously on the prop-pole, to which I fastened a long vine, as thick as my wrist.

Then I went alone through that primordial twilight jungle until an overpowering fetid odour assailed my nostrils, and from the rank vegetation in front of me Satha reared up his hideous head, swaying lethally from side to side, while his forked tongue jetted in and out, and his great yellow terrible eyes burned icily on me with all the evil wisdom of the black elder world that was when man was not. I backed away, feeling no fear, only an icy sensation along my spine, and Satha came sinuously after me, his shining 80-foot barrel rippling over the rotting vegetation in mesmeric silence. His wedge-shaped head was bigger than the head of the hugest stallion, his trunk was thicker than a man's body, and his scales shimmered with a thousand changing scintillations. I was to Satha as a mouse is to a king cobra, but I was fanged as no mouse ever was. Quick as I was, I knew I could not avoid the lightning stroke of that great triangular head; so I dared not let him come too close. Subtly I fled down the runway, and behind me the rush of the great supple body was like the sweep of wind through the grass.

He was not far behind me when I raced beneath the dead-fall, and as the great shining length glided under the trap, I gripped the vine with both hands and jerked desperately. With a crash the great trunk fell across Satha's scaly back, some 6 feet back of his wedge-shaped head.

I had hoped to break his spine but I do not think it did, for the great body coiled and knotted, the mighty tail lashed and thrashed, mowing down the bushes as if with a giant flail. At the instant of the fall, the huge head had whipped about and struck the tree with a terrific impact, the mighty fangs shearing through bark and wood like scimitars. Now, as if aware he fought an inanimate foe, Satha turned on me, standing out of his reach. The scaly neck writhed and arched, the mighty jaws gaped, disclosing fangs a foot in length, from which dripped venom that might have burned through solid stone.

I believe, what of his stupendous strength, that Satha would have writhed from under the trunk, but for a broken branch that had been driven deep into his side, holding him like a barb. The sound of his hissing filled the jungle and his eyes glared at me with such concentrated evil that I shook despite myself. Oh, he knew it was I who had trapped him! Now I came as close as I dared, and with a sudden powerful cast of my spear transfixed his neck just below the gaping jaws, nailing him to the tree-trunk. Then I dared greatly, for he was far from dead, and I knew he would in an instant tear the spear from the wood and be free to strike. But in that instant I ran in, and swinging my sword with all my great power, I hewed off his terrible head.

The heavings and contortions of Satha's prisoned form in life were naught to the convulsions of his headless length in death. I retreated, dragging the gigantic head after me with a crooked pole, and at a safe distance from the lashing, flying tail, I set to work. I worked with naked death then, and no man ever toiled more gingerly than did I. For I cut out the poison sacs at the base of the great fangs, and in the terrible venom I soaked the heads of eleven arrows, being careful that only the bronze points were in the liquid, which else had corroded away the wood of the tough shafts. While I was doing this, Grom, driven by comradeship and curiosity, came stealing nervously through the jungle, and his mouth gaped as he looked on the head of Satha.

For hours I steeped the arrowheads in the poison, until they were caked with a horrible green scum, and showed tiny flecks of corrosion where the venom had eaten into the solid bronze. I wrapped them carefully in broad, thick, rubber-like leaves, and then, though night had fallen and the hunting beasts were roaring on every hand, I went back through the jungled hills, Grom with me, until at dawn we came again to the high cliffs that loomed above the Valley of Broken Stones.

At the mouth of the valley I broke my spear, and I took all the unpoisoned shafts from my quiver, and snapped them. I painted my face and limbs as the Æsir painted themselves only when they went forth to certain doom, and I sang my death-song to the sun as it rose over the cliffs, my yellow mane blowing in the morning wind.

Then I went down into the valley, bow in hand.

Grom could not drive himself to follow me. He lay on his belly in the dust and howled like a dying dog.

I passed the lake and the silent camp where the pyre-ashes still smouldered, and came under the thickening trees beyond. About me the columns loomed, mere shapeless heads from the ravages of staggering aeons. The trees grew more dense, and under their vast leafy branches the very light was dusky and evil. As in twilight shadow I saw the ruined temple, cyclopean walls staggering up from masses of decaying masonry and fallen blocks of stone. About 600 yards in front of it a great column reared up in an open glade, 80 or 90 feet in height. It was so worn and pitted by weather and time that any child of my tribe could have climbed it, and I marked it and changed my plan.

I came to the ruins and saw huge crumbling walls upholding a domed roof from which many stones had fallen, so that it seemed like the lichen-grown ribs of some mythical monster's skeleton arching above me. Titanic columns flanked the open doorway through which ten elephants could have stalked abreast. Once there might have been inscriptions and hieroglyphics on the pillars and walls, but they were long worn away. Around the great room, on the inner side, ran columns in better state of preservation. On each of these columns was a flat pedestal, and some dim instinctive memory vaguely resurrected a shadowy scene wherein black drums roared madly, and on these pedestals monstrous beings squatted loathsomely in inexplicable rituals rooted in the black dawn of the universe.

There was no altar – only the mouth of a great well-like shaft in the stone floor, with strange obscene carvings all about the rim. I tore great pieces of stone from the rotting floor and cast them down the shaft which slanted down into utter darkness. I heard them bound along the side, but I did not hear them strike bottom. I cast down stone after stone, each with a searing curse, and at last I heard a sound that was not the dwindling rumble of the falling stones. Up from the well floated a weird demon-piping that was a symphony of madness. Far down in the darkness I glimpsed the faint fearful glimmering of a vast white bulk.

I retreated slowly as the piping grew louder, falling back through the broad doorway. I heard a scratching, scrambling noise, and up from the shaft and out of the doorway between the colossal columns came a prancing incredible figure. It went erect like a man, but it was covered with fur, that was shaggiest where its face should have been. If it had ears, nose and a mouth I did not discover them. Only a pair of staring red eyes leered from the furry mask. Its misshapen hands held a strange set of pipes, on which it blew weirdly as it pranced towards me with many a grotesque caper and leap.

Behind it I heard a repulsive obscene noise as of a quaking unstable mass heaving up out of a well. Then I nocked an arrow, drew the cord and sent the shaft singing through the furry breast of the dancing monstrosity. It went down as though struck by a thunderbolt, but to my horror the piping continued, though the pipes had fallen from the malformed hands. Then I turned and ran fleetly to the column, up which I swarmed before I looked back. When I reached the pinnacle I looked, and because of the shock and surprise of what I saw, I almost fell from my dizzy perch.

Out of the temple the monstrous dweller in the darkness had come, and I, who had expected a horror yet cast in some terrestrial mould, looked on the spawn of nightmare. From what subterranean hell it crawled in the long ago I know not, nor what black age it represented. But it was not a beast, as humanity knows beasts. I call it a worm for lack of a better term. There is no earthly language that has a name for it. I can only say that it looked somewhat more like a worm than it did an octopus, a serpent or a dinosaur.

It was white and pulpy, and drew its quaking bulk along the ground, worm-fashion. But it had wide flat tentacles, and fleshy feelers, and other adjuncts the use of which I am unable to explain. And it had a long proboscis which it curled and uncurled like an elephant's trunk. Its forty eyes, set in a horrific circle, were composed of thousands of facets of as many scintillant colours which changed and altered in never-ending transmutation. But through all interplay of hue and glint, they retained their evil intelligence – intelligence there was behind those flickering facets, not human nor yet bestial, but a night-born demoniac intelligence such as men in dreams vaguely sense throbbing titanically in the black gulfs outside our material universe. In size the monster was mountainous; its bulk would have dwarfed a mastodon.

But even as I shook with the cosmic horror of the thing, I drew a feathered shaft to my ear and arched it singing on its way. Grass and bushes were crushed flat as the monster came towards me like a moving mountain and shaft after shaft I sent with terrific force and deadly precision. I could not miss so huge a target. The arrows sank to the feathers or clear out of sight in the unstable bulk, each bearing enough poison to have stricken dead a bull elephant. Yet on it came, swiftly, appallingly, apparently heedless of both the shafts and the venom in which they were steeped. And all the time the hideous music played a maddening accompaniment, whining thinly from the pipes that lay untouched on the ground.

My confidence faded; even the poison of Satha was futile against this uncanny being. I drove my last shaft almost straight downward into the quaking white mountain, so close was the monster under my perch. Then suddenly its colour altered. A wave of ghastly blue surged over it, and the vast bulk heaved in earthquake-like convulsions. With a terrible plunge it struck the lower part of the column, which crashed to falling shards of stone. But even with the impact, I leaped far out and fell through the empty air full upon the monster's back.

The spongy skin yielded and gave beneath my feet, and I drove my sword hilt deep, dragging it through the pulpy flesh, ripping a horrible yard-long wound, from which oozed a green slime. Then a flip of a cable-like-tentacle flicked me from the titan's back and spun me 300 feet through the air to crash among a cluster of giant trees.

The impact must have splintered half the bones in my frame, for when I sought to grasp my sword again and crawl anew to the combat, I could not move hand or foot, could only writhe helplessly with my broken back. But I could see the monster and I knew that I had won, even in defeat. The mountainous bulk was heaving and billowing, the tentacles were lashing madly, the antennae writhing and knotting, and the nauseous whiteness had changed to a pale and grisly green. It turned ponderously and lurched back towards the temple, rolling like a crippled ship in a heavy swell. Trees crashed and splintered as it lumbered against them.

I wept with pure fury because I could not catch up my sword

and rush in to die glutting my berserk madness in mighty strokes. But the worm-god was death-stricken and needed not my futile sword. The demon pipes on the ground kept up their infernal tune, and it was like the fiend's death-dirge. Then as the monster veered and floundered, I saw it catch up the corpse of its hairy slave. For an instant the apish form dangled in mid-air, gripped round by the trunk-like proboscis, then was dashed against the temple wall with a force that reduced the hairy body to a mere shapeless pulp. At that the pipes screamed out horribly, and fell silent for ever.

The titan staggered on the brink of the shaft; then another change came over it – a frightful transfiguration the nature of which I cannot yet describe. Even now when I try to think of it clearly, I am only chaotically conscious of a blasphemous, unnatural transmutation of form and substance, shocking and indescribable. Then the strangely altered bulk tumbled into the shaft to roll down into the ultimate darkness from whence it came, and I knew that it was dead. And as it vanished into the well, with a rending, grinding groan the ruined walls quivered from dome to base. They bent inward and buckled with deafening reverberation, the columns splintered, and with a cataclysmic crash the dome itself came thundering down. For an instant the air seemed veiled with flying debris and stone-dust, through which the treetops lashed madly as in a storm or an earthquake convulsion. Then all was clear again and I stared, shaking the blood from my eyes. Where the temple had stood there lay only a colossal pile of shattered masonry and broken stones, and every column in the valley had fallen, to lie in crumbling shards.

In the silence that followed I heard Grom wailing a dirge over me. I bade him lay my sword in my hand, and he did so, and bent close to hear what I had to say, for I was passing swiftly.

"Let my tribe remember," I said, speaking slowly. "Let the tale be told from village to village, from camp to camp, from tribe to tribe, so that men may know that not man nor beast nor devil may prey in safety on the golden-haired people of Asgard. Let them build me a cairn where I lie and lay me therein with my bow and sword at hand, to guard this valley for ever; so if the ghost of the god I slew comes up from below, my ghost will ever be ready to give it battle."

And while Grom howled and beat his hairy breast, death came to me in the Valley of the Worm.

The Golden Key

George Macdonald

Tracing the fantasy thread back a long way brings us to George Macdonald. It is true to say that the earliest fantasies grew out of myths and legends and embellished stories of heroic adventures in strange lands. This remained part of the oral tradition for centuries. When authors came to write about these things much of them emerged as folk tales which in time evolved into fairy tales. But there were two writers in particular who took these tales rather more seriously, treating them as allegories of life. Hans Christian Andersen was one. The other was George Macdonald (1824–1905). Although he became known for his books for children, especially At the Back of the North Wind *(1871) and* The Princess and the Goblin *(1872) – a book that was a favourite of the young Tolkien and had a measurable influence on* Lord of the Rings *– Macdonald wrote the first truly adult fantasy of the Victorian era in* Phantastes *(1858). Macdonald experimented with fantasy all his life, most often developing themes of Christian allegory, but never preaching or moralizing. The following story will usually be found among Macdonald's collections of fairy tales – all of which should, of course, be compulsory reading – but it should not be restricted to any one age group. Tolkien regarded it as among the best of Macdonald's short fiction.*

T HERE WAS A BOY WHO USED TO SIT IN THE TWILIGHT and listen to his great-aunt's stories.

She told him that if he could reach the place where the end of the rainbow stands he would find there a golden key.

"And what is the key for?" the boy would ask. "What is it the key of? What will it open?"

"That nobody knows," his aunt would reply. "He has to find that out."

"I suppose, being gold," the boy once said, thoughtfully, "that I could get a good deal of money for it if I sold it."

"Better never find it than sell it," returned his aunt.

And then the boy went to bed and dreamed about the golden key.

Now all that his great-aunt told the boy about the golden key would have been nonsense, had it not been that their little house stood on the borders of Fairyland. For it is perfectly well known that out of Fairyland nobody ever can find where the rainbow stands. The creature takes such good care of its golden key, always flitting from place to place, lest anyone should find it! But in Fairyland it is quite different. Things that look real in this country look very thin indeed in Fairyland, while some of the things that here cannot stand still for a moment, will not move there. So it was not in the least absurd of the old lady to tell her nephew such things about the golden key.

"Did you ever know anybody find it?" he asked, one evening.

"Yes. Your father, I believe, found it."

"And what did he do with it, can you tell me?"

"He never told me."

"What was it like?"

"He never showed it to me."

"How does a new key come there always?"

"I don't know. There it is."

"Perhaps it is the rainbow's egg."

"Perhaps it is. You will be a happy boy if you find the nest."

"Perhaps it comes tumbling down the rainbow from the sky."

"Perhaps it does."

One evening, in summer, he went into his own room, and stood at the lattice-window, and gazed into the forest which fringed the outskirts of Fairyland. It came close up to his great-aunt's garden, and, indeed, sent some straggling trees into it. The forest lay to the east, and the sun, which was setting behind the cottage, looked straight into the dark wood with his level red eye. The trees were all old, and had few branches below, so that the sun could see a great way into the forest; and the boy, being keen-sighted, could see almost as far as the sun. The trunks stood like rows of red columns in the shine of the red sun, and he could see down aisle after aisle in the vanishing distance. And as he gazed into the forest he began to feel as if the trees were all waiting for him, and had something they could not go on with till he came to them. But he was hungry and wanted his supper. So he lingered.

Suddenly, far among the trees, as far as the sun could shine, he saw a glorious thing. It was the end of a rainbow, large and brilliant. He could count all seven colours, and could see shade after shade beyond the violet; while before the red stood a colour more gorgeous and mysterious still. It was a colour he had never seen before. Only the spring of the rainbow arch was visible. He could see nothing of it above the trees.

"The golden key!" he said to himself, and darted out of the house, and into the wood.

He had not gone far before the sun set. But the rainbow only glowed the brighter. For the rainbow of Fairyland is not dependent upon the sun as ours is. The trees welcomed him. The bushes made way for him. The rainbow grew larger and brighter; and at length he found himself within two trees of it.

It was a grand sight, burning away there in silence, with its gorgeous, its lovely, its delicate colours, each distinct, all combining. He could now see a great deal more of it. It rose high into the blue heavens, but bent so little that he could not tell how high the crown of the arch must reach. It was still only a small portion of a huge bow.

He stood gazing at it till he forgot himself with delight – even forgot the key which he had come to seek. And as he stood it grew more wonderful still. For in each of the colours, which was as large as the column of a church, he could faintly see beautiful forms slowly ascending as if by the steps of a winding stair. The forms appeared irregularly – now one, now many, now several, now none – men and women and children – all different, all beautiful.

He drew nearer to the rainbow. It vanished. He started back a step in dismay. It was there again, as beautiful as ever. So he contented himself with standing as near it as he might, and watching the forms that ascended the glorious colours towards the unknown height of the arch, which did not end abruptly but faded away in the blue air, so gradually that he could not say where it ceased.

When the thought of the golden key returned, the boy very wisely proceeded to mark out in his mind the space covered by the foundation of the rainbow, in order that he might know where to search, should the rainbow disappear. It was based chiefly upon a bed of moss.

Meantime it had grown quite dark in the wood. The rainbow alone was visible by its own light. But the moment the moon rose the rainbow vanished. Nor could any change of place restore the vision to the boy's eyes. So he threw himself down upon the mossy bed, to wait till the sunlight would give him a chance of finding the key. There he fell fast asleep.

When he woke in the morning the sun was looking straight into his eyes. He turned away from it, and the same moment saw a brilliant little thing lying on the moss within a foot of his face. It was the golden key. The pipe of it was of plain gold, as bright as gold could be. The handle was curiously wrought and set with sapphires. In a terror of delight he put out his hand and took it, and had it.

He lay for a while, turning it over and over, and feeding his eyes upon its beauty. Then he jumped to his feet, remembering that the pretty thing was of no use to him yet. Where was the lock to which the key belonged? It must be somewhere, for how could anybody be so silly as make a key for which there was no lock? Where should he go to look for it? He gazed about him, up into the air, down to the earth, but saw no keyhole in the clouds, in the grass, or in the trees.

Just as he began to grow disconsolate, however, he saw something glimmering in the wood. It was a mere glimmer that he saw, but he took it for a glimmer of rainbow, and went towards it.

And now I will go back to the borders of the forest.

Not far from the house where the boy had lived, there was another house, the owner of which was a merchant, who was much away from home. He had lost his wife some years before, and had only one child, a little girl, whom he left to the charge of two servants, who were very idle and careless. So she was neglected and left untidy, and was sometimes ill-used besides.

Now it is well known that the little creatures commonly called fairies, though there are many different kinds of fairies in Fairyland, have an exceeding dislike to untidiness. Indeed, they are quite spiteful to slovenly people. Being used to all the lovely ways of the trees and flowers, and to the neatness of the birds and all woodland creatures, it makes them feel miserable, even in their deep woods and on their grassy carpets, to think that within the same moonlight lies a dirty, uncomfortable, slovenly house. And this makes them angry with the people that live in it, and they would gladly drive them out of the world if they could. They want the whole earth nice and clean. So they pinch the maids black and blue, and play them all manner of uncomfortable tricks.

But this house was quite a shame, and the fairies in the forest could not endure it. They tried everything on the maids without effect, and at last resolved upon making a clean riddance, beginning with the child. They ought to have known that it was not her fault, but they have little principle and much mischief in them, and they thought that if they got rid of her the maids would be sure to be turned away.

So one evening, the poor little girl having been put to bed early, before the sun was down, the servants went off to the village, locking the door behind them. The child did not know she was alone, and lay contentedly looking out of her window towards the forest, of which, however, she could not see much, because of the ivy and other creeping plants which had straggled across her window. All at once she saw an ape making faces at her out of the mirror, and the heads carved upon a great old wardrobe grinning fearfully. Then two old spider-legged chairs came forward into the middle of the room, and began to dance a queer, old-fashioned dance. This set her laughing, and she forgot the ape and the grinning heads. So the fairies saw they had made a mistake, and sent the chairs back to their places. But they knew that she had been reading the story of Silverhair all day. So the next moment she heard the voices of the three bears upon the stair, big voice, middle voice and little voice, and she heard their soft, heavy tread, as if they had had stockings over their boots, coming nearer and nearer to the door of her room, till she could bear it no longer. She did just as Silverhair did, and as the fairies wanted her to do: she darted to the window, pulled it open, got upon the ivy, and so scrambled to the ground. She then fled to the forest as fast as she could run.

Now, although she did not know it, this was the very best way she could have gone; for nothing is ever so mischievous in its own place as it is out of it; and, besides, these mischievous creatures were only the children of Fairyland, as it were, and there are many other beings there as well; and if a wanderer gets in among them, the good ones will always help him more than the evil ones will be able to hurt him.

The sun was now set, and the darkness coming on, but the child thought of no danger but the bears behind her. If she had looked round, however, she would have seen that she was followed by a very different creature from a bear. It was a curious creature, made like a fish, but covered, instead of scales, with feathers of all colours, sparkling like those of a humming-bird. It had fins, not wings, and swam through the air as a fish does through the water. Its head was like the head of a small owl.

After running a long way, and as the last of the light was disappearing, she passed under a tree with drooping branches. It dropped its branches to the ground all about her, and caught her as in a trap. She struggled to get out, but the branches pressed her closer and closer to the trunk. She was in great terror and distress, when the air-fish, swimming into the thicket of branches, began tearing them with its beak. They loosened their hold at once, and the creature went on attacking them, till at length they let the child go. Then the air-fish came from behind her, and swam on in front, glittering and sparkling all lovely colours; and she followed.

It led her gently along till all at once it swam in at a cottage door. The child followed still. There was a bright fire in the middle of the floor, upon which stood a pot without a lid, full of water that boiled and bubbled furiously. The air-fish swam straight to the pot and into the boiling water, where it lay quiet. A beautiful woman rose from the opposite side of the fire and came to meet the girl. She took her up in her arms, and said, "Ah, you are come at last! I have been looking for you a long time."

She sat down with her on her lap, and there the girl sat staring at her. She had never seen anything so beautiful. She was tall and strong, with white arms and neck, and a delicate flush on her face. The child could not tell what was the colour of her hair, but could not help thinking it had a tinge of dark green. She had not one ornament upon her, but she looked as if she had just put off quantities of diamonds and emeralds. Yet here she was in the simplest, poorest little cottage, where she was evidently at home. She was dressed in shining green.

The girl looked at the lady, and the lady looked at the girl.

"What is your name?" asked the lady.

"The servants always called me Tangle."

"Ah, that was because your hair was so untidy. But that was their fault, the naughty women! Still, it is a pretty name, and I will call you Tangle too. You must not mind my asking you questions, for you may ask me the same questions, every one of them, and any others that you like. How old are you?"

"Ten," answered Tangle.

"You don't look like it," said the lady.

"How old are you, please?" returned Tangle.

"Thousands of years old," answered the lady.

"You don't look like it," said Tangle.

"Don't I? I think I do. Don't you see how beautiful I am!"

And her great blue eyes looked down on the little Tangle, as if all the stars in the sky were melted in them to make their brightness.

"Ah! but," said Tangle, "when people live long they grow old. At least I always thought so."

"I have not time to grow old," said the lady. "I am too busy for that. It is very idle to grow old. But I cannot have my little girl so untidy. Do you know I can't find a clean spot on your face to kiss!"

"Perhaps," suggested Tangle, feeling ashamed, but not too much so to say a word for herself, "perhaps that is because the tree made me cry so."

"My poor darling!" said the lady, looking now as if the moon were melted in her eyes, and kissing her little face, dirty as it was, "the naughty tree must suffer for making a girl cry."

"And what is your name, please?" asked Tangle.

"Grandmother," answered the lady.

"Is it really?"

"Yes, indeed. I never tell stories, even in fun."

"How good of you!"

"I couldn't if I tried. It would come true if I said it, and then I should be punished enough."

And she smiled like the sun through a summer shower.

"But now," she went on, "I must get you washed and dressed, and then we shall have some supper."

"Oh! I had supper long ago," said Tangle.

"Yes, indeed you had," answered the lady, "three years ago. You don't know that it is three years since you ran away from the bears. You are thirteen and more now."

Tangle could only stare. She felt quite sure it was true.

"You will not be afraid of anything I do with you, will you?" said the lady.

"I will try very hard not to be; but I can't be certain, you know," replied Tangle.

"I like your saying so, and I shall be quite satisfied," answered the lady.

She took off the girl's nightgown, rose with her in her arms, and going to the wall of the cottage, opened a door. Then Tangle saw a deep tank, the sides of which were filled with green plants, which had flowers of all colours. There was a roof over it like the roof of the cottage. It was filled with beautiful clear water, in which swam a multitude of such fishes as the one that had led her to the cottage. It was the light their colours gave that showed the place in which they were.

The lady spoke some words Tangle could not understand, and threw her into the tank.

The fishes came crowding about her. Two or three of them got under her head and kept it up. The rest of them rubbed themselves all over her, and with their wet feathers washed her quite clean. Then the lady, who had been looking on all the time, spoke again; whereupon some thirty or forty of the fishes rose out of the water underneath Tangle, and so bore her up to the arms the lady held out to take her. She carried her back to the fire, and, having dried her well, opened a chest, and taking out the finest linen garments, smelling of grass and lavender, put them upon her, and over all a green dress, just like her own, shining like hers, and soft like hers, and going into just such lovely folds from the waist, where it was tied with a brown cord, to her bare feet.

"Won't you give me a pair of shoes too, Grandmother?" said Tangle.

"No, my dear; no shoes. Look here. I wear no shoes."

So saying she lifted her dress a little, and there were the loveliest white feet, but no shoes. Then Tangle was content to go without shoes too. And the lady sat down with her again, and combed her hair, and brushed it, and then left it to dry while she got the supper.

First she got bread out of one hole in the wall; then milk out of another; then several kinds of fruit out a third; and then she went to the pot on the fire, and took out the fish, now nicely cooked, and, as soon as she had pulled off its feathered skin, ready to be eaten.

"But," exclaimed Tangle. And she stared at the fish, and could say no more.

"I know what you mean," returned the lady. "You do not like to eat the messenger that brought you home. But it is the kindest return you can make. The creature was afraid to go until it saw me put the pot on, and heard me promise it should be boiled the moment it returned with you. Then it darted out of the door at once. You saw it go into the pot of itself the moment it entered, did you not?"

"I did," answered Tangle, "and I thought it very strange; but then I saw you, and forgot all about the fish."

"In Fairyland," resumed the lady, as they sat down to the table, "the ambition of the animals is to be eaten by the people; for that is their highest end in that condition. But they are not therefore destroyed. Out of that pot comes something more than the dead fish, you will see."

Tangle now remarked that the lid was on the pot. But the lady took no further notice of it till they had eaten the fish, which Tangle found nicer than any fish she had ever tasted before. It was as white as snow, and as delicate as cream. And the moment she had swallowed a mouthful of it, a change she could not describe began to take place in her. She heard a murmuring all about her, which became more and more articulate, and at length, as she went on eating, grew intelligible. By the time she had finished her share, the sounds of all the animals in the forest came crowding through the door to her ears; for the door still stood wide open, though it was pitch-dark outside; and they were no longer sounds only; they were speech, and speech that she could understand. She could tell what the insects in the cottage were saying to each other too. She had even a suspicion that the trees and flowers all about the cottage were holding midnight communications with each other; but what they said she could not hear.

As soon as the fish was eaten, the lady went to the fire and took the lid off the pot. A lovely little creature in human shape, with large white wings, rose out of it, and flew round and round the roof of the cottage; then dropped, fluttering, and nestled in the lap of the lady. She spoke to it some strange words, carried it to the door, and threw it out into the darkness. Tangle heard the flapping of its wings die away in the distance.

"Now have we done the fish any harm?" she said, returning.

"No," answered Tangle, "I do not think we have. I should not mind eating one every day."

"They must wait their time, like you and me too, my little Tangle."

And she smiled a smile which the sadness in it made more lovely.

"But," she continued, "I think we may have one for supper tomorrow."

So saying, she went to the door of the tank, and spoke; and now Tangle understood her perfectly.

"I want one of you," she said, "the wisest."

Thereupon the fishes got together in the middle of the tank, with their heads forming a circle above the water, and their tails a larger circle beneath it. They were holding a council, in which their relative wisdom should be determined. At length one of them flew up into the lady's hand, looking lively and ready.

"You know where the rainbow stands?" she asked.

"Yes, Mother, quite well," answered the fish.

"Bring home a young man you will find there, who does not know where to go."

The fish was out of the door in a moment. Then the lady told Tangle it was time to go to bed; and, opening another door in the side of the cottage, showed her a little arbour, cool and green, with a bed of purple heath growing in it, upon which she threw a large wrapper made of the feathered skins of the wise fishes, shining gorgeous in the firelight. Tangle was soon lost in the strangest, loveliest dreams. And the beautiful lady was in every one of her dreams.

In the morning she woke to the rustling of leaves over her head, and the sound of running water. But, to her surprise, she could find no door – nothing but the moss-grown wall of the cottage. So she crept through an opening in the arbour, and stood in the forest. Then she bathed in a stream that ran merrily through the trees, and felt happier; for having once been in her grandmother's pond, she must be clean and tidy ever after; and, having put on her green dress, felt like a lady.

She spent that day in the wood, listening to the birds and beasts and creeping things. She understood all that they said, though she could not repeat a word of it; and every kind had a different language, while there was a common though more limited understanding between all the inhabitants of the forest. She saw nothing of the beautiful lady, but she felt that she was near her all the time; and she took care not to go out of sight of the cottage. It was round, like a snow-hut or a wigwam; and she could see neither door nor window in it. The fact was, it had no windows; and though it was full of doors, they all opened from the inside, and could not even be seen from the outside.

She was standing at the foot of a tree in the twilight, listening to a quarrel between a mole and a squirrel, in which the mole told the squirrel that the tail was the best of him, and the squirrel called the mole Spade-fists, when, the darkness having deepened around her, she became aware of something shining in her face, and looking round, saw that the door of the cottage was open, and the red light of the fire flowing from it like a river through the darkness. She left Mole and Squirrel to settle matters as they might, and darted off to the cottage. Entering, she found the pot boiling on the fire, and the grand, lovely lady sitting on the other side of it.

"I've been watching you all day," said the lady. "You shall have something to eat by-and-by, but we must wait till our supper comes home."

She took Tangle on her knee, and began to sing to her – such songs as made her wish she could listen to them for ever. But at length in rushed the shining fish; and snuggled down in the pot. It was followed by a youth who had outgrown his worn garments. His face was ruddy with health, and in his hand he carried a little jewel, which sparkled in the firelight.

The first words the lady said were, "What is that in your hand, Mossy?"

Now Mossy was the name his companions had given him, because he had a favourite stone covered with moss, on which he used to sit whole days reading; and they said the moss had begun to grow upon him too.

Mossy held out his hand. The moment the lady saw that it was the golden key, she rose from her chair, kissed Mossy on the forehead, made him sit down on her seat, and stood before him like a servant. Mossy could not bear this, and rose at once. But the lady begged him, with tears in her beautiful eyes, to sit, and let her wait on him.

"But you are a great, splendid, beautiful lady," said Mossy.

"Yes, I am. But I work all day long – that is my pleasure; and you will have to leave me so soon!"

"How do you know that, if you please, madam?" asked Mossy.

"Because you have got the golden key."

"But I don't know what it is for. I can't find the keyhole. Will you tell me what to do?"

"You must look for the keyhole. That is your work. I cannot help you. I can only tell you that if you look for it you will find it."

"What kind of box will it open? What is there inside?"

"I do not know. I dream about it, but I know nothing."

"Must I go at once?"

"You may stop here tonight, and have some of my supper. But you must go in the morning. All I can do for you is to give you clothes. Here is a girl called Tangle, whom you must take with you."

"That *will* be nice," said Mossy.

"No, no!" said Tangle. "I don't want to leave you, please, Grandmother."

"You must go with him, Tangle. I am sorry to lose you, but it will be the best thing for you. Even the fishes, you see, have to go into the pot, and then out into the dark. If you fall in with the Old Man of the Sea, mind you ask him whether he has not got some more fishes ready for me. My tank is getting thin."

So saying, she took the fish from the pot, and put the lid on as before. They sat down and ate the fish, and then the winged creature rose from the pot, circled the roof, and settled on the lady's lap. She talked to it, carried it to the door, and threw it out into the dark. They heard the flap of its wings die away in the distance.

The lady then showed Mossy into just such another chamber as that of Tangle; and in the morning he found a suit of clothes laid beside him. He looked very handsome in them. But the wearer of

Grandmother's clothes never thinks about how he or she looks, but thinks always how handsome other people are.

Tangle was very unwilling to go.

"Why should I leave you? I don't know the young man," she said to the lady.

"I am never allowed to keep my children long. You need not go with him except you please, but you must go some day; and I should like you to go with him, for he has the golden key. No girl need be afraid to go with a youth that has the golden key. You will take care of her, Mossy, will you not?"

"That I will," said Mossy.

And Tangle cast a glance at him, and thought she should like to go with him.

"And," said the lady, "if you should lose each other as you go through the – the – I never can remember the name of that country – do not be afraid, but go on and on."

She kissed Tangle on the mouth and Mossy on the forehead, led them to the door, and waved her hand eastward. Mossy and Tangle took each other's hand and walked away into the depth of the forest. In his right hand Mossy held the golden key.

They wandered thus a long way, with endless amusement from the talk of the animals. They soon learned enough of their language to ask them necessary questions. The squirrels were always friendly, and gave them nuts out of their own hoards; but the bees were selfish and rude, justifying themselves on the ground that Tangle and Mossy were not subjects of their queen, and charity must begin at home, though indeed they had not one drone in their poorhouse at the time. Even the blinking moles would fetch them an earth-nut or a truffle now and then, talking as if their mouths, as well as their eyes and ears, were full of cotton wool, or their own velvety fur. By the time they got out of the forest they were very fond of each other, and Tangle was not in the least sorry that her grandmother had sent her away with Mossy.

At length the trees grew smaller, and stood further apart, and the ground began to rise, and it got more and more steep, till the trees were all left behind, and the two were climbing a narrow

path with rocks on each side. Suddenly they came upon a rude
doorway, by which they entered a narrow gallery cut in the rock.
It grew darker and darker, till it was pitch-dark, and they had to
feel their way. At length the light began to return, and at last they
came out upon a narrow path on the face of a lofty precipice. This
path went winding down the rock to a wide plain, circular in
shape, and surrounded on all sides by mountains. Those opposite
to them were a great way off, and towered to an awful height,
shooting up sharp, blue, ice-enamelled pinnacles. An utter silence reigned where they stood. Not even the sound of water
reached them.

Looking down, they could not tell whether the valley below
was a grassy plain or a great still lake. They had never seen any
place look like it. The way to it was difficult and dangerous, but
down the narrow path they went, and reached the bottom in
safety. They found it composed of smooth, light-coloured sand-
stone, undulating in parts, but mostly level. It was no wonder to
them now that they had not been able to tell what it was, for this
surface was everywhere crowded with shadows. It was a sea of
shadows. The mass was chiefly made up of the shadows of leaves
innumerable, of all lovely and imaginative forms, waving to and
fro, floating and quivering in the breath of a breeze whose motion
was unfelt, whose sound was unheard. No forests clothed the
mountainsides, no trees were anywhere to be seen, and yet the
shadows of the leaves, branches and stems of all various trees
covered the valley as far as their eyes could reach. They soon
spied the shadows of flowers mingled with those of the leaves,
and now and then the shadow of a bird with open beak, and throat
distended with song. At times would appear the forms of strange,
graceful creatures, running up and down the shadow-boles and
along the branches, to disappear in the wind-tossed foliage. As
they walked they waded knee-deep in the lovely lake. For the
shadows were not merely lying on the surface of the ground, but
heaped up above it like substantial forms of darkness, as if they
had been cast upon a thousand different planes of the air. Tangle
and Mossy often lifted their heads and gazed upwards to descry
whence the shadows came; but they could see nothing more than

a bright mist spread above them, higher than the tops of the mountains, which stood clear against it. No forests, no leaves, no birds were visible.

After a while, they reached more open spaces, where the shadows were thinner; and came even to portions over which shadows only flitted, leaving them clear for such as might follow. Now a wonderful form, half bird-like half human, would float across on outspread sailing pinions. Anon an exquisite shadow group of gambolling children would be followed by the loveliest female form, and that again by the grand stride of a Titanic shape, each disappearing in the surrounding press of shadowy foliage. Sometimes a profile of unspeakable beauty or grandeur would appear for a moment and vanish. Sometimes they seemed lovers that passed linked arm in arm, sometimes father and son, sometimes brothers in loving contest, sometimes sisters entwined in gracefulest community of complex form. Sometimes wild horses would tear across, free, or bestrode by noble shadows of ruling men. But some of the things which pleased them most they never knew how to describe.

About the middle of the plain they sat down to rest in the heart of a heap of shadows. After sitting for a while, each, looking up, saw the other in tears: they were each longing after the country whence the shadows fell.

"We *must* find the country from which the shadows come," said Mossy.

"We must, dear Mossy," responded Tangle. "What if your golden key should be the key to *it*?"

"Ah! that would be grand," returned Mossy. "But we must rest here for a little, and then we shall be able to cross the plain before night."

So he lay down on the ground, and about him on every side, and over his head, was the constant play of the wonderful shadows. He could look through them, and see the one behind the other, till they mixed in a mass of darkness. Tangle, too, lay admiring, and wondering, and longing after the country whence the shadows came. When they were rested they rose and pursued their journey.

How long they were in crossing this plain I cannot tell; but before night Mossy's hair was streaked with grey, and Tangle had got wrinkles on her forehead.

As evening drew on, the shadows fell deeper and rose higher. At length they reached a place where they rose above their heads, and made all dark around them. Then they took hold of each other's hand, and walked on in silence and in some dismay. They felt the gathering darkness, and something strangely solemn besides, and the beauty of the shadows ceased to delight them. All at once Tangle found that she had not a hold of Mossy's hand, though when she lost it she could not tell.

"Mossy, Mossy!" she cried aloud in terror.

But no Mossy replied.

A moment after, the shadows sank to her feet, and down under her feet, and the mountains rose before her. She turned towards the gloomy region she had left, and called once more upon Mossy. There the gloom lay tossing and heaving, a dark stormy, foamless sea of shadows, but no Mossy rose out of it, or came climbing up the hill on which she stood. She threw herself down and wept in despair.

Suddenly she remembered that the beautiful lady had told them, if they lost each other in a country of which she could not remember the name, they were not to be afraid, but to go straight on.

"And besides," she said to herself, "Mossy has the golden key, and so no harm will come to him, I do believe."

She rose from the ground, and went on.

Before long she arrived at a precipice, in the face of which a stair was cut. When she had ascended halfway, the stair ceased, and the path led straight into the mountain. She was afraid to enter, and turning again towards the stair, grew giddy at sight of the depth beneath her, and was forced to throw herself down in the mouth of the cave.

When she opened her eyes, she saw a beautiful little creature with wings standing beside her, waiting.

"I know you," said Tangle. "You are my fish."

"Yes. But I am a fish no longer. I am an aëranth now."

"What is that?" asked Tangle.

"What you see I am," answered the shape. "And I am come to lead you through the mountain."

"Oh! thank you, dear fish – aëranth, I mean," returned Tangle, rising.

Thereupon the aëranth took to his wings, and flew on through the long, narrow passage, reminding Tangle very much of the way he had swum on before her when he was a fish. And the moment his white wings moved, they began to throw off a continuous shower of sparks of all colours, which lighted up the passage before them. All at once he vanished, and Tangle heard a low, sweet sound, quite different from the rush and crackle of his wings. Before her was an open arch, and through it came light, mixed with the sound of sea waves.

She hurried out, and fell, tired and happy, upon the yellow sand of the shore. There she lay, half asleep with weariness and rest, listening to the low plash and retreat of the tiny waves, which seemed ever enticing the land to leave off being land, and become sea. And as she lay, her eyes were fixed upon the foot of a great rainbow standing far away against the sky on the other side of the sea. At length she fell fast asleep.

When she awoke, she saw an old man with long white hair down to his shoulders, leaning upon a stick covered with green buds, and so bending over her.

"What do you want here, beautiful woman?" he said.

"Am I beautiful? I am so glad!" answered Tangle, rising. "My grandmother is beautiful."

"Yes. But what do you want?" he repeated, kindly.

"I think I want you. Are not you the Old Man of the Sea?"

"I am."

"Then Grandmother says, have you any more fishes ready for her?"

"We will go and see, my dear," answered the old man, speaking yet more kindly than before. "And I can do something for you, can I not?"

"Yes – show me the way up to the country from which the shadows fall," said Tangle.

For there she hoped to find Mossy again.

"Ah! indeed, that would be worth doing," said the old man. "But I cannot, for I do not know the way myself. But I will send you to the Old Man of the Earth. Perhaps he can tell you. He is much older than I am."

Leaning on his staff, he conducted her along the shore to a steep rock, that looked like a petrified ship turned upside down. The door of it was the rudder of a great vessel, ages ago at the bottom of the sea. Immediately within the door was a stair in the rock, down which the old man went, and Tangle followed. At the bottom the old man had his house, and there he lived.

As soon as she entered it, Tangle heard a strange noise, unlike anything she had ever heard before. She soon found that it was the fishes talking. She tried to understand what they said; but their speech was so old-fashioned, and rude, and undefined, that she could not make much of it.

"I will go and see about those fishes for my daughter," said the Old Man of the Sea.

And moving a slide in the wall of his house, he first looked out, and then tapped upon a thick piece of crystal that filled the round opening. Tangle came up behind him, and peeping through the window into the heart of the great deep green ocean, saw the most curious creatures, some very ugly, all very odd, and with especially queer mouths, swimming about everywhere, above and below, but all coming towards the window in answer to the tap of the Old Man of the Sea. Only a few could get their mouths against the glass; but those who were floating miles away yet turned their heads towards it.

The Old Man looked through the whole flock carefully for some minutes, and then turning to Tangle, said, "I am sorry I have not got one ready yet. I want more time than she does. But I will send some as soon as I can."

He then shut the slide.

Presently a great noise arose in the sea. The old man opened the slide again, and tapped on the glass, whereupon the fishes were all as still as sleep.

"They were only talking about you," he said. "And they do

speak such nonsense! Tomorrow," he continued, "I must show you the way to the Old Man of the Earth. He lives a long way from here."

"Do let me go at once," said Tangle.

"No. That is not possible. You must come this way first."

He led her to a hole in the wall, which she had not observed before. It was covered with the green leaves and white blossoms of a creeping plant.

"Only white-blossoming plants can grow under the sea," said the old man. "In there you will find a bath, in which you must lie till I call you."

Tangle went in, and found a smaller room or cave, in the further corner of which was a great basin hollowed out of a rock, and half full of the clearest seawater. Little streams were constantly running into it from cracks in the wall of the cavern. It was polished quite smooth inside, and had a carpet of yellow sand in the bottom of it. Large green leaves and white flowers of various plants crowded up and over it, draping and covering it almost entirely.

No sooner was she undressed and lying in the bath, than she began to feel as if the water were sinking into her, and she was receiving all the good of sleep without undergoing its forgetfulness. She felt the good coming all the time. And she grew happier and more hopeful than she had been since she lost Mossy. But she could not help thinking how very sad it was for a poor old man to live there all alone, and have to take care of a whole seaful of stupid and riotous fishes.

After about an hour, as she thought, she heard his voice calling her, and rose out of the bath. All the fatigue and aching of her long journey had vanished. She was as whole, and strong, and well as if she had slept for seven days.

Returning to the opening that led into the other part of the house, she started back with amazement, for through it she saw the form of a grand man, with a majestic and beautiful face, waiting for her.

"Come," he said; "I see you are ready."

She entered with reverence.

"Where is the Old Man of the Sea?" she asked, humbly.

"There is no one here but me," he answered, smiling. "Some people call me the Old Man of the Sea. Others have another name for me, and are terribly frightened when they meet me taking a walk by the shore. Therefore I avoid being seen by them, for they are so afraid, that they never see what I really am. You see me now. But I must show you the way to the Old Man of the Earth."

He led her into the cave where the bath was, and there she saw, in the opposite corner, a second opening in the rock.

"Go down that stair, and it will bring you to him," said the Old Man of the Sea.

With humble thanks Tangle took her leave. She went down the winding stair, till she began to fear there was no end to it. Still down and down it went, rough and broken, with springs of water bursting out of the rocks and running down the steps beside her. It was quite dark about her, and yet she could see. For after being in that bath, people's eyes always give out a light they can see by. There were no creeping things in the way. All was safe and pleasant though so dark and damp and deep.

At last there was not one step more, and she found herself in a glimmering cave. On a stone in the middle of it sat a figure with its back towards her – the figure of an old man bent double with age. From behind she could see his white beard spread out on the rocky floor in front of him. He did not move as she entered, so she passed round that she might stand before him and speak to him. The moment she looked in his face, she saw that he was a youth of marvellous beauty. He sat entranced with the delight of what he beheld in a mirror of something like silver, which lay on the floor at his feet, and which from behind she had taken for his white beard. He sat on, heedless of her presence, pale with the joy of his vision. She stood and watched him. At length, all trembling, she spoke. But her voice made no sound. Yet the youth lifted up his head. He showed no surprise, however, at seeing her – only smiled a welcome.

"Are you the Old Man of the Earth?" Tangle had said.

And the youth answered, and Tangle heard him, though not with her ears: "I am. What can I do for you?"

"Tell me the way to the country whence the shadows fall."

"Ah! that I do not know. I only dream about it myself. I see its shadows sometimes in my mirror: the way to it I do not know. But I think the Old Man of the Fire must know. He is much older than I am. He is the oldest man of all."

"Where does he live?"

"I will show you the way to his place. I never saw him myself."

So saying, the young man rose, and then stood for a while gazing at Tangle.

"I wish I could see that country too," he said. "But I must mind my work."

He led her to the side of the cave, and told her to lay her ear against the wall.

"What do you hear?" he asked.

"I hear," answered Tangle, "the sound of a great water running inside the rock."

"That river runs down to the dwelling of the oldest man of all – the Old Man of the Fire. I wish I could go to see him. But I must mind my work. That river is the only way to him."

Then the Old Man of the Earth stooped over the floor of the cave, raised a huge stone from it, and left it leaning. It disclosed a great hole that went plumb-down.

"That is the way," he said.

"But there are no stairs."

"You must throw yourself in. There is no other way."

She turned and looked him full in the face – stood so for a whole minute, as she thought: it was a whole year – then threw herself headlong into the hole.

When she came to herself, she found herself gliding down fast and deep. Her head was under water, but that did not signify, for, when she thought about it, she could not remember that she had breathed once since her bath in the cave of the Old Man of the Sea. When she lifted up her head a sudden and fierce heat struck her, and she sank it again instantly, and went sweeping on.

Gradually the stream grew shallower. At length she could hardly keep her head under. Then the water could carry her no further. She rose from the channel, and went step for step down the burning descent. The water ceased altogether. The heat was terrible. She felt scorched to the bone, but it did not touch her strength. It grew hotter and hotter. She said, "I can bear it no longer." Yet she went on.

At long last, the stair ended at a rude archway in an all but glowing rock. Through this archway Tangle fell exhausted into a cool mossy cave. The floor and walls were covered with moss – green, soft and damp. A little stream spouted from a rent in the rock and fell into a basin of moss. She plunged her face into it and drank. Then she lifted her head and looked around. Then she rose and looked again. She saw no one in the cave. But the moment she stood upright she had a marvellous sense that she was in the secret of the earth and all its ways. Everything she had seen, or learned from books; all that her grandmother had said or sung to her; all the talk of the beasts, birds and fishes; all that had happened to her on her journey with Mossy, and since then in the heart of the earth with the old man and the older man – all was plain: she understood it all, and saw that everything meant the same thing, though she could not have put it into words again.

The next moment she described, in a corner of the cave, a little naked child, sitting on the moss. He was playing with balls of various colours and sizes, which he disposed in strange figures upon the floor beside him. And now Tangle felt that there was something in her knowledge which was not in her understanding. For she knew there must be an infinite meaning in the change and sequence and individual forms of the figures into which the child arranged the balls, as well as in the varied harmonies of their colours, but what it all meant she could not tell. He went on busily, tirelessly, playing his solitary game, without looking up, or seeming to know that there was a stranger in his deep-with-drawn cell. Diligently as a lace-maker shifts her bobbins, he shifted and arranged his balls. Flashes of meaning would now pass from them to Tangle, and now again all would be not merely obscure, but utterly dark. She stood looking for a long time, for there was fascination in the sight; and the longer she looked the more an indescribable vague intelligence went on rousing itself in her mind. For seven years she had stood there watching the naked child with his coloured balls, and it seemed to her like seven hours, when all at once the shape the balls took, she knew not why, reminded her of the Valley of Shadows, and she spoke.

"Where is the Old Man of the Fire?" she said.

"Here I am," answered the child, rising and leaving his balls on the moss. "What can I do for you?"

There was such an awfulness of absolute repose on the face of the child that Tangle stood dumb before him. He had no smile, but the love in his large grey eyes was deep as the centre. And with the repose there lay on his face a shimmer as of moonlight, which seemed as if any moment it might break into such a ravishing smile as would cause the beholder to weep himself to death. But the smile never came, and the moonlight lay there unbroken. For the heart of the child was too deep for any smile to reach from it to his face.

"Are you the oldest man of all?" Tangle at length, although filled with awe, ventured to ask.

"Yes, I am. I am very, very old. I am able to help you, I know. I can help everybody."

And the child drew near and looked up in her face so that she burst into tears.

"Can you tell me the way to the country the shadows fall from?" she sobbed.

"Yes. I know the way quite well. I go there myself sometimes. But you could not go my way; you are not old enough. I will show you how you can go."

"Do not send me out into the great heat again," prayed Tangle.

"I will not," answered the child.

And he reached up, and put his little cool hand on her heart.

"Now," he said, "you can go. The fire will not burn you. Come."

He led her from the cave, and following him through another archway, she found herself in a vast desert of sand and rock. The sky of it was of rock, lowering over them like solid thunderclouds; and the whole place was so hot that she saw, in bright rivulets, the yellow gold and white silver and red copper trickling molten from the rocks. But the heat never came near her.

When they had gone some distance, the child turned up a great stone, and took something like an egg from under it. He next drew a long curved line in the sand with his finger, and laid the egg in it. He then spoke something Tangle could not understand. The egg broke, a small snake came out, and, lying in the line in the sand, grew and grew till he filled it. The moment he was thus full-grown, he began to glide away, undulating like a sea wave.

"Follow that serpent," said the child. "He will lead you the right way."

Tangle followed the serpent. But she could not go far without looking back at the marvellous child. He stood alone in the midst of the glowing desert, beside a fountain of red flame that had burst forth at his feet, his naked whiteness glimmering a pale rosy red in the torrid fire. There he stood, looking after her, till, from the lengthening distance, she could see him no more. The serpent went straight on, turning neither to the right nor left.

Meantime Mossy had got out of the lake of shadows, and, following his mournful, lonely way, had reached the seashore. It was a dark, stormy evening. The sun had set. The wind was blowing from the sea. The waves had surrounded the rock within which lay the Old Man's house. A deep water rolled between it and the shore, upon which a majestic figure was walking alone.

Mossy went up to him and said, "Will you tell me where to find the Old Man of the Sea?"

"I am the Old Man of the Sea," the figure answered.

"I see a strong kingly man of middle age," returned Mossy.

Then the Old Man looked at him more intently, and said, "Your sight, young man, is better than that of most who take this way. The night is stormy: come to my house and tell me what I can do for you."

Mossy followed him. The waves flew from before the footsteps of the Old Man of the Sea, and Mossy followed upon dry sand.

When they had reached the cave, they sat down and gazed at each other.

Now Mossy was an old man by this time. He looked much older than the Old Man of the Sea, and his feet were very weary.

After looking at him for a moment, the Old Man took him by the hand and led him into his inner cave. There he helped him to undress, and laid him in the bath. And he saw that one of his hands Mossy did not open.

"What have you in that hand?" he asked.

Mossy opened his hand, and there lay the golden key.

"Ah!" said the Old Man, "that accounts for your knowing me. And I know the way you have to go."

"I want to find the country whence the shadows fall," said Mossy.

"I dare say you do. So do I. But meantime, one thing is certain. What is that key for, do you think?"

"For a keyhole somewhere. But I don't know why I keep it. I never could find the keyhole. And I have lived a good while, I believe," said Mossy, sadly. "I'm not sure that I'm not old. I know my feet ache."

"Do they?" said the Old Man, as if he really meant to ask the question; and Mossy, who was still lying in the bath, watched his feet for a moment before he replied.

"No, they do not," he answered. "Perhaps I am not old either."

"Get up and look at yourself in the water."

He rose and looked at himself in the water, and there was not a grey hair on his head or a wrinkle on his skin.

"You have tasted of death now," said the Old Man. "Is it good?"

"It is good," said Mossy. "It is better than life."

"No," said the Old Man: "it is only more life. Your feet will make no holes in the water now."

"What do you mean?"

"I will show you that presently."

They returned to the outer cave, and sat and talked together for a long time. At length the Old Man of the Sea rose, and said to Mossy, "Follow me."

He led him up the stair again, and opened another door. They stood on the level of the raging sea, looking towards the east. Across the waste of waters, against the bosom of a fierce black cloud, stood the foot of a rainbow, glowing in the dark.

"This indeed is my way," said Mossy, as soon as he saw the rainbow, and stepped out upon the sea. His feet made no holes in the water. He fought the wind, and clomb the waves, and went on towards the rainbow.

The storm died away. A lovely day and a lovelier night followed. A cool wind blew over the wide plain of the quiet ocean. And still Mossy journeyed eastward. But the rainbow had vanished with the storm.

Day after day he held on, and he thought he had no guide. He did not see how a shining fish under the waters directed his steps. He crossed the sea, and came to a great precipice of rock, up which he could discover but one path. Nor did this lead him further than halfway up the rock, where it ended on a platform. Here he stood and pondered. It could not be that the way stopped here, else what was the path for? It was a rough path, not very plain, yet certainly a path. He examined the face of the rock. It was smooth as glass. But as his eyes kept roving hopelessly over it, something glittered, and he caught sight of a row of small sapphires. They bordered a little hole in the rock.

"The keyhole!" he cried.

He tried the key. It fitted. It turned. A great clang and clash, as of iron bolts on huge brazen caldrons, echoed thunderously within. He drew out the key. The rock in front of him began to fall. He retreated from it as far as the breadth of the platform would allow. A great slab fell at his feet. In front was still the solid rock, with this one slab fallen forward out of it. But the moment he stepped upon it, a second fell, just short of the edge of the first, making the next step of a stair, which thus kept dropping itself before him as he ascended into the heart of the precipice. It led him into a hall fit for such an approach – irregular and rude in formation, but floor, sides, pillars and vaulted roof, all one mass of shining stones of every colour that light can show. In the centre stood seven columns, ranged from red to violet. And on the pedestal of one of them sat a woman, motionless, with her face bowed upon her knees. Seven years had she sat there waiting. She lifted her head as Mossy drew near. It was Tangle. Her hair had grown to her feet, and was rippled like the windless sea on broad sands. Her face was beautiful, like her grandmother's, and as still and peaceful as that of the Old Man of the Fire. Her form was tall and noble. Yet Mossy knew her at once.

"How beautiful you are, Tangle!" he said, in delight and astonishment.

"Am I?" she returned. "Oh, I have waited for you so long! But you, you are the Old Man of the Sea. No. You are like the Old Man of the Earth. No, no. You are like the oldest man of all. You are like them all. And yet you are my own old Mossy! How did you come here? What did you do after I lost you? Did you find the keyhole? Have you got the key still?"

She had a hundred questions to ask him, and he a hundred more to ask her. They told each other all their adventures, and were as happy as man and woman could be. For they were younger and better, and stronger and wiser, than they had ever been before.

It began to grow dark. And they wanted more than ever to reach the country whence the shadows fall. So they looked about them for a way out of the cave. The door by which Mossy entered had closed again, and there was half a mile of rock between them and the sea. Neither could Tangle find the opening in the floor by which the serpent had led her thither. They searched till it grew so dark that they could see nothing, and gave it up.

After a while, however, the cave began to glimmer again. The light came from the moon, but it did not look like moonlight, for it gleamed through those seven pillars in the middle, and filled the place with all colours. And now Mossy saw that there was a pillar beside the red one, which he had not observed before. And it was of the same new colour that he had seen in the rainbow when he saw it first in the fairy forest. And on it he saw a sparkle of blue. It was the sapphires round the keyhole.

He took his key. It turned in the lock to the sounds of Æolian music. A door opened upon slow hinges, and disclosed a winding stair within. The key vanished from his fingers. Tangle went up.

Mossy followed. The door closed behind them. They climbed out of the earth; and, still climbing, rose above it. They were in the rainbow. Far abroad, over ocean and land, they could see through its transparent walls the earth beneath their feet. Stairs beside stairs wound up together, and beautiful beings of all ages climbed along with them.

They knew that they were going up to the country whence the shadows fall.

And by this time I think they must have got there.

The Hoard of the Gibbelins

Lord Dunsany

Lord Dunsany's influence upon fantasy fiction is immeasurable. There can scarcely have been a writer working in the field throughout the twentieth century who did not owe something to Dunsany's work. Dunsany was really Edward Plunkett (1878–1957), 18th Baron Dunsany. Although the ancestral home was at Dunsany Castle in County Meath, Ireland, Dunsany spent much of his time at Dunstall Priory at Shoreham in Kent, and the Kentish hills feature in many of his stories. Dunsany was fascinated with the creation of other, mythical worlds, and in The Gods of Pegana *(1905) he produced a series of short vignettes that brought to life the unsavoury world of the gods. The delight of Dunsany's work, as he progressed through* Time and the Gods *(1906),* The Sword of Welleran *(1908),* A Dreamer's Tales *(1910) and* The Book of Wonder *(1912), was that he did not focus solely on heroic adventures and action on a vast scale. Quite the contrary. He often looked at the minutiae of life or depicted the villains and anti-heroes, as the following story so aptly demonstrates. It was this vein of Dunsany's dark humour that influenced writers such as Clark Ashton Smith and Jack Vance, to whom we'll turn shortly.*

The Hoard of the Gibbelins

The Gibbelins eat, as is well known, nothing less good than man. Their evil tower is joined to Terra Cognita, to the lands we know, by a bridge. Their hoard is beyond reason; avarice has no use for it; they have a separate cellar for emeralds and a separate cellar for sapphires; they have filled a hole with gold and dig it up when they need it. And the only use that is known for their ridiculous wealth is to attract to their larder a continual supply of food. In times of famine they have even been known to scatter rubies abroad, a little trail of them to some city of man, and sure enough their larders would soon be full again.

Their tower stands on the other side of that river known to Homer – ὁ ῥόος ὠχεανοίο, as he called it – which surrounds the world. And where the river is narrow and fordable the tower was built by the Gibbelins' gluttonous sires, for they liked to see burglars rowing easily to their steps. Some nourishment that common soil has not the huge trees drained there with their colossal roots from both banks of the river.

There the Gibbelins lived and discreditably fed.

Alderic, Knight of the Order of the City and the Assault, hereditary Guardian of the King's Peace of Mind, a man not unremembered among the makers of myth, pondered so long upon the Gibbelins' hoard that by now he deemed it his. Alas that I should say of so perilous a venture, undertaken at dead of night by a valorous man, that its motive was sheer avarice! Yet upon avarice only the Gibbelins relied to keep their larders full, and once in every hundred years sent spies into the cities of men to see how avarice did, and always the spies returned again to the tower saying that all was well.

It may be thought that, as the years went on and men came by fearful ends on that tower's wall, fewer and fewer would come to the Gibbelins' table: but the Gibbelins found otherwise.

Not in the folly and frivolity of his youth did Alderic come to the tower, but he studied carefully for several years the manner in which burglars met their doom when they went in search of the treasure that he considered his. *In every case they had entered by the door.*

He consulted those who gave advice on this quest; he noted every detail and cheerfully paid their fees, and determined to do nothing that they advised, for what were their clients now? No more than examples of the savoury art, mere half-forgotten memories of a meal; and many, perhaps, no longer even that.

These were the requisites for the quest that these men used to advise: a horse, a boat, mail armour, and at least three men-at-arms. Some said, "Blow the horn at the tower door"; others said, "Do not touch it."

Alderic thus decided: he would take no horse down to the river's edge, he would not row along it in a boat, and he would go alone and by way of the Forest Unpassable.

How pass, you may say, by the unpassable? This was his plan: there was a dragon he knew of who if peasants' prayers are heeded deserved to die, not alone because of the number of maidens he cruelly slew, but because he was bad for the crops; he ravaged the very land and was the bane of a dukedom.

Now Alderic determined to go up against him. So he took horse and spear and pricked till he met the dragon, and the dragon came out against him breathing bitter smoke. And to him Alderic shouted, "Hath foul dragon ever slain true knight?" And well the dragon knew that this had never been, and he hung his head and was silent, for he was glutted with blood. "Then," said the knight, "if thou would'st ever taste maiden's blood again thou shalt be my trusty steed, and if not, by this spear there shall befall thee all that the troubadours tell of the dooms of thy breed."

And the dragon did not open his ravening mouth, nor rush upon the knight, breathing out fire; for well he knew the fate of those that did these things, but he consented to the terms imposed, and swore to the knight to become his trusty steed.

It was on a saddle upon this dragon's back that Alderic afterwards sailed above the unpassable forest, even above the tops of those measureless trees, children of wonder. But first he pondered that subtle plan of his which was more profound than merely to avoid all that had been done before; and he commanded a blacksmith, and the blacksmith made him a pickaxe.

Now there was great rejoicing at the rumour of Alderic's quest, for all folk knew that he was a cautious man, and they deemed that he would succeed and enrich the world, and they rubbed their hands in the cities at the thought of largesse; and there was joy among all men in Alderic's country, except perchance among the lenders of money, who feared they would soon be paid. And there was rejoicing also because men hoped that when the Gibbelins were robbed of their hoard, they would shatter their high-built bridge and break the golden chains that bound them to the world, and drift back, they and their tower, to the moon, from which they had come and to which they rightly belonged. There was little love for the Gibbelins, though all men envied their hoard.

So they all cheered, that day when he mounted his dragon, as though he was already a conqueror, and what pleased them more than the good that they hoped he would do to the world was that he scattered gold as he rode away; for he would not need it, he said, if he found the Gibbelins' hoard, and he would not need it more if he smoked on the Gibbelins' table.

When they heard that he had rejected the advice of those that gave it, some said that the knight was mad, and others said he was greater than those that gave the advice, but none appreciated the worth of his plan.

He reasoned thus: for centuries men had been well advised and had gone by the cleverest way, while the Gibbelins came to expect them to come by boat and to look for them at the door whenever their larder was empty, even as a man looketh for a snipe in the marsh; but how, said Alderic, if a snipe should sit in the top of a tree, and would men find him there? Assuredly never! So Alderic decided to swim the river and not to go by the door, but to pick his way into the tower through the stone. Moreover, it was in his mind to work below the level of the ocean, the river (as Homer knew) that girdles the world, so that as soon as he made a hole in the wall the water should pour in, confounding the Gibbelins, and flooding the cellars rumoured to be 20 feet in depth, and therein he would dive for emeralds as a diver dives for pearls.

And on the day that I tell of he galloped away from his home scattering largesse of gold, as I have said, and passed through many kingdoms, the dragon snapping at maidens as he went, but being unable to eat them because of the bit in his mouth, and earning no gentler reward than a spur-thrust where he was softest. And so they came to the swart arboreal precipice of the unpassable forest. The dragon rose at it with a rattle of wings. Many a farmer near the edge of the world saw him up there where yet the twilight lingered, a faint, black, wavering line; and mistaking him for a row of geese going inland from the ocean, went into their houses cheerily rubbing their hands and saying that winter was coming, and that we should soon have snow. Soon even there the twilight faded away, and when they descended at the edge of the world it was night and the moon was shining. Ocean, the ancient river, narrow and shallow there, flowed by and made no murmur. Whether the Gibbelins banqueted or whether they watched by the door, they also made no murmur. And Alderic dismounted and took his armour off, and saying one prayer to his lady, swam with his pickaxe. He did not part from his sword, for fear that he met with a Gibbelin. Landed the other side, he began to work at once, and all went well with him. Nothing put out its head from any window, and all were lighted so that nothing within could see him in the dark. The blows of his pickaxe were dulled in the deep walls. All night he worked, no sound came to molest him, and at dawn the last rock swerved and tumbled inwards, and the river poured in after. Then Alderic took a stone, and went to the bottom step, and hurled the stone at the door; he heard the echoes roll into the tower, then he ran back and dived through the hole in the wall.

He was in the emerald cellar. There was no light in the lofty vault above him, but, diving through 20 feet of water, he felt the floor all rough with emeralds, and open coffers full of them. By a faint ray of the moon he saw that the water was green with them, and, easily filling a satchel, he rose again to the surface; and there were the Gibbelins waist-deep in the water, with torches in their hands! And, without saying a word, *or even smiling*, they neatly hanged him on the outer wall – and the tale is one of those that have not a happy ending.

The Last Hieroglyph

Clark Ashton Smith

*One of Lord Dunsany's more immediate disciples was the
American author H. P. Lovecraft and he in turn had a
profound influence upon the Californian poet and author
Clark Ashton Smith (1893–1961). Although the mark of
Dunsany is apparent in Smith's work, Smith himself maintained he was not directly influenced by Dunsany but more by
the French decadent school of Théophile Gautier and Charles
Baudelaire. It is the blending of these two styles that makes
Smith's work so atmospheric. Smith delighted in words and
language and apparently spent much time reading a dictionary
and striving to use one new obscure word a day, and this choice
of unusual and frequently exotic words adds to the strangeness
of his worlds. The majority of Smith's output was squeezed into
a brief five years, between 1929 and 1934. Like Lovecraft and
Robert E. Howard, Smith was a frequent contributor to the
pulp magazine* Weird Tales. *Smith found it impossible to
interest commercial publishers in his work, and he was saved
from oblivion by author August Derleth who, through his own
specialist venture, Arkham House, published six collections of
Smith's work starting with* Out of Space and Time *(1942).
Many of Smith's stories are set in particular worlds that he
created such as Hyperborea or Atlantis. His own favourite was
Zothique, the world of the dying earth set millennia in the
future, and the following was one of the last stories he wrote
about that land.*

The world itself, in the end, shall be turned to a round cipher.
                                            – *Old prophecy of Zothique*

USHAIN THE ASTROLOGER HAD STUDIED THE CIRCLING orbs of night from many far-separated regions, and had cast, with such skill as he was able to command, the horoscopes of a myriad men, women and children. From city to city, from realm to realm he had gone, abiding briefly in any place: for often the local magistrates had banished him as a common charlatan; or elsewise, in due time, his consultants had discovered the error of his predictions and had fallen away from him. Sometimes he went hungry and shabby; and small honour was paid to him anywhere. The sole companions of his precarious fortunes were a wretched mongrel dog that had attached itself to him in the desert town of Zul-Bha-Sair, and a mute, one-eyed Negro whom he had bought very cheaply in Yoros. He had named the dog Ansarath, after the canine star, and had called the negro Mouzda, which was a word signifying darkness.

In the course of his prolonged itinerations, the astrologer came to Xylac and made his abode in its capital, Ummaos, which had been built above the shards of an elder city of the same name, long since destroyed by a sorcerer's wrath. Here Nushain lodged with Ansarath and Mouzda in a half-ruinous attic of a rotting tenement; and from the tenement's roof, Nushain was wont to observe the positions and movements of the sidereal bodies on evenings not obscured by the fumes of the city. At intervals some housewife or harlot, some porter or huckster or petty merchant, would climb the decaying stairs to his chamber, and would pay him a small sum for the nativity which he plotted with immense care by the aid of his tattered books of astrological science.

When, as often occurred, he found himself still at a loss regarding the significance of some heavenly conjunction or opposition after poring over his books, he would consult Ansarath, and would draw profound auguries from the variable motions of the dog's mangy tail or his actions in searching for fleas. Certain of these divinations were fulfilled, to the considerable benefit of Nushain's renown in Ummaos. People came to him more freely and frequently, hearing that he was a soothsayer of some note; and, moreover, he was immune from prosecution, owing to the liberal laws of Xylac, which permitted all the sorcerous and mantic arts.

It seemed, for the first time, that the dark planets of his fate were yielding to auspicious stars. For this fortune, and the coins which accrued thereby to his purse, he gave thanks to Vergama who, throughout the whole continent of Zothique, was deemed the most powerful and mysterious of the genii, and was thought to rule over the heavens as well as the earth.

On a summer night, when the stars were strewn thickly like a fiery sand on the black azure vault, Nushain went up to the roof of his lodging-place. As was often his custom, he took with him the negro Mouzda, whose one eye possessed a miraculous sharpness and had served well, on many occasions, to supplement the astrologer's own rather near-sighted vision. Through a well-codified system of signs and gestures, the mute was able to communicate the result of his observations to Nushain.

On this night the constellation of the Great Dog, which had presided over Nushain's birth, was ascendant in the east. Regarding it closely, the dim eyes of the astrologer were troubled by a sense of something unfamiliar in its configuration. He could not determine the precise character of the change till Mouzda, who evinced much excitement, called his attention to three new stars of the second magnitude which had appeared in close proximity to the Dog's hindquarters. These remarkable novae, which Nushain could discern only as three reddish blurs, formed a small equilateral triangle. Nushain and Mouzda were both certain that they had not been visible on any previous evening.

"By Vergama, this is a strange thing," swore the astrologer, filled with amazement and dumbfoundment. He began to compute the problematic influence of the novae on his future reading of the heavens, and perceived at once that they would exert, according to the law of astral emanations, a modifying effect on his own destiny, which had been so largely controlled by the Dog.

He could not, however, without consulting his books and

tables, decide the particular trend and import of this supervening influence; though he felt sure that it was most momentous, whether for his bale or welfare. Leaving Mouzda to watch the heavens for other prodigies, he descended at once to his attic. There, after collating the opinions of several old-time astrologers on the power exerted by novae, he began to re-cast his own horoscope. Painfully and with much agitation he laboured throughout the night, and did not finish his figurings till the dawn came to mix a deathly greyness with the yellow light of the candles.

There was, it seemed, but one possible interpretation of the altered heavens. The appearance of the triangle of novae in conjunction with the Dog signified clearly that Nushain was to start ere long on an unpremeditated journey which would involve the transit of no fewer than three elements. Mouzda and Ansarath were to accompany him; and three guides, appearing successively, at the proper times, would lead him towards a destined goal. So much his calculations had revealed, but no more: there was nothing to foretell whether the journey would prove auspicious or disastrous, nothing to indicate its bourn, purpose or direction.

The astrologer was much disturbed by this somewhat singular and equivocal augury. He was ill pleased by the prospect of an imminent journey, for he did not wish to leave Ummaos, among whose credulous people he had begun to establish himself not without success. Moreover, a strong apprehension was roused within him by the oddly manifold nature and veiled outcome of the journey. All this, he felt, was suggestive of the workings of some occult and perhaps sinister providence; and surely it was no common travelling which would take him through three elements and would require a triple guidance.

During the nights that followed, he and Mouzda watched the mysterious novae as they went over towards the west behind the bright-flaming Dog. And he puzzled interminably over his charts and volumes, hoping to discover some error in the reading he had made. But always, in the end, he was compelled to the same interpretation.

More and more, as time went on, he was troubled by the

thought of that unwelcome and mysterious journey which he must make. He continued to prosper in Ummaos, and it seemed that there was no conceivable reason for his departure from that city. He was as one who awaited a dark and secret summons, not knowing whence it would come, nor at what hour. Throughout the days, he scanned with fearful anxiety the faces of his visitors, deeming that the first of the three star-predicted guides might arrive unheralded and unrecognized among them.

Mouzda and the dog Ansarath, with the intuition of dumb things, were sensible of the weird uneasiness felt by their master. They shared it palpably, the negro showing his apprehension by wild and demoniac grimaces, and the dog crouching under the astrologer's table or prowling restlessly to and fro with his half-hairless tail between his legs. Such behaviour, in its turn, served to reconfirm the inquietude of Nushain, who deemed it a bad omen.

On a certain evening, Nushain pored for the fiftieth time over his horoscope, which he had drawn with sundry-coloured inks on a sheet of papyrus. He was much startled when, on the blank lower margin of the sheet, he saw a curious character which was no part of his own scribbling. The character was a hieroglyph written in dark bituminous brown, and seeming to represent a mummy whose shroudings were loosened about the legs and whose feet were set in the posture of a long stride. It was facing towards that quarter of the chart where stood the sign indicating the Great Dog, which, in Zothique, was a House of the Zodiac.

Nushain's surprise turned to a sort of trepidation as he studied the hieroglyph. He knew that the margin of the chart had been wholly clear on the previous night; and during the past day he had not left the attic at any time. Mouzda, he felt sure, would never have dared to touch the chart; and, moreover, the negro was little skilled in writing. Among the various inks employed by Nushain, there was none that resembled the sullen brown of the character, which seemed to stand out in a sad relief on the white papyrus.

Nushain felt the alarm of one who confronts a sinister and unexplainable apparition. No human hand, surely, had inscribed the mummy-shapen character, like the sign of a strange outer planet about to invade the Houses of his horoscope. Here, as in the advent of the three novae, an occult agency was suggested. Vainly, for many hours, he sought to unriddle the mystery: but in all his books there was naught to enlighten him; for this thing, it seemed, was wholly without precedent in astrology.

During the next day he was busied from morn till eve with the plotting of those destinies ordained by the heavens for certain people of Ummaos. After completing the calculations with his usual toilsome care, he unrolled his own chart once more, albeit with trembling fingers. An eeriness that was nigh to panic seized him when he saw that the brown hieroglyph no longer stood on the margin, but was now placed like a striding figure in one of the lower Houses, where it still fronted towards the Dog, as if advancing on that ascendant sign.

Henceforth the astrologer was fevered with the awe and curiosity of one who watches a fatal but inscrutable portent. Never, during the hours that he pondered above it, was there any change in the intruding character; and yet, on each successive evening when he took out the chart, he saw that the mummy had strode upwards into a higher House, drawing always nearer to the House of the Dog . . .

There came a time when the figure stood on the Dog's threshold. Portentous with mystery and menace that were still beyond the astrologer's divining, it seemed to wait while the night wore on and was shot through with the grey wefting of dawn. Then, overworn with his prolonged studies and vigils, Nushain slept in his chair. Without the troubling of any dream he slept; and Mouzda was careful not to disturb him; and no visitors came to the attic on that day. So the morn and the noon and the afternoon went over, and their going was unheeded by Nushain.

He was awakened at eve by the loud and dolorous howling of Ansarath, which appeared to issue from the room's furthest corner. Confusedly, ere he opened his eyes, he became aware of an odour of bitter spices and piercing natron. Then, with the dim webs of sleep not wholly swept from his vision, he beheld, by the yellowy tapers that Mouzda had lighted, a tall, mummy-like form that waited in silence beside him. The head, arms and body of the shape were wound closely with bitumen-coloured cerements; but the folds were loosened from the hips downward, and the figure stood like a walker, with one brown, withered foot in advance of its fellow.

Terror quickened in Nushain's heart, and it came to him that the shrouded shape, whether lich or phantom, resembled the weird, invasive hieroglyph that had passed from House to House through the chart of his destiny. Then, from the thick swathings of the apparition, a voice issued indistinctly, saying: "Prepare yourself, O Nushain, for I am the first guide of that journey which was foretold to you by the stars."

Ansarath, cowering beneath the astrologer's bed, was still howling his fear of the visitant; and Nushain saw that Mouzda had tried to conceal himself in company with the dog. Though a chill as of imminent death was upon him, and he deemed the apparition to be death itself, Nushain arose from his chair with that dignity proper to an astrologer, which he had maintained through all the vicissitudes of his lifetime. He called Mouzda and Ansarath from their hiding-place, and the two obeyed him, though with many cringings before the dark, muffled mummy.

With the comrades of his fortune behind him, Nushain turned to the visitant. "I am ready," he said, in a voice whose quavering was almost imperceptible. "But I would take with me certain of my belongings."

The mummy shook his mobled head. "It were well to take with you nothing but your horoscope: for this alone shall you retain in the end."

Nushain stooped above the table on which he had left his nativity. Before he began to roll the open papyrus, he noticed that the hieroglyph of the mummy had vanished. It was as if the written symbol, after moving athwart his horoscope, had materialized itself in the figure that now attended him. But on the chart's nether margin, in remote opposition to the Dog, was the sea-blue hieroglyph of a quaint merman with carp-like tail and head half human, half apish; and behind the merman was the black hieroglyph of a small barge.

Nushain's fear, for a moment, was subdued by wonder. But he rolled the chart carefully, and stood holding it in his right hand.

"Come," said the guide. "Your time is brief, and you must pass through the three elements that guard the dwelling-place of Vergama from unseasonable intrusion."

These words, in a measure, confirmed the astrologer's divinations. But the mystery of his future fate was in no wise lightened by the intimation that he must enter, presumably at the journey's end, the dim House of that being called Vergama, whom some considered the most secret of all the gods, and others the most cryptical of demons. In all the lands of Zothique, there were rumours and fables regarding Vergama; but these were wholly diverse and contradictory, except in their common attribution of almost omnipotent powers to this entity. No man knew the situation of his abode; but it was believed that vast multitudes of people had entered it during the centuries and millenniums, and that none had returned therefrom.

Ofttimes had Nushain called upon the name of Vergama, swearing or protesting thereby as men are wont to do by the cognomens of their shrouded lords. But now, hearing the name from the lips of his macabre visitor, he was filled with the darkest and most eerie apprehensions. He sought to subdue these feelings, and to resign himself to the manifest will of the stars. With Mouzda and Ansarath at his heels, he followed the striding mummy, which seemed little hampered, if at all, by its trailing cerements.

With one regretful backward glance at his littered books and papers, he passed from the attic room and down the tenement stairs. A wannish light seemed to cling about the swathings of the mummy; but, apart from this, there was no illumination; and Nushain thought that the house was strangely dark and silent, as if all its occupants had died or had gone away. He heard no sound from the evening city; nor could he see aught but close-encroaching darkness beyond the windows that should have gazed on a litten street. Also, it seemed that the stairs had changed and lengthened, giving no more on the courtyard of the tenement, but plunging deviously into an unsuspected region of stifling vaults and foul, dismal, nitrous corridors.

Here the air was pregnant with death, and the heart of Nushain failed him. Everywhere, in the shadow-curtained crypts and deep-shelved recesses, he felt the innumerable presence of the dead. He thought that there was a sad sighing of stirred cerements, a breath exhaled by long-stiffened cadavers, a dry clicking of lipless teeth beside him as he went. But darkness walled his vision, and he saw nothing save the luminous form of his guide, who stalked onwards as if through a natal realm.

It seemed to Nushain that he passed through boundless catacombs in which were housed the mortality and corruption of all the ages. Behind him still he heard the shuffling of Mouzda, and at whiles the low, frightened whine of Ansarath; so he knew that the twain were faithful to him. But upon him, with a chill of lethal damps, there grew the horror of his surroundings; and he shrank with all the repulsion of living flesh from the shrouded thing that he followed, and those other things that mouldered round about in the fathomless gloom.

Half thinking to hearten himself by the sound of his own voice, he began to question the guide; though his tongue clove to his mouth as if palsied. "Is it indeed Vergama, and none other, who has summoned me forth upon this journey? For what purpose has he called me? And in what land is his dwelling?"

"Your fate has summoned you," said the mummy. "In the end, at the time appointed and no sooner, you shall learn the purpose. As to your third question, you would be no wiser if I should name the region in which the house of Vergama is hidden from mortal trespass: for the land is not listed on any terrene chart, nor map of the starry heavens."

These answers seemed equivocal and disquieting to Nushain, who was possessed by frightful forebodings as he went deeper into the subterranean charnels. Dark, indeed, he thought, must be the goal of a journey whose first stage had led him so far amid the empire of death and corruption; and dubious, surely, was the being who had called him forth and had sent to him as the first guide a sere and shrunken mummy clad in the tomb's habiliments.

Now, as he pondered these matters almost to frenzy, the shelfy walls of the catacomb before him were outlined by a dismal light, and he came after the mummy into a chamber where tall candles of black pitch in sockets of tarnished silver burned about an immense and solitary sarcophagus. Upon the blank lid and sides of the sarcophagus, as Nushain neared it, he could see neither runes nor sculptures nor hieroglyphs engraven; but it seemed, from the proportions, that a giant must lie within.

The mummy passed athwart the chamber without pausing. But Nushain, seeing that the vaults beyond were full of darkness, drew back with a reluctance that he could not conquer; and though the stars had decreed his journey, it seemed to him that human flesh could go no further. Prompted by a sudden impulse, he seized one of the heavy yard-long tapers that burned stilly about the sarcophagus; and, holding it in his left hand, with his horoscope still firmly clutched in the right, he fled with Mouzda and Ansarath on the way he had come, hoping to retrace his footsteps through the gloomy caverns and return to Ummaos by the taper's light.

He heard no sound of pursuit from the mummy. But ever, as he fled, the pitch candle, flaring wildly, revealed to him the horrors that darkness had curtained from his eyes. He saw the bones of men that were piled in repugnant confusion with those of fell monsters, and the riven sarcophagi from which protruded the half-decayed members of innominate beings; members which were neither heads nor hands nor feet. And soon the catacomb divided and redivided before him, so that he must choose his way at random, not knowing whether it would lead him back to Ummaos or into the untrod depths.

Presently he came to the huge, browless skull of an uncouth creature, which reposed on the ground with upward-gazing orbits; and beyond the skull was the monster's mouldy skeleton, wholly blocking the passage. Its ribs were cramped by the narrowing walls, as if it had crept there and had died in the darkness, unable to withdraw or go forward. White spiders, demon-headed and large as monkeys, had woven their webs in the hollow arches of the bones; and they swarmed out interminably as Nushain approached; and the skeleton seemed to stir and quiver as they seethed over it abhorrently and dropped to the ground before the astrologer. Behind them others poured in a countless army, crowding and mantling every ossicle. Nushain fled with his companions; and running back to the forking of the caverns, he followed another passage.

Here he was not pursued by the demon spiders. But, hurrying on lest they or the mummy overtake him, he was soon halted by the rim of a great pit which filled the catacomb from wall to wall and was overwide for the leaping of man. The dog Ansarath, sniffing certain odours that arose from the pit, recoiled with a mad howling; and Nushain, holding the taper outstretched above it, discerned far down a glimmer of ripples spreading circle-wise on some unctuous black fluid; and two blood-red spots appeared to swim with a weaving motion at the centre. Then he heard a hissing as of some great cauldron heated by wizard fires; and it seemed that the blackness boiled upwards, mounting swiftly and evilly to overflow the pit; and the red spots, as they neared him, were like luminous eyes that gazed malignantly into his own . . .

So Nushain turned away in haste; and, returning upon his steps, he found the mummy awaiting him at the junction of the catacombs.

"It would seem, Nushain, that you have doubted your own horoscope," said the guide, with a certain irony. "However, even a bad astrologer, on occasion, may read the heavens aright. Obey, then, the stars that decreed your journey."

Henceforward, Nushain followed the mummy without recalcitrance. Returning to the chamber in which stood the immense sarcophagus, he was enjoined by his guide to replace in its socket the black taper he had stolen. Without other light than the phosphorescence of the mummy's cerements, he threaded the foul gloom of those profounder ossuaries which lay beyond. At last, through caverns where a dull dawning intruded upon the shadows, he came out beneath shrouded heavens, on the shore of a wild sea that clamoured in mist and cloud and spindrift. As if recoiling from the harsh air and light, the mummy drew back into the subterrance, and it said: "Here my dominion ends, and I must leave you to await the second guide."

Standing with the poignant sea-salt in his nostrils, with his hair and garments outblown on the gale, Nushain heard a metallic clangour, and saw that a door of rusty bronze had closed in the cavern entrance. The beach was walled by unscalable cliffs that ran sheerly to the wave on each hand. So perforce the astrologer waited; and from the torn surf he beheld erelong the emergence of a sea-blue merman whose head was half human, half apish; and behind the merman there hove a small black barge that was not steered or rowed by any visible being. At this, Nushain recalled the hieroglyphs of the sea creature and the boat which had appeared on the margin of his nativity; and unrolling the papyrus, he saw with wonderment that the figures were both gone; and he doubted not that they had passed, like the mummy's hieroglyph, through all the zodiacal Houses, even to that House which presided over his destiny; and thence, mayhap, they had emerged into material being. But in their stead now was the burning hieroglyph of a fire-coloured salamander, set opposite to the Great Dog.

The merman beckoned to him with antic gestures, grinning deeply, and showing the white serrations of his shark-like teeth. Nushain went forward and entered the barge in obedience to the signs made by the sea creature; and Mouzda and Ansarath, in faithfulness to their master, accompanied him. Thereupon the merman swam away through the boiling surf; and the barge, as if oared and ruddered by mere enchantment, swung about forthwith, and warring smoothly against wind and wave, was drawn straightly over that dim, unnamable ocean.

Half seen amid rushing foam and mist, the merman swam steadily on before. Time and space were surely outpassed during that voyage; and as if he had gone beyond mortal existence, Nushain experienced neither thirst nor hunger. But it seemed that his soul drifted upon seas of strange doubt and direst alienation; and he feared the misty chaos about him even as he had feared the nighted catacombs. Often he tried to question the mer-creature concerning their destination, but received no answer. And the wind blowing from shores unguessed, and the tide flowing to unknown gulfs, were alike filled with whispers of awe and terror.

Nushain pondered the mysteries of his journey almost to madness; and the thought came to him that, after passing through the region of death, he was now traversing the grey limbo of uncreated things; and, thinking this, he was loth to surmise the third stage of his journey; and he dared not reflect upon the nature of its goal.

Anon, suddenly, the mists were riven, and a cataract of golden rays poured down from a high-seated sun. Near at hand, to the lee of the driving barge, a tall island hove with verdurous trees and light, shell-shapen domes, and blossomy gardens hanging far up in the dazzlement of noon. There, with a sleepy purling, the surf was lulled on a low, grassy shore that had known not the anger of storm; and fruited vines and full-blown flowers were pendent above the water. It seemed that a spell of oblivion and slumber was shed from the island, and that any who landed thereon would dwell inviolable for ever in sun-bright dreams. Nushain was seized with a longing for its green, bowery refuge; and he wished to voyage no further into the dreadful nothingness of the mist-bound ocean. And between his longing and his terror, he quite forgot the terms of that destiny which had been ordained for him by the stars.

There was no halting nor swerving of the barge; but it drew still nearer to the isle in its coasting; and Nushain saw that the intervening water was clear and shallow, so that a tall man might easily wade to the beach. He sprang into the sea, holding his horoscope aloft, and began to walk towards the island; and Mouzda and Ansarath followed him, swimming side by side.

Though hampered somewhat by his long wet robes, the astrologer thought to reach that alluring shore; nor was there any movement on the part of the merman to intercept him. The water was mid-way between his waist and his armpits; and now it lapped at his girdle; and now at the knee-folds of his garment; and the island vines and blossoms drooped fragrantly above him.

Then, being but a step from that enchanted beach, he heard a great hissing, and saw that the vines, the boughs, the flowers, the very grasses, were intertwined and commingled with a million serpents, writhing endlessly to and fro in hideous agitation. From all parts of that lofty island the hissing came, and the serpents, with foully mottled volumes, coiled, crept and slithered upon it everywhere; and no single yard of its surface was free from their defilement, or clear for human treading.

Turning seaward in his revulsion, Nushain found the merman and the barge waiting close at hand. Hopelessly he re-entered the barge with his followers, and the magically driven boat resumed its course. And now, for the first time, the merman spoke, saying over his shoulder in a harsh, half-articulate voice, not without irony: "It would seem, O Nushain, that you lack faith in your own divinations. However, even the poorest of astrologers may sometimes cast a horoscope correctly. Cease, then, to rebel against that which the stars have written."

The barge drove on, and the mists closed heavily about it, and the noon-bright island was lost to view. After a vague interim the muffled sun went down behind inchoate waters and clouds; and a darkness as of primal night lay everywhere. Presently, through the torn rack, Nushain beheld a strange heaven whose signs and planets he could not recognize; and at this there came upon him the black horror of utmost dereliction. Then the mists and clouds returned, veiling that unknown sky from his scrutiny. And he could discern nothing but the merman, who was visible by a wan phosphor that clung always about him in his swimming.

Still the barge drove on; and in time it seemed that a red morning rose stifled and conflagrant behind the mists. The boat entered the broadening light, and Nushain, who had thought to behold the sun once more, was dazzled by a strange shore where flames towered in a high unbroken wall, feeding perpetually, to all appearance, on bare sand and rock. With a mighty leaping and a roar as of blown surf the flames went up, and a heat like that of many furnaces smote far on the sea. Swiftly the barge neared the shore; and the merman, with uncouth gestures of farewell, dived and disappeared under the waters.

Nushain could scarcely regard the flames or endure their heat. But the barge touched the strait tongue of land lying between them and the sea; and before Nushain, from the red wall of fire, a blazing salamander emerged, having the form and hue of that hieroglyph which had last appeared on his horoscope. And he knew, with ineffable consternation, that this was the third guide of his threefold journey.

"Come with me," said the salamander, in a voice like the crackling of faggots. Nushain stepped from the barge to that strand which was hot as an oven beneath his feet; and behind him, though with palpable lothness, Mouzda and Ansarath still followed. But, approaching the flames behind the salamander, and half swooning from their ardour, he was overcome by the weakness of mortal flesh; and seeking again to evade his destiny, he fled along the narrow scroll of beach between the fire and the water. But he had gone only a few paces when the salamander, with a great fiery roaring and racing, intercepted him; and it drove him straight towards the fire with terrible flailings of its dragon-like tail, from which showers of sparks were emitted. He could not face the salamander, and he thought the flames would consume him like paper as he entered them: but in the wall there appeared a sort of opening, and the fires arched themselves into an arcade, and he passed through with his followers, herded by the salamander, into an ashen land where all things were veiled with low-hanging smoke and steam. Here the salamander observed with a kind of irony: "Not wrongly, O Nushain, have you interpreted the stars of your horoscope. And now your journey draws to an end, and you will need no longer the services of a guide." So saying, it left him, going out like a quenched fire on the smoky air.

Nushain, standing irresolute, beheld before him a white stairway that mounted amid the veering vapours. Behind him the flames rose unbroken, like a topless rampart; and on either hand, from instant to instant, the smoke shaped itself into demon forms and faces that menaced him. He began to climb the stairs, and the shapes gathered below and about, frightful as a wizard's familiars, and keeping pace with him as he went upward, so that he dared not pause or retreat. Far up he climbed in the fumy dimness, and came unaware to the open portals of a house of grey stone rearing to unguessed height and amplitude.

Unwillingly, but driven by the thronging of the smoky shapes, he passed through the portals with his companions. The house was a place of long empty halls, tortuous as the folds of a sea-conch. There were no windows, no lamps; but it seemed that bright suns of silver had been dissolved and diffused in the air. Fleeing from the hellish wraiths that pursued him, the astrologer followed the winding halls and emerged ultimately in an inner chamber where space itself was immured. At the room's centre a cowled and muffled figure of colossal proportions sat upright on a marble chair, silent, unstirring. Before the figure, on a sort of table, a vast volume lay open.

Nushain felt the awe of one who approaches the presence of some high demon or deity. Seeing that the phantoms had vanished, he paused on the room's threshold: for its immensity made him giddy, like the void interval that lies between the worlds. He wished to withdraw; but a voice issued from the cowled being, speaking softly as the voice of his own inmost mind.

"I am Vergama, whose other name is Destiny; Vergama, on whom you have called so ignorantly and idly, as men are wont to call on their hidden lords; Vergama, who has summoned you on the journey which all men must make at one time or another, in one way or another way. Come forward, O Nushain, and read a little in my book."

The astrologer was drawn as by an unseen hand to the table. Leaning above it, he saw that the huge volume stood open at its middle pages, which were covered with a myriad signs written in inks of various colours, and representing men, gods, fishes, birds, monsters, animals, constellations, and many other things. At the end of the last column of the right-hand page, where little space was left for other inscriptions, Nushain beheld the hieroglyphs of an equal-sided triangle of stars, such as had lately appeared in proximity to the Dog; and, following these, the hieroglyphs of a mummy, a merman, a barge and a salamander, resembling the figures that had come and gone on his horoscope, and those that had guided him to the House of Vergama.

"In my book," said the cowled figure, "the characters of all things are written and preserved. All visible forms, in the beginning, were but symbols written by me; and at the last they shall exist only as the writing of my book. For a season they issue forth, taking to themselves that which is known as substance . . . It was I, O Nushain, who set in the heavens the stars that foretold your journey; I, who sent the three guides. And these things, having served their purpose, are now but infoliate ciphers, as before."

Vergama paused, and an infinite silence returned to the room, and a measureless wonder was upon the mind of Nushain. Then the cowled being continued.

"Among men, for a while, there was that person called Nushain the astrologer, together with the dog Ansarath and the negro Mouzda, who followed his fortunes . . . But now, very shortly, I must turn the page, and before turning it, must finish the writing that belongs thereon."

Nushain thought that a wind arose in the chamber, moving lightly with a weird sough and sigh, though he felt not the actual breath of its passing. But he saw that the fur of Ansarath, cowering close beside him, was ruffled by the wind. Then, beneath his marvelling eyes, the dog began to dwindle and wither, as if seared by a lethal magic; and he lessened to the size of a rat, and thence to the smallness of a mouse and the lightness of an insect, though preserving still his original form. After that, the tiny thing was caught up by the sighing air, and it flew past Nushain as a gnat might fly; and, following it, he saw that the hieroglyph of a dog was inscribed suddenly beside that of the salamander, at the bottom of the right-hand page. But, apart from this, there remained no trace of Ansarath.

Again a wind breathed in the room, touching not the astrologer, but fluttering the ragged raiment of Mouzda, who crouched near to his master, as if appealing for protection. And the mute became shrunken and shrivelled, turning at the last to a thing light and thin as the black, tattered wing-shard of a beetle, which the air bore aloft. And Nushain saw that the hieroglyph of a one-eyed negro was inscribed following that of the dog; but, aside from this, there was no sign of Mouzda.

Now, perceiving clearly the doom that was designed for him, Nushain would have fled from the presence of Vergama. He turned from the outspread volume and ran towards the chamber door, his worn, tawdry robes of an astrologer flapping about his thin shanks. But softly in his ear, as he went, there sounded the voice of Vergama.

"Vainly do men seek to resist or evade that destiny which turns them to ciphers in the end. In my book, O Nushain, there is room even for a bad astrologer."

Once more the weird sighing arose, and a cold air played upon Nushain as he ran; and he paused midway in the vast room as if a wall had arrested him. Gently the air breathed on his lean, gaunt figure, and it lifted his greying locks and beard, and it plucked softly at the roll of papyrus which he still held in his hand. To his dim eyes, the room seemed to reel and swell, expanding infinitely. Borne upward, around and around, in a swift vertiginous swirling, he beheld the seated shape as it loomed ever higher above him in cosmic vastness. Then the god was lost in light; and Nushain was a weightless and exile thing, the withered skeleton of a lost leaf, rising and falling on the bright whirlwind.

In the book of Vergama, at the end of the last column of the right-hand page, there stood the hieroglyph of a gaunt astrologer, carrying a furled nativity.

Vergama leaned forward from his chair, and turned the page.

The Sorcerer Pharesm

Jack Vance

Like Dunsany and Clark Ashton Smith, Jack Vance (b. 1916) delights in exotic language. His work is firmly in the tradition of both writers, most notably in the stories that he has set in the earth's last years. These first appeared in The Dying Earth *(1950) and were continued in* The Eyes of the Overworld *(1966),* Cugel's Saga *(1983) and* Rhialto the Marvellous *(1984). The following is one of the Cugel stories, which form part of a connected series. Cugel is a crafty but at times naïve thief who is caught while trying to burgle the manse of the wizard Iucounu. Iucounu despatches Cugel to the far side of the earth on a quest, after inserting into him the monitor, Firx, which ensures that Cugel will return. The stories follow Cugel's attempts to complete the wizard's quest and get back home.*

T HE MOUNTAINS WERE BEHIND: THE DARK DEFILES, the tarns, the echoing stone heights – all now a sooty bulk to the north. For a time Cugel wandered a region of low rounded hills the colour and texture of old wood, with groves of blue-black trees dense along the ridges, then came upon a faint trail which took him south by long swings and slants, and at last broke out over a vast dim plain. A half-mile to the right rose a line of tall cliffs, which instantly attracted his attention, bringing him a haunting pang of *déjà-vu*. He stared mystified. At some time in the past he had known these cliffs: how? when? His memory provided no response. He settled himself upon a low lichen-covered rock to rest, but now Firx, the monitor which Iucounu the Laughing Magician had implanted in Cugel's viscera, became impatient and inflicted a stimulating pang. Cugel leaped to his feet, groaning with weariness and shaking his fist to the south-west, the presumable direction of Almery. "Iucounu, Iucounu! If I could repay a tenth of your offences, the world would think me harsh!"

He set off down the trail, under the cliffs which had affected him with such poignant but impossible recollections. Far below spread the plain, filling three-quarters of the horizon with colours much like those of the lichened rock Cugel had just departed: black patches of woodland; a grey crumble where ruins filled an entire valley; nondescript streaks of grey-green, lavender, grey-brown; the leaden glint of two great rivers disappearing into the haze of distance.

Cugel's brief rest had only served to stiffen his joints; he limped, and the pouch chafed his hip. Even more distressing was the hunger gripping his belly. Another tally against Iucounu who had sent Cugel to the northern wastes on a mission of wanton frivolity! Iucounu, it must be allowed, had furnished an amulet converting such normally inedible substances as grass, wood, horn, hair, humus and the like into a nutritious paste. Unfortunately – and this was a measure of Iucounu's mordant humour – the paste retained the flavour of the native substance, and during his passage of the mountain Cugel had tasted little better than spurge, cullion, blackwort, oak twigs and galls, and on one occasion, when all else failed, certain refuse discovered in the cave of a bearded thawn. Cugel had eaten only minimally; his long spare frame had become gaunt; his cheekbones protruded like sponsons; the black eyebrows which once had crooked so jauntily now lay flat and dispirited. Truly, truly, Iucounu had much to answer for! And Cugel, as he proceeded, debated the exact quality of revenge he would take if ever he found his way back to Almery.

The trail swung down upon a wide stony flat where the wind had carved a thousand grotesque figures. Surveying the area Cugel thought to perceive regularity among the eroded shapes, and halted to rub his long chin in appraisal. The pattern displayed an extreme subtlety – so subtle indeed, that Cugel wondered if it had not been projected by his own mind. Moving closer, he discerned further complexities, and elaborations upon complexities: twists, spires, volutes; discs, saddles, wrenched spheres; torsions and flexions; spindles, cardioids, lanciform pinnacles: the most laborious, painstaking and intricate rock-carving conceivable, manifestly no random effort of the elements. Cugel frowned in perplexity, unable to imagine a motive for so complex an undertaking.

He went on and a moment later heard voices, together with the clank of tools. He stopped short, listened cautiously, then proceeded, to come upon a gang of about fifty men ranging in stature from 3 inches to well over 12 feet. Cugel approached on tentative feet, but after a glance the workers paid him no heed, continuing to chisel, grind, scrape, probe and polish with dedicated zeal.

Cugel watched for several minutes, then approached the overseer, a man 3 feet in height who stood at a lectern consulting the plans spread before him, comparing them to the work in progress by means of an ingenious optical device. He appeared to note everything at once, calling instructions, chiding, exhorting against error, instructing the least deft in the use of their tools. To exemplify his remarks he used a wonderfully extensible forefinger, which reached forth 30 feet to tap at a section of rock, to scratch a quick diagram, then as swiftly retract.

The foreman drew back a pace or two, temporarily satisfied with the work in progress, and Cugel came forward. "What intricate effort is this and what is its object?"

"The work is as you see," replied the foreman in a voice of penetrating compass. "From natural rock we produce specified shapes, at the behest of the sorcerer Pharesm . . . Now then! Now then!" The cry was addressed to a man 3 feet taller than Cugel, who had been striking the stone with a pointed maul. "I detect over-confidence!" The forefinger shot forth. "Use great care at this juncture; note how the rock tends to cleave? Strike here a blow of the sixth intensity at the vertical, using a semi-clenched grip; at this point a fourth-intensity blow groin-wise; then employ a quartergauge bant-iron to remove the swange."

With the work once more going correctly, he fell to studying his plans, shaking his head with a frown of dissatisfaction. "Much too slow! The craftsmen toil as if in a drugged torpor, or else display a mulish stupidity. Only yesterday Dadio Fessadil, he of 3 ells with the green kerchief yonder, used a 19-gauge freezing-bar to groove the bead of a small inverted quatrefoil."

Cugel shook his head in surprise, as if never had he heard of so egregious a blunder. And he asked: "What prompts this inordinate rock-hewing?"

"I cannot say," replied the foreman. "The work has been in progress 318 years, but during this time Pharesm has never clarified his motives. They must be pointed and definite, for he makes a daily inspection and is quick to indicate errors." Here he turned aside to consult with a man as tall as Cugel's knee, who voiced uncertainty as to the pitch of a certain volute. The foreman, consulting an index, resolved the matter; then he turned back to Cugel, this time with an air of frank appraisal. "You appear both astute and deft; would you care to take employment? We lack several craftsmen of the ½-ell category, or, if you prefer more forceful manifestations, we can nicely use an apprentice stone-breaker of 16 ells. Your stature is adjusted in either direction, there is identical scope for advancement. As you see I am a man of 4 ells. I reached the position of Striker in one year, Moulder of Forms in three, Assistant Chade in ten, and I have now served as Chief Chade for nineteen years. My predecessor was of 2 ells, and the Chief Chade before him was a 10-ell man." He went on to enumerate advantages of the work, which included sustenance, shelter, narcotics of choice, nympharium privileges, a stipend starting at ten terces a day, various other benefits including Pharesm's services as diviner and exorcizer. "Additionally, Pharesm maintains a conservatory where all may enrich their intellects. I myself take instruction in Insect Identification, the Heraldry of the Kings of Old Gomaz, Unison Chanting, Practical Catalepsy and Orthodox Doctrine. You will never find a master more generous than Pharesm the Sorcerer!"

Cugel restrained a smile for the Chief Chade's enthusiasm; still, his stomach was roiling with hunger and he did not reject the proffer out of hand. "I had never before considered such a career," he said. "You cite advantages of which I was unaware."

"True; they are not generally known."

"I cannot immediately say yes or no. It is a decision of consequence which I feel I should consider in all its aspects."

The Chief Chade gave a nod of profound agreement. "We encourage deliberation in our craftsmen, when every stroke must achieve the desired effect. To repair an inaccuracy of as much as a fingernail's width the entire block must be removed, a new block fitted into the socket of the old, whereupon all begins anew. Until the work has reached its previous stage nympharium privileges are denied to all. Hence, we wish no opportunistic or impulsive newcomers to the group."

Firx, suddenly apprehending that Cugel proposed a delay, made representations of a most agonizing nature. Clasping his abdomen, Cugel took himself aside and, while the Chief Chade watched in perplexity, argued heatedly with Firx. "How may I proceed without sustenance?" Firx's response was an incisive motion of the barbs. "Impossible!" exclaimed Cugel. "The amulet of Iucounu theoretically suffices, but I can stomach no more spurge; remember, if I fall dead in the trail, you will never rejoin your comrade in Iucounu's vats!"

Firx saw the justice of the argument and reluctantly became quiet. Cugel returned to the lectern, where the Chief Chade had been distracted by the discovery of a large tourmaline opposing the flow of a certain complicated helix. Finally Cugel was able to engage his attention. "While I weigh the proffer of employment and the conflicting advantages of diminution versus elongation, I will need a couch on which to recline. I also wish to test the perquisites you describe, perhaps for the period of a day or more."

"Your prudence is commendable," declared the Chief Chade. "The folk of today tend to commit themselves rashly to courses they later regret. It was not so in my youth, when sobriety and discretion prevailed. I will arrange for your admission into the compound, where you may verify each of my assertions. You will find Pharesm stern but just, and only the man who hacks the rock willy-nilly has cause to complain. But observe! Here is Pharesm the Sorcerer on his daily inspection!"

Up the trail came a man of imposing stature wearing a voluminous white robe. His countenance was benign; his hair was like yellow down; his eyes were turned upwards as if rapt in the contemplation of an ineffable sublimity. His arms were sedately folded, and he moved without motion of his legs. The workers, doffing their caps and bowing in unison, chanted a respectful salute, to which Pharesm returned an inclination of the head. Spying Cugel, he paused, made a swift survey of the work so far accomplished, then glided without haste to the lectern.

"All appears reasonably exact," he told the Chief Chade. "I believe the polish on the underside of Epi-projection 56–16 is uneven and I detect a minute chip on the secondary cinctor of the nineteenth spire. Neither circumstance seems of major import and I recommend no disciplinary action."

"The deficiencies shall be repaired and the careless artisans reprimanded: this at the very least!" exclaimed the Chief Chade in an angry passion. "Now I wish to introduce a possible recruit to our workforce. He claims no experience at the trade, and will deliberate before deciding to join our group. If he so elects, I envision the usual period as rubble-gatherer, before he is entrusted with tool-sharpening and preliminary excavation."

"Yes; this would accord with our usual practice. However . . ." Pharesm glided effortlessly forward, took Cugel's left hand and performed a swift divination upon the fingernails. His bland countenance became sober. "I see contradictions of four varieties. Still it is clear that your optimum bent lies elsewhere than in the hewing and shaping of rock. I advise that you seek another and more compatible employment."

"Well spoken!" cried the Chief Chade. "Pharesm the Sorcerer demonstrates his infallible altruism! In order that I do not fall short of the mark I hereby withdraw my proffer of employment! Since no purpose can now be served by reclining upon a couch or testing the perquisites, you need waste no more irreplaceable time."

Cugel made a sour face. "So casual a divination might well be inaccurate."

The Chief Chade extended his forefinger 30 feet vertically in outraged remonstrance, but Pharesm gave a placid nod. "This is quite correct, and I will gladly perform a more comprehensive divination, though the process requires six to eight hours."

"So long?" asked Cugel in astonishment.

"This is the barest minimum. First you are swathed head to foot in the intestines of fresh-killed owls, then immersed in a warm bath containing a number of secret organic substances. I must, of course, char the small toe of your left foot, and dilate your nose sufficiently to admit an explorer beetle, that he may study the conduits leading to and from your sensorium. But let us return to my divinatory, that we may commence the process in good time."

Cugel pulled at his chin, torn this way and that. Finally he said, "I am a cautious man, and must ponder even the advisability of undertaking such a divination; hence, I will require several days of calm and meditative somnolence. Your compound and the adjacent nympharium appear to afford the conditions requisite to such a state; hence—"

Pharesm indulgently shook his head. "Caution, like any other virtue, can be carried to an extreme. The divination must proceed at once."

Cugel attempted to argue further but Pharesm was adamant, and presently glided off down the trail.

Cugel disconsolately went to the side, considering first this stratagem, then that. The sun neared the zenith, and the work-men began to speculate as to the nature of the viands to be served for their midday meal. At last the Chief Chade signalled; all put down their tools and gathered about the cart which contained the repast.

Cugel jocularly called out that he might be persuaded to share the meal, but the Chief Chade would not hear of it. "As in all of Pharesm's activities, an exactitude of consequence must prevail. It is an unthinkable discrepancy that fifty-four men should consume the food intended for fifty-three."

Cugel could contrive no apposite reply, and sat in silence while the rock-hewers munched at meat pies, cheeses and salt fish. All ignored him save for one, a ¼-ell man whose generosity far exceeded his stature, and who undertook to reserve for Cugel a certain portion of his food. Cugel replied that he was not at all hungry, and rising to his feet wandered off through the project, hoping to discover some forgotten cache of food. He prowled here and there, but the rubble-gatherers had removed every trace of substance extraneous to the pattern. With appetite unassuaged Cugel arrived at the centre of the work, where sprawled on a carved disc he spied a most peculiar creature: essentially a gelatinous globe swimming with luminous particles from which a number of transparent tubes or tentacles dwindled away to nothing. Cugel bent to examine the creature, which pulsed with a slow internal rhythm. He prodded it with his finger, and bright little flickers rippled away from the point of contact. Interesting: a creature of unique capabilities! Removing a pin from his garments he prodded a tentacle, which emitted a peevish pulse of light, while the golden flecks in its substance surged back and forth. More intrigued than ever, Cugel hitched himself close, and gave himself to experimentation, probing here and there, watching the angry flickers and sparkles with great amusement.

A new thought occurred to Cugel. The creature displayed qualities reminiscent of both coelenterate and echinoderm. A terrene nudibranch? A mollusc deprived of its shell? More importantly, was the creature edible?

Cugel brought forth his amulet, applied it to the central globe and to each of the tentacles. He heard neither chime nor buzz: the creature was non-poisonous. He unsheathed his knife, sought to excise one of the tentacles, but found the substance too resilient and tough to be cut. There was a brazier nearby, kept aglow for forging and sharpening the workers' tools. He lifted the creature by two of its tentacles, carried it to the brazier and arranged it over the fire. He toasted it carefully and when he deemed it sufficiently cooked, sought to eat it. Finally, after various undignified efforts, he crammed the creature down his throat, finding it without taste or sensible nutritive volume.

The stone-carvers were returning to their work. With a significant glance for the foreman Cugel set off down the trail.

Not far distant was the dwelling of Pharesm the Sorcerer: a long low building of melted rock surmounted by eight oddly shaped domes of copper, mica and bright blue glass. Pharesm himself sat at leisure before the dwelling, surveying the valley with a serene and all-inclusive magnanimity. He held up a hand in calm salute. "I wish you pleasant travels and success in all future endeavours."

"The sentiment is naturally valued," said Cugel with some bitterness. "You might however have rendered a more meaningful service by extending a share of your noon meal."

Pharesm's placid benevolence was as before. "This would have been an act of mistaken altruism. Too fulsome a generosity corrupts the recipient and stultifies his resource."

Cugel gave a bitter laugh. "I am a man of iron principle, and I will not complain, even though, lacking any better fare, I was forced to devour a great transparent insect which I found at the heart of your rock-carving."

Pharesm swung about with a suddenly intent expression. "A great transparent insect, you say?"

"Insect, epiphyte; mollusc – who knows? It resembled no creature I have yet seen, and its flavour, even after carefully grilling at the brazier, was not distinctive."

Pharesm floated 7 feet into the air, to turn the full power of his gaze down at Cugel. He spoke in a low harsh voice: "Describe this creature in detail!"

Wondering at Pharesm's severity, Cugel obeyed. "It was thus and thus as to dimension." He indicated with his hands. "In colour it was a gelatinous transparency shot with numberless golden specks. These flickered and pulsed when the creature was disturbed. The tentacles seemed to grow flimsy and disappear rather than terminate. The creature evinced a certain sullen determination, and ingestion proved difficult."

Pharesm clutched at his head, hooking his fingers into the yellow down of his hair. He rolled his eyes upwards and uttered a tragic cry. "Ah! Five hundred years I have toiled to entice this creature, despairing, doubting, brooding by night, yet never abandoning hope that my calculations were accurate and my great talisman cogent. Then, when finally it appears, you fall upon it for no other reason then to sate your repulsive gluttony!"

Cugel, somewhat daunted by Pharesm's wrath, asserted his absence of malicious intent. Pharesm would not be mollified. He pointed out that Cugel had committed trespass and hence had forfeited the option of pleading innocence. "Your very existence is a mischief compounded by bringing the unpleasant fact to my notice. Benevolence prompted me to forbearance, which now I perceive for a grave mistake."

"In this case," stated Cugel with dignity, "I will depart your presence at once. I wish you good fortune for the balance of the day, and now, farewell."

"Not so fast," said Pharesm in the coldest of voices. "Exactitude has been disturbed; the wrong which has been committed demands a counter-act to validate the Law of Equipoise. I can define the gravity of your act in this manner: should I explode you on this instant into the most minute of your parts the atonement would measure one ten-millionth of your offence. A more stringent retribution becomes necessary."

Cugel spoke in great distress. "I understand that an act of consequence was performed, but remember! my participation was basically casual. I categorically declare first my absolute innocence, second my lack of criminal intent, and third my effusive apologies. And now, since I have many leagues to travel, I will—"

Pharesm made a peremptory gesture. Cugel fell silent. Pharesm drew a deep breath. "You fail to understand the calamity you have visited upon me. I will explain, so that you may not be astounded by the rigours which await you. As I have adumbrated, the arrival of the creature was the culmination of my great effort. I determined its nature through a perusal of 42,000 librams, all written in cryptic language: a task requiring a hundred years. During a second hundred years I evolved a pattern to draw it in upon itself and prepared exact specification. Next I assembled stone-cutters, and across a period of 300 years gave solid form to

my pattern. Since like subsumes like, the variates and intercon-
geles create a suprapullulation of all areas, qualities and internals
into a crystorrhoid whorl, eventually exciting the ponentiation of
a proubietal chute. Today occurred the concatenation; the 'creature', as you call it, pervolved upon itself; in your idiotic malice
you devoured it."

Cugel, with a trace of haughtiness, pointed out that the "idiotic
malice" to which the distraught sorcerer referred was in actuality
simple hunger. "In any event, what is so extraordinary about the
'creature'? Others equally ugly may be found in the net of any
fisherman."

Pharesm drew himself to his full height, glared down at Cugel.
"The 'creature'," he said in a grating voice, 'is TOTALITY.
The central globe is all of space, viewed from the inverse. The
tubes are vortices into various eras, and what terrible acts you
have accomplished with your prodding and poking, your boiling
and chewing, are impossible to imagine!"

"What of the effects of digestion?" enquired Cugel delicately.
"Will the various components of space, time and existence retain
their identity after passing the length of my inner tract?"

"Bah. The concept is jejune. Enough to say that you have
wreaked damage and created a serious tension in the ontological
fabric. Inexorably you are required to restore equilibrium."

Cugel held out his hands. "Is it not possible a mistake has been
made? That the 'creature' was no more than pseudo-TOTAL-
ITY? Or is it conceivable that the 'creature' may by some means
be lured forth once more?"

"The first two theories are untenable. As to the last, I must
confess that certain frantic expedients have been forming in my
mind." Pharesm made a sign, and Cugel's feet became attached to
the soil. "I must go to my divinatory and learn the full significance of the distressing events. In due course I will return."

"At which time I will be feeble with hunger," said Cugel
fretfully. "Indeed, a crust of bread and a bite of cheese would
have averted all the events for which I am now reproached."

"Silence!" thundered Pharesm. "Do not forget that your
penalty remains to be fixed; it is the height of impudent

recklessness to hector a person already struggling to maintain his judicious calm!"

"Allow me to say this much," replied Cugel. "If you return from your divining to find me dead and dessicated here on the path, you will have wasted much time fixing upon a penalty."

"The restoration of vitality is a small task," said Pharesm. "A variety of deaths by contrasting processes may well enter into your judgment." He started towards his divinatory, then turned back and made an impatient gesture. "Come; it is easier to feed you than return to the road."

Cugel's feet were once more free and he followed Pharesm through a wide arch into the divinatory. In a broad room with splayed grey walls, illuminated by three-coloured polyhedra, Cugel devoured the food Pharesm caused to appear. Meanwhile Pharesm secluded himself in his workroom, where he occupied himself with his divinations. As time passed Cugel grew restless, and on three occasions approached the arched entrance. On each occasion a Presentment came to deter him, first in the shape of a leaping ghoul, next as a zigzag blaze of energy, and finally as a score of glittering purple wasps.

Discouraged, Cugel went to a bench, and sat waiting with elbows on long legs, hands under his chin.

Pharesm at last reappeared, his robe wrinkled, the fine yellow down of his hair disordered into a multitude of small spikes. Cugel slowly rose to his feet.

"I have learned the whereabouts of TOTALITY," said Pharesm, in a voice like the strokes of a great gong. "In indignation, removing itself from your stomach, it has recoiled a million years into the past."

Cugel gave his head a solemn shake. "Allow me to offer my sympathy, and my counsel, which is: never despair! Perhaps the 'creature' will choose to pass this way again."

"An end to your chatter! TOTALITY must be recovered. Come."

Cugel reluctantly followed Pharesm into a small room walled with blue tile, roofed with a tall cupola of blue and orange glass.

Pharesm pointed to a black disc at the centre of the floor. "Stand there."

Cugel glumly obeyed. "In a certain sense, I feel that—"

"Silence!" Pharesm came forward. "Notice this object!" He displayed an ivory sphere the size of two fists, carved in exceedingly fine detail. "Here you see the pattern from which my great work is derived. It expresses the symbolic significance of NULLITY to which TOTALITY must necessarily attach itself, by Kratinjae's Second Law of Cryptorrhoid Affinites, with which you are possibly familiar."

"Not in every aspect," said Cugel. "But may I ask your intentions?"

Pharesm's mouth moved in a cool smile. "I am about to attempt one of the most cogent spells ever evolved: a spell so fractious, harsh, and coactive, that Phandaal, Ranking Sorcerer of Grand Motholam, barred its use. If I am able to control it, you will be propelled one million years into the past. There you will reside until you have accomplished your mission, when you may return."

Cugel stepped quickly from the black disc. "I am not the man for this mission, whatever it may be, I fervently urge the use of someone else!"

Pharesm ignored the expostulation. "The mission, of course, is to bring the symbol into contact with TOTALITY." He brought forth a wad of tangled grey tissue. "In order to facilitate your search, I endow you with this instrument which relates all possible vocables to every conceivable system of meaning." He thrust the net into Cugel's ear, where it swiftly engaged itself with the nerve of consonant expression. "Now," said Pharesm, "you need listen to a strange language for but three minutes when you become proficient in its use. And now, another article to enhance the prospect of success: this ring. Notice the jewel: should you approach to within a league of TOTALITY, darting lights within the gem will guide you. Is all clear?"

Cugel gave a reluctant nod. "There is another matter to be considered. Assume that your calculations are incorrect and that TOTALITY has returned only 900,000 years into the past: what then? Must I dwell out all my life in this possibly barbarous era?"

Pharesm frowned in displeasure. "Such a situation involves an error of 10 per cent. My system of reckoning seldom admits of deviation greater than 1 per cent."

Cugel began to make calculations, but now Pharesm signalled to the black disc. "Back! And do not again move hence!"

Sweat oozing from his glands, knees quivering and sagging, Cugel returned to his place.

Pharesm retreated to the far end of the room, where he stepped into a coil of gold tubing, which sprang spiralling up to clasp his body. From a desk he took four black discs, which he began to shuffle and juggle with such fantastic dexterity that they blurred in Cugel's sight. Pharesm at last flung the discs away; spinning and wheeling they hung in the air, gradually drifting towards Cugel.

Pharesm next took up a white tube, pressed it tight against his lips and spoke an incantation. The tube swelled and bulged into a great globe. Pharesm twisted the end shut and shouting a thunderous spell, hurled the globe at the spinning discs, and all exploded. Cugel was surrounded, seized, jerked in all directions outward, compressed with equal vehemence: the net result, a thrust in a direction contrary to all, with an impetus equivalent to the tide of a million years. Among dazzling lights and distorted visions, Cugel was transported beyond his consciousness.

Cugel awoke in a glare of orange-gold sunlight, of a radiance he had never known before. He lay on his back looking up into a sky of warm blue, of lighter tone and softer texture than the indigo sky of his own time.

He tested arms and legs and, finding no damage, sat upright, then slowly rose to his feet, blinking in the unfamiliar radiance.

The topography had changed only slightly. The mountains to the north were taller and of harsher texture, and Cugel could not identify the way he had come, or – more properly – the way he would come. The site of Pharesm's project was now a low forest of feathery-light green trees, on which hung clusters of red berries. The valley was as before, though the rivers flowed by different courses and three great cities were visible at varying distances. The air drifting up from the valley carried a strange tart fragrance mingled with an antique exhalation of moulder and must, and it seemed to Cugel that a peculiar melancholy hung in the air; in fact, he thought to hear music: a slow plaintive melody, so sad as to bring tears to his eyes. He searched for the source of the music, but it faded and disappeared even as he sought it, and only when he ceased to listen did it return.

For the first time Cugel looked towards the cliffs which rose to the west, and now the sense of *déjà-vu* was stronger than ever. Cugel pulled his chin in puzzlement. The time was a million years previous to that other occasion on which he had seen the cliffs, and hence, by definition, must be the first. But it was also the second time, for he well remembered his initial experience of the cliffs. On the other hand, the logic of time could not be contravened, and by such reckoning this view preceded the other. A paradox, thought Cugel: a puzzle indeed! Which experience had provided the background to the poignant sense of familiarity he had felt on both occasions? . . . Cugel dismissed the subject as unprofitable and started to turn away when movement caught his eye. He looked back up the face of the cliffs, and the air was suddenly full and rich with the music he had heard before, music of anguish and exalted despair . . . Cugel stared in wonder. A great winged creature wearing white robes flapped on high along the face of the cliff. The wings were long, ribbed with black chitin, sheathed with grey membrane. Cugel watched in awe as it swooped into a cave high up in the face of the cliff.

A gong tolled, from a direction Cugel could not determine. Overtones shuddered across the air and when they died, the unheard music became almost audible. From far over the valley came one of the Winged Beings, carrying a human form, of what age and sex Cugel could not determine. It hovered beside the cliff and dropped its burden. Cugel thought to hear a faint cry and the music was sad, stately, sonorous. The body seemed to fall slowly down the great height and struck at last at the base of the cliff. The Winged Being, after dropping the body, glided to a high ledge, where it folded its wings and stood like a man, staring over the valley. Cugel shrank back behind a rock. Had he been seen?

He could not be sure. He heaved a deep sigh. This sad golden world of the past was not to his liking; the sooner he could leave the better. He examined the ring which Pharesm had furnished, but the gem shone like dull glass, with none of the darting glitters which would point the direction to TOTALITY. It was as Cugel feared. Pharesm had erred in his calculations and Cugel could never return to his own time.

The sound of flapping wings caused him to look into the sky. He shrank back into such concealment as the rock offered. The music of woe swelled and sighed away, as in the light of the setting sun the winged creature hovered beside the cliff and dropped its victim. Then it landed on a ledge with a great flapping of wings and entered a cave.

Cugel rose to his feet and ran crouching down the path through the amber dusk.

The path presently entered a grove of trees and here Cugel paused to catch his breath, after which he proceeded more circumspectly. He crossed a patch of cultivated ground on which stood a vacant hut. Cugel considered it as shelter for the night, but thought to see a dark shape watching from the interior and passed it by.

The trail led away from the cliffs, across rolling downs, and just before the twilight gave way to night Cugel came to a village standing on the banks of a pond.

Cugel approached warily, but was encouraged by the signs of tidiness and good husbandry. In a park beside the pond stood a pavilion possibly intended for music, miming or declamation; surrounding the park were small narrow houses with high gables, the ridges of which were raised in decorative scallops. Opposite the pond was a larger building, with an ornate front of woven wood and enamelled plaques of red, blue and yellow. Three tall gables served as its roof, the central ridge supporting an intricate carved panel, while those to either side bore a series of small spherical blue lamps. At the front was a wide pergola sheltering benches, tables and an open space, all illuminated by red and green fire-fans. Here townsfolk took their ease, inhaling incense and drinking wine, while youths and maidens cavorted in an eccentric high-kicking dance, to the music of pipes and a concertina.

Emboldened by the placidity of the scene, Cugel approached. The villagers were of a type he had never before encountered, of no great stature, with generally large heads and long restless arms. Their skin was a rich pumpkin orange; their eyes and teeth were black; their hair, likewise black, hung smoothly down beside the faces of the men to terminate in a fringe of blue beads, while the women wound their hair around white rings and pegs, to arrive at a coiffure of no small complexity. The features were heavy at jaw and cheekbone; the long wide-spaced eyes drooped in a droll manner at the outer corners. The noses and ears were long and were under considerable muscular control, endowing the faces with great vivacity. The men wore flounced black kirtles, brown surcoats, headgear consisting of a wide black disc, a black cylinder, another lesser disc, surmounted by a gilded ball. The women wore black trousers, brown jackets with enamelled discs at the navel, and at each buttock a simulated tail of green or red plumes, possibly an indication as to marital status.

Cugel stepped into the light of the fire-fans; instantly all talk ceased. Noses became rigid, eyes stared, ears twisted about in curiosity. Cugel smiled to left and right, waved his hand in a debonair all-inclusive greeting, and took a seat at an empty table.

There were mutters of astonishment at the various tables, too quiet to reach Cugel's ears. Presently one of the elders arose and approaching Cugel's table spoke a sentence, which Cugel found unintelligible, for with insufficient scope, Pharesm's mesh as yet failed to yield meaning. Cugel smiled politely, held wide his hands in a gesture of well-meaning helplessness. The elder spoke once more, in a rather sharper voice, and again Cugel indicated his inability to understand. The elder gave his ears a sharp disapproving jerk and turned away. Cugel signalled to the proprietor, pointed to the bread and wine on a table and signified his desire that the same be brought to him.

The proprietor voiced a query which, for all its unintelligibility, Cugel was able to interpret. He brought forth a gold coin, and, satisfied, the proprietor turned away.

Conversation recommenced at the various tables and before long the vocables conveyed meaning to Cugel. When he had eaten and drunk, he rose to his feet and walked to the table of the elder who had first spoken to him, where he bowed respectfully. "Do I have permission to join you at your table?"

"Certainly; if you are so inclined. Sit." The elder indicated a seat. "From your behaviour I assumed that you were not only deaf and dumb, but also guilty of mental retardation. It is now clear, at least, that you hear and speak."

"I profess rationality as well," said Cugel. "As a traveller from afar, ignorant of your customs, I thought it best to watch quietly a few moments, lest in error I commit a solecism."

"Ingenious but peculiar," was the elder's comment. "Still, your conduct offers no explicit contradiction to orthodoxy. May I inquire the urgency which brings you to Farwan?"

Cugel glanced at his ring; the crystal was dull and lifeless; TOTALITY was clearly elsewhere. "My homeland is uncultured; I travel that I may learn the modes and styles of more civilized folk."

"Indeed!" The elder mulled the matter over for a moment, and nodded in qualified approval. "Your garments and physiognomy are of a type unfamiliar to me; where is this homeland of yours?"

"It lies in a region so remote," said Cugel, "that never till this instant had I knowledge of the land of Farwan!"

The elder flattened his ears in surprise. "What? Glorious Farwan, unknown? The great cities Impergos, Tharuwe, Rhaverjand – all unheard of? What of the illustrious Sembers? Surely the fame of the Sembers has reached you. They expelled the star-pirates; they brought the sea to the Land of Platforms; the splendour of Padara Palace is beyond description!"

Cugel sadly shook his head. "No rumour of this extraordinary magnificence has come to my ears."

The elder gave his nose a saturnine twitch. He said shortly: "Matters are as I state."

"I doubt nothing," said Cugel. "In fact I admit to ignorance. But tell me more, for I must be forced to abide long in this region.

For instance, what of the Winged Beings that reside in the cliff? What manner of creature are they?"

The elder pointed towards the sky. "If you had the eyes of a nocturnal titvit you might note a dark moon which reels around the earth, and which cannot be seen except when it casts its shadow upon the sun. The Winged Beings are denizens of this dark world and their ultimate nature is unknown. They serve the Great God Yelisea in this fashion: whenever comes the time for man or woman to die, the Winged Beings are informed by a despairing signal from the dying person's norn. They thereupon descend upon the unfortunate and convey him to their caves, which in actuality constitute a magic opening into the blessed land Byssom."

Cugel leaned back, black eyebrows raised in a somewhat quizzical arch. "Indeed, indeed," he said, in a voice which the elder found insufficiently earnest.

"There can be no doubt as to the truth of the facts as I have stated them. Orthodoxy derives from this axiomatic foundation, and the two systems are mutually reinforcing: hence each is doubly validated."

Cugel frowned. "The matter undoubtedly goes as you aver – but are the Winged Beings always accurate in their choice of victims?"

The elder rapped the table in annoyance. "The doctrine is irrefutable, for those whom the Winged Beings take never survive, even when they appear in the best of health. Admittedly the fall upon the rocks conduces towards death, but it is the mercy of Yelisea which sees fit to grant a speedy extinction, rather than the duration of a possibly agonizing canker. The system is wholly beneficent. The Winged Beings summon only the moribund, which are then thrust through the cliff into the blessed land Byssom. Occasionally a heretic argues otherwise and in this case – but I am sure that you share the orthodox view?"

"Wholeheartedly," Cugel asserted. "The tenets of your belief are demonstrably accurate." And he drank deep of his wine. Even as he set down the goblet a murmur of music whispered through the air: a concord infinitely sweet, infinitely melancholy. All sitting under the pergola became silent – though Cugel was unsure that he in fact had heard music.

The elder huddled forward a trifle, and drank. Only then did he glance up. "The Winged Beings are passing over even now."

Cugel pulled thoughtfully at his chin. "How does one protect himself from the Winged Beings?"

The question was ill-put; the elder glared, an act which included the curling forward of his ears. "If a person is about to die, the Winged Beings appear. If not, he need have no fear."

Cugel nodded several times. "You have clarified my perplexity. Tomorrow – since you and I are manifestly in the best of health – let us walk up the hill and saunter back and forth near the cliff."

"No," said the elder, "and for this reason: the atmosphere at such an elevation is insalubrious; a person is likely to inhale a noxious fume, which entails damage to the health."

"I comprehend perfectly," said Cugel. "Shall we abandon this dismal topic? For the nonce we are alive and concealed to some extent by the vines which shroud the pergola. Let us eat and drink and watch the merrymaking. The youths of the village dance with great agility."

The elder drained his goblet and rose to his feet. "You may do as you please; as for me, it is time for my Ritual Abasement, this act being an integral part of our belief."

"I will perform something of a like nature by and by," said Cugel. "I wish you the enjoyment of your rite."

The elder departed the pergola and Cugel was left by himself. Presently certain youths, attracted by curiosity, joined him, and Cugel explained his presence once again, though with less emphasis upon the barbaric crudity of his native land, for several girls had joined the group, and Cugel was stimulated by their exotic colouring and the vivacity of their attitudes. Much wine was served and Cugel was persuaded to attempt the kicking, jumping local dance, which he performed without discredit. The exercise brought him into close proximity with an especially beguiling girl, who announced her name to be Zhiaml Vraz. At the conclusion of the dance, she put her arm around his waist, conducted him back to the table, and settled herself upon his lap. This act of familiarity excited no apparent disapproval among the others of the group, and Cugel was emboldened further. "I have not yet arranged for a bedchamber; perhaps I should do so before the hour grows late."

The girl signalled the innkeeper. "Perhaps you have reserved a chamber for this chisel-faced stranger?"

"Indeed, I will display it for his approval."

He took Cugel to a pleasant chamber on the ground floor, furnished with couch, commode, rug and lamp. On one wall hung a tapestry woven in purple and black, on another was a representation of a peculiarly ugly baby which seemed trapped or compressed in a transparent globe. The room suited Cugel; he announced as much to the innkeeper and returned to the pergola, where now the merrymakers were commencing to disperse. The girl Zhiaml Vraz yet remained, and she welcomed Cugel with a warmth which undid the last vestige of his caution. After another goblet of wine, he leaned close to her ear. "Perhaps I am over-prompt; perhaps I over-indulge my vanity; perhaps I contravene the normal decorum of the village – but is there reason why we should not repair to my chamber, and there amuse ourselves?"

"None whatever," said the girl. "I am unwed and until this time may conduct myself as I wish, for this is our custom."

"Excellent," said Cugel. "Do you care to precede me, or walk discreetly to the rear?"

"We shall go together; there is no need for furtiveness!"

Together they went to the chamber and performed a number of erotic exercises, after which Cugel collapsed into a sleep of utter exhaustion, for his day had been taxing.

During the middle hours he awoke to find Zhiaml Vraz departed from the chamber, a fact which in his drowsiness caused him no distress and he once more returned to sleep.

The sound of the door angrily flung ajar aroused him; he sat up to find the sun not yet arisen, and a deputation led by the elder regarding him with horror and disgust.

The elder pointed a long quivering finger through the gloom. "I thought to detect heretical opinion; now the fact is known!

Notice: he sleeps with neither head-covering nor devotional salve on his chin. The girl Zhiaml Vraz reports that at no time in their congress did the villain call out for the approval of Yelisea!"

"Heresy beyond a doubt!" declared the others of the deputation.

"What else could be expected of an outlander?" asked the elder contemptuously. "Look! Even now he refuses to make the sacred sign."

"I do not know the sacred sign!" Cugel expostulated. "I know nothing of your rites! This is not heresy, it is simple ignorance!"

"I cannot believe this," said the elder. "Only last night I outlined the nature of orthodoxy."

"The situation is grievous," said another in a voice of portentous melancholy. "Heresy exists only through putrefaction of the Lobe of Correctitude."

"This is an incurable and fatal mortification," stated another, no less dolefully.

"True! Alas, too true!" sighed one who stood by the door. "Unfortunate man!"

"Come!" called the elder. "We must deal with the matter at once."

"Do not trouble yourself," said Cugel. "Allow me to dress myself and I will depart the village never to return."

"To spread your detestable doctrine elsewhere? By no means!"

And now Cugel was seized and hauled naked from the chamber. Out across the park he was marched, and to the pavilion at the centre. Several of the group erected an enclosure formed of wooden posts on the platform of the pavilion and into this enclosure Cugel was thrust. "What do you do?" he cried out. "I wish no part of your rites!"

He was ignored, and stood peering between the interstices of the enclosure while certain of the villagers sent aloft a large balloon of green paper buoyed by hot air, carrying three green fire-fans below.

Dawn showed sallow in the west. The villagers, with all arranged to their satisfaction, withdrew to the edge of the park. Cugel attempted to climb from the enclosure, but the wooden rods were of such dimension and spacing as to allow him no grip.

The sky lightened; high above burned the green fire-fans. Cugel, hunched and in goose-flesh from the morning chill, walked back and forth the length of the enclosure. He stopped short, as from afar came the haunting music. It grew louder, seeming to reach the very threshold of audibility. High in the sky appeared a Winged Being, white robes trailing and flapping. Down it settled and Cugel's joints became limp and loose. The Winged Being hovered over the enclosure, dropped, enfolded Cugel in its white robe, endeavoured to bear him aloft. But Cugel had seized a bar of the enclosure and the Winged Being flapped in vain. The bar creaked, groaned, cracked. Cugel fought free of the stifling cloak, tore at the bar with hysterical strength; it snapped and splintered. Cugel seized a fragment, stabbed at the Winged Being. The sharp stick punctured the white cloak, and the Winged Being buffeted Cugel with a wing. Cugel seized one of the chitin ribs and with a mighty effort twisted it around backwards, so that the substance cracked and broke and the wing hung torn. The Winged Being, aghast, gave a great bound which carried both it and Cugel out upon the pavilion, and now it hopped through the village trailing its broken wing.

Cugel ran behind belabouring it with a cudgel he had seized up. He glimpsed the villagers staring in awe; their mouths were wide and wet, and they might have been screaming but he heard nothing. The Winged Being hopped faster, up the trail towards the cliff, with Cugel wielding the cudgel with all his strength. The golden sun rose over the far mountains; the Winged Being suddenly turned to face Cugel, and Cugel felt the glare of its eyes, though the visage, if such there were, was concealed beneath the hood of the cloak. Abashed and panting, Cugel stood back, and now it occurred to him that he stood almost defenceless should others drop on him from on high. So now he shouted an imprecation at the creature and turned back to the village.

All had fled. The village was deserted. Cugel laughed aloud. He went to the inn, dressed himself in his garments, buckled on his sword. He went out into the taproom, and looking into the till, found a number of coins which he transferred to his pouch, alongside the ivory representation of NULLITY. He returned outdoors: best to depart while none was on hand to detain him. A flicker of light attracted his attention: the ring on his finger glinted with dozens of streaming sparks, and all pointed up the trail, towards the cliffs.

Cugel shook his head wearily, checked the darting lights once again. Without ambiguity they directed him back the way he had come. Pharesm's calculations, after all, had been accurate. He had best act with decision, lest TOTALITY once more drift beyond his reach.

He delayed only long enough to find an axe, and hastened up the trail, following the glittering sparks of the ring.

Not far from where he had left it, he came upon the maimed Winged Being, now sitting on a rock beside the road, the hood drawn over its head. Cugel picked up a stone, heaved it at the creature, which collapsed into sudden dust, leaving only a tumble of white cloth to signal the fact of its existence.

Cugel continued up the road, keeping to such cover as offered itself, but to no avail. Overhead hovered Winged Beings, flapping and swooping. Cugel made play with the axe, striking at the wings, and the creatures flew high, circling above.

Cugel consulted the ring and was led on up the trail, with the Winged Beings hovering just above. The ring coruscated with the intensity of its message: there was TOTALITY, resting blandly on a rock!

Cugel restrained the cry of exultation which rose in his throat. He brought forth the ivory symbol of NULLITY, ran forward and applied it to the gelatinous central globe.

As Pharesm had asserted, adherence was instant. With the contact Cugel could feel the spell which bound him to the olden time dissolving.

A swoop, a buffet of great wings! Cugel was knocked to the ground. White cloth enveloped him, and with one hand holding NULLITY he was unable to swing his axe. This was now wrenched from his grasp. He released NULLITY, gripped a rock, kicked, somehow freed himself, and sprang for his axe. The Winged Being seized NULLITY and with TOTALITY attached, bore it aloft towards a cave high in the cliffs.

Great forces were pulling at Cugel, whirling in all directions at once. There was a roaring in his ears, a flutter of violet lights, and Cugel fell a million years into the future.

He recovered consciousness in the blue-tiled room with the sting of an aromatic liquor at his lips. Pharesm, bending over him, patted his face, poured more of the liquor into his mouth. "Awake! Where is TOTALITY! How are you returned?"

Cugel pushed him aside, and sat up on the couch.

"TOTALITY!" roared Pharesm. "Where is it? Where is my talisman?"

"I will explain," said Cugal in a thick voice. "I had it in my grasp, and it was wrenched away by winged creatures in the service of Great God Yelisea."

"Tell me, tell me!"

Cugel recounted the circumstances which had led first to gaining and then losing that which Pharesm sought. As he talked, Pharesm's face became damp with grief and his shoulders sagged. At last he marched Cugel outside, into the dim red light of late afternoon. Together they scrutinized the cliffs which now towered desolate and lifeless above them. "To which cave did the creature fly?" asked Pharesm. "Point it out, if you are able!"

Cugel pointed. "There, or so it would seem. All was confusion, all a tumble of wings . . ."

"Remain here." Pharesm went inside the workroom and presently returned. "I give you light," and he handed Cugel a cold white flame tied into a silver chain. "Prepare yourself."

At Cugel's feet he cast a pellet which broke into a vortex, and Cugel was carried dizzily aloft to that crumbling ledge which he had indicated to Pharesm. Nearby was the dark opening into a cave. Cugel turned the flame within. He saw a dusty passage, three strides wide and higher than he could reach. It led back into the cliff, twisting slightly to the side. It seemed barren of all life.

Holding the lamp before him, Cugel slowly moved along the passage, heart thumping for dread of something he could not define. He stopped short: music? The memory of music? He listened and could hear nothing but when he tried to step forward fear clamped his legs. He held high the lantern and peered down the dusty passage. Where did it lead? What lay beyond? Dusty cave? Demonland? The blessed land Byssom? Cugel slowly proceeded, every sense alert. On a ledge he spied a shrivelled brown spheroid: the talisman he had carried into the past. TOTALITY had long since disengaged itself and departed.

Cugel carefully lifted the object, which was brittle with the age of a million years and returned to the ledge. The vortex, at a command from Pharesm, conveyed Cugel back to the ground.

Dreading the wrath of Pharesm, Cugel tendered the withered talisman.

Pharesm took it, held it between thumb and forefinger. "This was all?"

"There was nothing more."

Pharesm let the object fall. It struck and instantly became dust. Pharesm looked at Cugel, took a deep breath, then turned with a gesture of unspeakable frustration and marched back to his divinatory.

Cugel gratefully moved off down the trail, past the workmen standing in an anxious group waiting for orders. They eyed Cugel sullenly and a 2-ell man hurled a rock. Cugel shrugged and continued south along the trail. Presently he passed the site of the village, now a waste overgrown with gnarled old trees. The pond had disappeared and the ground was hard and dry. In the valley below were ruins, but none marked the sites of the ancient cities Impergos, Tharuwe and Rhaverjand, now gone beyond memory.

Cugel walked south. Behind him the cliffs merged with haze and presently were lost to view.

King Yvorian's Wager

Darrell Schweitzer

*For the last in this vein of "Dunsanian" fantasies I have
selected a story by Darrell Schweitzer (b. 1952). Schweitzer's
work covers the whole range of fantasy but he is perhaps best
known for his exotic, far-future fantasies set in his own version
of the Dying Earth, as depicted in* The Shattered Goddess
*(1982), and his stories of the youth of the world when the gods
are awakening and still deal with humans, as explored in* The
Mask of the Sorcerer *(1995). Schweitzer is also a scholar of
the fantasy field having edited a number of reference works. In
homage to Dunsany he wrote a study of the author's work,*
Pathways to Elfland *(1989) and compiled a volume of his
previously uncollected stories,* The Ghosts of the Heaviside
Layer *(1980). Schweitzer is also the editor of the current
incarnation of* Weird Tales, *where the following story first
appeared.*

ON THE MORNING OF HIS FATHER'S FUNERAL AND his own
accession, King Yvorian had a vision. It came to him as he
rode in solemn state on the golden throne of the Eagle Kings,
borne aloft at the head of a procession of priests and courtiers by
the former king's most trusted bearers. He sat stiffly in his metal-
feathered robes, in his helmet that gleamed golden and silver like
a second sunrise.

All around him the heralds chanted the dirge of the dead

monarch, and soldiers marched grimly, clad in black armour, with black banners draped from their spears. The common folk leaned out of windows and gathered on rooftops and walls, waving palm fronds and making their own lamentations. Each strove to outdo his neighbour, to tear his hair more painfully, to shred his garments more wretchedly, to show his face more streaked with tears, for the old king had been a tyrant, and they feared him even when he was dead.

Then, suddenly, the young King Yvorian stood up. His bearers struggled desperately to keep the throne level as the weight shifted, and the people gasped, and the chanters ceased their chanting.

The king spread his arms, and for an instant his robes were like burning wings in the bright morning light.

Someone shouted, "The king is going to fly!" and the whole multitude dropped to its knees, for they knew that the first king of the Eagle Dynasty had flown long ago, soaring into the sun to return with a fiery crown on his head, bestowed by the gods. Surely, if Yvorian too were about to fly, it was, at the very least, a miracle.

But the king merely stood swaying on the footrest at the throne's front. The beak-shaped visor of his helmet fell down over his face, and for an instant he did indeed look like a divine eagle sent by the gods to rule all the lands of the Crescent Sea.

Then he fell. His knees buckled, his head bowed, and he tumbled forward into the dusty street. His helmet rolled beneath the feet of the stumbling bearers.

The commoners cried out and began to flee in wild confusion. The bearers set the throne down and knelt, covering their faces with their hands. The courtiers and priests milled about, uncertain. Only the soldiers stood, stolidly, guarding their king who shouted words no one could make out and writhed like some drunkard or madman, tearing, hurling his metal-feathered robe aside, clawing at the dirt.

Overhead, shutters slammed closed.

Still the bearers knelt, calmly, knowing they had failed in their duty, while the prefect of the guards struck off their heads one by one. The youngest bearer wept, but he did not try to run away.

A soothsayer pushed his way through the soldiers and also knelt, trying to read the future in the spreading blood, but the prefect struck his head off too, lest he succeed.

Then the priests gathered around the boy-king in their black robes and black, beak-visored helmets, resembling nothing more than vultures gathered for the feast.

A more prudent soothsayer, watching from a balcony, remarked on this.

The priests dared not lay hands on the king, for they knew that he was touched by the gods, and when the gods touch a ruler so explicitly on the first day of his reign, it is an awesome portent. At such times, the whole history of the nation might be written anew.

And it was a holy thing. They let the vision run its course and waited patiently for more than an hour until the king sat up, dazed, and held out his hands to be helped to his feet. In silence the priests brushed him off as best they could and led him back to his throne. His helmet had been lost somewhere in the confusion. He sat with the wind blowing through his yellow hair. There was dirt down one side of his face.

The priests raised the throne up on their own shoulders.

It was only much later, after King Yvorian's father had been properly laid to rest in the necropolis of the Eagle Kings by the shore of the Crescent Sea, that Kaniphar, the chief priest, took the boy aside and asked him, "Mighty One, what did you see?"

"I saw the gods," said the young king. "I saw them as the poets describe them, huge and insubstantial as clouds, reclining on their couches as they moved men and armies across the face of the world, like pieces on a game board. All the while they were laughing. Then, as they turned and saw that I was among them, a god who had the face of a dog leaned down to me and said, '*Behold, thou shalt wager with Rada Vatu.*'"

"Many are the forms and aspects of the gods," said the priest. "It could have been any one of them that spoke to you."

"It does not matter," said the king. "Tell me of Rada Vatu."

The priest grew pale. "Majesty, I am afraid."

Then the king spoke in a low, grim voice, and for an instant it seemed that the dread former monarch had returned in the person of his fifteen-year-old son.

"The foremost of my priests must never be afraid to serve me."

Kaniphar fell to his knees and the king touched him lightly on the head, as if to bless him, but said nothing more, and the high priest was truly frightened.

"Very well then," he said. "You shall learn of Rada Vatu."

So, all night beneath the uncertain light of hanging lamps, the priest and the king pored over ancient books and unlocked many secrets, and spoke of Rada Vatu.

"This one is older and mightier than all the gods," said the priest, "and it is ill luck even to speak his name. For he is the lord of death and time and fate, and those are three of his other names. Sometimes, when the gods are at their games, a playing piece suddenly vanishes from the board. That is because Rada Vatu has taken it. Then the gods are silent and thoughtful, for they know that one day Rada Vatu will sweep them all away with a wave of his hand. In the end the gods are as men, and Rada Vatu erases them like old figures traced in the sand."

"But Rada Vatu shall *wager* with me!" said the king, leaning towards the priest, whispering in a low voice like a hiss.

"Yes, he does that. He is a trickster, and fond of games."

"I shall *beat* him," said the king. He jumped up, knocking his chair over backwards. He paced back and forth in his excitement, striking his fist into his palm. "Surely this means I shall be the greatest of the Eagle Kings!"

"Perhaps so, Majesty."

"No! It means more! It means I'll be greater even than the gods, and Rada Vatu will treat me as an *equal*. He won't snatch any playing pieces away from *me*!"

Now Kaniphar the priest was beside himself with terror and he shook his folded hands and wept, and his voice broke as he begged the king to put aside such thoughts.

"Majesty, know that Rada Vatu is death and that he comes to each of us at the ending of our days, but not before."

King Yvorian turned to him fiercely. Another vision had come to him, not from the gods, but out of his own mind.

"No, in my case it will be different. Rada Vatu shall come to me on my own terms, like an envoy I have deigned to receive."

Just then the gods looked down from their game and paused. One or two started to laugh, but were swiftly hushed into silence.

The next day King Yvorian (who had appointed a new chief priest that morning) gave the first of a seemingly endless stream of orders. The kingdom was transformed. Royal heralds shouted in every square in every town. Before the palace, trumpeters blew blasts, then the gates swung wide, and the armies of the Eagle King strode forth, to subdue and extract tribute from all the lands bordering the Crescent Sea, from all the islands, from all the cities on the banks of the rivers of the hinterlands.

The wars went on for years. Meanwhile, the people groaned under the exactions of King Yvorian, who taxed away the wealth of the rich and conscripted the poor for their labour.

The king began to build. A palace like none the earth had ever known rose in the capital of the Eagle Kings. Some said it was the king's very vision, a madman's dream made solid out of stone and wood and glass. Fantastic towers rose, and onion-domed minarets, and among them sat the colossal image of King Yvorian himself on a carven throne, as high as a mountain, carefully placed so that on the first day of the year the sun rose directly behind the king's crown, radiating his glory to all the world.

Inside, winding staircases turned so subtly that the eye could not follow them, until they ended up nowhere at all. There were rooms of gold and of silver, and chambers filled with clouds from which strange voices issued, and corridors suffused with red light, with green, and orange and blue. In one vast hall was only darkness, an enclosed abyss, infinite, bottomless. In these endless rooms amid the twisting corridors a whole other kingdom awaited the king's desire, a glittering court populated by bird-headed men and impossible beasts, by beautiful, nearly divine youths and maidens, all constructed of humming metal and a kind of marble that was somehow soft and warm and seemingly alive. There was, too, a library, with floor, ceiling, and walls, and even the shelves mirrored. The mirrors angled through time. The reflections multiplied the books until the library contained all that ever had been written, or ever would be, to an infinite number.

But nowhere in all the huge palace, which was greater than a city, would the king permit any clock or hourglass or other means to telling time. Nor would he allow anyone who entered there to speak of persons who had died – the new chief priest acted as if he had never had a predecessor – for the palace, he said, was a labyrinth designed to confuse Rada Vatu, and time and death were banished from it.

When he was twenty-five and had fathered a score of sons by his many wives, King Yvorian retired to his labyrinth. He entered alone, without any priests or ministers, for they were not like him, he said, but ordinary men who would inevitably age and be swept away by Rada Vatu. But he, in the prime of his manhood, was to remain ageless for ever, so that Rada Vatu would come and wager with him.

For a while, the king spoke to his ministers through a pool in the silver chamber, in which he could see their faces, from which their speech drifted up like something shouted in the depths of a cave. But the greyness of their beards and the weariness of their faces distressed him, until he could bear to look on them no more.

He devoted many years to pleasure in the company of his deathless, lifeless youths and maidens, in rooms filled with strange scents, with vapours and waters that brought impossible ecstasies.

Then he turned to his books, and a faceless automaton read to him the exquisite poetry of the ancients, and the sere, harsh words that are to come in the world's last age, when the sun is already dead and the remnants of mankind retreat into metal pyramids miles high to escape the darkness and the monsters that have inherited the earth.

And his thoughts were troubled, and he sent the automaton away, then read by himself for a while before withdrawing into the black room, the walled abyss. There he floated, his mind detached from his senses, and he pondered many things. He knew pain then, and shame, and he repented his follies, his excesses, his thousand petty cruelties.

He began to dream, there in the darkness, and his spirit drifted, and it seemed he looked down on the turning earth for century after century, as the history of mankind slowly passed.

Then he was walking, naked and cold, among the tombs of the gods. He looked down once, and realized that the dust stirring around his feet was not dust at all, but *suns*, countless billions to be kicked aside with each step.

The tombs rose on either side of him as if to line an endless avenue, black, vaster than worlds, silhouetted against faint stars and glowing nebulae, each of them carven to show some aspect of the god therein: an upraised hand, a bull's head, a cross, a salmon leaping.

Still King Yvorian journeyed along the avenue, among the dust of stars, until the tombs on either side of him were featureless and empty, their doors left open. At last there were no more of them, and he came to those grey, infinite plains which have never known the tread even of Rada Vatu.

His mind emptied, all thoughts, all knowledge, all pride pouring out like water on to the hungry sand – but a single spark remained like a final star in the endless night, the realization, the voice within him: *Yes, I am the greatest of all. I am worthy to treat with Rada Vatu.*

That was enough. It brought him back. He swam up, out of the darkness, out of the dream, out of the black chamber.

He stood in the silver room, by the pool, staring down into the motionless water. He wore only a plain white robe and was barefoot, for he knew that Rada Vatu was never impressed with finery. His own reflection showed himself unkempt but unaged, his yellow hair and beard wild, but his face as unwrinkled as it had been on the day he first entered the labyrinth.

"Surely I am ready," he said aloud. "Surely Rada Vatu will come to me now."

"*I have been with you all along,*" said a voice.

The king whirled around, searching for the one who spoke. But he was alone in the chamber. Carvings of men and beasts stared down at him from the walls, but he knew them incapable of speech. He walked towards a far corner of the room, away from the pool.

"Liar!" he shouted. "I have not allowed you to enter my house until now. I have shut you out."

"*No, I have merely spared you.*"

"Show yourself!"

Dust and plaster sprinkled from the ceiling, rattling on the marble floor. Then a draught billowed behind a tapestry. A hanging trembled like shaken bones. Darkness and dust whirled together and rose like a miniature whirlwind, then formed the likeness of a man clad in a black robe and barefoot. The face was that of Kaniphar, the chief priest Yvorian had slain on a morning long before.

"You!" He retreated back towards the centre of the room.

"*It is I.*" The voice was a cold whisper, like the wind between the tombs of the gods.

Then Rada Vatu tore away his Kaniphar face like a mask and revealed the glaring visage of the former tyrant, Yvorian's father. And the king retreated further, until he stood against the edge of the pool.

Rada Vatu removed his father face. Now his head was hollow like a hood, filled with pale blue fire. Two brilliant eyes floated there, like tiny stars.

"Why . . . why have you come?" said King Yvorian.

Rada Vatu strode to the edge of the pool, leaned down, and touched the water with his hand. The clear pool became blood-dark.

The king scurried away from the pool, across the room. Rada Vatu stood there, gazing into the water, his back to Yvorian.

"*Do you not know? I have come to wager with you.*"

The king regained some of his composure. "Yes. Of course. I knew that."

"*And I know all that you do,*" said Rada Vatu, "*for I can peer into your mind even as I peer into this pool.*"

"Yes. A wager."

"*Even so. I desire sport on occasion.*"

"A wager."

Rada Vatu turned around, and the fire of his face was blinding white, and his robes were white too, resplendent as the sunrise. Only his eyes were dark, huge, like shafts into an abyss.

"*This is my wager, King Yvorian of the Eagle Land: that you shall cast aside your glories of your own will, that you shall no longer even call yourself a king, that in the end you shall know yourself to be as other men. Until that time, I shall not touch you with death.*"

"Then I am truly immortal," said King Yvorian. He laughed loud and long. "It is an absurd wager. *I accept!*"

The king rubbed his dazzled eyes, looked again, and saw that Rada Vatu was gone. But the pool was still the colour of blood.

Because he no longer feared death or time or the touch of Rada Vatu, King Yvorian emerged from his labyrinth. It was a long journey to the gate. He walked for many days, still clad in his plain robe, barefoot, his hair wild, but wearing the beaked crown of the Eagle Kings. At last he came to a corridor he barely remembered, then into a darkened, pillared hall filled with debris. Rusted chains dangled where lanterns had once hung. Dust and leaves covered a tarnished throne. Some of the great roof beams had fallen, and even a few of the pillars. He climbed, then wriggled his way towards the outer door. Mice scattered before him, rustling under the leaves.

The door was gone, the doorway itself misshapen, like the mouth of a cave.

King Yvorian stepped outside, into the warm sunlight, on to soft grass. To see living grass again and a blue sky and trees rising around him seemed, for the moment, to be more a marvel than all the blackness of the outer spaces, all the infinite suns, all the tombs of the gods.

He walked a little ways, then turned to look back. He saw no palace, no colossal image of himself, no capital city, nor even the doorway from which he had emerged, but only a grassy hillside. Before him, a plain stretched all the way to a line of mountains which rose like an island glimpsed across the sea, a blue smear on the horizon that might be land, or perhaps a cloud. He found a path and followed it. The sun and wind on his face, the warmth of the earth beneath his feet were all startling, wonderful.

The path turned sharply around the hill. Suddenly a dog blocked his way, barking. King Yvorian jumped back, startled. He had nearly forgotten what such a creature was. He reached to touch it. The dog snapped at his hand, but then retreated, whining, puzzled.

The dog ran to a boy of about eight years and hid behind the child's legs. The boy wore a patchwork of wool and leather. He carried a staff.

"Who are you?" The boy's speech was strangely accented.

King Yvorian stood up straight and said sternly, "Do you not know? I am Yvorian the mighty! I am the king of legends! I rule all these lands!"

"You talk funny," said the boy. He turned and ran down the path, the dog running after him.

Yvorian continued on for several hours, until the sun began to set behind the blue mountains and the air grew cold. At last he sat down, exhausted, marvelling at the motion of the sun and the darkening sky. He slept by the side of the road on a pile of leaves and grass. When he awoke at dawn, he was stiff and sore, and weak with hunger. All these things were stranger to him than any of his dreams or visions within the labyrinth.

That morning he passed through a forest of scrubby trees and reached a village. Huts of stone and wood lined a single street. He walked among them, turning to either side, recalling the tombs of the gods.

Slowly the villagers emerged to stare at him, clad as the boy had been in leather and wool. They gathered before him, filling the street.

"Bow down before me," said Yvorian. "I am your king, returned to you at last."

At first the villagers just gaped. Some shook their heads. There was a low murmur of whispered questions.

"Behold! I am Yvorian of the Eagles! I am the greatest king of all! I *command* you!"

Then the child from the day before pushed through the crowd, tugged on the sleeve of a village elder, pointed at Yvorian and said, "That's him!"

Some of the villagers began to laugh. Others turned away, embarrassed or afraid. "A madman! A madman!" someone shouted.

The king raged at them. He shrieked for them to be still. He grabbed a man, then another, shoving them to their knees. But each merely leaped up again, laughing and shouting.

Yvorian struck about with his fists, truly like a madman in his fury. The villagers caught hold of him and beat him with clubs, tearing his robe, snatching the crown from his head. He fell to the ground, blind from the blood streaming over his face. Still the villagers kicked him and prodded him with their clubs.

Before he lost consciousness, he heard a woman say, "I wonder who he is, really."

A man said, "Where did he steal that crown?"

King Yvorian wandered for many days, ragged, covered with dirt and blood. He came to other towns, but no one would recognize him as king. Always, people laughed at him, or turned away sadly, or made signs to ward off evil. Sometimes their speech was strange, and he could not understand what they were saying at all.

So the king begged for bread and scraps. Occasionally he got some. More often, he stole. Oftener still, he went hungry.

Then soldiers seized him. This was the final outrage.

"Take your wretched hands *off* me! I am the king. I command all soldiers. I'll have your heads, all of you!"

The soldiers said nothing. Their captain barked a command, and all of them marched off, dragging King Yvorian. They did not wear the uniform of the Eagle Legions, Yvorian noticed. Their armour was not of scales shaped like feathers, but strangely supple plate like nothing he had ever seen before.

They brought him to a wooden lodge inside a stockade, where five judges sat in a semicircle around a table. The first judge wore a white robe, the second pale blue, the third green, the fourth orange – it seemed to Yvorian that the motif represented the seasons – but the fifth was clad in black and hid his face behind a silver mask fashioned like a skull.

The soldiers cast Yvorian roughly to his knees before the judges. A soldier flipped over an hourglass and the trial began.

"Who *are* you?" the first judge demanded, leaning forward in his carven chair.

Yvorian staggered to his feet. "I am the *king*, you fool. I am the mighty and eternal Yvorian, ruler of all the lands of the Crescent Sea, and all the islands."

The judges sat back, pondering.

"What you claim cannot be," said the second after a while. "There is no king here, nor has there been in the memory of any living man. We, the Five, rule the lands. As for the Crescent Sea, it is not known to us."

The third judge laughed. "Perhaps it has dried up."

"*Silence!*" Yvorian shouted. "*You are all ignorant men. Surely you have heard the mighty story—*"

The third judge laughed again. "I know many stories, and I've heard more, but never one about you."

"*I alone of all men have been found worthy to treat with Rada Vatu—*"

The four judges drew back with a simultaneous gasp. Then the fifth stirred, the black-clad one, his silver skull of a mask regarding Yvorian.

"*That* name we do know, but it is never spoken. Your own name is strange to us—"

The king stood still and said calmly, "But it is my name, and I am who I claim to be."

The masked judge banged his hand on the tabletop. The hourglass tumbled to the floor.

"We shall find that out, and much else besides."

The judge waved his hand, and Yvorian was seized by torturers, who tied him to a post and beat him till blood streamed over his back and thighs. They broke his legs with hammers, then turned him on a wheel over a fire. All the while he screamed and gasped, "I am King Yvorian. I am Yvorian, the greatest of all. I built the palace of the Eagles. I conquered all the lands. I am the mighty king. I am Yvorian."

But in the end, after many days, it seemed to him that perhaps he had only heard that name in a story somewhere.

The torturers nailed him to a tree and left him to die. Weeks passed, and he suffered beneath the hot sun and the cold of the night.

Crows rested on his shoulders. But Rada Vatu would not touch him, and he could not die. His broken bones mended. His wounds began to heal.

People gathered to marvel, to touch him, to bear away some of his hair or a cloth soaked in his blood, that they might be healed.

At last, a fearful torturer came in the night with a ladder and a pair of pinchers.

He drew out the nails, and Yvorian fled naked into the darkness.

King Yvorian thought back to the long years within the labyrinth, to the pleasures of his retreat, to the mysteries he had pondered, to his visions within the black room. More than once he tried to convince himself that *this* was yet another of those visions, more terrifying and painful than most, but a thing that would end.

Yet each morning he woke by the side of a road, or in a field or loft or cave, and he saw his sun-blackened body and his many scars, and he knew otherwise. Even his hands and feet were still marked where the nails had been.

So he retraced his path, avoiding the villages and towns, until he came again to the hillside from which he had emerged. He resolved to go inside once more, dress in his finest robes, and come forth, crown on his head, sceptre in his hand and sword at his side, with an army of automatons at his back. He would conquer the lands once again and put the unbelievers to death. Then he would command that his palace be unearthed, that it might stand more resplendent than ever before the eyes of men.

But he could not find the cave mouth. He wandered over the hill for weeks. He could not find it.

Finally, he knelt down and wept. He pounded the earth with his fists.

And a stranger stood before him. He looked up. The newcomer had the shape of a barefoot man in a black robe, but without any face or head. Only fire filled the robe's hood.

"*Who are you*?" said the stranger.

"I am King Yvorian, if I am anyone at all."

"*Who are you*?"

More firmly, the king replied, "I am Yvorian, lord of all the lands."

"*Ah*," said the other, and departed.

Clad in a kilt and shirt of woven grass, King Yvorian came down from the hills, into the broad valley where the Crescent Sea had once been in ages past. He followed a yellow-silted stream until he reached a river, and clear water.

Still he was king in his own mind, and each night he dreamed of his palace, and of his old ministers – he could still recall their names, every one, and their voices, and their individual manners, arrogant or servile or cold and expressionless. He remembered building the labyrinth. It seemed that still he heard the noise of hammers. It seemed that just a day or two before he himself had broken the ground with a spade and poured blood on the cornerstone.

And in his dreams his terrible father visited him many times, pacing back and forth, raging, proclaiming that a king is a king until he dies or abdicates, and to abdicate is to die.

"I have not abdicated," said Yvorian, in his dream.

Kaniphar, the chief priest he had killed, stood before him mournfully and said only, "A king lacking a kingdom is no king at all."

"I am still Yvorian," was his only reply. When he awoke from that dream, he was troubled.

Once more he declared his kingship openly in villages and towns along the river. Often he was laughed at or driven away with stones, but in other places men listened silently as he told the tale of his entire life, of his wager with Rada Vatu. This was a tale without an end.

Crowds gathered to hear him. Someone gave him fine clothing, and he threw away his grass kilt and shirt. Still the tale continued. Scribes came to write it down. Then heralds arrived for him, and bore him in a chair across many lands, until he came to a great city of black stone, which stood on a hill overlooking the river where it emptied into the grey, white-capped sea.

He was placed on a dais in the forum of the city. All around him pillars rose like trees in a forest, bearing up statues of gods and of kings. People swarmed out of black marble houses, out of wooden tenements, out of hovels; rich and poor alike, great lords in their canopied litters, beggars shoving against the levelled spears of the soldiers who held them back.

And Yvorian told his tale, and the people listened, and when Yvorian paused he could hear the wind blowing among the rooftops. And when he was done, the old and sick came to him, filing up to where he sat so they might be touched by his healing hands.

This went on for hours. It was nearly dawn when the place was empty but for a single youth, who stood before the dais. The boy was about fifteen, fair-haired, and richly clad. Rings gleamed on his fingers.

Yvorian regarded him.

"It feels so good to be a king once more."

"You are not a king," said the boy. "You are a madman. The mad are touched by the gods, even as kings are, and sometimes their hands can heal, even as those of a king can. Both are holy. But *I* am prince of this city. When my father dies, I shall be king. You, holy madman, shall remain what you are."

The prince left him, walking swiftly across the square.

Stunned, trembling, Yvorian rose from his seat and descended the dais. He saw another standing before him in the darkness among the pillars, a barefoot old man in a black robe, whose face rippled when he spoke like a thin, paper mask. His eyes were mere holes filled with fire.

"*Are you King Yvorian the mighty?*" the stranger asked.
"Yes."
"*Are you certain?*"

The madman cast off his fine robes and fled from the city, naked. He howled among the hills and in the depths of the forests. He crawled on all fours among the beasts of the fields, grazing. And he wept, and tore his hair, and dug in the earth with bloodied hands, searching for his kingdom.

But still he knew who he was, and when people came upon him he would rise and stand before them in great dignity, and try to tell them the story of King Yvorian. Often he was answered with laughter and stones, but sometimes with reverence. He touched many, and healed them.

At last when he lay shivering in the winter rain, feverish but unable to die, an anchorite found him and carried him to his hut high among the mountains. The holy man clothed him and gave him warm broth, and he told his story once again.

"It is a fine story," said the anchorite.

"It is *true*."

"Does that really matter? The pattern is interesting. It contains a moral."

Yvorian sat still for a while, warming his hands with the cup of broth. "I am not sure any more. My mind is filled with so many things, as if I have lived 10,000 years. I think all those things are true. But some of them must be only dreams. How can I tell?"

"Truth may be found both in waking things, and in dreams. So, again, does it really matter?"

"But I have no crown," said Yvorian. "Where is my palace? Where is my kingdom?"

Now it was the anchorite who paused. He sat still for a long time, gazing into the fire pit. Smoke rose gently up through the roof. Yvorian looked up at the smoke and the few stars he could see through the hole in the roof.

He waited patiently.

"I know where your kingdom is," the other said at last. "If that is what you desire, go to a certain town, as I shall direct you, and obey the first person you meet, whatever you are asked to do. Then you shall find your true kingdom."

And the king wept once more, for the very first time in his life out of gratitude.

The town the hermit named for him was far away. He walked throughout the winter and spring. By summer he had reached the edge of a vast desert. His fur clothing was too hot for him and he discarded it, once more weaving garments out of grass.

Slowly, painfully he crossed the wasteland, his grass clothing burned away by the sun, his bare skin darkened like old wood, his hair and beard streaming behind him in the wind like clouds crossing the face of the moon.

He reached his destination in the evening, as the last herdsmen drove their flocks into the town, as little bells rang to call the workmen home from their labours and the priests to their prayers.

A woman was drawing water from a well. She was neither young nor old, and three children clung to her brightly patterned skirt.

When he saw her, the wanderer did not proclaim himself king. He did not command her to bow down. He only said that he was very thirsty.

The woman looked up, startled. "If you'll carry this bucket for me," she said, "you may have some."

He nodded eagerly. She gave him the bucket and he stared into it. In the failing light he could still make out his own reflection, and he saw a man with a weathered face, whose hair and beard were purest white. He drank.

"And if you will work for me," the woman said, "I'll give you food and clothing. My husband has died, and I need all the help I can get."

Again he nodded, and followed her back to her house.

"You must tell me your name," she said.

"I am . . . Yvorian."

"I've heard that name before. In a story, I think."

"Yes, I know the story. I'll tell it to you some time."

The children stared at him, wide-eyed.

*   *   *

For Yvorian, every aspect of life in the town by the desert's edge was new to him, a marvel. He was no longer a naked wanderer, but wore comfortable, plain clothes, and ate regularly. That was a forgotten condition he was only beginning to recall. He performed many labours for the widow, whose name was Evadina. He tended her flocks. He cleaned her stable. He drew water from the well many, many times. Never before had he served another. It strengthened him.

After seven years, he married her. This, too, was utterly novel, for he had never loved anyone before in all his long life, or been loved, or even expected to be. It was like an opening of the eyes, an awakening for the first time.

Although he was taken to be a man of at least fifty, he fathered three sons by Evadina. As they grew, he told them, and his stepchildren too, the story of King Yvorian who dwelled beneath a magic mountain far to the west. Sometimes the story concentrated on the king's pride, or his cruelty, or his loneliness; sometimes it was merely a tale of marvels. At the town festivals, he told the story to all who would listen, and people applauded and left coins in his hat.

He tried to write the story down at the request of the priests, who wanted a copy to keep in their temple, but the only script he knew was an archaic one no one could read. Nevertheless, the priests admired his brush work and sometimes commissioned him to restore the icons of the gods, which hung in roadside shrines and faded from the sun and the weather.

On the night before the youngest of his sons was to go away and live elsewhere with his bride, Yvorian told the story of the king for the last time, extending it further than ever before, telling how the king emerged from his mountain and wandered through many lands, shedding his robes and his sceptre and his crown, until he found himself better off without them, relieved of their burden, and found a life no king could ever know.

"Father," said the young man. "I have loved that story since I was a child, and now you have made it such a beautiful thing that I think I have only now heard it for the first time. I shall remember you by it always."

The young man turned to go, then paused.

"What is it, son?"

"Still I do not understand. The story, it has no ending."

"Yes, it does. Come here." Yvorian rose, and led his son into the bedroom. His son followed, carrying a candle. The old man lay down beside Evadina, the boy's mother, who was already sleeping.

"Father?"

Yvorian put his finger to his lips. "Quiet. Don't wake her." Then he whispered, "This is the end of the story, that the teller came to recognize the end, and he knew that it didn't matter, for shortly before the end he had gained a great treasure, which was merely a life lived well, and not even Rada Vatu could take that away from him. Slowly, then, Rada Vatu began to touch him, and he started to age, as all men do, but it did not matter."

Then the young man saw that his father was tired and went away. He left the candle burning by the bedside. Yvorian lay still, gazing into the darkness, listening to his wife's breathing as she slept beside him.

After a time, he was aware of another person in the room. A stranger stood by the bed, clad in a black robe. His eyes glowed, like fireflies. He held a gleaming axe in his hand.

"Are you not the famous and mighty King Yvorian?"

"No. That is another Yvorian, a character in a story. I tell of him often."

"Ah." The stranger's face shrivelled inward, consumed in fire. The axe rose. *"I win the wager,"* said Rada Vatu.

"Are you certain?"

The axe fell.

The Howling Tower

Fritz Leiber

Another disciple of H. P. Lovecraft was Fritz Leiber (1910–92), but Leiber rapidly carved out his own worlds. He would soon become as adept at writing science fiction as he was at producing supernatural fiction and fantasy, but it will probably be for his fantasy that Leiber will be best remembered. And in particular for his long-running series featuring the tall Northern barbarian Fafhrd and his cunning sidekick, the Gray Mouser. Fafhrd was modelled on Leiber himself and the Mouser on his friend, Harry Fischer. Leiber began writing about them in a story called "Adept's Gambit" when he was still strongly under Lovecraft's influence and the early drafts of that story show Fafhrd and the Mouser in a world resembling ancient Greece under the influence of the Lovecraftian gods. Unable to sell the story Leiber gradually reworked it and developed others, establishing his own world of Newhon. Leiber was fortunate when the renowned editor of Astounding Science Fiction, *John W. Campbell, Jr, launched a companion magazine* Unknown *in 1939. Campbell wanted stories that treated the fantastic as if it were real, with real people and real situations. Leiber's characters were ideal for this. Although not Dunsanian, neither are they heroes. They have their scruples but otherwise operate only a shade on the right side of the law – depending on what law you mean. Their first published story was "Two Sought Adventure" (*Unknown, *August 1939, included in the first book* Two Sought Adventure, *1957) and Leiber continued to write about them for the* *next fifty years. They last appeared in* The Knight and Knave of Swords *(1988). In between Leiber produced stories that critic Brian Stableford has called "among the finest heroic fantasies ever written". The following is one of the early adventures from the June 1941 issue of* Unknown.

T HE SOUND WAS NOT LOUD, YET IT SEEMED TO fill the whole vast, darkening plain, and the palely luminous, hollow sky: a wailing and howling, so faint and monotonous that it might have been inaudible save for the pulsing rise and fall; an ancient, ominous sound that was somehow in harmony with the wild, sparsely vegetated landscape and the barbaric garb of the three men who sheltered in a little dip in the ground, lying close to a dying fire.

"Wolves, perhaps," Fafhrd said. "I have heard them howl that way on the Cold Waste when they hunted me down. But a whole ocean sunders us from the Cold Waste and there's a difference between the sounds, Gray Mouser."

The Mouser pulled his grey woollen cloak closer around him. Then he and Fafhrd looked at the third man, who had not spoken. The third man was meanly clad, and his cloak was ragged and the scabbard of his short sword was frayed. With surprise, they saw that his eyes stared, white-circled, from his pinched, leathery face and that he trembled.

"You've been over these plains many times before," Fafhrd said to him, speaking the guttural language of the guide. "That's why we've asked you to show us the way. You must know this country well." The last words pointed the question.

The guide gulped, nodded jerkily. "I've heard it before, not so loud," he said in a quick, vague voice. "Not at this time of year. Men have been known to vanish. There are stories. They say men hear it in their dreams and are lured away – not a good sound."

"No wolf's a good wolf," rumbled Fafhrd amusedly.

It was still light enough for the Mouser to catch the obstinate, guarded look on the guide's face as he went on talking.

"I never saw a wolf in these parts, nor spoke with a man who killed one." He paused, then rambled off abstractedly. "They tell of an old tower somewhere out on the plains. They say the sound is strongest there. I have not seen it. They say—"

Abruptly he stopped. He was not trembling now, seemed withdrawn into himself. The Mouser prodded him with a few tempting questions, but the answers were little more than mouth noises, neither affirmative nor negative.

The fire glowed through white ashes, died. A little wind rustled the scant grasses. The sound had ceased now, or else it had sunk so deeply into their minds that it was no longer audible. The Mouser, peering sleepily over the humped horizon of Fafhrd's great cloaked body, turned his thoughts to far-off, many-taverned Lankhmar, leagues and leagues away across alien lands and a whole uncharted ocean. The limitless darkness pressed down.

Next morning the guide was gone. Fafhrd laughed and made light of the occurrence as he stood stretching and snuffing the cool, clear air.

"Foh! I could tell these plains were not to his liking, for all his talk of having crossed them seven times. A bundle of superstitious fears! You saw how he quaked when the little wolves began to howl. My word on it, he's run back to his friends we left at the last water."

The Mouser, fruitlessly scanning the empty horizon, nodded without conviction. He felt through his pouch.

"Well, at least he's not robbed us – except for the two gold pieces we gave him to bind the bargain."

Fafhrd's laughter pealed and he thumped the Mouser between the shoulder blades. The Mouser caught him by the wrist, threw him with a twist and a roll, and they wrestled on the ground until the Mouser was pinned.

"Come on," grinned Fafhrd, springing up. "It won't be the first time we've travelled strange country alone."

They tramped far that day. The springiness of the Mouser's wiry body enabled him to keep up with Fafhrd's long strides. Towards evening a whirring arrow from Fafhrd's bow brought down a sort of small antelope with delicately ridged horns. A little earlier they had found an unsullied water hole and filled their skin bags. When the late summer sunset came, they made camp and munched carefully broiled loin and crisped bits of fat.

The Mouser sucked his lips and fingers clean, then strolled to the top of a nearby hummock to survey the line of their next day's march. The haze that had curtailed vision during the afternoon was gone now, and he could peer far over the rolling, swelling grasslands through the cool, tangy air. At that moment the road to Lankhmar did not seem so long, or so weary. Then his sharp eyes spied an irregularity in the horizon towards which they were tending. Too distinct for trees, too evenly shaped for rock; and he had seen no trees or rock in this country. It stood out sharp and tiny against the pale sky. No, it was built by man; a tower of some sort.

At that moment the sound returned. It seemed to come from everywhere at once; as if the sky itself were wailing faintly, as if the wide, solid ground were baying mournfully. It was louder this time, and there was in it a strange confusion of sadness and threat, grief and menace.

Fafhrd jumped to his feet and waved his arms strongly, and the Mouser heard him bellow out in a great, jovial voice, "Come, little wolves, come and share our fire and singe your cold noses. I will send my bronze-beaked birds winging to welcome you, and my friend will show you how a slung stone can buzz like a bee. We will teach you the mysteries of sword and axe. Come, little wolves, and be guests of Fafhrd and the Gray Mouser! Come, little wolves – or biggest of them all!"

The huge laugh with which he ended this challenge drowned out the alien sound and it seemed slow in reasserting itself, as though laughter were a stronger thing. The Mouser felt cheered and it was with a light heart that he told Fafhrd of what he had seen, and reminded him of what the guide had said about the noise and the tower.

Fafhrd only laughed again and guessed, "Perhaps the sad, furry ones have a den there. We shall find out tomorrow, since we go that way. I would like to kill a wolf."

The big man was in a jolly mood and would not talk with the Mouser about serious or melancholy things. Instead, he sang drinking songs and repeated old tavern jokes, chuckling hugely and claiming that they made him feel as drunk as wine. He kept up such an incessant clamour that the Mouser could not tell whether the strange howling had ceased, though he rather imagined he heard it once or twice. Certainly it was gone by the time they wrapped themselves up for sleep in the wraithlike starlight.

Next morning Fafhrd was gone. Even before the Mouser had halooed for him and scanned the nearby terrain, he knew that his foolish, self-ridiculed fears had become certainties. He could still see the tower, although in the flat, yellow light of morning it seemed to have receded, as though it were seeking to evade him. He even fancied he saw a tiny moving figure nearer to the tower than to him. That, he knew, was only imagination. The distance was too great. Nevertheless, he wasted little time in chewing and swallowing some cold meat, which still had a savoury taste, in wrapping up some more for his pouch, and in taking a gulp of water. Then he set out at a long, springy lope, a pace he knew he could hold for hours.

At the bottom of the next swell in the plain he found slightly softer ground, cast up and down it for Fafhrd's footprints and found them. They were wide-spaced, made by a man running.

Towards midday he found a water hole, lay down to drink and rest a little. A short way back he had again seen Fafhrd's prints. Now he noted another set in the soft earth; not Fafhrd's, but roughly parallel to his. They were at least a day older, wide-spaced, too, but a little wobbly. From their size and shape they might very well have been made by the guide's sandals; the middle of the print showed faintly the mark of thongs such as he had worn about the instep.

The Mouser loped doggedly on. His pouch, rolled cloak, water bag, and weapons were beginning to feel a burden. The tower was appreciably closer, although the sun haze masked any details. He calculated he had covered almost half the distance.

The slight successive swells in the prairieland seemed as endless as those in a dream. He noticed them not so much by sight as by the infinitesimal hindrance and easing they gave his lope. The little low clumps of bush and brush by which he measured his progress were all the same. The infrequent gullies were no wider than could be taken in a stride. Once a coiled greenish serpent raised its flat head from the rock on which it was sunning and observed his passing. Occasionally grasshoppers whirred out of his path. He ran with his feet close to the ground to conserve energy, yet there was a strong, forward leap to his stride, for he was used to matching that of a taller man. His nostrils flared wide, sucking and expelling air. The wide mouth was set. There was a grim, fixed look to the black eyes above the browned cheeks. He knew that even at his best he would be hard put to equal the speed in Fafhrd's rangy, long-muscled frame.

Clouds sailed in from the north, casting great, hurrying shadows over the landscape, finally blotting out the sun altogether. He could see the tower better now. It was of a dark colour, with black specks that might be small windows.

It was while he was pausing atop a rise for a breathing spell that the sound recommenced, taking him unaware, sending a shiver over his flesh. It might have been the low clouds that gave it greater power and an eerie, echoing quality. It might have been his being alone that made it seem less sorrowful and more menacing. But it was undeniably louder, and its rhythmic swells came like great gusts of wind.

The Mouser had counted on reaching the tower by sunset. But the early appearance of the sound upset his calculations and did not bode well for Fafhrd. His judgment told him he could cover the rest of the distance at something like top speed. Instantly he came to a decision. He tossed his big pouch, waterskin, bundled cloak, sword and harness into a clump of bushes; kept only his light inner jerkin, long dagger and sling. Thus lightened, he spurted ahead, feet flying. The low clouds darkened. A few drops of rain spattered. He kept his eyes on the ground, watching for inequalities and slippery spots. The sound seemed to intensify and gain new unearthliness of timbre with every bounding stride he took forward.

Away from the tower the plain had been empty and vast, but

here it was desolate. The sagging or tumbled wooden outbuild-
ings, the domestic grains and herbs run wild and dying out, the
lines of stunted and toppled trees, the suggestion of fences and
paths and ruts – all combined to give the impression that human
life had once been here but had long since departed. Only the
great stone tower, with its obstinate solidity, and with sound
pouring from it or seeming to pour from it, was alive.

The Mouser, pretty well winded though not shaky, now
changed his course and ran in an oblique direction to take
advantage of the cover provided by a thin line of trees and
wind-blown scrub. Such caution was second nature with him.
All his instincts clamoured against the possibility of meeting a
wolf or hound pack on open ground.

He had worked his way past and partway around the tower
before he came to the conclusion that there was no line of
concealment leading all the way up to the base. It stood a little
aloof from the ruins around it.

The Mouser paused in the shelter afforded by a weather-
silvered, buckled outbuilding; automatically searched about until
he found a couple of small stones whose weight suited his sling.
His sturdy chest still worked like a bellows, drinking air. Then he
peered around a corner at the tower and stood there crouched a
little, frowning.

It was not as high as he had thought: five storeys or perhaps six.
The narrow windows were irregularly placed, and did not give
any clear idea of inner configuration. The stones were large and
rudely hewn; seemed firmly set, save for those of the battlement,
which had shifted somewhat. Almost facing him was the dark,
uninformative rectangle of a doorway.

There was no rushing such a place, was the Mouser's thought;
no sense in rushing a place that had no sign of defenders. There
was no way of getting at it unseen; a watcher on the battlements
would have noted his approach long ago. One could only walk up
to it, tensely alert for unexpected attacks. And so the Mouser did
that.

Before he had covered half the distance his sinews were taut
and straining. He was mortally certain that he was being watched

by something more than unfriendly. A day's running had made
him a little light-headed, and his senses were abnormally clear.
Against the unending hypnotic background of the howling he
heard the splatters of the separate raindrops, not yet become a
shower. He noted the size and shape of each dark stone around
the darker doorway. He smelled the characteristic odour of stone,
wood, soil, but yet no heavy animal smell. For the thousandth
time he tried to picture some possible source for the sound. A
dozen hound packs in a cavern underground? That was close, but
not close enough. Something eluded him. And now the dark walls
were very near, and he strained his eyes to penetrate the gloom of
the doorway.

The remote grating sound might not have been enough of a
warning, for he was almost in a trance. It may have been the
sudden, very slight increase of darkness over his head that
twanged the taut bowstrings of his muscles and sent him lunging
with catlike rapidity into the tower – instinctively, without
pausing to glance up. Certainly he had not an instant to spare,
for he felt an unyielding surface graze his escaping body and flick
his heels. A spurt of wind rushed past him from behind, and the
jar of a mighty impact staggered him. He spun around to see a
great square of stone half obscuring the doorway. A few moments
before it had formed part of the battlement.

Looking at it as it lay there denting the ground, he grinned for
the first time that day and almost laughed in relief.

The silence was profound, startling. It occurred to the Mouser
that the howling had ceased utterly. He glanced around the
barren, circular interior, then started up the curving stone stair
that hugged the wall. His grin was dangerous now, businesslike.
On the first level above he found Fafhrd and – after a fashion –
the guide. But he found a puzzle, too.

Like that below, the room occupied the full circumference of
the tower. Light from the scattered, slit-like windows dimly
revealed the chests lining the walls and the dried herbs and
dessicated birds, small mammals and reptiles hanging from the
ceiling, suggesting an apothecary's shop. There was litter everywhere, but it was a tidy litter, seeming to have a tortuously logical

arrangement all its own. On a table was a hodgepodge of stoppered bottles and jars, mortars and pestles, odd instruments of horn, glass and bone, and a brazier in which charcoal smouldered. There was also a plate of gnawed bones and beside it a brassbound book of parchment, spread open by a dagger set across the pages.

Fafhrd lay face up on a bed of skins laced to a low wooden framework. He was pale and breathed heavily, looked as if he had been drugged. He did not respond when the Mouser shook him gently and whispered his name, then shook him hard and shouted it. But the thing that baffled the Mouser was the multitude of linen bandages wound around Fafhrd's limbs and chest and throat, for they were unstained and, when he parted them, there were no wounds beneath. They were obviously not bonds.

And lying beside Fafhrd, so close that his big hand touched the hilt, was Fafhrd's great sword, unsheathed.

It was only then that the Mouser saw the guide, huddled in a dark corner behind the couch. He was similarly bandaged. But the bandages were stiff with rusty stains, and it was easy to see that he was dead.

The Mouser tried again to wake Fafhrd, but the big man's face stayed a marble mask. The Mouser did not feel that Fafhrd was actually there, and the feeling frightened and angered him.

As he stood nervously puzzling he became aware of slow steps descending the stone stair. Slowly they circled the tower. The sound of heavy breathing was heard, coming in regular spaced gasps. The Mouser crouched behind the tables, his eyes glued on the black hole in the ceiling through which the stair vanished.

The man who emerged was old and small and bent, dressed in garments as tattered and uncouth and musty-looking as the contents of the room. He was partly bald, with a matted tangle of grey hair around his large ears. When the Mouser sprang up and menaced him with a drawn dagger he did not attempt to flee, but went into what seemed an ecstasy of fear – trembling, babbling throaty sounds, and darting his arms about meaninglessly.

The Mouser thrust a stubby candle into the brazier, held it to

the old man's face. He had never seen eyes so wide with terror –
they jutted out like little white balls – nor lips so thin and
unfeelingly cruel.

The first intelligible words that issued from the lips were
hoarse and choked; the voice of a man who has not spoken for
a long time.

"You are dead. You are dead!" he cackled at the Mouser,
pointing a shaky finger. "You should not be here. I killed you.
Why else have I kept the great stone cunningly balanced, so that a
touch would send it over? I knew you did not come because the
sound lured you. You came to hurt me and to help your friend. So
I killed you. I saw the stone fall. I saw you under the stone. You
could not have escaped it. You are dead."

And he tottered towards the Mouser, brushing at him as
though he could dissipate the Mouser like smoke. But when
his hands touched solid flesh he squealed and stumbled away.

The Mouser followed him, moving his knife suggestively.
"You are right as to why I came," he said. "Give me back my
friend. Rouse him."

To his surprise, the old man did not cringe, but abruptly stood
his ground. The look of terror in the unblinking eyes underwent a
subtle change. The terror was still there, but there was something
more. Bewilderment vanished and something else took its place.
He walked past the Mouser and sat down on a stool by the table.

"I am not much afraid of you," he muttered, looking sideways.
"But there are those of whom I am very much afraid. And I fear
you only because you will try to hinder me from protecting
myself against them or taking the measures I know I must take."
He became plaintive. "You must not hinder me. You must not."

The Mouser frowned. The ghastly look of terror – and something more – that warped the old man's face seemed a permanent
thing, and the strange words he spoke did not sound like lies.

"Nevertheless, you must rouse my friend."

The old man did not answer this. Instead, after one quick
glance at the Mouser, he stared vacantly at the wall, shaking his
head, and began to talk.

"I do not fear you. Yet I know the depths of fear. You do not.

Have you lived alone with *that sound* for years on years, knowing what it meant? I have.

"Fear was born into me. It was in my mother's bones and blood. And in my father's and in my brothers'. There was too much magic and loneliness in this, our home, and in my people. When I was a child they all feared and hated me – even the slaves and the great hounds that before me slavered and growled and snapped.

"But my fears were stronger than theirs, for did they not die one by one in such a way that no suspicion fell upon me until the end? I knew it was one against many, and I took no chances. When it began, they always thought I would be the next to go!" He cackled at this. "They thought I was small and weak and foolish. But did not my brothers die as if strangled by their own hands? Did not my mother sicken and languish? Did not my father give a great cry and leap from the tower's top?

"The hounds were the last to go. They hated me most – even more than my father hated me – and the smallest of them could have torn out my throat. They were hungry because there was no one left to feed them. But I lured them into the deep cellar, pretending to flee from them; and when they were all inside I slipped out and barred the door. For many a night thereafter they bayed and howled at me, but I knew I was safe. Gradually the baying grew less and less as they killed each other, but the survivors gained new life from the bodies of the slain. They lasted a long time. Eventually there was only one single thin voice left to howl vengefully at me. Each night I went to sleep, telling myself, 'Tomorrow there will be silence.' But each morning I was awakened by the cry. Then I forced myself to take a torch and go down and peer through the wicket in the door of the cellar. But though I watched for a long time there was no movement, save that of the flickering shadows, and I saw nothing but white bones and tatters of skin. And I told myself that the sound would soon go away."

The old man's thin lips were twisted into a pitiful and miserable expression that sent a chill over the Mouser.

"But the sound lived on, and after a long while it began to grow louder again. Then I knew that my cunning had been in vain. I had killed their bodies, but not their ghosts, and soon they would gain enough power to return and slay me, as they had always intended. So I studied more carefully my father's books of magic and sought to destroy their ghosts utterly or to curse them to such far-off places that they could never reach me. For a while I seemed to be succeeding, but the scales turned and they began to get the better of me. Closer and closer they came, and sometimes I seemed to catch my father's and brothers' voices, almost lost among the howling.

"It was on a night when they must have been very close that an exhausted traveller came running to the tower. There was a strange look in his eyes, and I thanked the beneficent god who had sent him to my door, for I knew what I must do. I gave him food and drink, and in his drink I mingled a liquid that enforced sleep and sent his naked ghost winging out of his body. *They* must have captured and torn it, for presently the man bled and died. But it satisfied them somewhat, for their howling went a long way off, and it was a long time before it began to creep back. Thereafter the gods were good and always sent me a guest before the sound came too close. I learned to bandage those I drugged so that they would last longer, and their deaths would satisfy the howling ones more fully."

The old man paused then, and shook his head queerly and made a vague, reproachful, clucking noise with his tongue.

"But what troubles me now," he said, "is that they have become greedier, or perhaps they have seen through my cunning. For they are less easy to satisfy, and press at me closely and never go far away. Sometimes I wake in the night, hearing them snuffing about, and feeling their muzzles at my throat. I must have more men to fight them for me. I must. He" – pointing at the stiff body of the guide – "was nothing to them. They took no more notice of him than a dry bone. That one" – his finger wavered over to Fafhrd – "is big and strong. He should hold them back for a long time."

It was dark outside now, and the only light came from the guttering candle. The Mouser glared at the old man where he sat perched on the stool like some ungainly plucked foul. Then he looked to where Fafhrd lay, watched the great chest rise and fall, saw the strong, pallid jaw jutting up over high wrappings. And at that, a terrible anger and an unnerving, boundless irritation took hold of him and he hurled himself upon the old man.

But at the instant he started his long dagger on the downward stroke the sound gushed back. It seemed to overflow from some pit of darkness, and to inundate the tower and plain so that the walls vibrated and dust puffed out from the dead things hanging from the ceiling.

The Mouser stopped the blade a hand's breadth from the throat of the old man, whose head, twisted back, jiggled in terror. For the return of the sound forcibly set the question: Could anyone but the old man save Fafhrd now? The Mouser wavered between alternatives, pushed the old man away, knelt by Fafhrd's side, shook him, spoke to him. There was no response. Then he heard the voice of the old man. It was shaky and half drowned by the sound, but it carried an almost gloating note of confidence.

"Your friend's body is poised on the brink of life. If you handle it roughly it may overbalance. If you strip off the bandages he will only die the quicker. You cannot help him." Then, reading the Mouser's question, "No, there is no antidote." Then hastily, as if he feared to take away all hope, "But he will not be defenceless against them. He is strong. His ghost may be strong, too. He may be able to weary them out. If he lives until midnight he may return."

The Mouser turned and looked up at him. Again the old man seemed to read something in the Mouser's merciless eyes, for he said, "My death by your hand will not satisfy those who howl. If you kill me, you will not save your friend, but doom him. Being cheated of my ghost, they will rend his utterly."

The wizened body trembled in an ecstasy of excitement and terror. The hands fluttered. The head bobbed back and forth, as if with the palsy. It was hard to read anything in that twitching, saucer-eyed face. The Mouser slowly got to his feet.

"Perhaps not," said the Mouser. "Perhaps as you say, your death will doom him." He spoke slowly and in a loud, measured tone. "Nevertheless, I shall take the chance of killing you right now unless you suggest something better."

"Wait," said the old man, pushing at the Mouser's dagger and drawing a pricked hand away. "Wait. There is a way you could help him. Somewhere out there" – he made a sweeping, upward gesture with his hand – "your friend's ghost is battling them. I have more of the drug left. I will give you some. Then you can fight them side by side. Together you may defeat them. But you must be quick. Look! Even now they are at him!"

The old man pointed at Fafhrd. The bandage on the barbarian's left arm was no longer unstained. There was a growing splotch of red on the left wrist – the very place where a hound might take hold. Watching it, the Mouser felt his insides grow sick and cold. The old man was pushing something into his hand. "Drink this. Drink this now," he was saying.

The Mouser looked down. It was a small glass vial. The deep purple of the liquid corresponded with the hue of a dried trickle he had seen at the corner of Fafhrd's mouth. Like a man bewitched, he plucked out the stopper, raised it slowly to his lips, paused.

"Swiftly! Swiftly!" urged the old man, almost dancing with impatience. "About half is enough to take you to your friend. The time is short. Drink! Drink!"

But the Mouser did not. Struck by a sudden, new thought, he eyed the old man over his upraised hand. And the old man must have instantly read the import of that thought, for he snatched up the dagger lying on the book and lunged at the Mouser with unexpected rapidity. Almost the thrust went home, but the Mouser recovered his wits and struck sideways with his free fist at the old man's hand so that the dagger clattered across the floor. Then, with a rapid, careful movement, the Mouser set the vial on the table. The old man darted after him, snatching at it, seeking to upset it, but the Mouser's iron grip closed on his wrists. He was forced to the floor, his arms pinioned, his head pushed back.

"Yes," said the Mouser, "I shall drink. Have no fear on that score. But you shall drink, too."

The old man gave a strangled scream and struggled

convulsively. "No! No!" he cried. "Kill me! Kill me with your knife! But not the drink! Not the drink!" The Mouser, kneeling on his arms to pinion them, pried at his jaw. Suddenly he became quiet and stared up, a peculiar lucidity in his white-circled, pinpoint-pupilled eyes. "It's no use. I sought to trick you," he said. "I gave the last of the drug to your friend. The stuff you hold is poison. We shall both die miserably, and your friend will be irrevocably doomed."

But when he saw that the Mouser did not heed this, he began once more to struggle like a maniac. The Mouser was inexorable. Although the base of his thumb was bitted deep, he forced the old man's jaws apart, held his nose and poured the thick purple liquor down. The face of the old man grew red and the veins stood out. When the gulp came it was like a death rattle. Then the Mouser drank off the rest – it was salty like blood and had a sickeningly sweet odour – and waited.

He was torn with revulsion at what he had done. Never had he inflicted such terror on man or woman before. He would much rather have killed. The look on the old man's face was grotesquely similar to that of a child under torture. Only that poor aged wretch, thought the Mouser, knew the full meaning of the howling that even now dinned menacingly in their ears. The Mouser almost let him reach the dagger towards which he was weakly squirming. But he thought of Fafhrd and gripped the old man tight.

Gradually the room filled with haze and began to swing and slowly spin. The Mouser grew dizzy. It was as if the sound were dissolving the walls. Something was wrenching at his body and prying at his mind. Then came utter blackness, whirled and shaken by a pandemonium of howling.

But there was no sound at all on the vast alien plain to which the blackness suddenly gave way. Only sight and a sense of great cold. A cloudless, sourceless moonlight revealed endless sweeps of smooth black rock and sharply edged the featureless horizon.

He was conscious of a thing that stood by him and seemed to be trying to hide behind him. Then, at a small distance, he noted a pale form which he instinctively knew to be Fafhrd. And around the pale form seethed a pack of black, shadowy animal shapes, leaping and retreating, worrying at the pale form, their eyes glowing like the moonlight, but brighter, their long muzzles soundlessly snarling. The thing beside him seemed to shrink closer. And then the Mouser rushed forward towards his friend.

The shadow pack turned on him and he braced himself to meet their onslaught. But the leader leaped past his shoulder, and the rest divided and flowed by him like a turbulent black stream. Then he realized that the thing which had sought to hide behind him was no longer there. He turned and saw that the black shapes pursued another small pale form.

It fled fast, but they followed faster. Over sweep after sweep of rock the hunt continued. He seemed to see taller, man-shaped figures among the pack. Slowly they dwindled in size, became tiny, vague. And still the Mouser felt the horrible hate and fear that flowed from them.

Then the sourceless moonlight faded, and only the cold remained, and that, too, dissipated, leaving nothing.

When he awoke, Fafhrd's face was looking down at him, and Fafhrd was saying, "Lie still, little man. Lie still. No, I'm not badly hurt. A torn hand. Not bad. No worse than your own."

But the Mouser shook his head impatiently and pushed his aching shoulder off the couch. Sunlight was knifing in through the narrow windows, revealing the dustiness of the air. Then he saw the body of the old man.

"Yes," Fafhrd said as the Mouser lay back weakly. "His fears are ended now. They've done with him. I should hate him. But who can hate such tattered flesh? When I came to the tower he gave me the drink. There was something wrong in my head. I believed what he said. He told me it would make me a god. I drank, and it sent me to a cold waste in hell. But now it's done with and we're still in Newhon."

The Mouser, eyeing the thoroughly and unmistakably dead things that dangled from the ceiling, felt content.

𝕶𝖎𝖓𝖌𝖘 𝖎𝖓 𝕯𝖆𝖗𝖐𝖓𝖊𝖘𝖘

Michael Moorcock and James Cawthorn

*Stories of sword-and-sorcery hit their peak in the early sixties.
The two last great series to appear were the Elric stories by
Michael Moorcock and the Dilvish stories by Roger Zelazny,
both represented here. In the late 1950s Moorcock (b. 1939),
along with his friend James Cawthorn, worked together in
developing an outline for a possible new Conan series which
Hans Stefan Santesson, editor of* Fantastic Universe, *had
requested, following the success of new Conan stories in that
magazine. In the end that project fell through, but Moorcock's
English editor, John Carnell, was interested in the stories for*
Science Fantasy. *Moorcock reworked them into a series about
a doomed albino prince, called Elric, who draws his strength
from his sword, Stormbringer, which devours the souls of those
it kills. The first run of stories was collected in* The Stealer of
Souls *(1963). In the next volume,* Stormbringer *(1965),
Moorcock killed off Elric in a cataclysmic finale, but, as with
all of Moorcock's characters, who are but reflections of the
Eternal Champion in the Multiverse, Elric returned for many
more adventures, the latest of which is* The Dreamthief's
Daughter *(2001). The following is the only one of the early
stories worked on jointly with artist and critic James Cawthorn
(b. 1929) who has collaborated with Moorcock on other
projects.*

Three Kings in Darkness lie,
Gutheran of Org, and I,
Under a bleak and sunless sky—
The third Beneath the Hill.
                    — Song of Veerkad

1

I T WAS ELRIC, LORD OF THE LOST AND sundered Empire of
Melniboné, who rode like a fanged wolf from a trap – all
slavering madness and mirth. He rode from Nadsokor, City of
Beggars, and there was hate in his wake. The citizens had judged
him rightly for what he was – a nigromancer of superlative
powers. Now they hounded him and also the grotesque little
man who rode laughing at Elric's side: Moonglum the Outlander,
from Elwher and the unmapped east.

The flames of brands devoured the velvet of the night as the
yelling, ragged throng pushed their bony nags in pursuit of the
pair.

Starvelings and tattered jackals that they were, there was
strength in their gaudy numbers and long knives and bone bows
glinted in the brandlight. They were too strong for a couple of
men to fight, too few to represent serious danger in a hunt, so
Elric and Moonglum had chosen to leave the city without dispute
and now sped towards the full and rising moon which stabbed its
sickly beams through the darkness to show them the disturbing
waters of the Varkalk River and a chance of escape from the
incensed mob.

They had half a mind to stand and face the mob, since the
Varkalk was their only alternative. But they knew well what the
beggars would do to them, whereas they were uncertain what
would become of them once they had entered the river. The
horses reached the sloping banks of the Varkalk and reared, with
hooves lashing.

Cursing, the two men spurred the steeds and forced them down
towards the water. Into the river the horses plunged, snorting and
spluttering. Into the river which led a roaring course towards the

hell-spawned Forest of Troos which lay within the borders of Org, country of necromancy and rotting, ancient evil.

Elric blew water away from his mouth and coughed. "They'll not follow us to Troos, I think," he shouted at his companion.

Moonglum said nothing. He only grinned, showing his white teeth and the unhidden fear in his eyes. The horses swam strongly with the current and behind them the ragged mob shrieked in frustrated bloodlust while some of their number laughed and jeered.

"Let the forest do our work for us!"

Elric laughed back at them, wildly, as the horses swam on down the dark, straight river, wide and deep, towards a sun-starved morning, cold and spiky with ice. Scattered, slim-peaked crags loomed on either side of the flat plain, through which the river ran swiftly. Green-tinted masses of jutting blacks and browns spread colour through the rocks and the grass was waving on the plain as if for some purpose. Through the dawnlight, the beggar crew chased along the banks, but eventually gave up their quarry to return, shuddering, to Nadsokor.

When they had gone, Elric and Moonglum made their mounts swim towards the banks and climb them, stumbling, to the top where rocks and grass had already given way to sparse forest land which rose starkly on all sides, staining the earth with sombre shades. The foliage waved jerkily, as if alive – sentient.

It was a forest of malignantly erupting blooms, blood-coloured and sickly mottled. A forest of bending, sinuously smooth trunks, black and shiny; a forest of spiked leaves of murky purples and gleaming greens – certainly an unhealthy place if judged only by the odour of rotting vegetation which was almost unbearable, impinging as it did upon the fastidious nostrils of Elric and Moonglum.

Moonglum wrinkled his nose and jerked his head in the direction they had come. "Back now?" he enquired. "We can avoid Troos and cut swiftly across a corner of Org to be in Bakshaan in just over a day. What say you, Elric?"

Elric frowned. "I don't doubt they'd welcome us in Bakshaan with the same warmth we received in Nadsokor. They'll not have forgotten the destruction we wrought there – and the wealth we acquired from their merchants. No, I have a fancy to explore the forest a little. I have heard tales of Org and its unnatural forest and should like to investigate the truth of them. My blade and sorcery will protect us, if necessary."

Moonglum sighed. "Elric – this once, let us not court the danger."

Elric smiled icily. His scarlet eyes blazed out of his dead white skin with peculiar intensity. "Danger? It can bring only death."

"Death is not to my liking, just yet," Moonglum said. "The fleshpots of Bakshaan, or if you prefer – Jadmar – on the other hand . . ."

But Elric was already urging his horse onward, heading for the forest. Moonglum sighed and followed.

Soon dark blossoms hid most of the sky, which was dark enough, and they could see only a little way in all directions. The rest of the forest seemed vast and sprawling; they could sense this, though sight of most of it was lost in the depressing gloom.

Moonglum recognized the forest from descriptions he had heard from mad-eyed travellers who drank purposefully in the shadows of Nadsokor's taverns.

"This is the Forest of Troos, sure enough," he said to Elric. "It's told of how the Doomed Folk released tremendous forces upon the earth and caused terrible changes among men, beasts and vegetation. This forest is the last they created, and the last to perish. They must have resented the planet giving them birth."

"A child will always hate its parents at certain times," Elric said impassively.

"Children of whom to be extremely wary, I should think," Moonglum retorted. "Some say that when they were at the peak of their power, they had no gods to frighten them."

"A daring people, indeed," Elric replied, with a faint smile. "They have my respect. But their lack of gods and fear was probably our downfall, if not theirs. Now fear and the gods are back and that, at least, is comforting."

Moonglum puzzled over this for a short time, and then, eventually, said nothing.

He was beginning to feel uneasy.

The place was full of malicious rustlings and whispers, though no living animal inhabited it, as far as they could tell. There was a discomforting absence of birds, rodents or insects and, though they normally had no love for such creatures, they would have appreciated their company in the disconcerting forest.

In a quavering voice, Moonglum began to sing a song in the hope that it would keep his spirits up and his thoughts off the lurking forest.

> A grin and a word is my trade;
> From these, my profit is made.
> Though my body's not tall and my courage is small,
> My fame will take longer to fade.

So singing, with his natural amiability returning, Moonglum rode after the man he regarded as a friend – a friend who possessed something akin to mastery over him, though neither admitted it.

Elric smiled at Moonglum's song. "To sing of one's own lack of size and absence of courage is not an action designed to ward off one's enemies, Moonglum."

"But this way I offer no provocation," Moonglum replied glibly. "If I sing of my shortcomings, I am safe. If I were to boast of my talents, then someone might consider this to be a challenge and decide to teach me a lesson."

"True," Elric assented gravely, "and well-spoken."

He began pointing at certain blossoms and leaves, remarking upon their alien tint and texture, referring to them in words that Moonglum could not understand, though he knew the words to be part of a sorcerer's vocabulary. The albino seemed to be untroubled by the fears which beset the Eastlander, but often, Moonglum knew, appearances with Elric could hide the opposite of what they indicated.

They stopped for a short break while Elric sifted through some of the samples he had torn from trees and plants. He carefully placed his prizes in his belt-pouch but would say nothing of why he did so to Moonglum.

"Come," he said, "Troos's mysteries await us."

But then a new voice, a woman's, said softly from the gloom: "Save the excursion for another day, strangers."

Elric reined his horse, one hand at Stormbringer's hilt. The voice had had an unusual effect upon him. It had been low, deep and had, for a moment, sent the pulse in his throat throbbing. Incredibly, he sensed that he was suddenly standing on one of fate's roads, but where the road would take him, he did not know. Quickly, he controlled his mind and then his body and looked towards the shadows from where the voice had come.

"You are very kind to offer us advice, madam," he said sternly. "Come, show yourself and give explanation . . ."

She rode out then, very slowly, on a black-coated gelding that pranced with a power she could barely restrain. Moonglum drew an appreciative breath, for although heavy-featured, she was incredibly beautiful. Her face and bearing was patrician, her eyes were grey-green, combining enigma and innocence. She was very young. For all her obvious womanhood and beauty, Moonglum aged her at seventeen or little more.

Elric frowned: "Do you ride alone?"

"I do now," she replied, trying to hide her obvious astonishment at the albino's weird lack of colouring. "I need aid – protection. Men who will escort me safely to Karlaak. There, they will be paid."

"Karlaak, by the Weeping Waste? It lies the other side of Ilmiora, 100 leagues away and a week's travelling at speed." Elric did not wait for her to reply to this statement. "We are not hirelings, madam. We are noblemen in our own lands."

"Then you are bound by the vows of chivalry, sir, and cannot refuse my request."

Elric laughed shortly. "Chivalry, madam? We come not from the upstart nations of the south with their strange codes and rules of behaviour. We are nobles of older stock whose actions are governed by our own desires. You would not ask what you do, if you knew our names."

She wetted her full lips with her tongue and said almost timidly: "You are . . . ?"

"Elric of Melniboné, madam, called Elric Woman-slayer in the west, and this is Moonglum of Elwher; he has no conscience."

She gasped. "I have heard of you. There are stories – legends – the white-faced reaver, the hell-driven sorcerer with a blade that drinks the souls of men . . ."

"Aye, that's true. And however magnified they are with the retelling, they cannot hint, those tales, at the darker truths which lie in their origin. Now, madam, do you still seek our aid?" Elric's voice was gentle, without menace, as he saw that she was very much afraid, although she had managed to control the signs of fear and her lips were tight with determination.

"I have no choice. I am at your mercy. My father, the Senior Senator of Karlaak, is very rich. Karlaak is called the City of the Jade Towers, as you will know, and such rare jades and ambers we have. Many could be yours."

"Be careful, madam, lest you anger me," warned Elric, although Moonglum's bright eyes lighted with avarice. "We are not nags to be hired or goods to be bought. Besides which" – he smiled disdainfully – "I am from crumbling Imrryr, the Dreaming City, from the Isle of the Dragon, hub of Ancient Melniboné, and I know what beauty really is. Your baubles cannot tempt one who has looked upon the milky Heart of Arioch, upon the blinding iridescence that throbs from the Ruby Throne, of the languorous and unnamable colours in the Actorios stone of the Ring of Kings. These are more than jewels, madam – they contain the life-stuff of the universe."

"I apologize, Lord Elric, and to you, Sir Moonglum."

Elric laughed, almost with affection. "We are grim clowns, lady, but the Gods of Luck aided our escape from Nadsokor and we owe them a debt. We'll escort you to Karlaak, City of the Jade Towers, and explore the Forest of Troos another time."

Her thanks was tempered with a wary look in her eyes.

"And now we have made introductions," said Elric, "perhaps you would be good enough to give your name and tell us your story."

"I am Zarozinia from Karlaak, a daughter of the Voashoon, the most powerful clan in south-eastern Ilmiora. We have kinsmen in the trading cities on the coasts of Pikarayd and I went with two cousins and my uncle to visit them."

"A perilous journey, Lady Zarozinia."

"Aye, and there are not only natural dangers, sir. Two weeks ago we made our good-byes and began the journey home. Safely we crossed the Straits of Vilmir and there employed men-at-arms, forming a strong caravan to journey through Vilmir and so to Ilmiora. We skirted Nadsokor since we had heard that the City of Beggars is inhospitable to honest travellers . . ."

Here, Elric smiled: "And sometimes to dishonest travellers, as we can appreciate."

Again the expression on her face showed that she had some difficulty in equating his obvious good humour with his evil reputation. "Having skirted Nadsokor," she continued, "we came this way and reached the borders of Org wherein, of course, Troos lies. Very warily we travelled, knowing dark Org's reputation, along the fringes of the forest. And then we were ambushed and our hired men-at-arms deserted us."

"Ambushed, eh?" broke in Moonglum. "By whom, madam, did you know?"

"By their unsavoury looks and squat shapes they seemed native Orgians. They fell upon the caravan and my uncle and cousins fought bravely but were slain. One of my cousins slapped the rump of my gelding and sent it galloping so that I could not control it. I heard terrible screams – mad, giggling shouts – and when I at last brought my horse to a halt, I was lost. Later I heard you approach and waited in fear for you to pass, thinking you also were Orgians, but when I heard your accents and some of your speech, I thought that you might help me."

"And help you we shall, madam," said Moonglum, bowing gallantly from the saddle. "And I am indebted to you for convincing Lord Elric here of your need. But for you, we should be deep in this awful forest by now and experiencing strange terrors no doubt. I offer my sorrow for your dead kinfolk and assure you that you will be protected from now onwards by more than swords and brave hearts, for sorcery can be called up if need be."

"Let's hope there'll be no need," frowned Elric. "You talk blithely of sorcery, friend Moonglum – you who hate me to use the art."

Moonglum grinned.

"I was consoling the young lady, Elric. And I've had occasion to be grateful for your horrid powers, I'll admit. Now I suggest that we make camp for the night and so refreshed be on our way at dawn."

"I'll agree to that," said Elric, glancing almost with embarrassment at the girl. Again he felt the pulse in his throat begin to throb and this time he had more difficulty in controlling it.

The girl also seemed fascinated by the albino. There was an attraction between them which might be strong enough to throw both their destinies along wildly different paths than any they had guessed.

Night came again quickly, for the days were short in those parts. While Moonglum tended the fire, nervously peering around him, Zarozinia, her richly embroidered cloth-of-gold gown shimmering in the firelight, walked gracefully to where Elric sat sorting the herbs he had collected. She glanced at him cautiously and then, seeing that he was absorbed, stared at him with open curiosity.

He looked up and smiled faintly, his eyes for once unprotected, his strange face frank and pleasant. "Some of these are healing herbs," he said, "and others are used in summoning spirits. Yet others give unnatural strength to the imbiber and some turn men mad. They will be useful to me."

She sat down beside him, her thick-fingered hands pushing her black hair back. Her full breasts lifted and fell rapidly.

"Are you really the terrible evil-bringer of the legends, Lord Elric? I find it hard to credit."

"I have brought evil to many places," he said, "but usually there has already been evil to match mine. I seek no excuses, for I know what I am and I know what I have done. I have slain malignant sorcerers and destroyed oppressors, but I have also been responsible for slaying fine men, and a woman, my cousin, whom I loved, I killed – or my sword did."

"And you are master of your sword?"

"Yes – perhaps. I often wonder. Without it, I am helpless." He put his hand around Stormbringer's hilt. "I should be grateful to it." Once again his red eyes seemed to become deeper, protecting some bitter emotion which was rooted at the core of his soul.

"I'm sorry if I revived unpleasant recollection . . ."

"Do not feel sorry, Lady Zarozinia. The pain is within me – you did not put it there. In fact I'd say you relieve it greatly by your presence."

Half startled, she glanced at him and smiled. "I am no wanton, sir," she said, "but . . ."

He got up quickly.

"Moonglum, is the fire going well?"

"Aye, Elric. She'll stay in for the night." Moonglum cocked his head on one side. It was unlike Elric to make such empty queries, but Elric said nothing further so the Eastlander shrugged, turned away to check his gear.

Since he could think of little else to say, Elric turned and said quietly, urgently: "I'm a killer and a thief, not fit to . . ."

"Lord Elric, I am . . ."

"You are infatuated by a legend, that is all."

"No! If you feel what I feel, then you'll know it's more."

"You are young."

"Old enough."

"Beware. I must fulfil my destiny."

"Your destiny?"

"It is no destiny at all, but an awful thing called doom. And I have no pity at all except when I see something in my own soul. Then I have pity – and I pity. But I hate to look and this is part of the doom which drives me. Not fate, nor the stars, nor men, nor demons, nor gods. Look at me, Zarozinia – it is Elric, poor white chosen plaything of the gods of time – Elric of Melniboné who causes his own gradual and terrible destruction."

"It is suicide!"

"Aye. Suicide of a dreadful sinning kind, for I drive myself to slow death. And those who go with me suffer also."

"You speak falsely, Lord Elric – from guilt-madness."

"Because I am guilty, lady."

"And does Sir Moonglum go to doom with you?"

"He is unlike others – he is indestructible in his own self-assurance."

"I am confident, also, Lord Elric."

"But your confidence is that of youth, it is different."

"Need I lose it with my youth?"

"You have strength. You are as strong as we are. I'll grant you that."

She opened her arms, rising. "Then be reconciled, Elric of Melniboné."

And he was. He seized her greedily, kissed her with a deeper need than that of passion. For the first time, Cymoril of Imrryr was forgotten as they dropped to the soft turf, oblivious of Moonglum who polished away at his curved sword with wry jealousy.

They all slept and the fire waned.

Elric, in his joy, had forgotten, or not heeded, that he had a watch to take and Moonglum, who had no source of strength but himself, stayed awake for as long as he could but sleep overcame him.

In the shadows of the awful trees, figures moved with shambling caution.

The misshapen men of Org began to creep inwards towards the sleepers.

Then Elric opened his eyes, aroused by instinct, stared at Zarozinia's peaceful face beside him, moved his eyes without turning his head and saw the danger. He rolled over, grasped Stormbringer and tugged the runeblade from its sheath. The sword hummed, as if in anger at being awakened.

"Moonglum! Danger!" Elric bellowed in fear, for he had more to protect than his own life. The little man's head jerked up. His curved sabre was already across his knees and he jumped to his feet, ran towards Elric as the Orgians closed in.

"I apologise," he said.

"My fault, I . . ."

And then the Orgians were at them. Elric and Moonglum stood over the girl as she came awake, saw the situation and did not scream. Instead she looked around for a weapon but found none. She remained still, where she was, the only thing to do.

Smelling like offal, the gibbering Orgians, some dozen of them, slashed at Elric and Moonglum with heavy blades like cleavers, long and dangerous.

Stormbringer whined and smote through a cleaver, cut into an Orgian's neck and beheaded him. Blood gurgled from the corpse as it slumped back across the fire. Moonglum ducked beneath a howling cleaver, lost his balance, fell, slashed at his opponent's legs and hamstrung him so that he collapsed shrieking. Moonglum stayed on the ground and lunged upwards, taking another in the heart. Then he sprang to his feet and stood shoulder to shoulder with Elric while Zarozinia got up behind them.

"The horses," grunted Elric. "If it's safe, try to get them."

There were still seven Orgians standing and Moonglum groaned as a cleaver sliced flesh from his left arm, retaliated, pierced the man's throat, turned slightly and sheared off another's face. They pressed forward, taking the attack to the incensed Orgians. His left hand covered with his own blood, Moonglum painfully pulled his long poignard from its sheath and held it with his thumb along the handle, blocked an opponent's swing, closed in and killed him with a ripping upward thrust of the dagger, the action of which caused his wound to pound with agony.

Elric held his great runesword in both hands and swung it in a semicircle, hacking down the howling misshapen things. Zarozinia darted towards the horses, leaped on to her own and led the other two towards the fighting men. Elric smote at another and got into his saddle, thanking his own forethought to leave the equipment on the horses in case of danger. Moonglum quickly joined him and they thundered out of the clearing.

"The saddlebags," Moonglum called in greater agony than that created by his wound. "We've left the saddlebags!"

"What of it? Don't press your luck, my friend."

"But all our treasure's in them!"

Elric laughed, partly in relief, partly from real humour. "We'll retrieve them, friend, never fear."

"I know you, Elric. You've no value for the realities."

But even Moonglum was laughing as they left the enraged Orgians behind them and slowed to a canter.

Elric reached and hugged Zarozinia. "You have the courage of your noble clan in your veins," he said.

"Thank you," she replied, pleased with the compliment, "but we cannot match such swordmanship as that displayed by you and Moonglum. It was fantastic."

"Thank the blade," he said shortly.

"No. I will thank you. I think you place too much reliance upon that hell weapon, however powerful it is."

"I need it."

"For what?"

"For my own strength and, now, to give strength to you."

"I'm no vampire," she smiled, "and need no such fearful strength as that supplies."

"Then be assured that I do," he told her gravely. "You would not love me if the blade did not give me what I need. I am like a spineless sea-thing without it."

"I do not believe that, but will not dispute with you now."

They rode for a while without speaking.

Later, they stopped, dismounted, and Zarozinia put herbs that Elric had given her upon Moonglum's wounded arm and began to bind it.

Elric was thinking deeply. The forest rustled with macabre, sensuous sounds. "We're in the heart of Troos," he said, "and our intention to skirt the forest has been forestalled. I have it in mind to call on the King of Org and so round off our visit."

Moonglum laughed. "Shall we send our swords along first? And bind our own hands?" His pain was already eased by the herbs which were having quick effect.

"I mean it. We owe, all of us, much to the Orgians. They slew Zarozinia's uncle and cousins, they wounded you and they now have our treasure. We have many reasons for asking the king for recompense. Also, they seem stupid and should be easy to trick."

"Aye. The king will pay us back for our lack of common sense by tearing our limbs off."

"I'm in earnest. I think we should go."

"I'll agree that I'd like our wealth returned to us. But we cannot risk the lady's safety, Elric."

"I am to be Elric's wife, Moonglum. Therefore if he visits the King of Org, I shall come too."

Moonglum lifted an eyebrow. "A quick courtship."

"She speaks the truth, however. We shall all go to Org – and sorcery will protect us from the king's uncalled-for wrath."

"And still you wish for death and vengeance, Elric," shrugged Moonglum, mounting. "Well, it's all the same to me since your roads, whatever else, are profitable ones. You may be the Lord of Bad Luck by your own reckoning, but you bring good luck to me, I'll say that."

"No more courting death," smiled Elric, "but we'll have some revenge, I hope."

"Dawn will be with us soon," Moonglum said. "The Orgian citadel lies six hours' ride from here by my working, south-south-east by the Ancient Star, if the map I memorized in Nadsokor was correct."

"You have an instinct for direction that never fails, Moonglum. Every caravan should have such a man as you."

"We base an entire philosophy on the stars in Elwher," Moonglum replied. "We regard them as the master plan for everything that happens on earth. As they revolve around the planet they see all things, past, present and future. They are our gods."

"Predictable gods, at least," said Elric and they rode off towards Org with light hearts considering the enormity of their risk.

2

Little was known of the tiny kingdom of Org save that the Forest of Troos lay within its boundaries and to that, other nations felt, it was welcome. The people were unpleasant to look upon, for the most part, and their bodies were stunted and strangely altered. Legend had it that they were the descendants of the Doomed Folk who had wrought such destruction upon the earth an entire Time Cycle before. Their rulers, it was said, were shaped like normal men in so far as their outward bodily appearance went, but their minds were warped more horribly than the limbs of their subjects.

The inhabitants were few and were generally scattered, ruled by their king from his citadel which was also called Org.

It was for this citadel that Elric and his companions rode and, as they did so, Elric explained how he planned to protect them all from the Orgians.

In the forest he had found a particular leaf which, when used with certain invocations (which were harmless in that the invoker was in little danger of being harmed by the spirits he marshalled), would invest that person, and anyone else to whom he gave the drug distilled from the leaf, with temporary invulnerability.

The spell somehow reknitted the skin and flesh structure so that it could withstand any edge and almost any blow. Elric explained, in a rare garrulous mood, how the drug and spell combined to achieve the effect, but his archaicisms and esoteric words meant little to the other two.

They stopped an hour's ride from where Moonglum expected to find the citadel so that Elric could prepare the drug and invoke the spell.

He worked swiftly over a small fire, using an alchemist's pestle and mortar, mixing the shredded leaf with a little water. As the brew bubbled on the fire, he drew peculiar runes on the ground, some of which were twisted into such alien forms that they seemed to disappear into a different dimension and reappear beyond it.

> Bone and blood and flesh and sinew,
> Spell and spirit bind anew;
> Potent potion work the life charm,
> Keep its takers safe from harm.

So Elric chanted as a small pink cloud formed in the air over the fire, wavered, reformed into a spiral shape which curled downwards into the bowl. The brew spluttered and then was still. The albino sorcerer said: "An old boyhood spell, so simple that I'd near forgotten it. The leaf for the potion grows only in Troos and therefore it is rarely possible to perform."

The brew, which had been liquid, had now solidified and Elric broke it into small pellets. "Too much," he warned, "taken at one time is poison, and yet the effect can last for several hours. Not always, though, but we must accept that small risk." He handed both of them a pellet which they received dubiously. "Swallow them just before we reach the citadel," he told them, "or in the event of the Orgians finding us first."

Then they mounted and rode on again.

Some miles to the south-east of Troos, a blind man sang a grim song in his sleep and so woke himself . . .

They reached the brooding citadel of Org at dusk. Guttural, drooling voices shouted at them from the battlements of the square-cut ancient dwelling place of the Kings of Org. The thick rock oozed moisture and was corroded by lichen and sickly, mottled moss. The only entrance large enough for a mounted man to pass through was reached by a path almost a foot deep in evil-smelling black mud.

"What's your business at the Royal Court of Gutheran the Mighty?"

They could not see who asked the question.

"We seek hospitality and an audience with your liege," called Moonglum cheerfully, successfully hiding his nervousness. "We bring important news to Org."

A twisted face peered down from the battlements. "Enter strangers and be welcome," it said unwelcomingly.

The heavy wooden drawgate shifted upwards to allow them entrance and the horses pushed their way slowly through the mud and so into the courtyard of the citadel.

Overhead, the grey sky was a racing field of black tattered

clouds which streamed towards the horizon as if to escape the horrid boundaries of Org and the disgusting Forest of Troos.

The courtyard was covered, though not so deeply, with the same foul mud as had impaired their progress to the citadel. It was full of heavy, unmoving shadow. On Elric's right, a flight of steps went up to an arched entrance which was hung, partially, with the same unhealthy lichen he had seen on the outer walls and, also, in the Forest of Troos.

Through this archway, brushing at the lichen with a pale, beringed hand, a tall man came and stood on the top step, regarding the visitors through heavy-lidded eyes. He was, in contrast to the other Orgians, handsome, with a massive, leonine head and long hair as white as Elric's; although the hair on the head of this great, solid man was somewhat dirty, tangled, unbrushed. He was dressed in a heavy jerkin of quilted, embossed leather, a yellow kilt which reached to his ankles and he carried a wide-bladed dagger, naked in his belt. He was older than Elric, aged between forty and fifty and his powerful if somewhat decadent face was seamed and pock-marked.

He stared at them in silence and did not welcome them; instead he signed to one of the battlement guards who caused the drawgate to be lowered. It came down with a crash, blocking off their way of escape.

"Kill the men and keep the woman," said the massive man in a low monotone. Elric had heard dead men speak in that manner.

As planned, Elric and Moonglum stood either side of Zarozinia and remained where they were, arms folded.

Puzzled, shambling Orgians came warily at them, their loose trousers dragging in the mud, their hands hidden by the long shapeless sleeves of their filthy garments. They swung their cleavers. Elric felt a faint shock as the blade thudded on to his arm, but that was all. Moonglum's experience was similar.

The Orgians fell back, amazement and confusion on their bestial faces.

The tall man's eyes widened. He put one ring-covered hand to his thick lips, chewing at a nail.

"Our swords have no effect upon them, King! They do not cut and they do not bleed. What are these folk?"

Elric laughed theatrically. "We are not common folk, little human, be assured. We are the messengers of the gods and come to your king with a message from our great masters. Do not worry, we shall not harm you since we are in no danger of being harmed. Stand aside and make us welcome."

Elric could see that King Gutheran was puzzled and not absolutely taken in by his words. Elric cursed to himself. He had measured the Orgians' intelligence by those he had seen. This king, mad or not, was much more intelligent, was going to be harder to deceive. He led the way up the steps towards glowering Gutheran.

"Greetings, King Gutheran. The gods have, at last, returned to Org and wish you to know this."

"Org has had no gods to worship for an eternity," said Gutheran hollowly, turning back into the citadel. "Why should we accept them now?"

"You are impertinent, King."

"And you are audacious. How do I know you come from the gods?" He walked ahead of them, leading them through the low-roofed halls.

"You saw that the swords of your subjects had no effect upon us."

"True. I'll take that incident as proof for the moment. I suppose there must be a banquet in your – honour. I shall order it. Be welcome, messengers." His words were ungracious but it was virtually impossible to detect anything from Gutheran's tone, since the man's voice stayed at the same pitch.

Elric pushed his heavy riding cloak back from his shoulders and said lightly: "We shall mention your kindness to our masters."

The court was a place of gloomy halls and false laughter and although Elric put many questions to Gutheran, the king would not answer them, or did so by means of ambiguous phrases which meant nothing. They were not given chambers wherein they could refresh themselves but instead stood about for several hours in the main hall of the citadel and Gutheran, while he was with them and not giving orders for the banquet, sat slumped on his throne and chewed at his nails, ignoring them.

"Pleasant hospitality," whispered Moonglum.

"Elric, how long will the effects of the drug last?" Zarozinia had remained close to him. He put his arm around her shoulders. "I do not know. Not much longer. But it has served its purpose. I doubt if they will try to attack us a second time. However, beware of other attempts, subtler ones, upon our lives."

The main hall, which had a higher roof than the others and was completely surrounded by a gallery which ran around it well above the floor, fairly close to the roof, was chilly and unwarmed. No fires burned in the several hearths, which were open and let into the floor, and the walls dripped moisture and were undecorated; damp, solid stone, timeworn and gaunt. There were not even rushes upon the floor which was strewn with old bones and pieces of decaying food.

"Hardly house-proud, are they?" commented Moonglum, looking around him with distaste and glancing at brooding Gutheran who was seemingly oblivious of their presence.

A servitor shambled into the hall and whispered a few words to the king. He nodded and arose, leaving the Great Hall.

Soon men came in, carrying benches and tables and began to place them about the hall.

The banquet was, at last, due to commence. And the air had menace in it.

The three visitors sat together on the right of the king who had donned a richly jewelled chain of kingship, while his son and several pale-faced female members of the royal line sat on the left, unspeaking even among themselves.

Prince Hurd, a sullen-faced youth who seemed to bear a resentment against his father, picked at the unappetising food which was served them all.

He drank heavily of the wine which had little flavour but was strong, fiery stuff and this seemed to warm the company a little.

"And what do the Gods want of us poor Orgians?" Hurd said, staring hard at Zarozinia with more than friendly interest.

Elric answered: "They ask nothing of you but your recognition. In return they will, on occasions, help you."

"That is all?" Hurd laughed. "That is more than those from the Hill can offer, eh, Father?"

Gutheran turned his great head slowly to regard his son.

"Yes," he murmured, and the word seemed to carry warning.

Moonglum said: "The Hill – what is that?"

He got no reply. Instead a high-pitched laugh came from the entrance to the Great Hall. A thin, gaunt man stood there staring ahead with a fixed gaze. His features, though emaciated, strongly resembled Gutheran's. He carried a stringed instrument and plucked at the gut so that it wailed and moaned with melancholy insistence.

Hurd said savagely: "Look, Father, 'tis blind Veerkad, the minstrel, your brother. Shall he sing for us?"

"Sing?"

"Shall he sing his songs, Father?"

Gutheran's mouth trembled and twisted and he said after a moment: "He may entertain our guests with an heroic ballad if he wishes, but . . ."

"But certain other songs he shall not sing . . ." Hurd grinned maliciously. He seemed to be tormenting his father deliberately in some way which Elric could not guess. Hurd shouted at the blind man: "Come, Uncle Veerkad – sing!"

"There are strangers present," said Veerkad hollowly above the wail of his own music. "Strangers in Org?"

Hurd giggled and drank more wine. Gutheran scowled and continued to tremble, gnawing at his nails.

Elric called: "We'd appreciate a song, minstrel."

"Then you'll have the song of the Three Kings in Darkness, strangers, and hear the ghastly story of the Kings of Org."

"No!" shouted Gutheran, leaping from his place, but Veerkad was already singing:

> Three kings in darkness lie,
> Gutheran of Org, and I,
> Under a bleak and sunless sky—
> The third Beneath the Hill.
> When shall the third arise?
> Only when another dies . . .

"Stop!" Gutheran got up in an obviously insane rage and stumbled across the table, trembling in terror, his face blanched, striking at the blind man, his brother. Two blows and the minstrel fell, slumping to the floor and not moving. "Take him out! Do not let him enter again," the king shrieked and foam flecked his lips.

Hurd, sober for a moment, jumped across the table, scattering dishes and cups and took his father's arm.

"Be calm, Father. I have a new plan for our entertainment."

"You! You seek my throne. 'Twas you who goaded Veerkad to sing his dreadful song. You know I cannot listen without . . ." He stared at the door. "One day the legend shall be realized and the Hill-King shall come. Then shall I, you and Org perish."

"Father" – Hurd was smiling horribly – "let the female visitor dance for us a dance of the gods."

"What?"

"Let the woman dance for us, Father."

Elric heard him. By now the drug must have worn off. He could not afford to show his hand by offering his companions further doses. He got to his feet.

"What sacrilege do you speak, Prince?"

"We have given you entertainment. It is the custom in Org for our visitors to give us entertainment also."

The hall was filled with menace. Elric regretted his plan to trick the Orgians, now. But there was nothing he could do. He had intended to exact tribute from them in the name of the gods, but obviously these mad men feared more immediate and tangible dangers than any the gods might represent.

He had made a mistake, put the lives of his friends in danger as well as his own. What should he do? Zarozinia murmured: "I have learned dances in Ilmiora where all ladies are taught the art. Let me dance for them. It might placate them and bedazzle them to make our work easier."

"Arioch knows our work is hard enough now. I was a fool to have conceived this plan. Very well, Zarozinia, dance for them, but with caution." He shouted at Hurd: "Our companion will dance for you, to show you the beauty that the gods create. Then you must pay the tribute, for our masters grow impatient."

"The tribute?" Gutheran looked up. "You mentioned nothing of tribute."

"Your recognition of the gods must take the form of precious stones and metals, King Gutheran. I thought you to understand that."

"You seem more like common thieves than uncommon messengers, my friends. We are poor in Org and have nothing to give away to charlatans."

"Beware of your words, King!" Elric's clear voice echoed warningly through the hall.

"We'll see the dance and then judge the truth of what you've told us."

Elric seated himself, grasped Zarozinia's hand beneath the table as she arose, giving her comfort.

She walked gracefully and confidently into the centre of the hall and there began to dance. Elric, who loved her, was amazed at her splendid grace and artistry. She danced the old, beautiful dances of Ilmiora, entrancing even the thick-skulled Orgians and, as she danced, a great golden Guest Cup was brought in.

Hurd leaned across his father and said to Elric: "The Guest Cup, Lord. It is our custom that our guests drink from it in friendship."

Elric nodded, annoyed at being disturbed in his watching of the wonderful dance, his eyes fixed on Zarozinia as she postured and glided. There was silence in the hall.

Hurd handed him the cup and absently he put it to his lips; seeing this Zarozinia danced on to the table and began to weave along it to where Elric sat. As he took the first sip, Zarozinia cried out and, with her foot, knocked the cup from his hand. The wine splashed on to Gutheran and Hurd who half rose, startled. "It was drugged, Elric. They drugged it!"

Hurd lashed at her with his hand, striking her across the face. She fell from the table and lay moaning slightly on the filthy floor. "Bitch! Would the messengers of the gods be harmed by a little drugged wine?"

Enraged, Elric pushed aside Gutheran and struck savagely at Hurd so that the young man's mouth gushed blood. But the drug was already having effect. Gutheran shouted something and Moonglum drew his sabre, glancing upwards. Elric was swaying, his senses were jumbled and the scene had an unreal quality. He saw servants grasp Zarozinia but could not see how Moonglum was faring. He felt sick and dizzy, could hardly control his limbs.

Summoning up his last remaining strength, Elric clubbed Hurd down with one tremendous blow. Then he collapsed into unconsciousness.

3

There was the cold clutch of chains about his wrists and a thin drizzle was falling directly on to his face which stung where Hurd's nails had ripped it.

He looked about him. He was chained between two stone menhirs upon an obvious burial barrow of gigantic size. It was night and a pale moon hovered in the heavens above him. He looked down at the group of men below. Hurd and Gutheran were among them. They grinned at him mockingly.

"Farewell, messenger. You will serve us a good purpose and placate the Ones from the Hill!" Hurd called as he and the others scurried back towards the citadel which lay, silhouetted, a short distance away.

Where was he? What had happened to Zarozinia – and Moonglum? Why had he been chained thus upon – realization and remembrance came – *the Hill*!

He shuddered, helpless in the strong chains which held him. Desperately he began to tug at them, but they would not yield. He searched his brain for a plan, but he was confused by torment and worry for his friends' safety. He heard a dreadful scuttling sound from below and saw a ghastly white shape dart into the gloom. Wildly he struggled in the rattling iron which held him.

In the Great Hall of the citadel, a riotous celebration was now reaching the state of an ecstatic orgy. Gutheran and Hurd were totally drunk, laughing insanely at their victory.

Outside the hall, Veerkad listened and hated. Particularly he hated his brother, the man who had deposed and blinded him to prevent his study of sorcery by means of which he had planned to raise the King from Beneath the Hill.

"The time has come, at last," he whispered to himself and stopped a passing servant.

"Tell me, where is the girl kept?"

"In Gutheran's chamber, master."

Veerkad released the man and began to grope his way through the gloomy corridors up twisting steps, until he reached the room he sought. Here he produced a key, one of many he'd had made without Gutheran's knowing, and unlocked the door.

Zarozinia saw the blind man enter and could do nothing. She was gagged and bound with her own dress and still dazed from the blow Hurd had given her. They had told her of Elric's fate, but Moonglum had so far escaped them; guards hunted him now in the stinking corridors of Org.

"I've come to take you to your companion, lady," smiled blind Veerkad, and, grasping her roughly with strength that his insanity had given him, picked her up and fumbled his way towards the door. He knew the passages of Org perfectly, for he had been born and grown up among them.

But two men were in the corridor outside Gutheran's chambers. One of them was Hurd, Prince of Org, who resented his father's appropriation of the girl and desired her for himself. He saw Veerkad bearing the girl away and stood silent while his uncle passed.

The other man was Moonglum, who observed what was happening from the shadows where he had hidden from the searching guards. As Hurd followed Veerkad, on cautious feet, Moonglum followed him.

Veerkad went out of the citadel by a small side door and carried his living burden towards the looming Burial Hill.

All about the foot of the monstrous barrow swarmed the leprous-white ghouls who sensed the presence of Elric, the Orgians' sacrifice to them.

Now Elric understood.

These were the things the Orgians feared more than the gods. These were the living-dead ancestors of those who now revelled in the Great Hall. Perhaps these were actually the Doomed Folk. Was that their doom? Never to rest? Never to die? Just to degenerate into mindless ghouls? Elric shuddered.

Now desperation brought back his memory.

He cried to Arioch, the Demon God of Melniboné, and his voice was an agonized wail to the brooding sky and the pulsing earth.

"Arioch! Destroy the stones. Save your servant! Arioch – master – aid me!"

It was not enough. The ghouls gathered together and began to scuttle, gibbering up the barrow towards the helpless albino.

"*Arioch! These are the things that would forsake your memory! Aid me to destroy them!*"

The earth trembled and the sky became overcast, hiding the moon but not the white-faced, bloodless ghouls who were now almost upon him.

And then a ball of fire formed in the sky above him and the very sky seemed to shake and sway around it. Then, with a roaring crash two bolts of lightning slashed down, pulverizing the stones and releasing Elric.

He got to his feet, knowing that Arioch would demand his price, as the first ghouls reached him.

He did not retreat, but in his rage and desperation leaped among them, smashing and flailing with the lengths of chain. The ghouls fell back and fled, gibbering in fear and anger, down the Hill and into the barrow.

Elric could now see that there was a gaping entrance to the barrow below him; black against the blackness. Breathing heavily, he found that his belt pouch had been left him. From it he

took a length of slim, gold wire and began frantically to pick at the
locks of the manacles.

Veerkad chuckled to himself and Zarozinia hearing him was
almost mad with terror. He kept drooling the words into her
ear: "When shall the third arise? Only when other dies. When
that other's blood flows red – we'll hear the footfalls of the dead.
You and I, we shall resurrect him and such vengeance will he
wreak upon my cursed brother. Your blood, my dear, it will be
that released him." He felt that the ghouls were gone and judged
them placated by their feast. "Your lover has been useful to me,"
he laughed as he began to enter the barrow. The smell of death
almost overpowered the girl as the blind madman bore her
downwards into the heart of the Hill.

Hurd, sobered after his walk in the colder air, was horrified
when he saw where Veerkad was going; the barrow, the Hill of the
King, was the most feared spot in the land of Org. Hurd paused
before the black entrance and turned to run. Then, suddenly, he
saw the form of Elric, looming huge and bloody, descending the
barrow slope, cutting off his escape.

With a wild yell he fled into the Hill passage.

Elric had not previously noticed the prince, but the yell startled
him and he tried to see who had given it but was too late. He
began to run down the steep incline towards the entrance of the
barrow. Another figure came scampering out of the darkness.

"Elric! Thank the stars and all the gods of earth! You live!"

"Thank Arioch, Moonglum. Where's Zarozinia?"

"In there – the mad minstrel took her with him and Hurd
followed. They are all insane, these kings and princes, I see no
sense to their actions."

"I have an idea that the minstrel means Zarozinia no good.
Quickly, we must follow."

"By the stars, the stench of death! I have breathed nothing like
it – not even at the great battle of the Eshmir Valley where the
armies of Elwher met those of Kaleg Vogun, usurper prince of the
Tanghensi, and half a million corpses strewed the valley from end
to end."

"If you've no stomach . . ."

"I wish I had none. It would not be so bad. Come . . ."

They rushed into the passage, led by the faraway sounds of Veerkad's maniacal laughter and the somewhat nearer movements of a fear-maddened Hurd who was now trapped between two enemies and yet more afraid of a third.

Hurd blundered along in the blackness, sobbing to himself in his terror.

In the weirdly phosphorescent Central Tomb, surrounded by the mummified corpses of his ancestors, Veerkad chanted the resurrection ritual before the great coffin of the Hill-King – a giant thing, half as tall again as Veerkad who was tall enough. Veerkad was forgetful for his own safety and thinking only of vengeance upon his brother Gutheran. He held a long dagger over Zarozinia who lay huddled and terrified upon the ground near the coffin.

The spilling of Zarozinia's blood would be the culmination of the ritual and then—

Then hell would, quite literally, be let loose. Or so Veerkad planned. He finished his chanting and raised the knife just as Hurd came screeching into the Central Tomb with his own sword drawn. Veerkad swung round, his blind face working in thwarted rage.

Savagely, without stopping for a moment, Hurd ran his sword into Veerkad's body, plunging the blade in up to the hilt so that its bloody point appeared sticking from his back. But the other, in his groaning death spasms, locked his hands about the prince's throat. Locked them immovably.

Somehow, the two men retained a semblance of life and, struggling with each other in a macabre death-dance, swayed about the glowing chamber. The coffin of the Hill-King began to tremble and shake slightly, the movement hardly perceptible.

So Elric and Moonglum found Veerkad and Hurd. Seeing that both were near dead, Elric raced across the Central Tomb to where Zarozinia lay, unconscious, mercifully, from her ordeal. Elric picked her up and made to return.

He glanced at the throbbing coffin.

"Quickly, Moonglum. That blind fool has invoked the dead, I can tell. Hurry, my friend, before the hosts of hell are upon us."

Moonglum gasped and followed Elric as he ran back towards the cleaner air of night.

"Where to now, Elric?"

"We'll have to risk going back to the citadel. Our horses are there and our goods. We need the horses to take us quickly away, for I fear there's going to be a terrible blood-letting soon if my instinct is right."

"There should not be too much opposition, Elric. They were all drunk when I left. That was how I managed to evade them so easily. By now, if they continued drinking as heavily as when last I saw them, they'll be unable to move at all."

"Then let's make haste."

They left the Hill behind them and began to run towards the citadel.

4

Moonglum had spoken truth. Everyone was lying about the Great Hall in drunken sleep. Open fires had been lit in the hearths and they blazed, sending shadows skipping around the hall.

Elric said softly: "Moonglum, go with Zarozinia to the stables and prepare our horses. I will settle our debt with Gutheran first." He pointed. "See, they have heaped their booty upon the table, gloating in their apparent victory."

Stormbringer lay upon a pile of burst sacks and saddlebags which contained the loot stolen from Zarozinia's uncle and cousins and from Elric and Moonglum.

Zarozinia, now conscious but confused, left with Moonglum to locate the stables and Elric picked his way towards the table, across the sprawled shapes of drunken Orgians, around the blazing fires and caught up, thankfully, his hell-forged rune-blade.

Then he leaped over the table and was about to grasp Gutheran, who still had his fabulously gemmed chain of kingship around his neck, when the great doors of the hall crashed open and a howling blast of icy air sent the torches dancing and leaping. Elric turned, Gutheran forgotten, and his eyes widened.

Framed in the doorway stood the King from Beneath the Hill.

The long-dead monarch had been raised by Veerkad whose own blood had completed the work of resurrection. He stood in rotting robes, his fleshless bones covered by tight, tattered skin. His heart did not beat, for he had none; he drew no breath, for his lungs had been eaten by the creatures which feasted on such things. But, horribly, he lived . . .

The King from the Hill. He had been the last great ruler of the Doomed Folk who had, in their fury, destroyed half the earth and created the Forest of Troos. Behind the dead king crowded the ghastly hosts who had been buried with him in a legendary past.

The massacre began!

What secret vengeance was being reaped, Elric could only guess at – but whatever the reason, the danger was still very real.

Elric pulled out Stormbringer as the awakened horde vented their anger upon the living. The hall became filled with the shrieking, horrified screams of the unfortunate Orgians. Elric remained, half paralysed in his horror, beside the throne. Aroused, Gutheran woke up and saw the King from the Hill and his host. He screamed, almost thankfully: "At last I can rest!"

And fell dying in a seizure, robbing Elric of his vengeance.

Veerkad's grim song echoed in Elric's memory. The Three Kings in Darkness: Gutheran, Veerkad and the King from Beneath the Hill. Now only the last lived – and he had been dead for millennia.

The king's cold, dead eyes roved the hall and saw Gutheran sprawled upon his throne, the ancient chain of office still about his throat. Elric wrenched it off the body and backed away as the King from Beneath the Hill advanced. And then his back was against a pillar and there were feasting ghouls everywhere else.

The dead king came nearer and then, with a whistling moan which came from the depths of his decaying body, launched himself at Elric who found himself fighting desperately against the Hill-King's clawing, abnormal strength, cutting at flesh that neither bled nor suffered pain. Even the sorcerous runeblade could do nothing against this horror that had no soul to take and no blood to let.

Frantically, Elric slashed and hacked at the Hill-King but ragged nails raked his flesh and teeth snapped at his throat. And above everything came the almost overpowering stench of death as the ghouls, packing the Great Hall with their horrible shapes, feasted on the living and the dead.

Then Elric heard Moonglum's voice calling and saw him upon the gallery which ran around the hall. He held a great oil jar.

"Lure him close to the central fire, Elric. There may be a way to vanquish him. Quickly, man, or you're finished!"

In a frantic burst of energy, the Melnibonéan forced the giant king towards the flames. Around them, the ghouls fed off the remains of their victims, some of whom still lived, their screams calling hopelessly over the sound of carnage.

The Hill-King now stood, unfeeling, with his back to the leaping central fire. He still slashed at Elric. Moonglum hurled the jar.

It shattered upon the stone hearth, spraying the king with blazing oil. He staggered, and Elric struck with his full power, the man and the blade combining to push the Hill-King backwards. Down went the king into the flames and the flames began to devour him.

A dreadful, lost howling came from the burning giant as he perished.

Flames licked everywhere throughout the Great Hall and soon the place was like hell itself, an inferno of licking fire through which the ghouls ran about, still feasting, unaware of their destruction. The way to the door was blocked.

Elric stared around him and saw no way of escape – save one.

Sheathing Stormbringer, he ran a few paces and leaped upwards, just grasping the rail of the gallery as flames engulfed the spot where he had been standing.

Moonglum reached down and helped him to clamber across the rail.

"I'm disappointed, Elric," he grinned, "you forgot to bring the treasure."

Elric showed him what he grasped in his left hand – the jewel-encrusted chain of kingship.

"This bauble is some reward for our hardships," he smiled, holding up the glittering chain. "I stole nothing, by Arioch! There are no kings left in Org to wear it! Come, let's join Zarozinia and get our horses."

They ran from the gallery as masonry began to crash downwards into the Great Hall.

They rode fast away from the halls of Org and looking back saw great fissures appear in the walls and heard the roar of destruction as the flames consumed everything that had been Org. They destroyed the seat of the monarchy, the remains of the Three Kings in Darkness, the present and the past. Nothing would be left of Org save an empty burial mound and two corpses, locked together, lying where their ancestors had lain for centuries in the Central Tomb. They destroyed the last link with the previous Time Cycle and cleansed the earth of an ancient evil. Only the dreadful Forest of Troos remained to mark the coming and the passing of the legendary Doomed Folk.

And the Forest of Troos was a warning.

Weary and yet relieved, the three saw the outlines of Troos in the distance, behind the blazing funeral pyre.

And yet, in his happiness, Elric had a fresh problem on his mind now that danger was past.

"Why do you frown now, love?" asked Zarozinia.

"Because I think you spoke the truth. Remember you said I placed too much reliance on my runeblade here?"

"Yes – and I said I would not dispute with you."

"Agreed. But I have a feeling that you were partially right. On the burial mound and in it I did not have Stormbringer with me – and yet I fought and won, because I feared for your safety." His voice was quiet. "Perhaps, in time, I can keep my strength by means of certain herbs I found in Troos and dispense with the blade for ever?"

Moonglum shouted with laughter hearing these words.

"Elric, I never thought I'd witness this. You daring to think of dispensing with that foul weapon of yours. I don't know if you ever shall, but the thought is comforting."

"It is, my friend, it is." He leaned in his saddle and grasped Zarozinia's shoulders, pulling her dangerously towards him as they galloped without slackening speed. And as they rode he kissed her, heedless of their pace.

"A new beginning!" he shouted above the wind. "A new beginning, my love!"

And then they all rode laughing towards Karlaak by the Weeping Waste, to present themselves, to enrich themselves, and to attend the strangest wedding the Northern Lands had ever witnessed. For it would be more than a marriage between the awful evil-bringer of legends and a senator's youthful daughter – it would be a marriage between the dark wisdom of the Ancient World and the bright hope of the New.

And who could tell what such a combination would bring about?

The earth would soon know, for Elric of Melniboné was the maker of legends and there were legends yet to make!

The Bells of Shoredan

Roger Zelazny

Roger Zelazny (1937–95) burst upon the fantasy scene in the early mid-sixties like a whirlwind. I can still feel the warmth of his blast. Over a short space of six or seven years he redefined the barriers of fantasy and science fiction, bringing an excitement and exuberance to a field that had been showing signs of senility. He is probably best remembered for his sequence of novels about Amber, the one true world of which the earth is but a shadow. This series began with Nine Princes in Amber *(1970) and ran through eight further books to* Prince of Chaos *(1991). In fact Zelazny was fascinated with shadow worlds and alternate existences.* Jack of Shadows *(1971) is set on a world one half of which is like our own, but the other half is ruled by magic.* Changeling *(1980), and its sequel* Madwand *(1981), is about two men who, as babies, were switched between earth and a world where magic works. Zelazny did so much more, of course, including his great science-fiction novels* This Immortal *(1966),* Lord of Light *(1967) and* Damnation Alley *(1969), but early in his career Zelazny introduced the character of Dilvish the Damned, and his metal horse Black. Dilvish is cast into hell by the sorcerer Jelerak but after 200 years returns, bent upon revenge. That is where the following story starts. The Dilvish stories were eventually collected as* Dilvish the Damned *(1982) and there is also a novel,* The Changing Land *(1980).*

NO LIVING THING DWELLED IN THE LAND OF RAHORINGHAST. Since an age before this age had the dead realm been empty of sound, save for the crashing of thunders and the *spit-spit* of raindrops ricocheting from off its stonework and the stones. The towers of the Citadel of Rahoring still stood; the great archway from which the gates had been stricken continued to gape, like a mouth frozen in a howl of pain and surprise, of death; the countryside about the place resembled the sterile landscape of the moon.

The rider followed the Way of the Armies, which led at last to that archway and on through into the citadel. Behind him lay a twisted trail leading downwards, downwards, and back, towards the south and the west. It ran through chill patterns of morning mist which clung, swollen, to the dark and pitted ground, like squadrons of gigantic leeches. It looped about the ancient towers, still standing only by virtue of enchantments placed upon them in foregone days. Black and awesome, high-rearing, and limned in nightmare's clarity, the towers and the citadel were the final visible extensions of the character of their dead maker: Hohorga, King of the World.

The rider, the green-booted rider who left no footprints when he walked, must have felt something of the dark power which still remained within the place, for he halted and sat silent, staring for a long while at the broken gates and the high battlements. Then he spoke a word to the black, horse-like thing he rode upon, and they pressed ahead.

As he drew near, he saw that something was moving in the shadows of the archway.

He knew that no living thing dwelled in the land of Rahoringhast . . .

The battle had gone well, considering the number of the defenders.

On the first day, the emissaries of Lylish had approached the walls of Dilfar, sought parley, requested surrender of the city, and been refused. There followed a brief truce, to permit single combat between Lance, the Hand of Lylish, and Dilvish called the Damned, Colonel of the East, Deliverer of Portaroy, scion of the Elvish House of Selar and the human House which hath been stricken.

The trial lasted but a quarter of an hour, until Dilvish, whose wounded leg had caused his collapse, did strike upwards from behind his buckler with the point of his blade. The armour of Lance, which had been deemed invincible, gave way then, when the blade of Dilvish smote at one of the two devices upon the breastplate – those which were cast in the form of cloven hoof-marks. Men muttered that these devices had not been present previously, and an attempt was made to take the colonel prisoner. His horse, however, which had stood on the sidelines like a steel statue, did again come to his aid, bearing him to safety within the city.

The assault was then begun, but the defenders were prepared and held well their walls. Well-fortified and well-provided was Dilfar. Fighting from a position of strength, the defenders cast down much destruction upon the Men of the West.

After four days the army of Lylish had withdrawn with the great rams which it had been unable to use. The Men of the West commenced the construction of helepoli, while they awaited the arrival of catapults from Bildesh.

Above the walls of Dilfar, high in the Keep of Eagles, there were two who watched.

"It will not go well, Lord Dilvish," said the king, whose name was Malacar the Mighty, though he was short of stature and long of year. "If they complete the towers-that-walk and bring catapults, they will strike us from afar. We will not be able to defend against this. Then the towers will walk when we are weakened from the bombardment."

"It is true," said Dilvish.

"Dilfar must not fall."

"No."

"Reinforcements have been sent for, but they are many leagues distant. None were prepared for the assault of Lord Lylish, and it will be long before sufficient troops will be mustered and be come here to the battle."

"That also is true, and by then it may be too late."

"You are said by some to be the same Lord Dilvish who liberated Portaroy in days long gone by."

"I am that Dilvish."

"If so, that Dilvish was of the House of Selar of the Invisible Blade."

"Yes."

"Is it true also, then – what is told of the House of Selar and the Bells of Shoredan in Rahoringhast?"

Malacar looked away as he said it.

"This thing I do not know," said Dilvish. "I have never attempted to raise the cursed legions of Shoredan. My grandmother told me that only twice in all the ages of time has this been done. I have also read of it in the Green Books of Time at the Keep of Mirata. I do not *know*, however."

"Only to one of the House of Selar will the bells respond. Else they swing noiseless, it is said."

"So is it said."

"Rahoringhast lies far to the north and the east and distressful is the way. One with a mount such as yours might make the journey, might ring there the bells, might call forth the doomed legions, though. It is said they will follow such a one of Selar to battle."

"Aye, this thought has come to me, also."

"Wilst essay this thing?"

"Aye, sir. Tonight. I am already prepared."

"Kneel then and receive thou my blessing, Dilvish of Selar. I knew thou wert he when I saw thee on the field before these walls."

And Dilvish did kneel and receive the blessing of Malacar, called the Mighty, Leige of the Eastern Reach, whose realm held Dilfar, Bildesh, Mystar, Mycar, Portaroy, Princeaton and Poind.

The way was difficult, but the passage of leagues and hours was as the movement of clouds. The western portal to Dilfar had within it a smaller passing-place, a man-sized door studded with spikes and slitted for the discharge of bolts.

Like a shutter in the wind, this door opened and closed.

Crouched low, mounted on a piece of the night, the colonel passed out through the opening and raced across the plain, entering for a moment the outskirts of the enemy camp.

A cry went up as he rode, and weapons rattled in the darkness.

Sparks flew from unshod steel hooves.

"All the speed at thy command now, Black, my mount!"

He was through the campsite and away before arrow could be set to bow.

High on the hill to the east, a small fire throbbed in the wind. Pennons, mounted on tall poles, flapped against the night, and it was too dark for Dilvish to read the devices thereon, but he knew that they stood before the tents of Lylish, Colonel of the West.

Dilvish spoke the words in the language of the damned, and as he spoke them the eyes of his mount glowed like embers in the night. The small fire on the hilltop leaped, one great leaf of flame, to the height of four men. It did not reach the tent, however. Then there was no fire at all, only the embers of all the fuels consumed in a single moment.

Dilvish rode on, and the hooves of Black made lightning on the hillside.

They pursued him a small while only. Then he was away and alone.

All that night did he ride through places of rock. Shapes reared high above him and fell again, like staggering giants surprised in their drunkenness. He felt himself launched, countless times, through empty air, and when he looked down on these occasions, there was only empty air beneath him.

With the morning, there came a levelling of his path, and the far edge of the Eastern Plain lay before him, then under him. His leg began to throb beneath its dressing, but he had lived in the Houses of Pain for more than the lifetimes of men, and he put the feeling far from his thoughts.

After the sun had raised itself over the jagged horizon at his back, he stopped to eat and to drink, to stretch his limbs.

In the sky then, he saw the shapes of the nine black doves who must circle the world for ever, never to land, seeing all things on the earth and on the sea, and passing all things by.

"An omen," he said. "Be it a good one?"

"I know not," replied the creature of steel.

"Then let us make haste to learn."

He remounted.

For four days did he pass over the plain, until the yellow and green waving grasses gave way and the land lay sandy before him.

The winds of the desert cut at his eyes. He fixed his scarf as a muffle, but it could not stop the entire assault. When he would cough and spit, he needed to lower it, and the sand entered again. He would blink and his face would burn, and he would curse, but no spell he knew could lay the entire desert like yellow tapestry, smooth and unruffled below him. Black was an opposing wind, and the airs of the land rushed to contest his passage.

On the third day in the desert, a mad wight flew invisible and gibbering at his back. Even Black could not outrun it, and it ignored the foulest imprecations of Mabrahoring, language of the demons and the damned.

The following day, more joined with it. They would not pass the protective circle in which Dilvish slept, but they screamed across his dreams – meaningless fragments of a dozen tongues – troubling his sleep.

He left them when he left the desert. He left them as he entered the land of stone and marshes and gravel and dark pools and evil openings in the ground from which the fumes of the underworld came forth.

He had come to the border of Rahoringhast.

It was damp and grey, everywhere.

It was misty in places, and the water oozed forth from the rocks, came up from out of the ground.

There were no trees, shrubs, flowers, grasses. No birds sang, no insects hummed.

No living thing dwelled in the land of Rahoringhast.

Dilvish rode on and entered through the broken jaws of the city.

All within was shadow and ruin.

He passed up the Way of the Armies.

Silent was Rahoringhast, a city of the dead.

He could feel this, not as the silence of nothingness now, but as the silence of a still presence.

Only the steel cloven hooves sounded within the city.

There came no echoes.

Sound . . . Nothing. Sound . . . Nothing. Sound . . .

It was as though something unseen moved to absorb every evidence of life as soon as it noised itself.

Red was the palace, like bricks hot from the kiln and flushed with the tempers of their making. But of one piece were the walls. No seams nor cracks, no divisions were there in the sheet of red. It was solid, was imponderable, broad of base, and reached with its thirteen towers higher than any building Dilvish had ever seen, though he had dwelled in the high Keep of Mirata itself, where the Lords of Illusion hold sway, bending space to their will.

Dilvish dismounted and regarded the enormous stairway that lay before him.

"That which we seek lies within."

Black nodded and touched the first stair with his hoof. Fire rose from the stone. He drew back his hoof and smoke curled about it. There was no mark upon the stair to indicate where he had touched.

"I fear I cannot enter this place and preserve my form," he stated. "At the least, my form."

"What compels thee?"

"An ancient enchantment to preserve this place against the assault of any such as I."

"Can it be undone?"

"Not by any creature which walks this world, or flies above it or writhes beneath it, or I'm a horse. Though the seas some day rise and cover the land, this place will exist at their bottom. This was torn from Chaos by Order in the days when those Principles stalked the land, naked, just beyond the hills. Whoever compelled them was one of the First, and powerful even in terms of the Mighty."

"Then I must go alone."

"Perhaps not. One is approaching even now with whom you had best wait and parley."

Dilvish waited, and a single horseman emerged from a distant street and advanced upon them.

"Greetings," called the rider, raising his right hand, open.

"Greetings." Dilvish returned the gesture.

The man dismounted. His costume was deep violet in colour, the hood thrown back, the cloak all-engulfing. He bore no visible arms.

"Why stand you here before the Citadel of Rahoring?" he asked.

"Why stand you here to ask me, priest of Babrigore?" said Dilvish, and not ungently.

"I am spending the time of a moon in this place of death, to dwell upon the ways of evil. It is to prepare myself as head of my temple."

"You are young to be head of a temple."

The priest shrugged and smiled. "Few come to Rahoringhast," he observed.

"Small wonder," did Dilvish reply. "I trust I shall not remain here long."

"Were you planning on entering this – place?" He gestured.

"I was, and am."

The man was half a head shorter than Dilvish, and it was impossible to guess at his form beneath the robes he wore. His eyes were blue and he was swarthy of complexion. A mole on his left eyelid danced when he blinked.

"Let me beg you reconsider this action," he stated. "It would be unwise to enter this building."

"Why is that?"

"It is said that it is still guarded within by the ancient warders of its lord."

"Have you ever been inside?"

"Yes."

"Were you troubled by any ancient wardens?"

"No, but as a priest of Babrigore I am under the protection of – of – Jelerak."

Dilvish spat. "May his flesh be flayed from his bones and its life yet remain."

The priest dropped his eyes.

"Though he fought the creature which dwelled within this place," said Dilvish, "he became as foul himself afterwards."

"Many of his deeds do lie like stains upon the land," said the priest, "but he was not always such a one. He was a white wizard who matched his powers against the Dark One, in days when the world was young. He was not sufficient. He fell. He was taken as servant by the Maleficent. For centuries he endured this bondage, until it changed him, as such must. He, too, came to glory in the ways of darkness. But then, when Selar of the Unseen Blade bought the life of Hohorga with his own, Jel – he fell as if dead and lay as such for the space of a week. Near-delirious, when he awakened he worked with counterspell at one last act of undoing: to free the cursed legions of Shoredan. He essayed that thing. He did. He stood upon this very stairway for two days and two nights, until the blood mingled with the perspiration on his brow, but he could not break the hold of Hohorga. Even dead, the dark strength was too great for him. Then he wandered mad about the countryside, until he was taken in and cared for by the priests of Babrigore. Afterwards, he lapsed back into the ways he had learned, but he has always been kindly disposed towards the Order which cared for him. He has never asked anything more of us. He has sent us food in times of famine. Speak no evil of him in my presence."

Dilvish spat again. "May he thrash in the darkness of darknesses for the ages of ages, and may his name be cursed for ever."

The priest looked away from the sudden blaze in his eyes. "What want you in Rahoring?" he asked, finally.

"To go within – and do a thing."

"If you must, then I shall accompany you. Perhaps my protection shall also extend to yourself."

"I do not solicit your protection, priest."

"The asking is not necessary."

"Very well. Come with me then."

He started up the stairway.

"What is that thing you ride?" asked the priest, gesturing back. "Like a horse in form, but now it is a statue."

Dilvish laughed. "I, too, know something of the ways of darkness, but my terms with it are my own."

"No man may have special terms with darkness."

"Tell it to a dweller in the Houses of Pain, priest. Tell it to a statue. Tell it to one who is all of the race of men! Tell it not to me."

"What is your name?"

"Dilvish. What is yours?"

"Korel. I shall speak to you no more of darkness then, Dilvish, but I will still go with you into Rahoring."

"Then stand not talking." Dilvish turned and continued upward.

Korel followed him.

When they had gone halfway, the daylight began to grow dim about them. Dilvish looked back. All he could see was the stairway leading down and down, back. There was nothing else in the world but the stairs. With each step upward, the darkness grew.

"Did it happen thus when last you entered this place?" he asked.

"No," said Korel.

They reached the top of the stair and stood before the dim portal. By then it was as though night lay upon the land.

They entered.

A sound, as of music, came from far ahead and there was a flickering light within. Dilvish laid his hand upon the hilt of his sword. The priest whispered to him: "It will do you no good."

They moved up the passageway and came at length into a vacant hall. Braziers spewed flame from high sockets in the walls. The ceiling was lost in shadow and smoke.

They crossed that hall to where a wide stair led up into a blaze of light and sound.

Korel looked back. "It begins with the light," said he, "all this

newness," gesturing. "The outer passage bore only rubble and
. . . dust . . ."

"What else is the matter?" Dilvish looked back.

Only one set of footprints led into the hall through the dust.
Dilvish then laughed, saying: "I tread lightly."

Korel studied him. Then he blinked and his mole jerked across
his eye.

"When I entered here before," he said, "there were no sounds,
no torches. Everything lay empty and still, ruined. Do you know
what is happening?"

"Yes," said Dilvish, "for I read of it in the Green Books of
Time at the Keep of Mirata. Know, oh priest of Babrigore, that
within the hall above the ghosts do play at being ghosts. Know,
too, that Hohorga dies again and again so long as I stand within
this place."

As he spoke the name Hohorga a great cry was heard within the
high hall. Dilvish raced up the stairs, the priest rushing after him.

Now, within the halls of Rahoring there came up a mighty
wailing.

They stood at the top of the stairs, Dilvish like a statue, blade
half drawn from its sheath; Korel, hands within his sleeves,
praying after the manner of his order.

The remains of a great feast were strewn about the hall; the
light came down out of the air from coloured globes which circled
like planets through the great heaven-design within the vaulted
ceiling; the throne on the high dais beside the far wall was empty.
That throne was too large for any of this age to occupy. The walls
were covered all over with ancient devices, strange, on alternate
slabs of white and orange marble. In the pillars of the wall were
set gems the size of doubled fists, burning yellow and emerald,
infra-ruby and ultra-blue, casting a fire-radiance, transparent
and illuminating, as far as the steps to the throne. The canopy of
the throne was wide and all of white gold, worked in the manner
of mermaids and harpies, dolphins and goat-headed snakes; it was
supported by wyvern, hippogriff, fire-drake, chimaera, unicorn,
cockatrice, griffin and pegasus, sejant erect. It belonged to the
one who lay dying upon the floor.

In the form of a man, but half again as large, Hohorga lay upon the tiles of his palace and his intestines filled his lap. He was supported by three of his Guard, while the rest attended to his slayer. It had been said in the Books of Time that Hohorga the Maleficent was indescribable. Dilvish saw that this was both true and untrue.

He was fair to look upon and noble of feature; but so blindingly fair was he that all eyes were averted from that countenance now lined with pain. A faint bluish halo was diminishing about his shoulders. Even in the death-pain he was as cold and perfect as a carved gemstone set upon the red-green cushion his blood; his was the hypnotic perfection of a snake of many colours. It is said that eyes have no expression of their own, and that one could not reach into a barrel of eyes and separate out those of an angry man or those of one's beloved.

Hohorga's eyes were the eyes of a ruined god: infinitely sad, as proud as an ocean of lions.

One look and Dilvish knew this thing, though he could not tell their colour.

Hohorga was of the blood of the First.

The guards had cornered the slayer. He fought them, apparently empty-handed, but parrying and thrusting as though he gripped a blade. Wherever his hand moved, there were wounds.

He wielded the only weapon which might have slain the King of the World, who permitted none to go armed in his presence, save for his own Guard.

He bore the Invisible Blade.

He was Selar, first of the Elvish House of that name, great-gone sire of Dilvish, who at that moment cried out his name.

Dilvish drew his blade and rushed across the hall. He cut at the attackers, but his blade passed through them as through smoke.

They beat down Selar's guard. A mighty blow sent something unseen ringing across the hall. Then they dismembered him, slowly, Selar of Shoredan, as Dilvish wept, watching.

And then Hohorga spoke, in a voice held firm though soft, without inflection, like the steady beating of surf or the hooves of horses.

"I have outlived the one who presumed to lay hands upon me, which is as it must be. Know that it was written that eyes would never see the blade that could slay me. Thus do the Powers have their jokes. Much of what I have done shall never be undone, O children of men and elves and salamanders. Much more than you know do I take with me from this world into the Silence. You have slain that which was greater than yourselves, but do not be proud. It matters no longer to me. Nothing does. Have my curses."

Those eyes closed and there was a clap of thunder.

Dilvish and Korel stood alone in the darkened ruins of a great hall.

"Why did this thing appear today?" asked the priest.

"When one of the blood of Selar enters here," said Dilvish, "it is re-enacted."

"Why have you come here, Dilvish, son of Selar?"

"To ring the Bells of Shoredan."

"It cannot be."

"If I am to save Dilfar and re-deliver Portaroy it *must* be.

"I go now to seek the bells," he said.

He crossed through the near-blackness of night without stars, for neither were his eyes the eyes of men, and he was accustomed to much dark.

He heard the priest following after him.

They circled behind the broken bulk of the Earth-Lord's throne. Had there been sufficient light as they passed, they would have seen darkened spots upon the floor turning to stain, then crisp sand-brown, and then to red-green blood, or something like blood, as Dilvish moved near them, and vanishing once again as he moved away.

Behind the dais was the door to the central tower. Fevera Mirata, Queen of Illusion, had once shown Dilvish this hall in a mirror the size of six horsemen riding abreast, and broidered about with a frame of golden daffodils which hid their heads till it cleared of all save their reflections.

Dilvish opened the door and halted. Smoke billowed forth, engulfing him. He was seized with coughing but he kept his guard before him.

"It is the Warden of the Bells!" cried Korel. "Jelerak deliver us!"

"Damn Jelerak!" said Dilvish. "I'll deliver myself!"

But as he spoke, the cloud swirled away and spun itself into a glowing tower that held the doorway, illuminating the throne and the places about the throne. Two red eyes glowed within the smoke.

Dilvish passed his blade through and through the cloud, meeting with no resistance.

"If you remain incorporeal, I shall pass through you," he called out. "If you take a shape, I shall dismember it. Make your choice," and he said it in Mabrahoring, the language spoken in hell.

"Deliverer, Deliverer, Deliverer," hissed the cloud, "my pet Dilvish, little creature of hooks and chains. Do you not know your master? Is your memory so short?" and the cloud collapsed upon itself and coalesced into a bird-headed creature with the hindquarters of a lion and two serpents growing up from its shoulders, curling and engendering about its high crest of flaming quills.

"Cal-den!"

"Aye, your old tormentor, Elf-man. I have missed you, for few depart my care. It is time you returned."

"This time," said Dilvish, "I am not chained and unarmed, and we meet in my world," and he cut forward with his blade, striking the serpent head from Cal-den's left shoulder.

A piercing bird-cry filled the hall and Cal-den sprang forward. Dilvish struck at his breast but the blade was turned aside, leaving only a smallish gash from which a pale liquor flowed.

Cal-den struck him then backwards against the dais, catching his blade in a black claw, shattering it, and he raised his other arm to smite him. Dilvish did then stab upwards with what remained of the sword, nine inches of jagged length.

It caught Cal-den beneath the jaw, entering there and remaining, the hilt torn from Dilvish's hand as the tormentor shook his head, roaring.

Then was Dilvish seized about the waist so that his bones did sigh and creak within him. He felt himself raised into the air, the serpent tearing at his ear, claws piercing his sides. Cal-den's face was turned up towards him, wearing the hilt of his blade like a beard of steel.

Then did he hurl Dilvish across the dais, so as to smash him against the tiles of the floor.

But the wearer of the green boots of Elfland may not fall or be thrown to land other than on his feet.

Dilvish did recover him then, but the shock of his landing caused pain in the thigh wound he bore. His leg collapsed beneath him, so that he put out his hand to the side.

Cal-den did then spring upon him, smiting him sorely about the head and shoulders. From somewhere, Korel hurled a stone which struck upon the demon's crest.

Dilvish scrambled backwards, until his hand came upon a thing in the rubble which drew the blood from it.

A blade.

He snatched at the hilt and brought it up off the floor with a side-armed cut that struck Cal-den across the back, stiffening him into a bellow that near burst the ears to hear. Smoke arose from the wound.

Dilvish stood, and saw that he held nothing.

Then did he know that the blade of his ancestor, which no eyes may look upon, had come to him from the ruins where it had lain across the ages, to serve him, scion of the House of Selar, in this moment of his need.

He directed it towards the breast of Cal-den.

"My rabbit, you are unarmed, yet you have cut me," said the creature. "Now shall we return to the Houses of Pain."

They both lunged forward.

"I always knew," said Cal-den, "that my little Dilvish was something special," and he fell to the floor with an enormous crash and the smokes arose from his body.

Dilvish placed his heel upon the carcass and wrenched free the blade outlined in steaming ichor.

"To you, Selar, do I owe this victory," he said, and raised a length of smouldering nothingness in salute. Then he sheathed the sword.

Korel was at his side. He watched as the creature at their feet vanished like embers and ice, leaving behind a stench that was most foul to smell.

Dilvish turned him again to the door of the tower and entered there, Korel at his side.

The broken bell-pull lay at his feet. It fell to dust when he touched it with his toe.

"It is said," he told Korel, "that the bell-pull did break in the hands of the last to ring it, half an age ago."

He raised his eyes, and there was only darkness above him.

"The legions of Shoredan did set forth to assault the Citadel of Rahoring," said the priest, as though reading it from some old parchment, "and word of their movement came soon to the King of the World. Then did he lay upon three bells cast in Shoredan a weird. When these bells were rung a great fog came over the land and engulfed the columns of marchers and those on horseback. The fog did disperse upon the second ringing of the bells, and the land was found to be empty of the troop. It was later written by Merda, Red Wizard of the South, that somewhere still do these marchers and horsemen move, through regions of eternal fog. 'If these bells be rung again by a hand of that House which despatched the layer of the weird, then will these legions come forth from a mist to serve that one for a time in battle. But when they have served, they will vanish again into the places of gloom, where they will continue their march upon a Rahoringhast which no longer exists. How they may be freed to rest, this thing is not known. One mightier than I has tried and failed.' "

Dilvish bowed his head a moment, then he felt the walls. They were not like the outer walls. They were cast of blocks of that same material, and between those blocks were scant crevices wherein his fingers found purchase.

He raised himself above the floor and commenced to climb, the soft green boots somehow finding toeholds wherever they struck.

The air was hot and stale, and showers of dust descended upon him each time he raised an arm above his head.

He pulled himself upwards, until he counted a hundred such movements and the nails of his hands were broken. Then he clung to the wall like a lizard, resting, and felt the pains of his last encounter burning like suns within him.

He breathed the fetid air and his head swam. He thought of the Portaroy he had once delivered, long ago, the city of friends, the place where he had once been feted, the land whose need for him had been strong enough to free him from the Houses of Pain and break the grip of stone upon his body; and he thought of that Portaroy in the hands of the Colonel of the West, and he thought of Dilfar now resisting that Lylish who might sweep the bastions of the east before him.

He climbed once again.

His head touched the metal lip of a bell.

He climbed around it, bracing himself on the crossbars which now occurred.

There were three bells suspended from a single axle.

He set his back against the wall and clung to the crossbars, placing his feet upon the middle bell.

He pushed, straightening his legs.

The axle protested, creaking and grinding within its sockets.

But the bell moved, slowly. It did not return, however, but stayed in the position into which it had been pushed.

Cursing, he worked his way through the crossbars and over to the opposite side of the belfry.

He pushed it back and it stuck on the other side. All the bells moved with the axle, though.

Nine times more did he cross over in darkness to push at the bells.

Then they moved more easily.

Slowly, they fell back as he released the pressure of his legs. He pushed them out again and they returned again. He pushed them again, and again.

A click came from one of the bells as the clapper struck. Then another. Finally, one of them rang.

He kicked out harder and harder, and then did the bells swing free and fill the tower about him with a pealing which vibrated the roots of his teeth and filled his ears with pain. A storm of dust came down over him and his eyes were full of tears. He coughed and closed them. He let the bells grow still.

Across some mighty distance he thought he heard the faint winding of a horn.

He began the downward climb.

"Lord Dilvish," said Korel, when he had reached the floor. "I have heard the blowing of horns."

"Yes," said Dilvish.

"I have a flask of wine with me. Drink."

Dilvish rinsed his mouth and spat, then drank three mighty swallows.

"Thank you, priest. Let us be gone from here now."

They crossed through the hall once more and descended the inner stair. The smaller hall was now unlighted and lay in ruin. They made their way out, Dilvish leaving no tracks to show where he had gone; and halfway down the stairs the darkness departed from them.

Through the bleak day that now clung to the land, Dilvish looked back along the Way of the Armies. A mighty fog filled the air far beyond the broken gates, and from within that fog there came again the notes of the horn and the sounds of the movements of troops. Almost, Dilvish could see the outlines of the columns of marchers and riders, moving, moving, but not advancing.

"My troops await me," said Dilvish upon the stair. "Thank you, Korel, for accompanying me."

"Thank you, Lord Dilvish. I came to this place to dwell upon the ways of evil. You have shown me much that I may meditate upon."

They descended the final stairs. Dilvish brushed dust from his garments and mounted Black.

"One thing more, Korel, priest of Babrigore," he said. "If you ever meet with your patron, who should provide you much more evil to meditate upon than you have seen here, tell him that, when all the battles have been fought, his statue will come to kill him."

The mole danced as Korel blinked up at him. "Remember," he replied, "that once he wore a mantle of light."

Dilvish laughed, and the eyes of his mount glowed red through the gloom. "There!" he said, gesturing. "There is your sign of his goodness and light!"

Nine black doves circled in the heavens.

Korel bowed his head and did not answer.

"I go now to lead my legions."

Black reared on steel hooves and laughed along with his rider.

Then they were gone, up the Way of the Armies, leaving the Citadel of Rahoring and the priest of Babrigore behind them in the gloom.

𝕬 𝕳𝖊𝖗𝖔 𝖆𝖙 𝖙𝖍𝖊 𝕲𝖆𝖙𝖊𝖘

Tanith Lee

Heroic fantasy hasn't entirely been the domain of male writers. Back in the 1930s Catherine L. Moore produced a wonderfully innovative series featuring the warrior woman, Jirel of Joiry, and later Leigh Brackett and Marion Zimmer Bradley virtually cornered the market in planetary romances. Tanith Lee (b. 1947) writes material in the entire range of fantasy fiction, and she is almost impossible to define. She began with books for children, such as The Dragon Hoard *(1971) and* Animal Castle *(1972). Her first adult book,* The Birthgrave *(1975), about a woman searching for her true name, blended the fields of sword-and-sorcery and planetary romance.* The Flat Earth *series, which began with* Night's Master *(1978), mixes the oriental and the exotic in almost Dunsanian tradition. The collection* Red as Blood *(1983) reworks well-known fairy tales in darker mode while* Sung in Shadow *(1983) takes us back to a Shakespearean Renaissance Italy. And there's a lot more. The following comes from Lee's collection* Cyrion *(1982) about a wandering hero who is not quite as traditional as he might at first seem.*

T HE CITY LAY IN THE MIDST OF THE DESERT.

At the onset it could resemble a mirage; next, one of the giant mesas that were the teeth of the desert, filmy blue with distance and heat. But Cyrion had found the road which led to the city, and taking the road, presently the outline of the place came clear. High walls and higher towers within, high gates of hammered bronze. And above, the high and naked desert sky, that reflected back from its sounding-bowl no sound at all from the city, and no smoke.

Cyrion stood and regarded the city. He was tempted to believe it a desert too, one of those hulks of men's making, abandoned centuries ago as the sands of the waste crept to their threshold. Certainly, the city was old. Yet it had no aspect of neglect, none of the indefinable melancholy of the unlived-in house.

Intuitively, Cyrion knew that as he stood regarding the city from without, so others stood noiselessly within, regarding Cyrion.

What did they perceive? This: a young man, tall and deceptively slim, deceptively elegant, which elegance itself was something of a surprise, for he had been months travelling in the desert, on the caravan routes and the rare and sand-blown roads. He wore the loose dark clothing of a nomad, but with the generous hood thrust back to show he did not have a nomad's pigmentation. At his side a sword was sheathed in red leather. The sunlight struck a silver-gold burnish on the pommel of the sword that was also the colour of his hair. His left hand was mailed in rings which apparently no bandit had been able to relieve him of. If the watchers in the city had remarked that Cyrion was as handsome as the Arch-Demon himself, they would not have been the first to do so.

Then there came the booming scraping thunder of two bronze gates unbarred and dragged inward on their runners. The way into the city was exposed – yet blocked now by a crowd. Silent they were, and clad in black, the men and the women; even the children. And their faces were all the same, and gazed at Cyrion in the same way. They gazed at him as if he were the last bright day of their lives, the last bright coin in the otherwise empty coffer.

The sense of his dynamic importance to them was so strong that Cyrion swept the crowd a low, half-mocking bow. As he swept the bow, from his keen eyes' corner, Cyrion saw a man walk through the crowd and come out of the gate.

The man was as tall as Cyrion. He had a hard face, tanned but sallow, wings of black hair beneath a shaved crown, and a collar of swarthy gold set with gems. But his gaze also clung on Cyrion. It was like a lover's look. Or the starving lion's as it beholds the deer.

"Sir," said the black-haired man, "what brings you to this, our city?"

Cyrion gestured lazily with the ringed left hand. "The nomads have a saying: 'After a month in the desert, even a dead tree is an object of wonder.'"

"Only curiosity, then," said the man.

"Curiosity; hunger; thirst; loneliness; exhaustion," enlarged Cyrion. By looking at Cyrion, few would think him affected by any of these things.

"Food we will give you, drink and rest. Our story we may not give. To satisfy the curious is not our fate. Our fate is darker and more savage. We await a saviour. We await him in bondage."

"When is he due?" Cyrion enquired.

"You, perhaps, are he."

"Am I? You flatter me. I have been called many things, never saviour."

"Sir," said the black-haired man, "do not jest at the wretched trouble of this city, nor at its solitary hope."

"No jest," said Cyrion, "but I hazard you wish some service of me. Saviours are required to labour, I believe, in behalf of their people. What do you want? Let us get it straight."

"Sir," said the man, "I am Memled, prince of this city."

"Prince, but not saviour?" interjected Cyrion, his eyes widening with the most insulting astonishment.

Memled lowered his gaze. "If you seek to shame me with that, it is your right. But you should know, I am prevented by circumstance."

"Oh, indeed. Naturally."

"I bear your gibe without complaint. I ask again if you will act for the city."

"And I ask you again what I must do."

Memled raised his lids and directed his glance at Cyrion once more. "We are in the thrall of a monster, a demon-beast. It dwells in the caverns beneath the city, but at night it roves at will. It demands the flesh of our men to eat; it drinks the blood of our women and our children. It is protected through ancient magic, by a pact made a hundred years before between the princes of the city (cursed be they!) and the hordes of the Fiend. None born of the city has power to slay the beast. Yet there is a prophecy. A stranger, a hero who ventures to our gates, will have the power."

"And how many heroes," said Cyrion gently, "have you persuaded to an early death with this enterprise, you and your demon-beast?"

"I will not lie to you. Upward of a score. If you turn aside, no one here will speak ill of you. Your prospects of success would be slight, should you set your wits and sword against the beast. And our misery is nothing to you."

Cyrion ran his eyes over the black-clad crowd. The arid faces were all still fixed towards his. The children, like miniature adults, just as arid, immobile, noiseless. If the tale were true, they had learned the lessons of fear and sorrow early, nor would they live long to enjoy their lessoning.

"Other than its dietary habits," Cyrion said, "what can you tell me of your beast?"

Memled shivered. His sallowness increased. "I can reveal no more. It is a part of the foul sorcery that binds us. We may say nothing to aid you, do nothing to aid you. Only pray for you, if you should decide to pit your skill against the devil."

Cyrion smiled. "You have a cool effrontery, my friend, that is altogether delightful. Inform me then merely of this. If I conquer your beast, what reward is there – other, of course, than the blessing of your people?"

"We have our gold, our silver, our jewels. You may take them all away with you, or whatever you desire. We crave safety, not wealth. Our wealth has not protected us from horror and death."

"I think we have a bargain," said Cyrion. He looked at the children again. "Providing the treasury tallies with your description."

*   *   *

It was noon, and the desert sun poured its merciless light upon the city. Cyrion walked in the company of Prince Memled and his guard – similarly black-clad men, but with weighty blades and daggers at their belts, none, presumably, ever stained by beast-blood. The crowd moved circumspectly in the wake of their prince. Only the rustle of feet shuffling the dust was audible, and no speech. Below the bars of overhanging windows, here and there, a bird cage had been set out in the violet shade. The birds in the cages did not sing.

They reached a market-place, sun-bleached, unpeopled and without merchandise of any sort. A well at the market's centre proclaimed the water which would, in the first instance, have caused the building of a city here. Further evidence of water lay across from the market, where a broad stairway, flanked by stone columns, led to a massive battlemented wall and doors of bronze this time plated by pure flashing gold. Over the wall-top, the royal house showed its peaks and pinnacles, and the heads of palm trees. There was a green perfume in the air, heady as incense in the desert.

The crowd faltered in the market-place. Memled, and his guard conducted Cyrion up the stairway. The gold-plated doors were opened. They entered a cool palace, blue as an under-sea cave, buzzing with slender fountains, sweet with the scent of sun-scorched flowers.

Black-garmented servants brought chilled wine. The food was poor and did not match the wine. Had the flocks and herds gone to appease the demon-beast? Cyrion had spied not a goat nor a sheep in the city. For that matter, not a dog, nor even the sleek lemon cats and striped marmosets rich women liked to nurse instead of babies.

After the food and drink, Memled, near wordless yet courteous, led Cyrion to a treasury where wealth lay as thick as dust, and spilling on the ground.

"I would have thought," said Cyrion, fastidiously investigating ropes of pearls and chains of rubies, "such stuff might have bought you a hero, had you sent for one."

"This, too, is our limitation. We may not send. He must come to us, by accident."

"As the nomads say," said Cyrion, charmingly, innocently, "'No man knows the wall better than he who built it.'"

At that instant, something thundered in the guts of the world. It was a fearful bellowing cacophony. It sounded hot with violence and the lust for carnage. It was like a bull, or a pen of bulls, with throats of brass and sinews of molten iron, roaring in concert underground. The floor shook a little. A sapphire tumbled from its heap and fell upon another heap below.

Cyrion seemed interested rather than disturbed.

Certainly, there was nothing more than interest in his voice as he asked Prince Memled: "Can that be your beast, contemplating tonight's dinner?"

Memled's face took on an expression of the most absolute anguish and despair. His mouth writhed. He uttered a sudden sharp cry, as if a dreaded, well-remembered pain had seized him. He shut his eyes.

Intrigued, Cyrion observed: "It is fact then, you cannot speak of it? Calm yourself, my friend. It speaks very ably for itself."

Memled covered his face with his hands, and turned away.

Cyrion walked out through the door. Presently, pallid, but sufficiently composed, Memled followed his hero-guest. Black guards closed the treasury.

"Now," said Cyrion, "since I cannot confront your beast until it emerges from its caverns by night, I propose to sleep. My journey through the desert has been arduous, and, I am sure you agree, freshness in combat is essential."

"Sir," said Memled, "the palace is at your disposal. But, while you sleep, I and some others shall remain at your side."

Smiling, Cyrion assured him, "Indeed, my friend, you and they will not."

"Sir, it is best you are not left alone. Forgive my insistence."

"What danger is there? The beast is no threat till the sun goes down. There are some hours yet."

Memled seemed troubled. He spread his hand, indicating the city beyond the palace walls. "You are a hero, sir. Certain of the people may bribe the guard. They may enter the palace and disrupt your rest with questions and clamour."

"It seemed to me," said Cyrion, "your people are uncommonly quiet. But if not, they are welcome. I sleep deeply. I doubt if anything would wake me till sunset, when I trust you, Prince, or another, will do so."

Memled's face, such an index of moods, momentarily softened with relief. "That deeply do you sleep? Then I will agree to let you sleep alone. Unless, perhaps a girl might be sent to you?"

"You are too kind. However, I decline the girl. I prefer to select my own ladies, after a fight rather than before."

Memled smiled his own stiff and rusty smile. Behind his eyes, sluggish currents of self-dislike, guilt and shame stirred cloudily.

The doors were shut on the sumptuous chamber intended for Cyrion's repose. Aromatics burned in silver bowls. The piercing afternoon sun was excluded behind shutters of painted wood and embroidered draperies. Beyond the shut doors, musicians made sensuous low music on pipes, drums and ghirzas. All was conducive to slumber. Though not to Cyrian's.

In contrast to his words, he was a light sleeper. In the city of the beast, he had no inclination to sleep at all. Privacy was another case. Having secured the chamber doors on the inside, he prowled soundlessly, measuring the room for its possibilities. He prised open a shutter, and scanned across the blistering roofs of the palace into the dry green palm shade of the gardens.

All about, the city kept its tongueless vigil. Cyrion thoughtfully felt of its tension. It was like a great single heart, poised between one beat and the next. A single heart, or two jaws about to snap together—

"Cyrion," said a voice urgently.

To see him spin about was to discover something of the nature of Cyrion. A nonchalant idler at the window one second, a coiled spring let fly the split second after. The sword was ready in his bare right hand. He had drawn too fast almost for a man's eye to register. Yet he was not even breathing quickly. And, finding the vacant chamber before him, as he had left it, no atom altered in his stance.

"Cyrion," cried the voice again, out of nothing and nowhere. "I pray heaven you had the cunning to lie to them, Cyrion."

Cyrion appeared to relax his exquisite vigilance. He had not.

"Heaven, no doubt, enjoys your prayers," he said. "And am I to enjoy the sight of you?"

The voice was female, expressive and very beautiful.

"I am in a prison," said the voice. There was the smallest catch in it, swiftly mastered. "I speak to warn you. Do not credit them, Cyrion."

Cyrion began to move about the room. Casually and delicately he lifted aside the draperies with his sword.

"They offered me a girl," he said reflectively.

"But they did not offer you certain death."

Cyrion had completed his circuit of the room. He looked amused and entertained.

He knelt swiftly, then stretched himself flat. A circular piece was missing in the mosaic pattern of the floor. He set one acute eye there and looked through into a dim area, lit by one murky source of light beyond his view. Directly below, a girl lay prone on the darkness which must itself be a floor, staring up at him from luminous wild eyes. In the half-glow she was more like a bloom of light herself than a reality; a trembling crystalline whiteness on the air, hair like the gold chains in the treasury, a face like that of a carved goddess, the body of a beautiful harlot before she gets in the trade – still virgin – and at her waist, her wrists, her ankles, drawn taut to pegs in the ground, iron chains.

"So there you are."

"It is a device of the stonework that enabled you to hear me and I you. In former days, princes would sit in your room above, drinking and making love, listening to the cries of those being tortured in this dungeon, and sometimes they would peer through to increase their pleasure. But either Memled has forgotten, or he thought me past crying out. I glimpsed your shadow pass over the aperture. Earlier, the jailor spoke your name to me. Oh, Cyrion, I am to die, and you with me."

She stopped, and tears ran like drops of silver from her wild eyes.

"You have a captive audience, lady," said Cyrion.

"It is this way," she whispered. "The beast they have pretended to seek rescue from is, in fact, the familiar demon of the city. They love the brute, and commit all forms of beastliness in its name. How else do you suppose they have amassed such stores of treasure, here in the wilderness? And once a year they honour the beast by giving to it a beautiful maiden and a notable warrior. I was to have been the bride of a rich and wise lord in a city by the sea. But I am thought beautiful; Memled heard of me. Men of this city attacked the caravan in which I rode, and carried me here, to this, where I have lingered a month. You arrived by unlucky destiny, unless some of Memled's sorcery enticed you here, unknowingly. Tonight, we shall share each other's fate."

"You are their prisoner, I am not. How do they plan to reconcile me to sacrifice?"

"That is but too simple. At dusk a hundred men will come. You do not seem afraid, but even fearless, before a hundred men you cannot prevail. They will take your sword, stun you, bind you. There is a trick door in the western wall that gives on a stairway. Through the door and down the stair they will thrust you. Below are the caverns where the beast roams, bellowing for blood. I too must pass that way to death."

"A fascinating tale," said Cyrion, "What prompts you to tell it me?"

"Are you not a hero?" the girl demanded passionately. "Have you not promised to slay the beast for them, to be their saviour, though admittedly in return for gold. Can you not instead be your own saviour, and mine?"

"Forgive me, lady," said Cyrion, in a tone verging subtly on naïveté, "I am at a loss. Besides, our dooms seem written with a firm hand. Perhaps we should accept them."

Cyrion rose from the mosaic. On his feet he halted, just aside from the hole.

After a moment, the girl screamed: "You are a coward, Cyrion. For all your looks and your fine sword, for all your nomad's garments, the wear of those they name the Lions of the Desert – for all that – *coward* and *fool*."

Cyrion seemed to be considering.

After a minute, he said amiably: "I suppose I might open the trick door now, and seek the monster of my own volition, sword in hand and ready. Then, if I slay him, I might return for you, and free you."

The girl wept. Through her tears she said, with a knife for a voice: "If you are a *man*, you will do it."

"Oh no, lady. Only if I am your notion of a man."

The stair was narrow, and by design lightlessly invisible – save that Cyrion had filched one of the scented tapers from the room above to give him eyes. The trick door had been easy to discover, an ornamental knob that turned, a slab that slid. Thirty steps down, he passed another kind of door, of iron, on his right. Faintly, beyond the door, he heard a girl weeping.

The stair descended through the western wall of the palace, and proceeded underground. Deep in the belly of the caverns that sprawled, as yet unseen, at the end of the stair, no ominous rumour was manifested. At length, the stair reached bottom, and ceased. Ahead stretched impenetrable black, and from the black an equally black and featureless silence.

Cyrion advanced, the taper held before him. The dark toyed with the taper, surrendering a miniature oasis of half-seen things, such as trunks of rock soaring up towards the ceiling. The dark mouthed Cyrion. It licked him, rolled him around on its tongue. The lit taper was just a garnish to its palate; it liked the light with Cyrion, as a man might like salt with his meat.

Then there came a huge wind from out of the nothing ahead. A metallic heated blast, as if from a furnace. Cyrion stopped, pondering. The beast, closeted in the caverns, had sighed? An instant after, it roared.

Above, in the treasury, the roaring had seemed to stagger the foundations of the house. Here, it peeled even the darkness, and dissected it like a fruit. The broken pieces of the dark rattled on the trunks of rock. Shards erupted from the rock and rained to the ground. The caverns thrummed, murmured, fell dumb. The dark did not re-congeal.

There was a new light. A flawless round of light, pale, smoky red. Then it blinked. Then there were two. Two flawless rounds of simmering raw rose. Two eyes.

Cyrion dropped the taper and put his heel on it.

This beast you witnessed by its own illumination. It swelled from the black as the eyes brightened with its interest. It was like no other beast; you could liken it to nothing else. It was like itself, unique. Only its size was comparable to anything. To a tower, a wall – one eye alone, that rosy window, could have fit tall Cyrion in its socket.

So radiant now, those eyes, the whole cavern was displayed, the mounting rocks, the floor piled with dusts, the dust curtains floating in the air. From the dust, the beast lifted itself. It gaped its mouth. Cyrion ducked, and the blast of burning though non-incendiary breath rushed over his head. It was not fetid breath, simply very hot. Cyrion planted his sword point down in the dust, and indolently leaned on it. He looked like a marvellous statue. For someone who could move like lightning, he had chosen now to become stone, and the pink fires settled on his pale hair, staining it the colour of diluted wine.

In this fashion Cyrion watched the demon-beast, by the light of its vast eyes, slink towards him. He watched, motionless, leaning on his sword.

Then a sinewy taloned forefoot, lengthy as a column, struck at him, and Cyrion was no longer in that spot, motionless, leaning on his sword, as he had been an instant before. Away in the shadow, Cyrion stood again unmoving, sword poised, negligently waiting. Again, the batting of scythefringed death; again missing him.

The jaws clashed, and slaver exploded forth, like a waterfall. Cyrion was gone, out of reach. Stone had returned to lightning. The fourth blow was his. He neither laughed at the seriousness of his mission nor frowned. No meditation was needed, the target no challenge, facile . . .

Cyrion swung back his arm, and sent the sword plummeting, like a straight white rent through the cavern. It met the beast's left eye, shattered it like pink glass, plunged to the brain.

Like a cat, Cyrion sprang to a ledge and crouched there.

Black ichor spouted to the cavern's top. Now, once more gradually, the light faded. The thunderous roaring ebbed like a colossal sea withdrawing from these dry caves beneath the desert.

On his ledge, Cyrion waited, pitiless and without triumph, for the beast, in inevitable stages, to fall, to be still, to die.

In the reiterated blackness, blind, but remembering infallibly his way, as he remembered all things, once disclosed, Cyrion went to the demon-beast and plucked out his sword, and returned with it up the pitchy stairway to the iron dungeon door set in the wall.

The iron door was bolted from without. He shot the bolts and pushed open the door.

He paused, just inside the prison, sword in hand, absorbing each detail. A stone box the prison was, described by dull fluttering torches. The girl lay on the floor, pegged and chained as he had regarded her through the peep-hole. He glanced towards the peep-hole, which was barely to be seen against the torch murk.

"Cyrion," the girl murmured, "the beast's black blood is on your sword, and you live."

Her white and lovely face was turned to him, the rich strands of golden hair swept across the floor, her silken breasts quivered to the tumult of her heart. Her tears fell again, but now her eyes were yielding. They showed no amazement or inquisition, only love.

He went to her, and, raising his sword a second time, chopped the head from her body.

Thirty steps up, a door crashed wide. Cyrion stooped gracefully, straightened, took the thirty steps in a series of fine-flexed leaps. He stepped through the trick door and was in the upper chamber, the sword yet stark in his bare right hand. And in his left hand, mailed with rings, a woman's head held by its shining hair.

Opposite, in the forced doorway of the chamber, Memled stared with a face like yellow cinders.

Then he collapsed on his knees, and behind him, the guards also dropped down.

Memled began to sob. The sobs were rough, racking him. He plainly could not keep them back, and his whole body shuddered.

Cyrion remained where he was, ignoring his bloody itinerary. Finally Memled spoke.

"After an eternity, heaven has heard our lament, replied to our entreaty. You, the hero of the city, after the eternity, our saviour. But we were bound by the hell-pact, and could neither warn nor advise you. How did you fathom the truth?"

"And what is the truth?" asked Cyrion, with unbelievable sweetness, as he stood between blotched blade and dripping head.

"The truth – that the monster is illusion set to deceive those heroes who would fight for us, set to deceive by the bitch-sorceress whose head you have lopped. Year in and out, she has drained us, roaming by night, feasting on the flesh and blood of my people, unrelenting and vile she-wolf that she was. And our fragile chance, a prophecy, the solitary weakness in the hell-pact – that only if a heroic traveller should come to the gates and agree to rid us of our torment, might we see her slain. But always she bewitched and duped these heroes, appearing in illusory shackles, lying that we would sacrifice her, sending each man to slay a phantom beast that did not exist save while her whim permitted it. And then the hero would go to her, trustingly, and she would seize him and murder him too. Over a score of champions we sent to their deaths in this manner, because we were bound and could not direct them where the evil lay. And so, again, sir hero, how did you fathom truth in this sink of witchery?"

"Small things," said Cyrion laconically.

"But you will list them for me?" Memled proffered his face, all wet with tears, and brimming now with a feverish joy.

"Her proximity to me, which seemed unlikely if she were what she claimed. Her extreme beauty which had survived a month's imprisonment and terror, and her wrists and ankles which were unchafed by her chains. That, a stranger to this place, she knew so much of its by-ways and its history. More interesting, that she knew so much of me – besides my name, which I did not see why a jailor should have given her – for instance, that I wore a nomad's garment, and that she thought me presentable, though she could not have seen me herself. She claimed she beheld my shadow pass over the peep-hole, but no more. She knew all our bargain, too, yours and mine, as if she had been listening to it. Would you hear more?"

"Every iota of it!"

"Then I will cite the beast, which patently was unreal. So huge a voice it could make the floors tremble, and yet the house was still intact. And the creature itself so untiny it could have shaken the city to flour, but confined in a cavern where it had not even stirred the dust. And then, the absence of bones, and its wholesome breath, meant to impress by volume and heat, and which smelled of nothing else. A cat which chews rats will have a fouler odour. And this thing, which supposedly ate men and drank their blood and was big enough to fill the air with stink, clean as a scoured pot on the stove. Lastly, I came above and saw the peep-hole would show nothing of what went on in this room, let alone a shadow passing. And I noticed too, the lady's sharp teeth, if you like."

Memled got to his feet.

Halfway to Cyrion, he checked and turned to the guards.

"Inform the city our terror has ended."

The guards, round-eyed, rushed away.

Memled came to Cyrion, glaring at the head, which Cyrion had prudently set down in a convenient bowl, and which was beginning to crumble to a sort of rank powder.

"We are free of her," Memled cried. "And the treasury is yours to despoil. Take all I have. Take – take this, the royal insignia of the city," and he clutched the collar of swarthy gold at his throat.

"Unnecessary," said Cyrion lightly. He wiped his sword upon a drapery. Memled paid no heed. Cyrion sheathed the sword. Memled smiled, still rusty, but his face vivid with excitement. "The treasury, then," suggested Cyrion.

Cyrion dealt cannily in the treasury. The light of day was gone by now, and by the smooth amber of the lamps, Cyrion chose from among the ropes of jewels and skeins of metal, from the cups and gemmy daggers, the armlets and the armour. Shortly, there was sufficient to weigh down a leather bag, which Cyrion slung upon his back. Memled would have pressed further gifts on him. Cyrion declined.

"As the nomads say," said Cyrion, " 'three donkeys cannot get their heads into the same bucket.' I have enough."

Outside in the city, now ablaze with windows under a sky ablaze with stars, songs and shouting of celebration rose into the cool hollow of the desert night.

"A night without blood and without horror," said Memled.

Cyrion walked down the palace stairway. Memled remained on the stair, his guards scattered loosely about him. In the market-place a fire burned, and there was dancing. The black clothes were all gone; the women had put on their finery and earrings sparkled and clinked as they danced together. The men drank, eyeing the women.

Near the edge of the group, two children poised like small stones, dressed in their best, and Cyrion saw their faces.

A child's face, incorrigible calendar of the seasons of the soul. Men learn pretence, if they must. A child has not had the space to learn.

Cyrion hesitated. He turned about, and strolled back towards the steps of the palace, and softly up the steps.

"One last thing, my friend, the prince," he called to Memled.

"What is that?"

Cyrion smiled. "You were too perfect and I did not quite see it, till just now a child showed me." Cyrion swung the bag from his shoulder exactly into Memled's belly. Next second the sword flamed to Cyrion's hand, and Memled's black-winged head hopped down the stair.

Around the fire, the dancers had left off dancing. The guards were transfixed in stammering shock, though no hand flew to a blade. Cyrion wiped his own blade, this time on Memled's already trembling torso.

"That one, too," said Cyrion.

"Yes, sir," said the nearest of the guard, thickly. "There were the two of them."

"And they diced nightly over who should batten on the city, did they not, your prince-demon and his doxy. He could not avoid the prophecy, either, of a hero at the gates. He was obliged to court me, and, in any event, reckoned the lady would deal with me as with the others. But when she did not, he was content I should have killed her, if he could escape me and keep the city for himself to feed him. He rendered himself straightly. He never once uttered for his own demonic side. He acted as a man, as Memled, the prince – fear and joy. He was too good. Yet I should never have been sure but for the children's agonized blankness down there, in the crowd."

"You are undeniably a hero, and heaven will bless you," said the guard. It was easy to see he was a true human man, and the rest of them were human too. Unpredictable and bizarre was their relief at rescue, as with all true men, who do not get their parts by heart beforehand, when to cry or when to grin.

Cyrion laughed low at the glittering sky. "Then bless me, heaven."

He went down the stair again. Both children were howling now, as they had not dared do formerly, untrammelled, healthy. Cyrion opened the leather bag, and released the treasure on the square, for adults and children alike to play with.

Empty-handed, as he came, Cyrion went away into the desert, under the stars.

Lady of the Skulls

Patricia A. McKillip

Like Ursula K. Le Guin and Tanith Lee, Patricia McKillip (b. 1948) was one of those authors who emerged in the wake of the Tolkien fantasy explosion and became popular, at least initially, for books written for a teenage market. With McKillip it was The Throme of the Erril of Sherill *(1973) followed by the wonderfully imaginative* The Forgotten Beasts of Eld *(1976), which won the very first World Fantasy Award. Since then McKillip has produced the Morgon of Hed trilogy, starting with* The Riddle-Master of Hed *(1976) – a series redolent of Tolkien and Le Guin – and the continuing Cygnet series, which began with* The Sorceress and the Cygnet *(1991). The following is one of McKillip's rare short stories.*

THE LADY SAW THEM RIDE ACROSS THE PLAIN: a company of six. Putting down her watering can, which was the bronze helm of some unfortunate knight, she leaned over the parapet, chin on her hand. They were all armed, their war-horses caparisoned; they glittered under the noon sun with silver-edged shields, jewelled bridles and sword hilts. What, she wondered as always in simple astonishment, did they imagine they had come to fight? She picked up the helm, poured water into a skull containing a miniature rose bush. The water came from within the tower, the only source on the entire barren, sun-cracked plain. The knights would ride around the tower under the hot sun for hours, looking for entry. At sunset, she would greet them, carrying water.

She sighed noiselessly, trowelling around the little rose bush with a dragon's claw. If they were too blind to find the tower door, why did they think they could see clearly within it? They, she thought in sudden impatience. They, they, they . . . they fed the plain with their bleached bones; they never learned . . .

A carrion-bird circled above her, counting heads. She scowled at it; it cried back at her, mocking. You, its black eye said, *never die. But you bring the dead to me.*

"They never listen to me," she said, looking over the plain again, her eyes prickling dryly. In the distance, lightning cracked apart the sky; purple clouds rumbled. But there was no rain in them, never any rain; the sky was as tearless as she. She moved from skull to skull along the parapet wall, watering things she had grown stubbornly from seeds that blew from distant, placid gardens in peaceful kingdoms. Some were grasses, weeds, or wildflowers. She did not care; she watered anything that grew.

The men below began their circling. Their mounts kicked up dust, snorting; she heard cursing, bewildered questions, then silence as they paused to rest. Sometimes they called her, pleading. But she could do nothing for them. They churned around the tower, bright, powerful, richly armed. She read the devices on their shields: three of Grenelief, one of Stoney Head, one of Dulcis Isle, one of Carnelaine. After a time, one man dropped out of the circle, stood back. His shield was simple: a red rose on white. Carnelaine, she thought, looking down at him, and then realized he was looking up at her.

He would see a puff of airy sleeve, a red geranium in an upside-down skull. Lady of the Skulls, they called her, clamouring to enter. Sometimes they were more courteous, sometimes less. She watered, waiting for this one to call her. He did not; he guided his horse into the tower's shadow and dismounted. He took his helm off, sat down to wait, burrowing idly in the ground and flicking stones as he watched her sleeve sometimes, and sometimes the distant storm.

Drawn to his calm, the others joined him finally, flinging off pieces of armour. They cursed the hard ground and sat, their voices drifting up to her in the windless air as she continued her watering.

Like others before them, they spoke of what the most precious thing of the legendary treasure might be, besides elusive. They had made a pact, she gathered: if one obtained the treasure, he would divide it among those left living. She raised a brow.

The one of Dulcis Isle, a dark-haired man wearing red jewels in his ears, said, "Anything of the dragon for me. They say it was a dragon's hoard, once. They say that dragon bones are wormholed with magic, and if you move one bone the rest will follow. The bones will bring the treasure with them."

"I heard," said the man from Stoney Head, "there is a well and a fountain rising from it, and when the drops of the fountain touch ground they turn to diamonds."

"Don't talk of water," one of the three thick-necked, nut-haired men of Grenelief pleaded. "I drank all mine."

"All we must do is find the door. There's water within."

"What are you going to do?" the man of Carnelaine asked. "Hoist the water on your shoulder and carry it out?"

The straw-haired man from Stoney Head tugged at his long moustaches. He had a plain, blunt, energetic voice devoid of any humour. "I'll carry it out in my mouth. When I come back alive for the rest of it, there'll be plenty to carry it in. Skulls, if nothing else. I heard there's a sorceress's cauldron, looks like a rusty old pot—"

"May be that," another of Grenelief said.

"May be, but I'm going for the water. What else could be most precious in this heat-blasted place?"

"That's a point," the man of Dulcis Isle said. Then: "But no, it's dragon bone for me."

"More to the point," the third of Grenelief said, aggrieved, "how do we get in the cursed place?"

"There's a lady up there watering plants," the man of Carnelaine said, and there were all their faces staring upwards, she could have tossed jewels into their open mouths. "She knows we're here."

"It's the Lady," they murmured, hushed.

"Lady of the Skulls."

"Does she have hair? I wonder."

"She's old as the tower. She must be a skull."

"She's beautiful," the man of Stoney Head said shortly. "They always are, the ones who lure, the ones who guard, the ones who give death."

"Is it her tower?" the one of Carnelaine asked. "Or is she trapped?"

"What's the difference? When the spell is gone, so will she be. She's nothing real, just a piece of the tower's magic."

They shifted themselves as the tower shadow shifted. The Lady took a sip of water out of the helm, then dipped her hand in it and ran it over her face. She wanted to lean over the edge and shout at them all: Go home, you silly, brainless fools. If you know so much, what are you doing here sitting on bare ground in front of a tower without a door waiting for a woman to kill you? They moved to one side of the tower, she to the other, as the sun climbed down the sky. She watched the sun set. Still the men refused to leave, though they had not a stick of wood to burn against the dark. She sighed her noiseless sigh and went down to greet them.

The fountain sparkled in the midst of a treasure she had long ceased to notice. She stepped around gold armour, black, gold-rimmed dragon bones, the white bones of princes. She took the plain silver goblet beside the rim of the well, and dipped it into the water, feeling the cooling mist from the little fountain. The man of Dulcis Isle was right about the dragon bones. The doorway was the dragon's open yawning maw, and it was invisible by day.

The last ray of sunlight touched the bone, limned a black, toothed opening that welcomed the men. Mute, they entered, and she spoke.

"You may drink the water, you may wander throughout the tower. If you make no choice, you may leave freely. Having left, you may never return. If you choose, you must make your choice by sunset tomorrow. If you choose the most precious thing in the tower, you may keep all that you see. If you choose wrongly, you will die before you leave the plain."

Their mouths were open again, their eyes stunned at what hung like vines from the old dragon's bones, what lay heaped upon the floor. Flicking, flicking, their eyes came across her finally, as she stood patiently holding the cup. Their eyes stopped at her: a tall, broad-shouldered, barefoot woman in a coarse white linen smock, her red hair bundled untidily on top of her head, her long skirt still splashed with the wine she had spilled in the tavern so long ago. In the torchlight it looked like blood.

They chose to sleep, as they always did, tired by the long journey, dazed by too much rich, vague colour in the shadows. She sat on the steps and watched them for a little. One cried in his sleep. She went to the top of the tower after a while, where she could watch the stars. Under the moon, the flowers turned odd, secret colours, as if their true colours blossomed in another land's daylight, and they had left their pale shadows behind by night. She fell asleep naming the moon's colours.

In the morning, she went down to see who had had sense enough to leave.

They were all still there, searching, picking, discarding among the treasures on the floor, scattered along the spiralling stairs. Shafts of light from the narrow windows sparked fiery colours that constantly caught their eyes, made them drop what they had, reach out again. Seeing her, the one from Dulcis Isle said, trembling, his eyes stuffed with riches, "May we ask questions? What is this?"

"Don't ask her, Marlebane," the one from Stoney Head said brusquely. "She'll lie. They all do."

She stared at him. "I will only lie to you," she promised. She took the small treasure from the hand of the man from Dulcis Isle. "This is an acorn made of gold. If you swallow it, you will speak all the languages of humans and animals."

"And this?" one of Grenelief said eagerly, pushing next to her, holding something of silver and smoke.

"That is a bracelet made of a dragon's nostril bone. The jewel in it is its petrified eye. It watches for danger when you wear it."

The man of Carnelaine was playing a flute made from a wizard's thigh bone. His eyes, the odd grey-green of the dragon's eye, looked dream-drugged with the music. The man of Stoney Head shook him roughly.

"Is that your choice, Ran?"

"No." He lowered the flute, smiling. "No, Corbeil."

"Then drop it before it seizes hold of you and you choose it. Have you seen yet what you might take?"

"No. Have you changed your mind?"

"No." He looked at the fountain, but, prudent, did not speak.

"Bram, look at this," said one brother of Grenelief to another. "Look!"

"I am looking, Yew."

"Look at it! Look at it, Ustor! Have you ever seen such a thing? Feel it! And watch: it vanishes, in light."

He held a sword; its hilt was solid emerald, its blade like water falling in clear light over stone. The Lady left them, went back up the stairs, her bare feet sending gold coins and jewels spinning down through the cross-hatched shafts of light. She stared at the place on the horizon where the flat dusty gold of the plain met the parched dusty sky. Go, she thought dully. Leave all this and go back to the places where things grow. Go, she willed them, go go, go, with the beat of her heart's blood. But no one came out the door beneath her. Someone, instead, came up the stairs.

"I have a question," said Ran of Carnelaine.

"Ask."

"What is your name?"

She had all but forgotten; it came to her again, after a beat of surprise. "Amaranth." He was holding a black rose in one hand, a silver lily in the other. If he chose one, the thorns would kill him; the other, flashing its pure light, would sear through his eyes into his brain.

"Amaranth. Another flower."

"So it is," she said indifferently. He laid the magic flowers on the parapet, picked a dying geranium leaf, smelled the miniature rose. "It has no smell," she said. He picked another dead leaf. He seemed always on the verge of smiling; it made him look sometimes wise and sometimes foolish. He drank out of the bronze watering helm; it was the colour of his hair.

"This water is too cool and sweet to come out of such a barren plain," he commented. He seated himself on the wall, watching her. "Corbeil says you are not real. You look real enough to me." She was silent, picking dead clover out of the clover pot. "Tell me where you came from."

She shrugged. "A tavern."

"And how did you come here?"

She gazed at him. "How did you come here, Ran of Carnelaine?"

He did smile then, wryly. "Carnelaine is poor; I came to replenish its coffers."

"There must be less chancy ways."

"Maybe I wanted to see the most precious thing there is to be found. Will the plain bloom again, if it is found? Will you have a garden instead of skull-pots?"

"Maybe," she said levelly. "Or maybe I will disappear. Die when the magic dies. If you choose wisely, you'll have answers to your questions."

He shrugged. "Maybe I will not choose. There are too many precious things."

She glanced at him. He was trifling, wanting hints from her, answers couched in riddles. Shall I take rose or lily? Or wizard's thigh bone? Tell me. Sword or water or dragon's eye? Some had questioned her so before.

She said simply, "I cannot tell you what to take. I do not know myself. As far as I have seen, everything kills." It was as close as she could come, as plain as she could make it: leave.

But he said only, his smile gone, "Is that why you never left?" She stared at him again. "Walked out the door, crossed the plain on some dead king's horse and left?"

She said, "I cannot." She moved away from him, tending some wildflower she called wind-bells, for she imagined their music as the night air tumbled down from the mountains to race across the plain. After a while, she heard his steps again, going down.

A voice summoned her: "Lady of the Skulls!" It was the man

of Stoney Head. She went down, blinking in the thick, dusty light. He stood stiffly, his face hard. They all stood still, watching.

"I will leave now," he said. "I may take anything?"

"Anything," she said, making her heart stone against him, a ghost's heart, so that she would not pity him. He went to the fountain, took a mouthful of water. He looked at her, and she moved to show him the hidden lines of the dragon's mouth. He vanished through the stones.

They heard him scream a moment later. The three of Grenelief stared towards the sound. They each wore pieces of a suit of armour that made the wearer invisible: one lacked an arm, another a thigh, the other his hands. Subtly their expressions changed, from shock and terror into something more complex. Five, she saw them thinking. Only five ways to divide it now.

"Anyone else?" she asked coldly. The man of Dulcis Isle slumped down on to the stairs, swallowing. He stared at her, his face gold-green in the light. He swallowed again. Then he shouted at her.

She had heard every name they could think of to shout before she had ever come to the tower. She walked up the stairs past him; he did not have the courage to touch her. She went to stand among her plants. Corbeil of Stoney Head lay where he had fallen, a little brown patch of wet earth beside his open mouth. As she looked, the sun dried it, and the first of the carrion-birds landed.

She threw bones at the bird, cursing, though it looked unlikely that anyone would be left to take his body back. She hit the bird a couple of times, then another came. Then someone took the bone out of her hand, drew her back from the wall.

"He's dead," Ran said simply. "It doesn't matter to him whether you throw bones at the birds or at him."

"I have to watch," she said shortly. She added, her eyes on the jagged line the parapet made against the sky, like blunt worn dragon's teeth, "You keep coming, and dying. Why do you all keep coming? Is treasure worth being breakfast for the carrion crows?"

"It's worth many different things. To the brothers of Grenelief it means adventure, challenge, adulation if they succeed. To Corbeil it was something to be won, something he would have that no one else could get. He would have sat on top of the pile, and let men look up to him, hating and envying."

"He was a cold man. Cold men feed on a cold fire. Still," she added, sighing, "I would have preferred to see him leave on his feet. What does the treasure mean to you?"

"Money." He smiled his vague smile. "It's not in me to lose my life over money. I'd sooner walk empty-handed out the door. But there's something else."

"What?"

"The riddle itself. That draws us all, at heart. What is the most precious thing? To see it, to hold it, above all to recognize it and choose it – that's what keeps us coming and traps you here." She stared at him, saw, in his eyes, the wonder that he felt might be worth his life.

She turned away; her back to him, she watered bleeding heart and columbine, stonily ignoring what the crows were doing below. "If you find the thing itself," she asked dryly, "what will you have left to wonder about?"

"There's always life."

"Not if you are killed by wonder."

He laughed softly, an unexpected sound, she thought, in that place. "Wouldn't you ride across the plain, if you heard tales of this tower, to try to find the most precious thing in it?"

"Nothing's precious to me," she said, heaving a cauldron of dandelions into shadow. "Not down there, anyway. If I took one thing away with me, it would not be sword or gold or dragon bone. It would be whatever is alive."

He touched the tiny rose. "You mean, like this? Corbeil would never have died for this."

"He died for a mouthful of water."

"He thought it was a mouthful of jewels." He sat beside the rose, his back to the air, watching her pull pots into shade against the noon light. "Which makes him twice a fool, I suppose. Three times a fool: for being wrong, for being deluded, and for dying.

What a terrible place this is. It strips you of all delusions and then it strips your bones."

"It is terrible," she said sombrely. "Yet those who leave without choosing never seem to get the story straight. They must always talk of the treasure they didn't take, not of the bones they didn't leave."

"It's true. Always, they take wonder with them out of this tower and they pass it on to every passing fool." He was silent a little, still watching her. "Amaranth," he said slowly. "That's the flower in poetry that never dies. It's apt."

"Yes."

"And there is another kind of Amaranth, that's fiery and beautiful and it dies . . ." Her hands stilled, her eyes widened, but she did not speak. He leaned against the hot, crumbling stones, his dragon's eyes following her like a sunflower following the sun. "What were you," he asked, "when you were the Amaranth that could die?"

"I was one of those faceless women who brought you wine in a tavern. Those you shout at, and jest about, and maybe give a coin to and maybe not, depending how we smile."

He was silent, so silent she thought he had gone, but when she turned, he was still there; only his smile had gone. "Then I've seen you," he said softly, "many times, in many places. But never in a place like this."

"The man from Stoney Head expected someone else, too."

"He expected a dream."

"He saw what he expected: Lady of the Skulls." She pulled wild mint into a shady spot under some worn tapestry. "And so he found her. That's all I am now. You were better off when all I served was wine."

"You didn't build this tower."

"How do you know? Maybe I got tired of the laughter and the coins and I made a place for myself where I could offer coins and give nothing."

"Who built this tower?"

She was silent, crumbling a mint leaf between her fingers. "I did," she said at last. "The Amaranth who never dies."

"Did you?" He was oddly pale; his eyes glittered in the light as if at the shadow of danger. "You grow roses out of thin air in this blistered plain; you try to beat back death for us with our own bones. You curse our stupidity and our fate, not us. Who built this tower for you?" She turned her face away, mute. He said softly, "The other Amaranth, the one that dies, is also called Love-lies-bleeding."

"It was the last man," she said abruptly, her voice husky, shaken with sudden pain, "who offered me a coin for love. I was so tired of being touched and then forgotten, of hearing my name spoken and then not, as if I were only real when I was looked at, and just something to forget after that, like you never remember the flowers you toss away. So I said to him: no, and no, and no. And then I saw his eyes. They were like amber with thorns of dark in them: sorcerer's eyes. He said, 'Tell me your name.' And I said, 'Amaranth,' and he laughed and laughed and I could only stand there, with the wine I had brought him overturned on my tray, spilling down my skirt. He said, 'Then you shall make a tower of your name, for the tower is already built in your heart.'"

"Love-lies-bleeding," he whispered.

"He recognized that Amaranth."

"Of course he did. It was what died in his own heart."

She turned then, wordless, to look at him. He was smiling again, though his face was still blanched under the hard, pounding light, and the sweat shone in his hair. She said, "How do you know him?"

"Because I have seen this tower before and I have seen in it the woman we all expected, the only woman some men ever know . . . And every time we come expecting her, the woman who lures us with what's most precious to us and kills us with it, we build the tower around her again and again and again . . ."

She gazed at him. A tear slid down her cheek, and then another. "I thought it was my tower," she whispered. "The Amaranth that never dies but only lives for ever to watch men die."

"It's all of us," he sighed. In the distance, thunder rumbled. "We all build towers, then dare each other to enter . . ." He picked up the little rose in its skull pot and stood abruptly; she followed him to the stairs.

"Where are you going with my rose?"

"Out."

She followed him down, protesting. "But it's mine!"

"You said we could choose anything."

"It's just a worthless thing I grew, it's nothing of the tower's treasure. If you must take after all, choose something worth your life!"

He glanced back at her, as they rounded the tower stairs to the bottom. His face was bone-white, but he could still smile. "I will give you back your rose," he said, "if you will let me take the Amaranth."

"But I am the only Amaranth."

He strode past his startled companions, whose hands were heaped with *this*, *no this*, and *maybe this*. As if the dragon's magical eye had opened in his own eye, he led her himself into the dragon's mouth.

The Sunlight on the Water

Louise Cooper

Louise Cooper (b. 1952) was first discovered in America with The Book of Paradox *(1973) – a wonderfully exotic novel drawing upon the magic of the tarot – and it was some years before she really became established in Britain, starting with her Time Master series (which began with* The Initiate *in 1985) and then with the long-running Indigo series, starting with* Nemesis *(1988). Cooper's work never draws upon sword-wielding heroes or epic battles. Her stories depict the world of individuals trapped by fate within their world of everyday magic. Such is the nature of the following story, written especially for this anthology, and the closest we come to the literary fairy tale.*

EVERYONE HAD ALWAYS SAID THAT TAIZU AND POLYENKA were the perfect couple. From the day they had first held hands in the crocodile of small children walking solemnly to learn their letters at fierce old Aunt Chanka's, the stars of their mutual fate had been set in their courses. Time passed, and dame school was soon exchanged for the hard realities of work: Taizu went as apprentice to the blacksmith, while Polyenka joined the chattering gaggle of girls labouring year-round in the fields. His gangling frame filled out, she blossomed from gawky child to slender young woman, and neither they nor anybody else in the village doubted what their future would be. Made for each other, everyone said. One more summer, perhaps two, and there would be a wedding in the village. Even the shaman and his three wise-wives nodded knowing approval and smiled as they anticipated the ceremony and the rituals and the gifts that would be heaped upon them to bring the couple good luck.

And so it had been. Taizu worked well and diligently at his trade; Polyenka learned to cook and sew and generally prepare for a change in her status. Both kept their virginity, encouraged (or intimidated) by lectures from the shaman, who promised the gods' disfavour if either should dare to experiment before the magical night of their marriage. The nuptials were to take place on the winter solstice – an auspicious date, said the shaman – and it seemed that piety was its own reward, for just one month before the appointed time the old blacksmith died and, as he had no sons to succeed him, the forge and its adjacent small cottage and garden were Taizu's to inherit.

The wedding was a wonderful excuse for drinking and dancing and general merriment, and by the time the young couple were allowed to escape to their new home half the village's adult population (and a few of the more unruly children, who would be punished for it tomorrow) were laid out in a glorious stupor on or under the tables where the feast had been served. Taizu had drunk his fair share, too, but when the door was bolted and the fire was banked up, and for the first time in their lives they lay together under the goosedown quilt that was the traditional village gift to newly-weds, the dizziness fell away from him and a new, deep emotion took its place. He cupped Polyenka's face between his hands and, in the firelight's glow, gazed with a kind of wonder at her warm grey eyes, the smiling curve of her mouth, the luxuriance of her fair hair. He wanted to speak, but his heart was so full that words would not come. Polyenka, though, found them for him. She said, "I love you, husband."

Husband. Wife. *His* wife. Always and for ever; the bond sealed and indissoluble. Taizu had not known it was possible for a man to be so happy.

"Wife," he said, trying the word for the very first time. "Dearest wife."

Her smile became still sweeter. "Promise you'll never leave me, Taizu."

"I promise, my love," he said.

For five years that promise was kept, to such a degree that a running joke grew up in the village: the shaman, people said, must have anointed Taizu and Polyenka with glue rather than holy water when he joined them in wedlock. The joke was good-spirited and Taizu and Polyenka laughed at it, just as they laughed at everything. They were blissfully content. His business prospered, while she – when she was not helping in the forge for the sheer pleasure of being with him – discovered a natural talent for growing things, so that the flourishing fruit and vegetables in their garden were the envy of their neighbours. The only cloud that could have shadowed their happiness was the fact that there were, as yet, no children of their union. But neither minded too much. They were young and healthy, and the shaman's wise-wives assured them there was plenty of time. Better, they agreed, to enjoy their youth and their modest prosperity without the added responsibilities of a family.

Then, in the fifth summer of their marriage, the plague came.

It was an outbreak of the small plague; less deadly than its greater cousin but still capable of taking a serious toll. The previous summer's harvest had not been good, and the resulting winter shortages had been followed by a wet spring, making people more vulnerable than they might otherwise have been. The very old and the very young took it first; with nine days still to go before the midsummer solstice, six funerals had already taken place and the shaman held out little hope for several others who lay sick. Five days before the solstice, the shaman's second wise-wife died. Three days to go, and the twin sons of Taizu and Polyenka's nearest neighbour were put to bed with a high fever . . .

Taizu could not have forbidden his wife to do what she did, any more than he could have foreseen the consequences. Polyenka was young and robustly healthy; with their own garden to provide food, they had not been hit so hard by the crop failure of the previous year. And someone had to help the children, for their father was away working in another district and their mother had started to show the first unmistakable symptoms. Anyone with a grain of humanity would have gone into the house and nursed and cared for the sick family. Anyone.

But the one who did was Polyenka, and capricious fate decreed that, on the eve of the solstice, as the children and their mother began to pull through the worst of the fever, Taizu's beloved wife lurched suddenly forward in her chair by the hearth and whispered, "Oh, Taizu . . . my head *hurts* so . . ."

Taizu ran for the shaman, and the shaman came. But there was nothing he could do, for even the small plague had no cure beyond hope and prayer and a few herbs that might or might not have some minor effect. The fever came quickly, and the shaman stayed in the house all through the short summer night, intoning prayers and entreaties to the gods while Taizu wiped Polyenka's sweating brow, held a bowl for her as she retched black bile and tried vainly to soothe her when she cried with pain and fear.

Two hours after dawn she seemed to rally, and Taizu dared to allow himself to hope. She was young, she was strong – surely, *surely* she would live?

But at sunset the brief remission ended. And precisely at midnight on Midsummer Day, Polyenka died.

At the shaman's decree, she was buried by the holy well at the edge of the woodland, where it was said that the goddess of the trees came to bathe. Polyenka, the shaman said, deserved the honour of a sacred resting-place, for she was pure of heart and soul and the gods themselves would weep for her passing. Taizu felt as if his own tears would never stop. Day and night he cried for his wife, and nothing and no one could console him. She had been his life, his world, the joy of his heart, and without her nothing had any meaning. When the last rites were over and the women and children of the village had all laid flowers on Polyenka's new grave, he turned away without a word to anyone, went in to his house and quietly closed the door. He wanted to die. But to take one's own life was forbidden by the gods, and those who did so were not gathered into the joyful elysium of the afterworld but must languish for ever in the outer dark. Polyenka was in the joyful elysium; the shaman had said so, and Taizu believed him. So Taizu knew he must endure, and wait for the day when his natural term was over and he could rejoin his love again.

He remained in his shuttered home for three days and three nights, before, on a bright, warm morning with a sweet wind frisking through the village, he emerged to take up the reins of his life again. But he was a changed man. Gone was the briskly cheerful manner, the ready smile, the infectious laughter. He worked diligently in his forge through all the daylight hours, but when work was done he closed himself away in his house and was not seen again until the next morning. He rarely spoke, never smiled, and refused all invitations to join in the life of the village once more. He existed, but he no longer lived.

The small plague faded, the summer went on, and life returned to normal. Autumn came and went, and soon it was winter again. As the winter solstice approached, Taizu was seen less about the village than usual. Everyone knew why: the day was – or would have been – the fifth anniversary of his marriage to Polyenka. But even if he had wanted their sympathy nobody could find any words that seemed adequate. Better, they thought, to let him grieve in peace.

On solstice night Taizu stood at his window and silently watched the procession winding its way out of the village towards the high hilltop 2 miles away. As the last cluster of burning torches bobbed away into the dark, he closed the shutter and moved slowly to his familiar chair by the fire. Tonight they would celebrate the rebirth of the sun: a beacon fire would be lit, toasts drunk and prayers sent flying upwards, and tomorrow a new year would begin. Last year, he and Polyenka had been at the heart of the revels. Now . . .

He had thought he was done with crying, but the wave of misery caught him unawares and he laid his head down on the chair arm and gave way to it. He was still its grip when, with a detached part of his mind, he became aware of a sudden increase in the room's light. Thinking that perhaps a log had fallen out of

the fire, and reacting instinctively to the possible danger, he
raised his head.

The light was not a burning log. A pale, glowing golden oval
had appeared beside the hearth. And in the oval stood Polyenka.

The chair skidded back and crashed over as shock brought
Taizu lurching to his feet. For several moments all he could do
was stare, mouth working but incapable of making any sound.
Polyenka smiled and held out her hands towards him . . . then,
with a thrill that all but tore the heart out of him, Taizu saw her
step out of the shining oval and fully into the room.

His voice broke from its paralysis with a harsh sound, and he
croaked, "My love . . . oh, my love . . . you have come home!"

"And that is the boon we have been granted," said Polyenka.
"Because of the strength of our love, and the manner in which
fate took me from you, I may return to you on each solstice night,
summer and winter, until your own earthly life is over." She
gazed into his eyes with a look that had always melted him, and
melted him still. "Dearest Taizu, I am the happiest creature in
this or any other world!"

Taizu still knelt on the floor where he had collapsed before
her as though he were a worshipper before a goddess. His face
was rapturous as he drank in her words. Each solstice night.
Summer and winter. His wife. His beloved. Back with him.
Home . . . He wanted to shout his joy to the rafters. He wanted
to run outside into the cold and the crackling frost, and dance
and sing wildly among the bare trees of his garden. He wanted to
race to the hilltop where the villagers were celebrating, and
scream his own praises to the gods who had plucked him from
the dead ashes of his life and rekindled the flame of his soul. He
did neither of these things. Instead, he ran to the kitchen and
brought meat and bread and apples and beer and laid them
before his beloved like a sacrificial offering. No matter that
ghosts did not eat or drink and thus she could not join his feast
of thanksgiving; no matter, even, that he could not touch her or
kiss her or hold her in his arms as he used to do. She was *here*,
and that was enough, *enough*.

Through the blissfully long winter night, Taizu sat beside the fire and talked with his Polyenka. She told him of the afterworld and its beauties that were beyond mortal ability to imagine, and he told her of the harvest and the doings of the village and of all her old friends. And they laughed and they joked, just as they used to do in the old, happy times.

When the first glimmer of dawn showed in the east, she left him, with a last blown kiss and the promise that he would see her again in half a year. It was an age to wait and yet it was nothing, and Taizu went to his bed and slept a deep, peaceful sleep that was filled with contented dreams of her. When he woke at noon, some of the memories had faded; he could no longer recall, for instance, her stories of the spirit world. But that, perhaps, was only right and proper; and anyway, it did not matter. Nothing mattered, but that his Polyenka had come back to him, and would return twice each year until his life's end.

Taizu's neighbours puzzled greatly at the change in him, but he gently and smilingly evaded all their attempts to discover what had brought it about. He wanted no one to know of his boon; not even the shaman. He wanted to keep it close and private, a precious secret to be hoarded and nurtured and savoured. At last the neighbours gave up their efforts and agreed that Taizu must simply have recovered from his bereavement. A wonderful thing, to see him return to his old self again. No one should mourn for ever, and Taizu was young and resilient and had the best of his life before him. Another year, or perhaps two, and who could say that he might not marry again?

Taizu, though, had no intention of marrying again. He lived the next half-year in a state of growing anticipation, and only as the summer solstice drew very near did he suffer pangs of terror, fearing that perhaps he had had a bout of madness and Polyenka's return had been an illusion. But it was not an illusion. As darkness fell on the solstice night, she came to him again. And again they talked and laughed, and he forgot that she could not eat, and he became a little drunk with beer and happiness and the relief that his fears were unfounded. The summer night was brief and the visit ended all too soon. But she would come again at midwinter. She would *always* come again.

Ten years passed. Taizu, mid-thirties now, was in the prime of his strength, and very handsome. A number of girls in the village still had hopes of him, but he continued to disappoint them, until even the most optimistic gossips gave up their matchmaking. All the same, Taizu had a man's natural urges, and being fundamentally honest he privately admitted to himself that he *did* sometimes yearn for a woman to share his home and his bed, and give him children to carry on his name. But his love was for Polyenka; and even though that love could never be consummated again, to go with another would be to betray her. On their wedding night she had said: "*Promise you'll never leave me.*" He had kept that promise, and he always would. The sacrifice was worth while.

So each solstice Polyenka continued to return to her husband's hearth, and Taizu continued to live for her visits. No one in the village knew, or even began to guess, what took place in the blacksmith's house on those secret nights. More years passed. The old shaman went to the gods, and his eldest son took on his role and chose three new wise-wives of his own. People died of age or sickness, children were born and most survived, crops were good or bad as the capricious elements dictated. Taizu's business thrived, for he had nothing else to distract him from his work. At fifty he was a man of considerable substance, with two apprentices and a share in one of the largest grain-barns in the district. But still he lived for nothing else except Polyenka's next return.

The winter solstice after Taizu's fiftieth birthday was also the thirtieth anniversary of his and Polyenka's marriage. To Taizu it was a very special occasion, so as dusk fell he set to tidying the cottage, sweeping it from top to bottom, and then prepared a feast (he was no cook, but it was the intention that mattered) that he considered fit for such a celebration.

Polyenka came a little later than usual. At first Taizu did not notice the slight change in her manner. But after a while it occurred to him that she seemed . . . *distracted* was the best word he could find for it. Her eyes kept straying towards the window or the wall, though there was nothing there worth anyone's attention. And though she made a show of listening to his talk and laughing at his stories, he could not shake off the feeling that a part of her mind was elsewhere.

At last he ventured to ask, "My love, is anything wrong?"

"Wrong?" Polyenka's head came round quickly, and she smiled her familiar smile. (Though was there something a little too ready about it? He could not be sure . . .) "No, beloved, of course not."

Taizu was not entirely satisfied, and persisted. "It's just that you seem . . . a little apart from me tonight. As if you are not entirely happy."

"I am happy," said Polyenka. "How could I not be, when I am with you?" A pause. "Only . . ."

Alarm filled him. "What, sweet wife? What is it?"

She shook her head and her ghost-hair shimmered, making Taizu's heart turn over with love. She was *so* beautiful . . . 'Nothing of any importance, dearest. I was just somewhat surprised when I first saw you." Again, that smile. "You have changed a little, Taizu."

"Changed? How?"

She laughed. (Did he imagine a faintly false note in the laughter? No; it was his imagination . . .) "Your hair. You are going grey. And there is a bald patch on your crown."

Taizu put his hand up to his head in surprise. He only looked in a glass when shaving, and he had not noticed anything untoward. But she was right: his pate *was* thinning. Embarrassed, he, too, laughed.

"Well, perhaps you are right. But it's only natural in a man when he grows older. Beddo – you remember Beddo? – hadn't a single hair on his head by the time he was my age. And as for grey: well, they say it's distinguishing, don't they?"

"Yes," said Polyenka, not meeting his eyes. "And they are right, of course; it is most distinguishing. I simply noticed. That's all."

Taizu was reassured, and the rest of the night passed in comfortable talk. Afterwards, he did reflect for a little, wondering idly how Polyenka herself would have looked now, if she still lived a mortal life. She, of course, had not changed since the day of her death; she would always be the young and lovely girl he had married. But would *her* hair have been grey by now? Would she have stayed as slender as she was, or would she have become plump and spreading, like so many of the village women? The questions could not be answered, and so there was no point speculating. It was a curiosity. That was all.

Taizu passed his fifty-fifth birthday, and as his sixtieth approached, his friends planned a celebration party for him. The birthday would fall twelve days after the summer solstice, and though, out of neighbourliness, Taizu did his best to show enthusiasm for the occasion, he was far more preoccupied by excitement at the prospect of Polyenka's next visit. Last winter she had been very late (it had happened on a number of occasions in the past few years), and he hoped with all his heart that this time she would appear promptly.

She did not. In fact it was almost midnight when the glowing golden oval began to glimmer by the hearth, and when Polyenka stepped out of it she did not greet him with her customary loving affection, but stood in the middle of the room, staring at him with an expression that he could not interpret. Though he could not believe it possible in her, she looked *sulky*.

"My love," he began, holding out his arms to her.

"Hello, Taizu." Polyenka shifted restlessly, and seemed reluctant to look at him. Taizu felt the stirrings of a deep dread. In truth he had felt it before, but in the past he had refused to acknowledge it, pushing it away down into a part of his mind where it could not creep out and assail him. This time, though, it would not be quieted. This time, it could not be ignored.

He opened his mouth, not knowing what to say but desperate to say *something* that would turn the tide and make everything all right again. Polyenka, though, took the reins from his hands before he could utter a sound.

She said, "Taizu, I don't want to come any more."

Taizu's world crashed into shards around him. He stared at her, feeling that he was falling into a bottomless pit of bewilderment and betrayal. "Why?" he asked in a tiny, helpless whisper.

She turned away, her hair rippling. "Oh, Taizu . . . Don't you
see? You've *changed* so. These last years . . . it's been growing
each time, and I can't . . . I just can't . . . Taizu, you're *old*!"

Tears began to trickle down the lines on Taizu's face. "Old
. . .?" he repeated.

"Yes, *old*! Look at yourself! Your hair's gone grey – what hair
you have left – and your skin is wrinkled, and you've put on
weight and are starting to stoop. You're an old man, and it makes
me shudder just to look at you!"

Appalled, he tried to protest. "But I'm still Taizu!"

"No, you're not! Not the Taizu I married. He was young, like
me, and handsome. But all that's gone, and it will never come
back. *I* don't want to come back, Taizu, and I won't, not after
tonight." At last she did look at him, and what he saw in her eyes
scattered the last ashes of Taizu's hopes. "I can't love a man as
old as you. I *can't*."

Taizu pleaded with her. He begged, he wept, he reasoned, he
railed and even screamed. But Polyenka was immovable, and the
inevitable moment came when she gazed at him one final time – a
pitying gaze, with distaste lurking behind it – and said, "I'm
sorry, Taizu. But I'm going now. Goodbye . . . my dear."

Those last two words, "my dear", were like a viper's bite to
Taizu. As the golden oval faded, taking Polyenka with it, he sank
to his knees on the floor, crying like an abandoned child. The
tears flowed on and on, and did not stop until dawn began to
break. Then, he rose stiffly to his feet and walked slowly, dull-
eyed, to his bedroom, where his little shaving-glass hung on the
wall. By the trickle of early light coming in at the window he
stared at his own reflection, and truly saw for the first time the old
man that Polyenka could no longer love. The young and handsome Taizu of the past was still there, he knew; if he unfocused
his eyes he could almost glimpse him, smiling and merry, behind
the reflection. But Polyenka had chosen to look only at the
surface, like a child admiring the dazzle of sunlight on water
and not caring what lay beneath.

Taizu turned away from the glass, and lay for an hour on his
bed, and then rose and began his work, as he always did. The

birthday party took place, for it would have been churlish to spurn his neighbours' kindness. But through it all he did not smile, and rarely spoke, and though the village wondered at the change in him, no one had the courage – or the discourtesy – to probe.

Life went on as it always had, and for Taizu the sun no longer shone. Each solstice night he kept a lonely vigil, but Polyenka did not return. Ten years passed and Taizu was seventy. By an ironic joke of fate he showed no signs of failing. He had not died of overwork, or disease, or accident; indeed, he looked set to continue on for many more years yet. The winter solstice came again. If Polyenka had lived, they would have been wed fifty years, but Taizu sternly forbade himself to think of that. It was just a day, like any other.

No one paid much heed when, two days before the occasion, Taizu went down with a sneezing rheum. He was old, but he was strong; the ailment was nothing and would soon pass. But it did not pass. The morning of the solstice eve found Taizu confined to his bed; through the day he weakened rapidly, and by nightfall his neighbours were seriously concerned. They nursed him, tried to feed him, tried to rally him, but he did not rally, and shortly before midnight the shaman was sent for.

One look at Taizu told the shaman all, and he prayed by the bedside until it was over. Taizu died surrounded by his good friends and neighbours, and the last words he spoke before his eyes closed for the final time were: "Ah, my Polyenka . . ." He was smiling.

There were trees and fields and rivers, and a strange and wonderful golden light shone over all as Taizu gazed around him. In the distance he could hear laughter and music, and a scent of flowers and something even headier came to him on the warm breeze. It took him a little while to understand, and when he did, his spirit rejoiced. The gods judged him worthy, and he had come to elysium.

He began to walk, not with any aim in mind but simply for the delight of it. Walking was easier than it had been, and he marvelled at that, until a pool of water showed him the answer to the conundrum. The pool was deep and the water pure and shining, and when he knelt to drink from it he saw his face reflected clearly in the smooth surface. The old man with his wrinkles and white hair and stooping back was gone. From the water young Taizu was smiling back at him, and he would never be old again.

Taizu's soul bloomed with a happiness that he had never known before. He walked on, striding now with new confidence, a spring in his step. As he neared a grove of trees, more laughter came on the breeze, and a group of nymphs appeared. They ran to him, still laughing, and danced around him, playful and coquettish. They were beautiful. In fact, Taizu thought, they were the most beautiful creatures he had ever seen . . .

The nymphs led him in to the grove, their eyes promising delight. Taizu rejoiced in their attentions. Was he not a man? Did he not feel as a man felt? This was what the gods promised in the afterlife; the old shaman had said so, long ago, and now Taizu knew that he had been right. He would meet the shaman again, here. He would meet old friends. He would meet—

He saw her then, as she ran towards him through the trees with the light dappling on her golden hair. Her face smiled radiantly, and she held out her arms to him and she cried, "Taizu! Oh, my beloved husband, you have come home!"

Oh, my beloved husband. But it had not been so, had it, ten years ago, when he was old and grey and no longer handsome. *I can't love a man as old as you*, she had told him. And she had left him, abandoned him, because all she could or would look for was the sunlight on the surface of the pool.

Old Taizu gazed wisely out of young Taizu's eyes, and with an honesty and clear-sightedness that only comes with age he thought that perhaps she was not as beautiful as he had once believed. A little too broad in the face. A little too heavy in the leg. And that sulky look, which he had seen in her face on the night of her last visit . . . it had always been a trait of hers, though in the old days he had been too much in love to notice. The sunlight on the water had, perhaps, dazzled him, too . . .

He glanced at the nymphs, who had withdrawn from him and clustered together a short way off. One of them, seeing, waved to him and blew a kiss. Taizu smiled, then turned to his wife. She had stopped, and there was sudden doubt on her face. For all that he was no longer mortal, Taizu's nature was still human, and thus imperfect. So it was surely forgivable that he should feel just a *small* sense of pleasure and justice at her chagrin. Just a *small* one.

He bowed to her, and he said with meticulous but cool courtesy, "Polyenka." Then he turned and, with the nymphs drifting like enchanter's smoke behind him, walked away into the grove.

Paladin of the Lost Hour

Harlan Ellison

No matter what conventions there are in fantasy, Harlan Ellison (b. 1934) will turn them inside out, shake them and rebuild them until they buzz anew. I know of no other writer who, solidly for over forty years, has railed and fought so strongly against convention. That was why he compiled the ground-breaking anthology Dangerous Visions *(1967) and it's almost certainly why he has won more awards for his fiction than any other writer. Just check out his collections* Strange Wine *(1978),* Shatterday *(1980) or the huge* The Essential Ellison *(1987), if you want to see what I mean. The following story remixes many of the elements we've encountered in the stories so far and then lights the blue touch paper.*

T HIS WAS AN OLD MAN. NOT AN INCREDIBLY OLD MAN: obsolete, spavined; not as worn as the sway-backed stone steps ascending the Pyramid of the Sun to an ancient temple; not yet a relic. But even so, a *very* old man, this old man perched on an antique shooting-stick, its handles opened to form a seat, its spike thrust at an angle into the soft ground and trimmed grass of the cemetery. Grey, thin rain misted down at almost the same angle as that at which the spike pierced the ground. The winter-barren trees lay flat and black against an aluminium sky, unmoving in the chill wind. An old man sitting at the foot of a grave mound whose headstone had tilted slightly when the earth had settled; sitting in the rain and speaking to someone below.

"They tore it down, Minna.

"I tell you, they must have bought off a councilman.

"Came in with bulldozers at six o'clock in the morning, and you *know* that's not legal. There's a Municipal Code. Supposed to hold off till at least seven on weekdays, eight on the weekend; but there they were at six, even *before* six, barely light for godsakes. Thought they'd sneak in and do it before the neighbourhood got wind of it and called the landmarks committee. Sneaks: they come on *holidays*, can you imagine!

"But I was out there waiting for them, and I told them, 'You can't do it, that's Code number 91.3002, sub-section E,' and they lied and said they had special permission, so I said to the big muckymuck in charge, 'Let's see your waiver permit,' and he said the Code didn't apply in this case because it was supposed to be only for grading, and since they were demolishing and not grading, they could start whenever they felt like it. So I told him I'd call the police, then, because it came under the heading of Disturbing the Peace, and he said . . . well, I know you hate that kind of language, old girl, so I won't tell you what he said, but you can imagine.

"So I called the police, and gave them my name, and of course they didn't get there till almost quarter after seven (which is what makes me think they bought off a councilman), and by then those 'dozers had levelled most of it. Doesn't take long, you know that.

"And I don't suppose it's as great a loss as, maybe, say, the Great Library of Alexandria, but it was the last of the authentic Deco design drive-ins, and the carhops still served you on roller skates, and it was a landmark, and just about the only place left in the city where you could still get a decent grilled cheese sandwich pressed very flat on the grill by one of those weights they used to use, made with real cheese and not that rancid plastic they cut into squares and call it 'cheese food'.

"Gone, old dear, gone and mourned. And I understand they plan to put up another one of those mini-malls on the site, just ten blocks away from one that's already there, and you know what's going to happen: this new one will drain off the traffic from the older one, and then that one will fail the way they all do when the next one gets built, you'd think they'd see some history in it; but no, they never learn. And you should have seen the crowd by seven-thirty. All ages, even some of those kids painted like aborigines, with torn leather clothing. Even they came to protest. Terrible language, but at least they were concerned. And nothing could stop it. They just whammed it, and down it went.

"I do so miss you today, Minna. No more good grilled cheese." Said the *very* old man to the ground. And now he was crying softly, and now the wind rose, and the mist rain stippled his overcoat.

Nearby, yet at a distance, Billy Kinetta stared down at another grave. He could see the old man over there off to his left, but he took no further notice. The wind whipped the vent of his trenchcoat. His collar was up but rain trickled down his neck. This was a younger man, not yet thirty-five. Unlike the old man, Billy Kinetta neither cried nor spoke to memories of someone who had once listened. He might have been a geomancer, so silently did he stand, eyes towards the ground.

One of these men was black; the other was white.

Beyond the high, spiked-iron fence surrounding the cemetery two boys crouched, staring through the bars, through the rain; at the men absorbed by grave matters, by matters of graves. These were not really boys. They were legally young men. One was nineteen, the other two months beyond twenty. Both were legally old enough to vote, to drink alcoholic beverages, to drive a car. Neither would reach the age of Billy Kinetta.

One of them said, "Let's take the old man."

The other responded, "You think the guy in the trenchcoat'll get in the way?"

The first one smiled; and a mean little laugh. "I sure as shit hope so." He wore, on his right hand, a leather carnaby glove with the fingers cut off, small round metal studs in a pattern along the line of his knuckles. He made a fist, flexed, did it again.

They went under the spiked fence at a point where erosion had created a shallow gully. "Sonofabitch!" one of them said, as he slid through on his stomach. It was muddy. The front of his sateen roadie jacket was filthy. "Sonofabitch!" He was speaking in general of the fence, the sliding under, the muddy ground, the universe in total. And the old man, who would now *really* get the crap kicked out of him for making this fine sateen roadie jacket filthy.

They sneaked up on him from the left, as far from the young guy in the trenchcoat as they could. The first one kicked out the shooting-stick with a short, sharp, downward movement he had learned in his Tae Kwon-Do class. It was called the *yup-chagi*. The old man went over backwards.

Then they were on him, the one with the filthy sonofabitch sateen roadie jacket punching at the old man's neck and the side of his face as he dragged him around by the collar of the overcoat. The other one began ransacking the coat pockets, ripping the fabric to get his hand inside.

The old man commenced to scream. "Protect me! You've got to protect me . . . it's necessary to protect me!"

The one pillaging pockets froze momentarily. What the hell kind of thing is that for this old fucker to be saying? Who the hell does he think'll protect him? Is he asking *us* to protect him? I'll protect you, scumbag! I'll kick in your fuckin' lung! "Shut 'im up!" he whispered urgently to his friend. "Stick a fist in his mouth!" Then his hand, wedged in an inside jacket pocket, closed over something. He tried to get his hand loose, but the jacket and coat and the old man's body had wound around his wrist. "C'mon loose, motherfuckah!" he said to the very old man, who was still screaming for protection. The other young man was making huffing sounds, as dark as mud, as he slapped at the rain-soaked hair of his victim. "I can't . . . he's all twisted 'round . . . getcher hand outta there so's I can . . ." Screaming, the old man had doubled under, locking their hands on his person.

And then the pillager's fist came loose, and he was clutching – for an instant – a gorgeous pocket watch.

What used to be called a turnip watch.

The dial face was *cloisonné*, exquisite beyond the telling.

The case was of silver, so bright it seemed blue.

The hands, cast as arrows of time, were gold. They formed a shallow V at precisely eleven o'clock. This was happening at 3.45 in the afternoon, with rain and wind.

The timepiece made no sound, no sound at all.

Then: there was space all around the watch, and in that space in the palm of the hand, there was heat. Intense heat for just a moment, just long enough for the hand to open.

The watch glided out of the boy's palm and levitated.

"Help me! You *must* protect me!"

Billy Kinetta heard the shrieking, but did not see the pocket watch floating in the air above the astonished young man. It was silver, and it was end-on towards him, and the rain was silver and slanting; and he did not see the watch hanging free in the air, even when the furious young man disentangled himself and leaped for it. Billy did not see the watch rise just so much, out of reach of the mugger.

Billy Kinetta saw two boys, two young men of ratpack age, beating someone much older; and he went for them. Pow, like that!

Thrashing his legs, the old man twisted around – over, under – as the boy holding him by the collar tried to land a punch to put him away. Who would have thought the old man to have had so much battle in him?

A flapping shape, screaming something unintelligible, hit the centre of the group at full speed. The carnaby-gloved hand reaching for the watch grasped at empty air one moment, and the next was buried under its owner as the boy was struck a crackback block that threw him face-first into the soggy ground. He tried to rise, but something stomped him at the base of his spine; something kicked him twice in the kidneys; something rolled over him like a flash flood.

Twisting, twisting, the very old man put his thumb in the right eye of the boy clutching his collar.

The great trenchcoated maelstrom that was Billy Kinetta whirled into the boy as he let loose of the old man on the ground and, howling, slapped a palm against his stinging eye. Billy locked his fingers and delivered a roundhouse wallop that sent the boy reeling backwards to fall over Minna's tilted headstone.

Billy's back was to the old man. He did not see the miraculous pocket watch smoothly descend through rain that did not touch it, to hover in front of the old man. He did not see the old man reach up, did not see the timepiece snuggle into an arthritic hand, did not see the old man return the turnip to an inside jacket pocket.

Wind, rain and Billy Kinetta pummelled two young men of a legal age that made them accountable for their actions. There was no thought of the knife stuck down in one boot, no chance to reach it, no moment when the wild thing let them rise. So they crawled. They scrabbled across the muddy ground, the slippery grass, over graves and out of his reach. They ran; falling, rising, falling again; away, without looking back.

Billy Kinetta, breathing heavily, knees trembling, turned to help the old man to his feet; and found him standing, brushing dirt from his overcoat, snorting in anger and mumbling to himself.

"Are you all right?"

For a moment the old man's recitation of annoyance continued, then he snapped his chin down sharply as if marking end to the situation, and looked at his cavalry to the rescue. "That was very good, young fella. Considerable style you've got there."

Billy Kinetta stared at him wide-eyed. "Are you sure you're okay?" He reached over and flicked several blades of wet grass from the shoulder of the old man's overcoat.

"I'm fine. I'm fine but I'm wet and I'm cranky. Let's go somewhere and have a nice cup of Earl Grey."

There had been a look on Billy Kinetta's face as he stood with lowered eyes, staring at the grave he had come to visit. The emergency had removed that look. Now it returned.

"No, thanks. If you're okay, I've got to do some things."

The old man felt himself all over, meticulously, as he replied, "I'm only superficially bruised. Now if I were an old woman, instead of a spunky old man, same age though, I'd have lost considerable of the calcium in my bones, and those two would have done me some mischief. Did your know that women lose a considerable part of their calcium when they reach my age? I read a report." Then he paused, and said shyly, "Come on, why don't you and I sit and chew the fat over a nice cup of tea?"

Billy shook his head with bemusement, smiling despite himself. "You're something else, Dad. I don't even know you."

"I like that."

"What: that I don't know you?"

"No, that you called me 'Dad' and not 'Pop'. I *hate* 'Pop'. Always makes me think the wise-apple wants to snap off my cap with a bottle opener. Now *Dad* has a ring of respect to it. I like that right down to the ground. Yes, I believe we should find someplace warm and quiet to sit and get to know each other. After all, you saved my life. And you know what that means in the Orient."

Billy was smiling continuously now. "In the first place, I doubt very much I saved your life. Your wallet, maybe. And in the second place, I don't even know your name; what would we have to talk about?"

"Gaspar," he said, extending his hand. "That's a first name. Gaspar. Know what it means?"

Billy shook his head.

"See, already we have something to talk about."

So Billy, still smiling, began walking Gaspar out of the cemetery. "Where do you live? I'll take you home."

They were on the street, approaching Billy Kinetta's 1979 Cutlass. "Where I live is too far for now. I'm beginning to feel a bit peaky. I'd like to lie down for a minute. We can just go on over to your place, if that doesn't bother you. For a few minutes. A cup of tea. Is that all right?"

He was standing beside the Cutlass, looking at Billy with an old man's expectant smile, waiting for him to unlock the door and hold it for him till he'd placed his still-calcium-rich but nonetheless old bones in the passenger seat. Billy stared at him, trying to figure out what was at risk if he unlocked that door. Then he snorted a tiny laugh, unlocked the door, held it for Gaspar as he seated himself, slammed it and went around to unlock the other

side and get in. Gaspar reached across and thumbed up the door
lock knob. And they drove off together in the rain.

Through all of this the timepiece made no sound, no sound at
all.

Like Gaspar, Billy Kinetta was alone in the world.

His three-room apartment was the vacuum in which he existed.
It was furnished, but if one stepped out into the hallway and, for
all the money in all the numbered accounts in all the banks in
Switzerland, one were asked to describe those furnishings, one
would come away no richer than before. The apartment was
charisma poor. It was a place to come when all other possibilities
had been expended. Nothing green, nothing alive, existed in
those boxes. No eyes looked back from the walls. Neither warmth
nor chill marked those spaces. It was a place to wait.

Gaspar leaned his closed shooting-stick, now a walking-stick
with handles, against the bookcase. He studied the titles of the
paperbacks stacked haphazardly on the shelves.

From the kitchenette came the sound of water running into a
metal pan. Then tin on cast iron. Then the hiss of gas and the
flaring of a match as it was struck; and the pop of the gas being lit.

"Many years ago," Gaspar said, taking out a copy of Moravia's
The Adolescents and thumbing it as he spoke, "I had a library of
books, oh, thousands of books – never could bear to toss one out,
not even the bad ones – and when folks would come to the house
to visit they'd look around at all the nooks and crannies stuffed
with books; and if they were the sort of folks who don't snuggle
with books, they'd always ask the same dumb question." He
waited a moment for a response and when none was forthcoming
(the sound of china cups on sink tile), he said, "Guess what the
question was."

From the kitchen, without much interest: "No idea."

"They'd always ask it with the kind of voice people use in the
presence of large sculptures in museums. They'd ask me, 'Have
you read all these books?'" He waited again, but Billy Kinetta
was not playing the game. "Well, young fella, after a while the
same dumb question gets asked a million times, you get sorta

snappish about it. And it came to annoy me more than a little bit. Till I finally figured out the right answer.

"And you know what that answer was? Go ahead, take a guess."

Billy appeared in the kitchenette doorway. "I suppose you told them you'd read a lot of them but not all of them."

Gaspar waved the guess away with a flapping hand. "Now what good would that have done? They wouldn't know they'd asked a dumb question, but I didn't want to insult them, either. So when they'd ask if I'd read all those books, I'd say, 'Hell, no. Who wants a library full of books you've already read?' "

Billy laughed despite himself. He scratched at his hair with idle pleasure, and shook his head at the old man's verve. "Gaspar, you are a wild old man. You retired?"

The old man walked carefully to the most comfortable chair in the room, an overstuffed thirties-style lounge that had been reupholstered many times before Billy Kinetta had purchased it at the American Cancer Society Thrift Shop. He sank into it with a sigh. "No sir, I am not by any means retired. Still very active."

"Doing what, if I'm not prying?"

"Doing ombudsman."

"You mean, like a consumer advocate? Like Ralph Nader?"

"Exactly. I watch out for things. I listen, I pay some attention; and if I do it right, sometimes I can even make a little difference. Yes, like Mr Nader. A very fine man."

"And you were at the cemetery to see a relative?"

Gaspar's face settled into an expression of loss. "My dear old girl. My wife, Minna. She's been gone, well, it was twenty years in January." He sat silently staring inward for a while, then: "She was everything to me. The nice part was that I knew how important we were to each other; we discussed, well, just *every-thing*. I miss that the most, telling her what's going on.

"I go to see her every other day.

"I used to go every day. But. It. Hurt. Too much."

They had tea. Gaspar sipped and said it was very nice, but had Billy ever tried Earl Grey? Billy said he didn't know what that was, and Gaspar said he would bring him a tin, that it was splendid. And they chatted. Finally, Gaspar asked, "And who were you visiting?"

Billy pressed his lips together. "Just a friend." And would say no more. Then he sighed and said, "Well, listen, I have to go to work."

"Oh? What do you do?"

The answer came slowly. As if Billy Kinetta wanted to be able to say that he was in computers, or owned his own business, or held a position of import. "I'm night manager at a 7-Eleven."

"I'll bet you meet some fascinating people coming in late for milk or one of those slushies," Gaspar said gently. He seemed to understand.

Billy smiled. He took the kindness as it was intended. "Yeah, the cream of high society. That is, when they're not threatening to shoot me through the head if I don't open the safe."

"Let me ask you a favour," Gaspar said. "I'd like a little sanctuary, if you think it's all right. Just a little rest. I could lie down on the sofa for a bit. Would that be all right? You trust me to stay here while you're gone, young fella?"

Billy hesitated only a moment. The very old man seemed okay, not a crazy, certainly not a thief. And what was there to steal? Some tea that wasn't even Earl Grey?

"Sure. That'll be okay. But I won't be coming back till 2 a.m. So just close the door behind you when you go; it'll lock automatically."

They shook hands, Billy shrugged into his still-wet trenchcoat, and he went to the door. He paused to look back at Gaspar sitting in the lengthening shadows as evening came on. "It was nice getting to know you, Gaspar."

"You can make that a mutual pleasure, Billy. You're a nice young fella."

And Billy went to work, alone as always.

When he came home at two, prepared to open a can of Hormel chili, he found the table set for dinner; with the scent of an elegant beef stew enriching the apartment. There were new potatoes and stir-fried carrots and zucchini that had been lightly battered to delicate crispness. And cupcakes. White cake with chocolate frosting. From a bakery.

And in that way, as gently as that, Gaspar insinuated himself into Billy Kinetta's apartment and his life.

As they sat with tea and cupcakes, Billy said, "You don't have anyplace to go, do you?"

The old man smiled and made one of those deprecating movements of the head. "Well, I'm not the sort of fella who can bear to be homeless, but at the moment I'm what vaudevillians used to call 'at liberty'."

"If you want to stay on a time, that would be okay," Billy said. "It's not very roomy here, but we seem to get on all right."

"That's strongly kind of you, Billy. Yes, I'd like to be your roommate for a while. Won't be too long, though. My doctor tells me I'm not long for this world." He paused, looked into the teacup and said softly, "I have to confess . . . I'm a little frightened. To go. Having someone to talk to would be a great comfort."

And Billy said, without preparation, "I was visiting the grave of a man who was in my rifle company in Vietnam. I go there sometimes." But there was such pain in his words that Gaspar did not press him for details.

So the hours passed, as they will with or without permission, and when Gaspar asked Billy if they could watch the television, to catch an early newscast, and Billy tuned in the old set just in time to pick up dire reports of another aborted disarmament talk, and Billy shook his head and observed that it wasn't only Gaspar who was frightened of something like death, Gaspar chuckled, patted Billy on the knee and said, with unassailable assurance, "Take my word for it, Billy . . . it isn't going to happen. No nuclear holocaust. Trust me, when I tell you this: it'll never happen. Never, never, not ever."

Billy smiled wanly. "And why not? What makes *you* so sure . . . got some special inside information?"

And Gaspar pulled out the magnificent timepiece, which Billy was seeing for the first time, and he said, "It's not going to happen because it's only eleven o'clock."

Billy stared at the watch, which read 11:00 precisely. He consulted his wristwatch. "Hate to tell you this, but your watch has stopped. It's almost five-thirty."

Gaspar smiled his own certain smile. "No, it's eleven." And they made up the sofa for the very old man, who placed his pocket change and his fountain pen and the sumptuous turnip watch on the now-silent television set, and they went to sleep.

One day Billy went off while Gaspar was washing the lunch dishes, and when he came back, he had a large paper bag from Toys R Us.

Gaspar came out of the kitchenette rubbing a plate with a souvenir dish towel from Niagara Falls, New York. He stared at Billy and the bag. "What's in the bag?" Billy inclined his head, and indicated the very old man should join him in the middle of the room. Then he sat down cross-legged on the floor, and dumped the contents of the bag. Gaspar stared with startlement, and sat down beside him.

So for two hours they played with tiny cars that turned into robots when the sections were unfolded.

Gaspar was excellent at figuring out all the permutations of the Transformers, Starriors and GoBots. He played well.

Then they went for a walk. "I'll treat you to a matinee," Gaspar said. "But no films with Karen Black, Sandy Dennis or Meryl Streep. They're always crying. Their noses are always red. I can't stand that."

They started to cross the avenue. Stopped at the light was this year's Cadillac Brougham, vanity licence plates, ten coats of acrylic lacquer and two coats of clear (with a little retarder in the final "colour coat" for a slow dry) of a magenta hue so rich that it approximated the shade of light shining through a decanter filled with Château Lafite-Rothschild 1945.

The man driving the Cadillac had no neck. His head sat thumped down hard on the shoulders. He stared straight ahead, took one last deep pull on the cigar, and threw it out the window. The still-smoking butt landed directly in front of Gaspar as he passed the car. The old man stopped, stared down at this

coprolitic metaphor, and then stared at the driver. The eyes
behind the wheel, the eyes of a macaque, did not waver from
the stoplight's red circle. Just outside the window, someone was
looking in, but the eyes of the rhesus were on the red circle.

A line of cars stopped behind the Brougham.

Gaspar continued to stare at the man in the Cadillac for a
moment, and then, with creaking difficulty, he bent and picked
up the smouldering butt of stogie.

The old man walked the two steps to the car – as Billy watched
in confusion – thrust his face forward till it was mere inches from
the driver's profile, and said with extreme sweetness, "I think
you dropped this in our living-room."

And as the glazed simian eyes turned to stare directly into the
pedestrian's face, nearly nose-to-nose, Gaspar casually flipped
the butt with its red glowing tip into the back seat of the Cadillac,
where it began to burn a hole in the fine Corinthian leather.

Three things happened simultaneously:

The driver let out a howl, tried to see the butt in his rear-view
mirror, could not get the angle, tried to look over his shoulder
into the back seat but without a neck could not perform that feat
of agility, put the car into neutral, opened his door and stormed
into the street trying to grab Gaspar. "You fuckin' bastid,
whaddaya think you're doin' tuh my car you asshole bastid, I'll
kill ya . . ."

Billy's hair stood on end as he saw what Gaspar was doing; he
rushed back the short distance in the crosswalk to grab the old
man; Gaspar would not be dragged away, stood smiling with
unconcealed pleasure at the mad bull rampaging and screaming
of the hysterical driver. Billy yanked as hard as he could and
Gaspar began to move away, around the front of the Cadillac,
towards the far kerb. Still grinning with octogeneric charm.

The light changed.

These three things happened in the space of five seconds,
abetted by the impatient honking of the cars behind the
Brougham as the light turned green.

Screaming, dragging, honking, as the driver found he could not
do three things at once: he could not go after Gaspar while the

traffic was clanging at him; could not let go of the car door to crawl into the back seat from which now came the stench of charring leather that could not be rectified by an inexpensive Tijuana tuck'n'roll; could not save his back seat and at the same time stave off the hostility of a dozen drivers cursing and honking. He trembled there, torn three ways, doing nothing.

Billy dragged Gaspar.

Out of the crosswalk. Out of the street. On to the kerb. Up the side street. Into the alley. Through a backyard.

To the next street over away from the avenue.

Puffing with the exertion, Billy stopped at last, five houses up the street. Gaspar was still grinning, chuckling softly with unconcealed pleasure at his puckish ways. Billy turned on him with wild gesticulations and babble.

"You're *nuts!*"

"How about that?" the old man said, giving Billy an affectionate poke in the biceps.

"Nuts! Looney! That guy would've torn off your head! What the hell's wrong with you, old man? Are you out of your boots?"

"I'm not crazy. I'm responsible."

"Responsible!?! Re*spon*sible, fer chrissakes? For what? For all the butts every yotz throws into the street?"

The old man nodded. "For butts, and trash, and pollution, and toxic waste dumping in the dead of night; for bushes, and cactus, and the baobab tree; for pippin apples and even lima beans, which I despise. You show me someone who'll eat lima beans without being at gunpoint, I'll show you a pervert!"

Billy was screaming. "What the hell are you talking about?"

"I'm also responsible for dogs and cats and guppies and cockroaches and the President of the United States and Jonas Salk and your mother and the entire chorus line at the Sands Hotel in Las Vegas. Also their choreographer."

"Who do you think you are? God?"

"Don't be sacrilegious. I'm too old to wash your mouth out with laundry soap. Of course I'm not God. I'm just an old man. *But I'm responsible.*"

Gaspar started to walk away, towards the corner and the

avenue, and a resumption of their route. Billy stood where the old man's words had pinned him.

"Come on, young fella," Gaspar said, walking backwards to speak to him, "we'll miss the beginning of the movie. I hate that."

Billy had finished eating, and they were sitting in the dimness of the apartment, only the lamp in the corner lit. The old man had gone to the County Art Museum and had bought inexpensive prints – Max Ernst, Gérôme, Richard Dadd, a subtle Feininger – which he had mounted in Insta-Frames. They sat in silence for a time, relaxing; then murmuring trivialities in a pleasant undertone.

Finally, Gaspar said, "I've been thinking a lot about my dying. I like what Woody Allen said."

Billy slid to a more comfortable position in the lounger. "What was that?"

"He said: I don't mind dying, I just don't want to be there when it happens."

Billy snickered.

"I feel something like that, Billy. I'm not afraid to go, but I don't want to leave Minna entirely. The times I spend with her, talking to her, well, it gives me the feeling we're still in touch. When I go, that's the end of Minna. She'll be well and truly dead. We never had any children, almost everyone who knew us is gone, no relatives. And we never did anything important that anyone would put in a record book, so that's the end of us. For me, I don't mind; but I wish there was someone who knew about Minna . . . she was a remarkable person."

So Billy said, "Tell me. I'll remember for you."

Memories in no particular order. Some as strong as ropes that could pull the ocean ashore. Some that shimmered and swayed in the faintest breeze like spiderwebs. The entire person, all the little movements, that dimple that appeared when she was amused at something foolish he had said. Their youth together, their love, the procession of their days towards middle age. The small cheers and the pain of dreams never realized. So much about *him* as he spoke of *her*. His voice soft and warm and filled with a longing so deep and true that he had to stop frequently because the words broke and would not come out till he had thought away some of the passion. He thought of her and was glad. He had gathered her together, all her dowry of love and taking care of him, her clothes and the way she wore them, her favourite knick-knacks, a few clever remarks: and he packed it all up and delivered it to a new repository.

The very old man gave Minna to Billy Kinetta for safekeeping.

Dawn had come. The light filtering in through the blinds was saffron. "Thank you, Dad," Billy said. He could not name the feeling that had taken him hours earlier. But he said this: "I've never had to be responsible for anything, or anyone, in my whole life. I never belonged to anybody . . . I don't know why. It didn't bother me, because I didn't know any other way to be."

Then his position changed, there in the lounger. He sat up in a way that Gaspar thought was important. As if Billy were about to open the secret box buried at his centre. And Billy spoke so softly the old man had to strain to hear him.

"I didn't even know him.

"We were defending the airfield at Danang. Did I tell you we were 1st Battalion, 9th Marines? Charlie was massing for a big push out of Quang Ngai province, south of us. Looked as if they were going to try to take the provincial capital. My rifle company was assigned to protect the perimeter. They kept sending in patrols to bite us. Every day we'd lose some poor bastard who scratched his head when he shouldn't of. It was June, late in June, cold and a lot of rain. The foxholes were hip-deep in water.

"Flares first. Our howitzers started firing. Then the sky was full of tracers, and I started to turn towards the bushes when I heard something coming, and these two main-force regulars in dark blue uniforms came towards me. I could see them so clearly. Long black hair. All crouched over. And they started firing. And that goddam carbine seized up, wouldn't fire; and I pulled out the banana clip, tried to slap in another, but they saw me and just turned a couple of AK-47s on me . . . God, I remember everything slowed down . . . I looked at those things, seven-point-six-two millimetre assault rifles they were . . . I got crazy for a second, tried to figure out in my own mind if they were Russian-made, or Chinese, or Czech, or North Korean. And it was so bright from the flares I could see them starting to squeeze off the rounds, and then from out of nowhere this lance corporal jumped out at them and yelled somedamnthing like, 'Hey, you VC fucks, looka here!' except it wasn't that . . . I never could recall what he said actually . . . and they turned to brace him . . . and they opened him up like a Baggie full of blood . . . and he was all over me, and the bushes, and oh, God there was pieces of him floating on the water I was standing in . . .''

Billy was heaving breath with impossible weight. His hands moved in the air before his face without pattern or goal. He kept looking into far corners of the dawn-lit room as if special facts might present themselves to fill out the reasons behind what he was saying.

"Aw, geezus, he was *floating* on the water . . . aw, Christ, he *got in my boots!*" Then a wail of pain so loud it blotted out the sound of traffic beyond the apartment; and he began to moan, but not cry; and the moaning kept on; and Gaspar came from the sofa and held him and said such words as *it's all right*, but they might not have been those words, or *any* words.

And pressed against the old man's shoulder, Billy Kinetta ran on only half sane: "He wasn't my friend, I never knew him, I'd never talked to him, but I'd seen him, he was just this guy, and there wasn't any reason to do that, he didn't know whether I was a good guy or a shit or anything, so why did he do that? He didn't need to do that. They wouldn't of seen him. He was dead before I killed them. He was gone already. I never got to say thank you or thank you or . . . *anything!*

"Now he's in that grave, so I came here to live, so I can go there, but I try and try to say thank you, and he's dead, and he can't hear me, he can't hear nothin', he's just down there, down in the ground, and I can't say thank you . . . oh, geezus, geezus, why don't he hear me, I just want to say thanks . . .''

Billy Kinetta wanted to assume the responsibility for saying thanks, but that was possible only on a night that would never come again; and this was the day.

Gaspar took him to the bedroom and put him down to sleep in exactly the same way he would soothe an old, sick dog.

Then he went to his sofa, and because it was the only thing he could imagine saying, he murmured, "He'll be all right, Minna. Really he will."

When Billy left for the 7-Eleven the next evening, Gaspar was gone. It was an alternate day, and that meant he was out at the cemetery. Billy fretted that he shouldn't be there alone, but the old man had a way of taking care of himself. Billy was not smiling as he thought of his friend, and the word *friend* echoed as he realized that, yes, this was his friend, truly and really his friend. He wondered how old Gaspar was, and how soon Billy Kinetta would be once again what he had always been: alone.

When he returned to the apartment at two-thirty, Gaspar was asleep, cocooned in his blanket on the sofa. Billy went in and tried to sleep, but hours later, when sleep would not come, when thoughts of murky water and calcium night light on dark foliage kept him staring at the bedroom ceiling, he came out of the room for a drink of water. He wandered around the living-room, not wanting to be by himself even if the only companionship in this sleepless night was breathing heavily, himself in sleep.

He stared out the window. Clouds in chiffon strips across the sky. The squealing of tyres from the street.

Sighing, idle in his movement around the room, he saw the old man's pocket watch lying on the coffee table beside the sofa. He walked to the table. If the watch was still stopped at eleven o'clock, perhaps he would borrow it and have it repaired. It would be a nice thing to do for Gaspar. The old man loved that beautiful timepiece.

Billy bent to pick it up.

The watch, stopped at the V of eleven precisely, levitated at an angle, floating away from him.

Billy Kinetta felt a shiver travel down his back to burrow in at the base of his spine. He reached for the watch hanging in air before him. It floated away just enough that his fingers massaged empty space. He tried to catch it. The watch eluded him, lazily turning away like an opponent who knows he is in no danger of being struck from behind.

Then Billy realized Gaspar was awake. Turned away from the sofa, nonetheless he knew the old man was observing him. And the blissful floating watch.

He looked at Gaspar.

They did not speak for a long time.

Then: "I'm going back to sleep," Billy said. Quietly.

"I think you have some questions," Gaspar replied.

"Questions? No, of course not, Dad. Why in the world would I have questions? I'm still asleep." But that was not the truth, because he had not been asleep that night.

"Do you know what 'Gaspar' means? Do you remember the three wise men of the Bible, the Magi?"

"I don't want any frankincense and myrrh. I'm going back to bed. I'm going now. You see, I'm going right now."

" 'Gaspar' means master of the treasure, keeper of the secrets, paladin of the palace." Billy was staring at him, not walking into the bedroom; just staring at him. As the elegant timepiece floated to the old man, who extended his hand palm-up to receive it. The watch nestled in his hand, unmoving, and it made no sound, no sound at all.

"You go back to bed. But will you go out to the cemetery with me tomorrow? It's important."

"Why?"

"Because I believe I'll be dying tomorrow."

It was a nice day, cool and clear. Not at all a day for dying, but neither had been many such days in South-East Asia, and death had not been deterred.

They stood at Minna's gravesite, and Gaspar opened his shooting-stick to form a seat; and he thrust the spike into the ground; and he settled onto it, and sighed, and said to Billy Kinetta, "I'm growing cold as that stone."

"Do you want my jacket?"

"No, I'm cold inside." He looked around at the sky, at the grass, at the rows of markers. "I've been responsible, for all of this, and more."

"You've said that before."

"Young fella, are you by any chance familiar, in your reading, with an old novel by James Hilton called *Lost Horizon*? Perhaps you saw the movie. It was a wonderful movie. It was a wonderful movie, actually much better than the book. Mr Capra's greatest achievement. A human testament. Ronald Colman was superb. Do you know the story?"

"Yes."

"Do you remember the High Lama, played by Sam Jaffe? His name was Father Perrault?"

"Yes."

"Do you remember how he passed on the caretakership of that magical hidden world, Shangri-La, to Ronald Colman?"

"Yes, I remember that." Billy paused. "Then he died. He was very old, and he died."

Gaspar smiled up at him. "Very good, Billy. I knew you were a good boy. So now, if you remember all that, may I tell you a story? It's not a very long story."

Billy nodded, smiling at his friend.

"In 1582 Pope Gregory XIII decreed that the civilized world would no longer observe the Julian calendar. October 4th, 1582 was followed, the next day, by October 15th. Eleven days vanished from the world. One hundred and seventy years later, the British parliament followed suit, and September 2nd, 1752 was followed, the next day, by September 14th. Why did he do that, the Pope?"

Billy was bewildered by the conversation. "Because he was bringing it into synch with the real world. The solstices and equinoxes. When to plant, when to harvest."

Gaspar waggled a finger at him with pleasure. "Excellent, young fella. And you're correct when you say Gregory abolished the Julian calendar because its error of one day in every 128 years had moved the vernal equinox to March 11th. That's what the history books say. It's what *every* history book says. But what if?"

"What if *what*? I don't know what you're talking about."

"What if: Pope Gregory had the knowledge revealed to him that he *must* readjust time in the minds of men? What if: the excess time in 1582 was eleven days and one hour? What if: he accounted for those eleven days, vanished those eleven days, but that one hour slipped free, was left loose to bounce through eternity? A very special hour . . . an hour that must *never* be used . . . an hour that must never toll. What if?"

Billy spread his hands. "What if, what if, what if! It's all just philosophy. It doesn't mean anything. Hours aren't real, time isn't something that you can bottle up. So what if there *is* an hour out there somewhere that . . ."

And he stopped.

He grew tense, and leaned down to the old man. "The watch. Your watch. It doesn't work. It's stopped."

Gaspar nodded. "At eleven o'clock. My watch works; it keeps very special time, for one very special hour."

Billy touched Gaspar's shoulder. Carefully he asked, "Who are you, Dad?"

The old man did not smile as he said, "Gaspar. Keeper. Paladin. Guardian."

"Father Perrault was hundreds of years old."

Gaspar shook his head with a wistful expression on his old face. "I'm eighty-six years old, Billy. You asked me if I thought I was God. Not God, not Father Perrault, not an immortal, just an old man who will die too soon. Are you Ronald Colman?"

Billy nervously touched his lower lip with a finger. He looked at Gaspar as long as he could, then turned away. He walked off a few paces, stared at the barren trees. It seemed suddenly much chillier here in this place of entombed remembrances. From a distance he said, "But it's only . . . what? A chronological convenience. Like daylight saving time; Spring forward, Fall back. We don't actually *lose* an hour; we get it back."

Gaspar stared at Minna's grave. "At the end of April I lost an hour. If I die now, I'll die an hour short in my life. I'll have been cheated out of one hour I want, Billy." He swayed towards all he had left of Minna. "One last hour I could have with my old girl.

That's what I'm afraid of, Billy. I have that hour in my possession. I'm afraid I'll use it, God help me, I want so much to use it."

Billy came to him. Tense, and chilled, he said, "Why must that hour never toll?"

Gaspar drew a deep breath and tore his eyes away from the grave. His gaze locked with Billy's. And he told him.

The years, all the days and hours, exist. As solid and as real as mountains and oceans and men and women and the baobab tree. Look, he said, at the lines in my face and deny that time is real. Consider these dead weeds that were once alive and try to believe it's all just vapour or the mutual agreement of Popes and Caesars and young men like you.

"The lost hour must never come, Billy, for in that hour it all ends. The light, the wind, the stars, this magnificent open place we call the universe. It all ends, and in its place – waiting, always waiting – is eternal darkness. No new beginnings, no world without end, just the infinite emptiness."

And he opened his hand, which had been lying in his lap, and there, in his palm, rested the watch, making no sound at all, and stopped dead at eleven o'clock. "Should it strike twelve, Billy, eternal night falls; from which there is no recall."

There he sat, this very old man, just a perfectly normal old man. The most recent in the endless chain of keepers of the lost hour, descended in possession from Caesar and Pope Gregory XIII, down through the centuries of men and women who had served as caretakers of the excellent timepiece. And now he was dying, and now he wanted to cling to life as every man and woman clings to life no matter how awful or painful or empty, even if it is for one more hour. The suicide, falling from the bridge, at the final instant, tries to fly, tries to climb back up the sky. This weary old man, who only wanted to stay one brief hour more with Minna. Who was afraid that his love would cost the universe.

He looked at Billy, and he extended his hand with the watch waiting for its next paladin. So softly Billy could barely hear him, knowing that he was denying himself what he most wanted at this last place in his life, he whispered, "If I die without passing it on . . . it will begin to tick."

"Not me," Billy said. "Why did you pick me? I'm no one special. I'm not someone like you. I run an all-night service mart. There's nothing special about me the way there is about you! I'm *not* Ronald Colman! I don't want to be responsible, I've *never* been responsible!"

Gaspar smiled gently. "You've been responsible for me."

Billy's rage vanished. He looked wounded.

"Look at us, Billy. Look at what colour you are; and look at what colour I am. You took me in as a friend. I think of you as worthy, Billy. Worthy."

They remained there that way, in silence, as the wind rose. And finally, in a timeless time, Billy nodded.

Then the young man said, "You won't be losing Minna, Dad. Now you'll go to the place where she's been waiting for you, just as she was when you first met her. There's a place where we find everything we've ever lost through the years."

"That's good, Billy, that you tell me that. I'd like to believe it, too. But I'm a pragmatist. I believe in what exists . . . like rain and Minna's grave and the hours that pass that we can't see, but they *are*. I'm afraid, Billy. I'm afraid this will be the last time I can speak to her. So I ask a favour. As payment, in return for my life spent protecting the watch.

"I ask for one minute of the hour, Billy. One minute to call her back so we can stand face-to-face and I can touch her and say goodbye. You'll be the new protector of this watch, Billy, so I ask you please, just let me steal one minute."

Billy could not speak. The look on Gaspar's face was without horizon, empty as tundra, bottomless. The child left alone in darkness; the pain of eternal waiting. He knew he could never deny this old man, no matter what he asked, and in the silence he heard a voice say: "*No!*" And it was his own.

He had spoken without conscious volition. Strong and determined, and without the slightest room for reversal. If a part of his heart had been swayed by compassion, that part had been instantly overridden. No. A final, unshakable no.

For an instant Gaspar looked crestfallen. His eyes clouded with tears; and Billy felt something twist and break within himself at the sight. He knew he had hurt the old man. Quickly, but softly, he said urgently, "You know that would be wrong, Dad. We mustn't . . ."

Gaspar said nothing. Then he reached out with his free hand and took Billy's. It was an affectionate touch.

"That was the last test, young fella. Oh, you know I've been testing you, don't you? This important item couldn't go to just anyone.

"And you passed the test, my friend: my last, best friend. When I said I could bring her back from where she's gone, here in this place we've both come to so often, to talk to someone lost to us, I knew you would understand that *anyone* could be brought back in that stolen minute. I knew you wouldn't use it for yourself, no matter how much you wanted it; but I wasn't sure that as much as you like me, it might not sway you. But you wouldn't even give it to *me*, Billy."

He smiled up at him, his eyes now clear and steady.

"I'm content, Billy. You needn't have worried. Minna and I don't need that minute. But if you're to carry on for me, I think you *do* need it. You're in pain, and that's no good for someone who carries this watch. You've got to heal, Billy.

"So I give you something you would never take for yourself. I give you a going-away present . . ."

And he started the watch, whose ticking was as loud and as clear as a baby's first sound; and the sweep-second hand began to move away from eleven o'clock.

Then the wind rose, and the sky seemed to cloud over, and it grew colder, with a remarkable silver-blue mist that rolled across the cemetery; and though he did not see it emerge from that grave at a distance far to the right, Billy Kinetta saw a shape move towards him. A soldier in the uniform of a day past, and his rank was Lance Corporal. He came towards Billy Kinetta, and Billy went to meet him as Gaspar watched.

They stood together and Billy spoke to him. And the man whose name Billy had never known when he was alive, answered. And then he faded, as the seconds ticked away. Faded, and faded, and was gone. And the silver-blue mist rolled through them, and past them, and was gone; and the soldier was gone.

Billy stood alone.

When he turned back to look across the grounds to his friend, he saw that Gaspar had fallen from the shooting-stick. He lay on the ground. Billy rushed to him, and fell to his knees and lifted him onto his lap. Gaspar was still.

"Oh, God, Dad, you should have heard what he said. Oh, geez, he let me go. He let me go so I didn't even have to say I was sorry. He told me he didn't even *see* me in that foxhole. He never knew he'd saved my life. I said thank you and he said no, thank *you*, that he hadn't died for nothing. Oh, please, Dad, please don't be dead yet. I want to tell you . . ."

And, as it sometimes happens, rarely but wonderfully, sometimes they come back for a moment, for an instant before they go, the old man, this very old man, opened his eyes, just before going on his way, and he looked through the dimming light at his friend, and he said, "May I remember you to my old girl, Billy?"

And his eyes closed again, after only a moment; and his caretakership was at an end; as his hand opened and the most excellent timepiece, now stopped again at one minute past eleven, floated from his palm and waited till Billy Kinetta extended his hand; and then it floated down and lay there silently, making no sound, no sound at all. Safe. Protected.

There in the place where all lost things returned, the young man sat on the cold ground, rocking the body of his friend. And he was in no hurry to leave. There was time.

A blessing of the 18th Egyptian Dynasty:
God be between you and harm in
all the empty places you walk.

𝔜esterday was 𝔐onday

Theodore Sturgeon

In the days before Harlan Ellison shook fantasy by the throat
there were a few others who strove for daring and originality.
Avram Davidson was one, Philip Jose Farmer another, and
king of the castle was Theodore Sturgeon (1918–85). Sturgeon
was another who came alive under the editorial eye of John W.
Campbell in Astounding *and* Unknown *in the forties, and in*
the early fifties was probably the single most creative writer in
science fiction and fantasy. Currently Sturgeon's entire corpus
of short fiction is being repackaged and reprinted in a ten-
volume series from North Atlantic Books but if that's a bit too
much then try and track down his long out-of-print collections
such as Sturgeon in Orbit *(1964) or* A Touch of Sturgeon
(1987). You'll never be the same again.

HARRY WRIGHT ROLLED OVER and said something spelled
"Bzzzzhha-a-aw!" He chewed a bit on a mouthful of
dry air and spat it out, opened one eye to see if it really would
open, opened the other and closed the first, closed the second,
swung his feet on to the floor, opened them again and stretched.
This was a daily occurrence, and the only thing that made it
remarkable at all was that he did it on a Wednesday morning,
and—

Yesterday was Monday.

Oh, he knew it was Wednesday all right. It was partly that,

even though he knew yesterday was Monday, there was a gap between Monday and now; and that must have been Tuesday. When you fall asleep and lie there all night without dreaming, you know, when you wake up, that time has passed. You've done nothing that you can remember; you've had no particular thoughts, no way to gauge time, and yet you know that some hours have passed. So it was with Harry Wright. Tuesday had gone wherever your eight hours went last night.

But he hadn't slept through Tuesday. Oh no. He never slept, as a matter of fact, more than six hours at a stretch, and there was no particular reason for him doing so now. Monday was the day before yesterday; he had turned in and slept his usual stretch, he had awakened, and it was Wednesday.

If *felt* like Wednesday. There was a Wednesdayish feel to the air.

Harry put on his socks and stood up. He wasn't fooled. He knew what day it was. "What happened to yesterday?" he muttered. "Oh – yesterday was Monday." That sufficed until he got his pyjamas off. "Monday," he mused, reaching for his underwear, "was quite a while back, seems as though." If he had been the worrying type, he would have started then and there. But he wasn't. He was an easy-going sort, the kind of man that gets himself into a rut and stays there until he is pushed out. That was why he was an automobile mechanic at twenty-three dollars a week; that's why he had been one for eight years now, and would be from now on, if he could only find Tuesday and get back to work.

Guided by his reflexes, as usual, and with no mental effort at all, which was also usual, he finished washing, dressing, and making his bed. His alarm clock, which never alarmed because he was of such regular habits, said, as usual, six twenty-two when he paused on the way out, and gave his room the once-over. And there was a certain something about the place that made even this phlegmatic character stop and think.

It wasn't finished.

The bed was there, and the picture of Joe Louis. There were the two chairs sharing their usual seven legs, the split table, the pipe-organ bedstead, the beige wallpaper with the two swans over and over and over, the tiny corner sink, the tilted bureau. But none of them was finished. Not that there were any holes in anything. What paint there had been in the first place was still there. But there was an odour of old cut lumber, a subtle, insistent air of building, about the room and everything in it. It was indefinable, inescapable, and Harry Wright stood there caught up in it, wondering. He glanced suspiciously around but saw nothing he could really be suspicious of. He shook his head, locked the door and went out into the hall.

On the steps a little fellow, just over 3 feet tall, was gently stroking the third step from the top with a razor-sharp chisel, shaping up a new scar in the dirty wood. He looked up as Harry approached, and stood up quickly.

"Hi," said Harry, taking in the man's leather coat, his peaked cap, his wizened, bright-eyed little face. "Whatcha doing?"

"Touch-up," piped the little man. "The actor in the third floor front has a nail in his right heel. He came in late Tuesday night and cut the wood here. I have to get it ready for Wednesday."

"This is Wednesday," Harry pointed out.

"Of course. Always has been. Always will be."

Harry let that pass, started on down the stairs. He had achieved his amazing bovinity by making a practice of ignoring things he could not understand. But one thing bothered him—

"Did you say that feller in the third floor front was an actor?"

"Yes. They're all actors, you know."

"You're nuts, friend," said Harry bluntly. "That guy works on the docks."

"Oh, yes – that's his part. That's what he acts."

"No kiddin'. An' what does he do when he isn't acting?"

"But he – Well, that's all he does do! That's all any of the actors do!"

"Gee – I thought he looked like a reg'lar guy, too," said Harry. "An actor? 'Magine!"

"Excuse me," said the little man, "but I've got to get back to work. We mustn't let anything get by us, you know. They'll be through Tuesday before long, and everything must be ready for them."

Harry thought: this guy's crazy nuts. He smiled uncertainly and went down to the landing below. When he looked back the man was cutting skilfully into the stair, making a neat little nail scratch. Harry shook his head. This was a screwy morning. He'd be glad to get back to the shop. There was a '39 sedan down there with a busted rear spring. Once he got his mind on that he could forget this nonsense. That's all that matters to a man in a rut. Work, eat, sleep, payday. Why even try to think anything else out?

The street was a riot of activity, but then it always was. But not quite this way. There were automobiles and trucks and buses around, aplenty, but none of them was moving. And none of them was quite complete. This was Harry's own field; if there was anything he didn't know about motor vehicles, it wasn't very important. And through that medium he began to get the general idea of what was going on.

Swarms of little men who might have been twins of the one he had spoken to were crowding around the cars, the sidewalks, the stores and buildings. All were working like mad with every tool imaginable. Some were touching up the finish of the cars with fine wire brushes, laying on networks of microscopic cracks and scratches. Some, with ball peens and mallets, were denting fenders skilfully, bending bumpers in an artful crash pattern, spider-webbing safety glass windshields. Others were ageing top dressing with high-pressure, needlepoint sandblasters. Still others were pumping dust into upholstery, sandpapering the dashboard finish around light switches, throttles, chokes, to give a finger-worn appearance. Harry stood aside as a half-dozen of the workers scampered down the street bearing a fender which they riveted to a 1930 coupé. It was freshly bloodstained.

Once awakened to this highly unusual activity, Harry stopped, slightly open-mouthed, to watch what else was going on. He saw the same process being industriously accomplished with the houses and stores. Dirt was being laid on plate-glass windows over a coat of clear sizing. Woodwork was being cleverly scored and the paint peeled to make it look correctly weather-beaten, and dozens of leather-clad labourers were on their hands and knees, poking dust and dirt into the cracks between the paving blocks. A line of them went down the sidewalk, busily chewing gum and spitting it out; they were followed by another crew who carefully placed the wads according to diagrams they carried, and stamped them flat.

Harry set his teeth and muscled his rocking brain into something like its normal position. "I ain't never seen a day like this or crazy people like this," he said, "but I ain't gonna let it be any of my affair. I got my job to go to." And trying vainly to ignore the hundreds of little, hardworking figures, he went grimly on down the street.

When he got to the garage he found no one there but more swarms of stereotyped little people climbing over the place, dulling the paintwork, cracking the cement flooring, doing their hurried, efficient little tasks of ageing. He noticed, only because he was so familiar with the garage, that they were actually *making* the marks that had been there as long as he had known the place. "Hell with it," he gritted, anxious to submerge himself into his own world of wrenches and grease guns. "I got my job; this is none o' my affair."

He looked about him, wondering if he should clean these interlopers out of the garage. Naw – not his affair. He was hired to repair cars, not to police the joint. Long as they kept away from him – and, of course, animal caution told him that he was far, far outnumbered. The absence of the boss and the other mechanics was no surprise to Harry; he always opened the place.

He climbed out of his street clothes and into coveralls, picked up a tool case and walked over to the sedan, which he had left up on the hydraulic rack yester – that is, Monday night. And that is when Harry Wright lost his temper. After all, the car was his job, and he didn't like having anyone else mess with a job he had started. So when he saw his job – his '39 sedan – resting steadily on its wheels over the rack, which was down under the floor, and when he saw that the rear spring was repaired, he began to burn. He dived under the car and ran deft fingers over the rear wheel suspensions. In spite of his anger at this unprecedented occurrence, he had to admit to himself that the job had been done well. "Might have done it myself," he muttered.

A soft clank and a gentle movement caught his attention. With a roar he reached out and grabbed the leg of one of the ubiquitous little men, wriggled out from under the car, caught his culprit by his leather collar, and dangled him at arm's length.

"What are you doing to my job?" Harry bellowed.

The little man tucked his chin into the front of his shirt to give his windpipe a chance, and said, "Why, I was just finishing up that spring job."

"Oh. So you were just finishing up on that spring job," Harry whispered, choked with rage. Then, at the top of his voice, "Who told you to touch that car?"

"Who told me? What do you – Well, it just had to be done, that's all. You'll have to let me go. I must tighten up those two bolts and lay some dust on the whole thing."

"You must *what*? You get within 6 feet o' that car and I'll twist your head off your neck with a Stillson!"

"But – it has to be done!"

"You won't do it! Why, I oughta—"

"Please let me go! If I don't leave that car the way it was Tuesday night—"

"When was Tuesday night?"

"The last act, of course. Let me go, or I'll call the district supervisor!"

"Call the devil himself. I'm going to spread you on the sidewalk outside; and heaven help you if I catch you near here again!"

The little man's jaw set, his eyes narrowed, and he whipped his feet upwards. They crashed into Wright's jaw; Harry dropped him and staggered back. The little man began squealing, "Supervisor! Supervisor! Emergency!"

Harry growled and started after him; but suddenly, in the air between him and the midget workman, a long white hand appeared. The empty air was swept back, showing an aperture from the garage to blank, blind nothingness. Out of it stepped a tall man in a single loose-fitting garment literally studded with pockets. The opening closed behind the man.

Harry cowered before him. Never in his life had he seen such noble, powerful features, such strength of purpose, such broad shoulders, such a deep chest. The man stood with the backs of his hands on his hips, staring at Harry as if he were something somebody forgot to sweep up.

"That's him," said the little man shrilly. "He is trying to stop me from doing the work!"

"Who are you?" asked the beautiful man, down his nose.

"I'm the m-mechanic on this j-j – Who wants to know?"

"Iridel, supervisor of the district of Futura, wants to know."

"Where in hell did you come from?"

"I did not come from hell. I came from Thursday."

Harry held his head. "What *is* all this?" he wailed. "Why is today Wednesday? Who are all these crazy little guys? What happened to Tuesday?"

Iridel made a slight motion with his finger, and the little man scurried back under the car. Harry was frenzied to hear the wrench busily tightening bolts. He half started to dive under after the little fellow, but Iridel said, "Stop!" and when Iridel said, "Stop!" Harry stopped.

"This," said Iridel calmly, "is an amazing occurrence." He regarded Harry with unemotional curiosity. "An actor on stage before the sets are finished. Extraordinary."

"What stage?" asked Harry. "What are you doing here anyhow, and what's the idea of all these little guys working around here?"

"You ask a great many questions, actor," said Iridel. "I shall answer them, and then I shall have a few to ask you. These little men are stagehands – I am surprised that you didn't realize that. They are setting the stage for Wednesday. Tuesday? That's going on now."

"Arrgh!" Harry snorted. "How can Tuesday be going on when today's Wednesday?"

"Today isn't Wednesday, actor."

"Huh?"

"Today is Tuesday."

Harry scratched his head. "Met a feller on the steps this

mornin' – one of these here stagehands of yours. He said this was Wednesday."

"It *is* Wednesday. Today is Tuesday. Tuesday is today. 'Today' is simply the name for the stage set which happens to be in use. 'Yesterday' means the set that has just been used; 'Tomorrow' is the set that will be used after the actors have finished with 'today'. This is Wednesday. Yesterday was Monday; today is Tuesday. See?"

Harry said, "No."

Iridel threw up his long hands. "My, you actors are stupid. Now listen carefully. This is Act Wednesday, Scene 6.22. That means that everything you see around you here is being readied for 6.22 a.m. on Wednesday. Wednesday isn't a time; it's a place. The actors are moving along towards it now. I see you still don't get the idea. Let's see . . . ah. Look at that clock. What does it say?"

Harry Wright looked at the big electric clock on the wall over the compressor. It was corrected hourly and highly accurate, and it said 6.22. Harry looked at it amazed. "Six tw— but my gosh, man, that's what time I left the house. I walked here, an' I been here ten minutes already!"

Iridel shook his head. "You've been here no time at all, because there is no time until the actors make their entrances."

Harry sat down on a grease drum and wrinkled up his brains with the effort he was making. "You mean that this time proposition ain't something that moves along all the time? Sorta – well, like a road. A road don't go no place – You just go places along it. Is that it?"

"That's the general idea. In fact, that's a pretty good example. Suppose we say that it's a road; a highway built of paving blocks. Each block is a day; the actors move along it, and go through day after day. And our job here – mine and the little men – is to . . . well, pave that road. This is the clean-up gang here. They are fixing up the last little details, so that everything will be ready for the actors."

Harry sat still, his mind creaking with the effects of this information. He felt as if he had been hit with a lead pipe, and the shock of it was being drawn out infinitely. This was the craziest-sounding thing he had ever run into. For no reason at all he remembered a talk he had had once with a drunken aviation mechanic who had tried to explain to him how the air flowing over an aeroplane's wings makes the machine go up in the air. He hadn't understood a word of the man's discourse, which was all about eddies and chords and cambers and foils, dihedrals and the Bernoulli effect. That didn't make any difference; the things flew whether he understood how or not; he knew that because he had seen them. This guy Iridel's lecture was the same sort of thing. If there was nothing in all he said, how come all these little guys were working around here? Why wasn't the clock telling time? Where was Tuesday?

He thought he'd get that straight for good and all. "Just where is Tuesday?" he asked.

"Over there," said Iridel, and pointed. Harry recoiled and fell off the drum; for when the man extended his hand, it *disappeared*!

Harry got up off the floor and said tautly, "Do that again."

"What? Oh – point towards Tuesday? Certainly." And he pointed. His hand appeared again when he withdrew it.

Harry said, "My gosh!" and sat down again on the drum, sweating and staring at the supervisor of the district of Futura. "You point, an' your hand – ain't," he breathed. "What direction is that?"

"It is a direction like any other direction," said Iridel. "You know yourself there are four directions: forwards, sidewards, upwards, and" – he pointed again, and again his hand vanished – "*that* way!"

"They never tole me that in school," said Harry. "Course, I was just a kid then, but—"

Iridel laughed. "It is the fourth dimension – it is *duration*. The actors move through length, breadth and height, anywhere they choose to within the set. But there is another movement – one they can't control – and that is duration."

"How soon will they come . . . eh . . . here?" asked Harry, waving an arm. Iridel dipped into one of his numberless pockets and pulled out a watch. "It is now eight thirty-seven Tuesday morning," he said. "They'll be here as soon as they finish the act, and the scenes in Wednesday that have already been prepared."

Harry thought again for a moment, while Iridel waited patiently, smiling a little. Then he looked up at the supervisor and asked, "Hey, this 'actor' business – what's that all about?"

"Oh, that. Well, it's a play, that's all. Just like any play – put on for the amusement of an audience."

"I was to a play once," said Harry. "Who's the audience?"

Iridel stopped smiling. "Certain – Ones who may be amused," he said. "And now I'm going to ask you some questions. How did you get here?"

"Walked."

"You *walked* from Monday night to Wednesday morning?"

"Naw – from the house to here."

"Ah – but how did you get to Wednesday, six twenty-two?"

"Well I – Damfino. I just woke up an' came to work as usual."

"This is an extraordinary occurrence," said Iridel, shaking his head in puzzlement. "You'll have to see the producer."

"Producer? Who's he?"

"You'll find out. In the meantime, come along with me. I can't leave you here; you're too close to the play. I have to make my rounds anyway."

Iridel walked towards the door. Harry was tempted to stay and find himself some more work to do, but when Iridel glanced back at him and motioned him out, Harry followed. It was suddenly impossible to do anything else.

Just as he caught up with the supervisor, a little worker ran up, whipping off his cap.

"Iridel, sir," he piped, "the weather makers put .006 of 1 per cent too little moisture in the air on this set. There's three-sevenths of an ounce too little gasoline in the storage tanks under here."

"How much is in the tanks?"

"Four thousand two hundred and seventy-three gallons, three pints, seven and twenty-one thirty-fourths ounces."

Iridel grunted. "Let it go this time. That was very sloppy work. Someone's going to get transferred to Limbo for this."

"Very good, sir," said the little man. "Long as you know we're not responsible." He put on his cap, spun around three times and rushed off.

"Lucky for the weather makers that the amount of gas in that tank doesn't come into Wednesday's script," said Iridel. "If anything interferes with the continuity of the play, there's the devil to pay. Actors haven't sense enough to cover up, either. They are liable to start whole series of miscues because of a little thing like that. The play might flop and then we'd all be out of work."

"Oh," Harry oh-ed. "Hey, Iridel, what's the idea of that patchy-looking place over there?"

Iridel followed his eyes. Harry was looking at a corner lot. It was tree-lined and overgrown with weeds and small saplings. The vegetation was true to form around the edges of the lot, and around the path that ran diagonally through it; but the spaces in between were a plane surface. Not a leaf nor a blade of grass grew there; it was naked-looking, blank, and absolutely without any colour whatever.

"Oh, that," answered Iridel. "There are only two characters in Act Wednesday who will use that path. Therefore it is as grown-over as it should be. The rest of the lot doesn't enter into the play, so we don't have to do anything with it."

"But – suppose someone wandered off the path on Wednesday," Harry offered.

"He'd be due for a surprise, I guess. But it could hardly happen. Special prompters are always detailed to spots like that, to keep the actors from going astray or missing any cues."

"Who are they – the prompters, I mean?"

"Prompters? GAs – Guardian Angels. That's what the script writers call them."

"I heard o' them," said Harry.

"Yes, they have their work cut out for them," said the supervisor. "Actors are always forgetting their lines when they shouldn't, or remembering them when the script calls for a lapse. Well, it looks pretty good here. Let's have a look at Friday."

"Friday? You mean to tell me you're working on Friday already?"

"Of course! Why, we work years in advance! How on earth do you think we could get our trees grown otherwise? Here – step in!" Iridel put out his hand, seized empty air, drew it aside to show the kind of absolute nothingness he had first appeared from, and waved Harry on.

"Y-you want me to go in there?" asked Harry diffidently.

"Certainly. Hurry, now!"

Harry looked at the section of void with a rather weak-kneed look, but could not withstand the supervisor's strange compulsion. He stepped through.

And it wasn't so bad. There were no whirling lights, no sensations of falling, no falling unconscious. It was just like stepping into another room – which is what had happened. He found himself in a great round chamber, whose roundness was touched a bit with the indistinct. That is, it had curved walls and a domed roof, but there was something else about it. It seemed to stretch off in that direction towards which Iridel had so astonishingly pointed. The walls were lined with an amazing array of control machinery: switches and ground-glass screens, indicators and dials, knurled knobs and levers. Moving deftly before them was a crew of men, each looking exactly like Iridel except that their garments had no pockets. Harry stood wide-eyed, hypnotized by the enormous complexity of the controls and the ease with which the men worked among them. Iridel touched his shoulder. "Come with me," he said. "The producer is in now; we'll find out what is to be done with you."

They started across the floor. Harry had not quite time to wonder how long it would take them to cross that enormous room, for when they had taken perhaps a dozen steps they found themselves at the opposite wall. The ordinary laws of space and time simply did not apply in the place.

They stopped at a door of burnished bronze, so very highly polished that they could see through it. It opened and Iridel pushed Harry through. The door swung shut. Harry, panic-stricken lest he be separated from the only thing in this weird world he could begin to get used to, flung himself against the great bronze portal. It bounced him back, head over heels, into the middle of the floor. He rolled over and got up to his hands and knees.

He was in a tiny room, one end of which was filled by a colossal teakwood desk. The man sitting there regarded him with amusement. "Where'd you blow in from?" he asked; and his voice was like the angry bee sound of an approaching hurricane.

"Are you the producer?"

"Well, I'll be damned," said the man, and smiled. It seemed to fill the whole room with light. He was a big man, Harry noticed; but in this deceptive place, there was no way of telling how big. "I'll be most verily damned. An actor. You're a persistent lot, aren't you? Building houses for me that I almost never go into. Getting together and sending requests for better parts. Listening carefully to what I have to say and then ignoring or misinterpreting my advice. Always asking for just one more chance, and when you get it, messing that up too. And now one of you crashes the gate. What's your trouble, anyway?"

There was something about the producer that bothered Harry, but he could not place what it was, unless it was the fact that the man awed him and he didn't know why. "I woke up in Wednesday," he stammered, "and yesterday was Tuesday. I mean Monday. I mean –" He cleared his throat and started over. "I went to sleep Monday night and woke up Wednesday, and I'm looking for Tuesday."

"What do you want me to do about it?"

"Well, couldn't you tell me how to get back there? I got work to do."

"Oh – I get it," said the producer. "You want a favour from me. You know, some day, some one of you fellows is going to come to me wanting to give me something, free and for nothing, and then I am going to drop quietly dead. Don't I have enough trouble running this show without taking up time and space by doing favours for the likes of you?" He drew a couple of breaths and then smiled again. "However – I have always tried to be just, even if it is a tough job sometimes. Go out and tell Iridel to show you the way back. I think I know what happened to you; when you made your exit from the last act you played in, you somehow managed to walk out behind the wrong curtain when you reached the wings. There's going to be a prompter sent to Limbo for this. Go on now – beat it."

Harry opened his mouth to speak, thought better of it and scuttled out the door, which opened before him. He stood in the huge control chamber, breathing hard. Iridel walked up to him.

"Well?"

"He says for you to get me out of here."

"All right," said Iridel. "This way." He led the way to a curtained doorway much like the one they had used to come in. Beside it were two dials, one marked in days and the other in hours and minutes.

"Monday night good enough for you?" asked Iridel.

"Swell," said Harry.

Iridel set the dials for 9.30 p.m. on Monday. "So long, actor. Maybe I'll see you again some time."

"So long," said Harry. He turned and stepped through the door.

He was back in the garage, and there was no curtained doorway behind him. He turned to ask Iridel if this would enable him to go to bed again and do Tuesday right from the start, but Iridel was gone.

The garage was a blaze of light. Harry glanced up at the clock: it was fifteen seconds after nine thirty. That was funny; everyone should be home by now except Slim Jim, the night man, who hung out until four in the morning serving up gas at the pumps outside. A quick glance around sufficed. This might be Monday night, but it was a Monday night he hadn't known.

The place was filled with the little men again!

Harry sat on the fender of a convertible and groaned. "Now what have I got myself into?" he asked himself.

He could see that he was at a different place-in-time from the one in which he had met Iridel. There, they had been working to build, working with a precision and nicety that was a pleasure to watch. But here . . .

The little men were different, in the first place. They were tired-looking, sick, slow. There were scores of overseers about,

and Harry winced with one of the little fellows when one of the
men in white lashed out with a long whip. As the Wednesday
crews worked, so the Monday gangs slaved. And the work they
were doing was different. For here they were breaking down,
breaking up, carting away. Before his eyes, Harry saw sections of
paving lifted out, pulverized, toted away by the sackload by lines
of trudging, browbeaten little men. He saw great beams upended
to support the roof, while bricks were pried out of the walls. He
heard the gang working on the roof, saw patches of roofing torn
away. He saw walls and roof both melt away under that driving,
driven onslaught, and before he knew what was happening he was
standing alone on a section of the dead white plain he had noticed
before on the corner lot.

It was too much for his overburdened mind; he ran out into the
night, breaking through lines of laden slaves, through neat and
growing piles of rubble, screaming for Iridel. He ran for a long
time, and finally dropped down behind a stack of lumber out
where the Unitarian church used to be, dropped because he could
go no further. He heard footsteps and tried to make himself
smaller. They came on steadily; one of the overseers rounded the
corner and stood looking at him. Harry was in deep shadow, but
he knew the man in white could see in the dark.

"Come out o' there," grated the man. Harry came out.

"You the guy was yellin' for Iridel?"

Harry nodded.

"What makes you think you'll find Iridel in Limbo?" sneered
his captor. "Who are you, anyway?"

Harry had learned by this time. "I'm an – actor," he said in a
small voice. "I got into Wednesday by mistake, and they sent me
back here."

"What for?"

"Huh? Why – I guess it was a mistake, that's all."

The man stepped forward and grabbed Harry by the collar. He
was about eight times as powerful as a hydraulic jack. "Don't give
me no guff, pal," said the man. "Nobody gets sent to Limbo by
mistake, or if he didn't do somethin' up there to make him
deserve it. Come clean, now."

"I didn't do nothin'," Harry wailed. "I asked them the way back, and they showed me a door, and I went through it and came here. That's all I know. Stop it, you're choking me!"

The man dropped him suddenly. "Listen, babe, you know who I am? Hey?" Harry shook his head. "Oh – you don't. Well, I'm Gurrah!"

"Yeah?" Harry said, not being able to think of anything else at the moment.

Gurrah puffed on his chest and appeared to be waiting for something more from Harry. When nothing came, he walked up to the mechanic, breathed in his face. "Ain't scared, huh? Tough guy, huh? Never heard of Gurrah, supervisor of Limbo an' the roughest, toughest son of the devil from Incidence to Eternity, huh?"

Now Harry was a peaceable man, but if there was anything he hated, it was to have a stranger breathe his bad breath pugnaciously at him. Before he knew it had happened, Gurrah was sprawled 8 feet away, and Harry was standing alone rubbing his left knuckles – quite the more surprised of the two.

Gurrah sat up, feeling his face. "Why, you . . . you hit me!" he roared. He got up and came over to Harry. "You hit me!" he said softly, his voice slightly out of focus in amazement. Harry wished he hadn't – wished he was in bed or in Futura or dead or something. Gurrah reached out with a heavy fist and – patted him on the shoulder. "Hey," he said, suddenly friendly, "you're all right. Heh! Took a poke at me, didn't you? Be damned! First time in a month o' Mondays anyone ever made a pass at me. Last was a feller named Orton. I killed 'im." Harry paled.

Gurrah leaned back against the lumber pile. "Dam'f I didn't enjoy that, feller. Yeah. This is a hell of a job they palmed off on me, but what can you do? Breakin' down – breakin' down. No sooner get through one job, workin' top speed, drivin' the boys till they bleed, than they give you the devil for not bein' halfway through another job. You'd think I'd been in the business long enough to know what it was all about, after more than 820 million acts, wouldn't you? Heh. Try to tell *them* that. Ship a load of dog houses up to Wednesday, sneakin' it past backstage nice as you please. They turn right around and call me up. 'What's the matter with you, Gurrah? Them dog houses is no good. We sent you a list o' worn-out items two acts ago. One o' the items was dog houses. Snap out of it or we send someone back there who can read an' put you on a toteline.' That's what I get – act in and act out. An' does it do any good to tell 'em that my aide got the message an' dropped dead before he got it to me? No. Uh-uh. If I say anything about that, they tell me to stop workin' 'em to death. If I do that, they kick because my shipments don't come in fast enough."

He paused for breath. Harry had a hunch that if he kept Gurrah in a good mood it might benefit him. He asked, "What's your job, anyway?"

"Job?" Gurrah howled. "Call this a job? Tearin' down the sets, shippin' what's good to the act after next, junkin' the rest?" He snorted.

Harry asked, "You mean they use the same props over again?"

"That's right. They don't last, though. Six, eight acts, maybe. Then they got to build new ones and weather them and knock 'em around to make 'em look as if they was used."

There was silence for a time. Gurrah, having got his bitterness off his chest for the first time in literally ages, was feeling pacified. Harry didn't know how to feel. He finally broke the ice. "Hey, Gurrah, how'm I goin' to get back into the play?"

"What's it to me? How'd you – Oh, that's right, you walked in from the control room, huh? That it?"

Harry nodded.

"An' how," growled Gurrah, "did you get inta the control room?"

"Iridel brought me."

"Then what?"

"Well, I went to see the producer, and—"

"Th' *producer*! Holy – You mean you walked right in and –" Gurrah mopped his brow. "What'd he say?"

"Why – he said he guessed it wasn't my fault that I woke up in Wednesday. He said to tell Iridel to ship me back."

"An' Iridel threw you back to Monday." And Gurrah threw back his shaggy head and roared.

"What's funny?" asked Harry, a little peeved.

"Iridel," said Gurrah. "Do you realize that I've been trying for 50,000 acts or more to get something on that pretty ol' heel, and he drops you right in my lap. Pal, I can't thank you enough! He was supposed to send you back into the play, and instead o' that you wind up in yesterday! Why, I'll blackmail him till the end of time!" He whirled exultantly, called to a group of bedraggled little men who were staggering under a cornerstone on their way to the junkyard. "Take it easy, boys," he called. "I got ol' Iridel by the short hair. No more busted backs! No more snotty messages! *Haw haw haw*!"

Harry, a little amazed at all this, put in a timid word, "Hey, Gurrah. What about me?"

Gurrah turned. "You? Oh. *Tel-e-phone!*" At his shout two little workers, a trifle less bedraggled than the rest, trotted up. One hopped up and perched on Gurrah's right shoulder; the other draped himself over the left, with his head forward. Gurrah grabbed the latter by the neck, brought the man's head close and shouted into his ear, "Give me Iridel!" There was a moment's wait, then the little man on his other shoulder spoke in Iridel's voice, into Gurrah's ear, "Well?"

"Hiyah, fancy pants!"

"Fancy – I beg your – Who is this?"

"It's Gurrah, you futuristic parasite. I got a couple things to tell you."

"Gurrah! How *dare* you talk to me like that! I'll have you—"

"You'll have me in your job if I tell all I know. You're a wart on the nose of progress, Iridel."

"What is the meaning of this?"

"The meaning of this is that you had instructions sent to you by the producer an' you muffed them. Had an actor there, didn't you? He saw the boss, didn't he? Told you he was to be sent back, didn't he? Sent him right over to me instead of to the play, didn't you? You're slippin', Iridel. Gettin' old. Well, get off the wire. I'm callin' the boss, right now."

"The boss? Oh – don't do that, old man. Look, let's talk this thing over. Ah – about that shipment of three-legged dogs I was wanting you to round up for me; I guess I can do without them. Any little favour I can do for you—"

"You'll damn well do, after this. You better, Goldilocks." Gurrah knocked the two small heads together, breaking the connection and probably the heads, and turned grinning to Harry. "You see," he explained, "that Iridel feller is a damn good supervisor, but he's a stickler for detail. He sends people to Limbo for the silliest little mistakes. He never forgives anyone and he never forgets a slip. He's the cause of half the misery back here, with his hurry-up orders. Now things are gonna be different. The boss has wanted to give Iridel a dose of his own medicine for a long time now, but Irrie never gave him a chance."

Harry said patiently, "About me getting back now—"

"My fran'!" Gurrah bellowed. He delved into a pocket and pulled out a watch like Iridel's. "It's eleven forty on Tuesday," he said. "We'll shoot you back there now. You'll have to dope out your own reasons for disappearing. Don't spill too much, or a lot of people will suffer for it – you the most. Ready?"

Harry nodded; Gurrah swept out a hand and opened the curtain to nothingness. "You'll find yourself quite a ways from where you started," he said, "because you did a little moving around here. Go ahead."

"Thanks," said Harry.

Gurrah laughed. "Don't thank me, chum. You rate all the thanks! Hey – if, after you kick off, you don't make out so good up there, let them toss you over to me. You'll be treated good; you've my word on it. Beat it; luck!"

Holding his breath, Harry Wright stepped through the doorway.

He had to walk thirty blocks to the garage, and when he got there the boss was waiting for him.

"Where you been, Wright?"

"I – lost my way."

"Don't get wise. What do you think this is – vacation time? Get going on the spring job. Damn it, it won't be finished now till tomorra."

Harry looked him straight in the eye and said, "Listen. It'll be finished tonight. I happen to know." And, still grinning, he went back into the garage and took out his tools.

Pixel Pixies

Charles de Lint

This story and the previous are the only light fantasies in this volume. By and large I wanted to avoid comic fantasy, as I've covered those in other anthologies, but since I want to explore as wide a range of fantasy as possible, I can't avoid them completely. Sturgeon's story was the kind that became known as the Unknown-*style fantasy. It was really slick fantasy, of the type also appearing in* Collier's *or the* Saturday Evening Post, *and had hitherto been the domain of Thorne Smith or Lord Dunsany (in his later period) or Stephen Vincent Benet, but had not previously been seen in the pulps. It wasn't always light-hearted, but it treated the fantasy elements as real and explored what would happen if our everyday world suddenly took a turn for the impossible. Thankfully that type of story is still being published and often represents fantasy at its best. Charles de Lint (b. 1951) is a Canadian musician and writer whose early works, such as* A Pattern of Silver Strings *(1981), published by his own Triskell Press, were heavily influenced by Celtic folklore. Later books, such as* Moonheart *(1984) and* Ghostwood *(1990), developed the Celtic background into contemporary urban fantasies about the clash between civilization and older cultures.*

ONLY WHEN MISTRESS HOLLY HAD RETIRED TO HER apartment above the store would Dick Bobbins peep out from behind the furnace where he'd spent the day dreaming and drowsing and reading the books he borrowed from the shelves upstairs. He would carefully check the basement for unexpected visitors and listen for a telltale floorboard to creak from above. Only when he was very very sure that the mistress, and especially her little dog, had both, indeed, gone upstairs, would he creep all the way out of his hidden hobhole.

Every night, he followed the same routine.

Standing on the cement floor, he brushed the sleeves of his drab little jacket and combed his curly brown hair with his fingers. Rubbing his palms briskly together, he plucked last night's borrowed book from his hidey-hole and made his way up the steep basement steps to the store. Standing only 2 feet high, this might have been an arduous process all on its own, but he was quick and agile, as a hob should be, and in no time at all he'd be standing in among the books, considering where to begin the night's work.

There was dusting and sweeping to do, books to be put away. Lovely books. It didn't matter to Dick if they were serious leather-bound tomes or paperbacks with garish covers. He loved them all, for they were filled with words, and words were magic to this hob. Wise and clever humans had used some marvellous spell to imbue each book with every kind of story and character you could imagine, and many you couldn't. If you knew the key to unlock the words, you could experience them all.

Sometimes Dick would remember a time when he hadn't been able to read. All he could do then was riffle the pages and try to smell the stories out of them. But now, oh now, he was a magician, too, for he could unearth the hidden enchantment in the books any time he wanted to. They were his nourishment and his joy, weren't they just.

So first he worked, earning his keep. Then he would choose a new book from those that had come into the store while he was in his hobhole, drowsing away the day. Sitting on top of one of the bookcases, he'd read until it got light outside and it was time to return to his hiding-place behind the furnace, the book under his arm in case he woke early and wanted to finish the story while he waited for the mistress to go to bed once more.

⋆   ⋆   ⋆

I hate computers.

Not when they do what they're supposed to. Not even when I'm the one who's made some stupid mistake, like deleting a file I didn't intend to, or exiting one without saving it. I've still got a few of those old warhorse programs on my machine that don't pop up a reminder asking if I want to save the file I was working on.

No, it's when they seem to have a mind of their own. The keyboard freezing for no apparent reason. Getting an error message that you're out of disk space when you know you've got at least a couple of gigs free. Passwords becoming temporarily, and certainly arbitrarily, obsolete. Those and a hundred other, usually minor, but always annoying, irritations.

Sometimes it's enough to make you want to pick up the nearest component of the machine and fling it against the wall.

For all the effort they save, the little tasks that they automate and their wonderful storage capacity, at times like this – when everything's going as wrong as it can go – their benefits can't come close to outweighing their annoyances.

My present situation was partly my own fault. I'd been updating my inventory all afternoon and before saving the file and backing it up, I'd decided to go on the Internet to check some of my competitors' prices. The used-book business, which is what I'm in, has probably the most arbitrary pricing in the world. Though I suppose that can be expanded to include any business specializing in collectibles.

I logged on without any trouble and went merrily browsing through listings on the various book search pages, making notes on the particularly interesting items, a few of which I actually had in stock. It wasn't until I tried to exit my browser that the trouble started. My browser wouldn't close and I couldn't switch to another window. Nor could I log off the Internet.

Deciding it had something to do with the page I was on – I know that doesn't make much sense, but I make no pretence to being more than vaguely competent when it comes to knowing how the software actually interfaces with the hardware – I called up the drop-down menu of "My Favorites" and clicked on my own home page. What I got was a fan shrine to pro wrestling star Steve Austin.

I tried again and ended up at a commercial software site.

The third time I was taken to the site of someone named Cindy Margolis – the most downloaded woman on the Internet, according to the *Guinness Book of World Records*. Not on this computer, my dear.

I made another attempt to get off-line, then tried to access my home page again. Each time I found myself in some new outlandish and unrelated site.

Finally I tried one of the links on the last page I'd reached. It was supposed to bring me to Netscape's home page. Instead I found myself on the Web site of a real estate company in Santa Fe, looking at a cluster of pictures of the vaguely Spanish-styled houses that they were selling.

I sighed, tried to break my Internet connection for what felt like the hundredth time, but the "Connect to" window still wouldn't come up.

I could have rebooted, of course. That would have got me off-line. But it would also mean that I'd lose the whole afternoon's work because, being the stupid woman I was, I hadn't had the foresight to save the stupid file before I went gadding about on the stupid Internet.

"Oh, you stupid machine," I muttered.

From the front window display where she was napping, I heard Snippet, my Jack Russell terrier, stir. I turned to reassure her that, no, she was still my perfect little dog. When I swivelled my chair to face the computer again, I realized that there was a woman standing on the other side of the counter.

I'd seen her come into the store earlier, but I'd lost track of everything in my one-sided battle of wits with the computer – it having the wits, of course. She was a very striking woman, her dark brown hair falling in Pre-Raphaelite curls that were streaked with green, her eyes both warm and distant, like an odd mix of a perfect summer's day and the mystery you can feel swell up inside you when you look up into the stars on a crisp, clear autumn night. There was something familiar about her, but I couldn't quite place it. She wasn't one of my regulars.

She gave me a sympathetic smile.

"I suppose it was only a matter of time before they got into the computers," she said.

I blinked. "What?"

"Try putting your sweater on inside-out."

My face had to be registering the confusion I was feeling, but she simply continued to smile.

"I know it sounds silly," she said. "But humour me. Give it a try."

Anyone in retail knows, you get all kinds. And the secondhand market gets more than its fair share, trust me on that. If there's a loopy person anywhere within a hundred blocks of my store, you can bet they'll eventually find their way inside. The woman standing on the other side of my counter looked harmless enough, if somewhat exotic, but you just never know any more, do you?

"What have you got to lose?" she asked.

I was about to lose an afternoon's work as things stood, so what was a little pride on top of that?

I stood up and took my sweater off, turned it inside out, and put it back on again.

"Now give it a try," the woman said.

I called up the "Connect to" window and this time it came up. When I put the cursor on the "Disconnect" button and clicked, I was logged off. I quickly shut down my browser and saved the file I'd been working on all afternoon.

"You're a life-saver," I told the woman. "How did you know that would work?" I paused, thought about what I'd just said, what had just happened. "*Why* would that work?"

"I've had some experience with pixies and their like," she said.

"Pixies," I repeated. "You think there are pixies in my computer?"

"Hopefully, not. If you're lucky, they're still on the Internet and didn't follow you home."

I gave her a curious look. "You're serious, aren't you?"

"At times," she said, smiling again. "And this is one of them."

I thought about one of my friends, an electronic pen pal in Arizona, who had this theory that the first atom bomb detonation for ever changed the way that magic would appear in the world. According to him, the spirits live in the wires now instead of the trees. They travel through phone and modem lines, take up residence in computers and appliances where they live on electricity and lord knows what else.

It looked like Richard wasn't alone in his theories, not that I pooh-poohed them myself. I'm part of a collective that originated this electronic database called the Wordwood. After it took on a life of its own, I pretty much keep an open mind about things that most people would consider preposterous.

"I'd like to buy this," the woman went on.

She held up a trade paperback copy of *The Beggars' Shore* by Zak Mucha.

"Good choice," I said.

It never surprises me how many truly excellent books end up in the secondary market. Not that I'm complaining – it's what keeps me in business.

"Please take it as thanks for your advice," I added.

"You're sure?"

I looked down at my computer, where my afternoon's work was now safely saved in its file.

"Oh, yes," I told her.

"Thank you," she said. Reaching into her pocket, she took out a business card and gave it to me. "Call me if you ever need any other advice along the same lines."

The business card simply said "The Kelledys" in a large script. Under it were the names "Meran and Cerin" and a phone number. Now I knew why, earlier, she'd seemed familiar. It had just been seeing her here in the store, out of context, that had thrown me.

"I love your music," I told her. "I've seen you and your husband play several times."

She gave me another of those kind smiles of hers.

"You can probably turn your sweater around again now," she said as she left.

Snippet and I watched her walk by the window. I took off my sweater and put it back on properly.

"Time for your walk," I told Snippet. "But first let me back up this file to a zip disk."

That night, after the mistress and her little dog had gone upstairs, Dick Bobbins crept out of his hobhole and made his nightly journey up to the store. He replaced the copy of *The Woods Colt* that he'd been reading, putting it neatly back on the fiction shelf under "W" for Williamson, fetched the duster, and started his work. He finished the "History" and "Local Interest" sections, dusting and straightening the books, and was climbing up on to the "Poetry" shelves near the back of the store when he paused, hearing something from the front of the store.

Reflected in the front window, he could see the glow of the computer's monitor and realized that the machine had turned on by itself. That couldn't be good. A faint giggle spilled out of the computer's speakers, quickly followed by a chorus of other voices, tittering and snickering. That was even less good.

A male face appeared on the screen, looking for all the world as though it could see out of the machine. Behind him other faces appeared, a whole gaggle of little men in green clothes, good-naturedly pushing and shoving each other, whispering and giggling. They were red-haired like the mistress, but there the resemblance ended. Where she was pretty, they were ugly, with short faces, turned-up noses, squinting eyes and pointed ears.

This wasn't good at all, Dick thought, recognizing the pixies for what they were. Everybody knew how you spelled "trouble". It was "P-I-X-Y".

And then they started to clamber out of the screen, which shouldn't have been possible at all, but Dick was a hob and he understood that just because something shouldn't be able to happen, didn't mean it couldn't. Or wouldn't.

"Oh, this is bad," he said mournfully. "Bad, bad, bad."

He gave a quick look up to the ceiling. He had to warn the mistress. But it was already too late. Between one thought and the next, a dozen or more pixies had climbed out of the computer on to her desk, not one of them taller than his own waist. They began riffling through her papers, using her pens and ruler as swords to poke at each other. Two of them started a pushing match that resulted in a small stack of books falling off the side of the desk. They landed with a bang on the floor.

The sound was so loud that Dick was sure the mistress would come down to investigate, she and her fierce little dog. The pixies all stood like little statues until first one, then another, started to giggle again. When they all began to shove at a bigger stack of books, Dick couldn't wait any longer.

Quick as a monkey, he scurried down to the floor.

"Stop!" he shouted as he ran to the front of the store.

And, "Here, you!"

And, "Don't!"

The pixies turned at the sound of his voice and Dick skidded to a stop.

"Oh, oh," he said.

The little men were still giggling and elbowing each other, but there was a wicked light in their eyes now, and they were all looking at him with those dark, considering gazes. Poor Dick realized that he hadn't thought any of this through in the least bit properly, for now that he had their attention, he had no idea what to do with it. They might only be a third his size, individually, but there were at least twenty of them and everybody knew just how mean a pixy could be, did he set his mind to it.

"Well, will you look at that," one of the pixies said. "It's a little hobberdy man." He looked at his companions. "What shall we do with him?"

"Smash him!"

"Whack him!"

"Find a puddle and drown him!"

Dick turned and fled, back the way he'd come. The pixies streamed from the top of Mistress Holly's desk, laughing wickedly and shouting threats as they chased him. Up the "Poetry" shelves Dick went, all the way to the very top. When he looked back down, he saw that the pixies weren't following the route he'd taken.

He allowed himself a moment's relief. Perhaps he was safe. Perhaps they couldn't climb. Perhaps they were afraid of heights.

Or, he realized with dismay, perhaps they meant to bring the whole bookcase crashing down, and him with it.

For the little men had gathered at the bottom of the bookcase and were putting their shoulders to its base. They might be small, but they were strong, and soon the tall stand of shelves was tottering unsteadily, swaying back and forth. A loose book fell out. Then another.

"No, no! You mustn't!" Dick cried down to them.

But he was too late.

With cries of "Hooray!" from the little men below, the bookcase came tumbling down, spraying books all around it. It smashed into its neighbour, bringing that stand of shelves down as well. By the time Dick hit the floor, hundreds of books were scattered all over the carpet and he was sitting on top of a tall, unsteady mountain of poetry, clutching his head, awaiting the worst.

The pixies came clambering up its slopes, the wicked lights in their eyes shining fierce and bright. He was, Dick realized, about to become an ex-hob. Except then he heard the door to Mistress Holly's apartment open at the top of the back stairs.

Rescued, he thought. And not a moment too soon. She would chase them off.

All the little men froze and Dick looked for a place to hide from the mistress's gaze.

But the pixies seemed unconcerned. Another soft round of giggles arose from them as, one by one, they transformed into soft, glittering lights no bigger than the mouth of a shot glass. The lights rose up from the floor where they'd been standing and went sailing towards the front of the store. When the mistress appeared at the foot of the stairs, her dog at her heels, she didn't even look at the fallen bookshelves. She saw only the lights, her eyes widening with happy delight.

Oh, no, Dick thought. They're pixy-leading her.

The little dog began to growl and bark and tug at the hem of her long flannel nightgown, but she paid no attention to it.

Smiling a dreamy smile, she lifted her arms above her head like a ballerina and began to follow the dancing lights to the front of the store. Dick watched as pixy magic made the door pop open and a gust of chilly air burst in. Goosebumps popped up on the mistress's forearms but she never seemed to notice the cold. Her gaze was locked on the lights as they swooped, around and around in a gallitrap circle, then went shimmering out on to the street beyond. In moments she would follow them, out into the night and who knew what terrible danger.

Her little dog let go of her hem and ran ahead, barking at the lights. But it was no use. The pixies weren't frightened and the mistress wasn't roused.

It was up to him, Dick realized.

He ran up behind her and grabbed her ankle, bracing himself. Like the pixies, he was much stronger than his size might give him to appear. He held firm as the mistress tried to raise her foot. She lost her balance and down she went, down and down, toppling like some enormous tree. Dick jumped back, hands to his mouth, appalled at what he'd had to do. She banged her shoulder against a display at the front of the store, sending yet another mass of books cascading on to the floor.

Landing heavily on her arms, she stayed bent over for a long time before she finally looked up. She shook her head as though to clear it. The pixy lights had returned to the store, buzzing angrily about, but it was no use. The spell had been broken. One by one, they zoomed out of the store, down the street and were quickly lost from sight. The mistress's little dog ran back out on to the sidewalk and continued to bark at them, long after they were gone.

"Please let me be dreaming . . ." the mistress said.

Dick stooped quickly out of sight as she looked about at the sudden ruin of the store. He peeked at her from his hiding-place, watched her rub at her face, then slowly stand up and massage her shoulder where it had hit the display. She called the dog back in, but stood in the doorway herself for a long time, staring out at the street, before she finally shut and locked the door behind her.

Oh, it was all such a horrible, terrible, awful mess.

"I'm sorry, I'm sorry, I'm sorry," Dick murmured, his voice barely a whisper, tears blurring his eyes.

The mistress couldn't hear him. She gave the store another survey, then shook her head.

"Come on, Snippet," she said to the dog. "We're going back to bed. Because this is just a dream."

She picked her way through the fallen books and shelves as she spoke.

"And when we wake up tomorrow everything will be back to normal."

But it wouldn't be. Dick knew. This was more of a mess than even the most industrious of hobs could clear up in just one night. But he did what he could until the morning came, one eye on the task at hand, the other on the windows in case the horrible pixies decided to return. Though what he'd do if they did, probably only the moon knew, and she wasn't telling.

Did you ever wake up from the weirdest, most unpleasant dream, only to find that it wasn't a dream at all?

When I came down to the store that morning, I literally had to lean against the wall at the foot of the stairs and catch my breath. I felt all faint and woozy. Snippet walked daintily ahead of me, sniffing the fallen books and whining softly.

An earthquake, I told myself. That's what it had been. I must have woken up right after the main shock, come down half-asleep and seen the mess, and just gone right back to bed again, thinking I was dreaming.

Except there'd been those dancing lights. Like a dozen or more Tinkerbells. Or fireflies. Calling me to follow, follow, follow, out into the night, until I'd tripped and fallen . . .

I shook my head slowly, trying to clear it. My shoulder was still sore and I massaged it as I took in the damage.

Actually, the mess wasn't as bad as it had looked at first. Many of the books appeared to have toppled from the shelves and landed in relatively alphabetical order.

Snippet whined again, but this time it was her "I really have to go" whine, so I grabbed her leash and a plastic bag from behind the desk and out we went for her morning constitutional.

It was brisk outside, but warm for early December, and there still wasn't any snow. At first glance, the damage from the quake appeared to be fairly marginal, considering it had managed to topple a couple of the bookcases in my store. The worst I could see were that all garbage canisters on the block had been overturned, the wind picking up the paper litter and carrying it in eddying pools up and down the street. Other than that, everything seemed pretty much normal. At least it did until I stopped into Café Joe's down the street to get my morning latte.

Joe Lapegna had originally operated a sandwich bar at the same location, but with the coming of Starbucks to town, he'd quickly seen which way the wind was blowing and renovated his place into a café. He'd done a good job with the décor. His café was every bit as contemporary and urban as any of the other high-end coffee bars in the city, the only real difference being that, instead of young college kids with rings through their noses, you got Joe serving the lattes and espressos. Joe with his broad shoulders and meaty, tattooed forearms, a fat caterpillar of a black moustache perched on his upper lip.

Before I could mention the quake, Joe started to tell me how he'd opened up this morning to find every porcelain mug in the store broken. None of the other breakables, not the plates or coffeemakers. Nothing else was even out of place.

"What a weird quake it was," I said.

"Quake?" Joe said. "What quake?"

I waved a hand at the broken china he was sweeping up.

"This was vandals," he said. "Some little bastards broke in and had themselves a laugh."

So I told him about the bookcases in my shop, but he only shook his head.

"You hear anything about a quake on the radio?" he asked.

"I wasn't listening to it."

"I was. There was nothing. And what kind of a quake only breaks mugs and knocks over a couple of bookcases?"

Now that I thought of it, it was odd that there hadn't been any other disruption in my own store. If those bookcases had come down, why hadn't the front window display? I'd noticed a few books had fallen off my desk, but that was about it.

"It's so weird," I repeated.

Joe shook his head. "Nothing weird about it. Just some punks out having their idea of fun."

By the time I got back to my own store, I didn't know what to think. Snippet and I stopped in at a few other places along the strip and while everyone had damage to report, none of it was what could be put down to a quake. In the bakery, all the pies had been thrown against the front windows. In the hardware store, each and every electrical bulb was smashed – though they looked as though they'd simply exploded. All the rolls of paper towels and toilet paper from the grocery store had been tossed up into the trees behind their shipping and receiving bays, turning the bare-branched oaks and elms into bizarre mummy-like versions of themselves. And on it went.

The police arrived not long after I returned to the store. I felt like such a fool when one of the detectives came by to interview me. Yes, I'd heard the crash and come down to investigate. No, I hadn't seen anything.

I couldn't bring myself to mention the dancing lights.

No, I hadn't thought to phone it in.

"I thought I was dreaming," I told him. "I was half-asleep when I came downstairs and didn't think it had really happened. It wasn't until I came back down in the morning . . ."

The detective was of the opinion that it had been gang-related, kids out on the prowl, egging each other on until it had got out of control.

I thought about it when he left and knew he had to be right. The damage we'd sustained was all on the level of pranks – mean-spirited, to be sure, but pranks nonetheless. I didn't like the idea of our little area being the sudden target of vandals, but there really wasn't any other logical explanation. At least none occurred to me until I stepped back into the store and glanced at my computer. That's when I remembered Meran Kelledy, how she'd got me to turn my sweater inside out and the odd things she'd been saying about pixies on the Web.

If you're lucky, they're still on the Internet and didn't follow you home.

Of course that wasn't even remotely logical. But it made me think. After all, if the Wordwood database could take on a life of its own, who was to say that pixies on the Internet was any more improbable? As my friend Richard likes to point out, everyone has odd problems with their computers that could as easily be attributed to mischievous spirits as to software glitches. At least they could be if your mind was inclined to think along those lines, and mine certainly was.

I stood for a long moment, staring at the screen of my computer. I don't know exactly at what point I realized that the machine was on. I'd turned it off last night before Snippet and I went up to the apartment. And I hadn't stopped to turn it on this morning before we'd gone out. So either I was getting monumentally forgetful, or I'd turned it on while sleepwalking last night, or . . .

I glanced over at Snippet, who was once again sniffing every-thing as though she'd never been in the store before. Or as if someone or something interesting and strange *had*.

"This is silly," I said.

But I dug out Meran's card and called the number on it all the same, staring at the computer screen as I did. I just hoped nobody had been tinkering with my files.

Bookstore hobs are a relatively recent phenomenon, dating back only a couple of hundred years. Dick knew hobs back home in the old country who'd lived in the same household for three times that length of time. He'd been a farm hob himself, once, living on a Devon steading for 212 years until a new family moved in and began to take his services for granted. When one year they actually dared to complain about how poorly the harvest had been put away, he'd thrown every bit of it down into a nearby ravine and set off to find new habitation.

A cousin who lived in a shop had suggested to Dick that he try the same, but there were fewer commercial establishments in those days and they all had their own hob by the time he went looking, first up into Somerset, then back down through Devon, finally moving west to Cornwall. In the end, he made his home in a small cubby-hole of a bookstore he found in Penzance. He lived there for years until the place went out of business, the owner setting sail for North America with plans to open another shop in the new land once he arrived.

Dick had followed, taking up residence in the new store when it was established. That was where he'd taught himself to read.

But he soon discovered that stores didn't have the longevity of a farm. They opened and closed up business seemingly on nothing more than a whim, which made it a hard life for a hob, always looking for a new place to live. By the latter part of this century, he had moved twelve times in the space of five years before finally settling into the place he now called home, the bookstore of his present mistress with its simple sign out front:

Holly Rue – Used Books

He'd discovered that a quality used-book store was always the best. Libraries were good, too, but they were usually home to displaced gargoyles and the ghosts of writers and had no room for a hob as well. He'd tried new book stores, but the smaller ones couldn't keep him busy enough and the large ones were too bright, their hours of business too long. And he loved the wide and eclectic range of old and new books to be explored in a shop such as Mistress Holly's, titles that wandered far from the beaten path, or worthy books no longer in print, but nonetheless inspired. The stories he found in them sustained him in a way that nothing else could, for they fed the heart and the spirit.

But this morning, sitting behind the furnace, he only felt old and tired. There'd been no time to read at all last night, and he hadn't thought to bring a book down with him when he finally had to leave the store.

"I hate pixies," he said, his voice soft and lonely in the darkness. "I really really do."

Faeries and pixies had never got along, especially not since the last pitched battle between them in the old country when the faeries had been driven back across the River Parrett, leaving everything west of the Parrett as pixyland. For years, hobs such as Dick had lived a clandestine existence in their little steadings, avoiding the attention of pixies whenever they could.

Dick hadn't needed last night's experience to tell him why.

After a while he heard the mistress and her dog leave the store, so he crept out from behind the furnace to stand guard in case the pixies returned while the pair of them were gone. Though what he would do if the pixies did come back, he had no idea. He was an absolute failure when it came to protecting anything; that had been made all too clear last night.

Luckily the question never arose. Mistress Holly and the dog returned and he slipped back behind the furnace, morosely clutching his knees and rocking back and forth, waiting for the night to come. He could hear life go on upstairs. Someone came by to help the mistress right the fallen bookcases. Customers arrived and left with much discussion of the vandalism on the street. Most of the time he could hear only the mistress, replacing the books on their shelves.

"I should be doing that," Dick said. "That's my job."

But he was only an incompetent hob, concealed in his hidey-hole, of no use to anyone until they all went to bed and he could go about his business. And even then, any ruffian could come along and bully him and what could he do to stop them?

Dick's mood went from bad to worse, from sad to sadder still. It might have lasted all the day, growing unhappier with each passing hour, except at mid-morning he suddenly sat up, ears and nose quivering. A presence had come into the store above. A piece of an old mystery, walking about as plain as could be.

He realized that he'd sensed it yesterday as well, while he was dozing. Then he'd put it down to the dream he was wandering in, forgetting all about it when he woke. But today, wide awake, he couldn't ignore it. There was an oak king's daughter upstairs, an old and powerful spirit walking far from her woods. He began to shiver. Important faerie such as she wouldn't be out and about unless the need was great. His shiver deepened. Perhaps she'd come to reprimand him for the job so poorly done. She might turn him into a stick or a mouse.

Oh, this was very bad. First pixies, now this.

Whatever was he going to do? However could he even begin to explain that he'd meant to chase the pixies away, truly he had, but he simply wasn't big enough, nor strong enough. Perhaps not even brave enough.

He rocked back and forth, harder now, his face burrowed against his knees.

After I'd made my call to Meran, David, who works at the deli down the street, came by and helped me stand the bookcases upright once more. The deli hadn't been spared a visit from the vandals either. He told me that they'd taken all the sausages out of the freezer and used them to spell out rude words on the floor.

"Remember when all we had to worry about was some graffiti on the walls outside?" he asked when he was leaving.

I was still replacing books on the shelves when Meran arrived. She looked around the store while I expanded on what I'd told her over the phone. Her brow furrowed thoughtfully and I was wondering if she was going to tell me to put my sweater on backwards again.

"You must have a hob in here," she said.

"A what?"

It was the last thing I expected her to say.

"A hobgoblin," she said. "A brownie. A little faerie man who dusts and tidies and keeps things neat."

"I just thought it didn't get all that dirty," I said, realizing as I spoke how ridiculous that sounded.

Because, when I thought about it, a helpful brownie living in the store explained a lot. While I certainly ran the vacuum cleaner over the carpets every other morning or so, and dusted when I could, the place never seemed to need much cleaning. My apartment upstairs required more and it didn't get a fraction of the traffic.

And it wasn't just the cleaning. The store, for all its clutter, was organized, though half the time I didn't know how. But I always seemed to be able to lay my hand on whatever I needed to find without having to root about too much. Books often got put away without my remembering I'd done it. Others mysteriously vanished, then reappeared a day or so later, properly filed in their appropriate section – even if they had originally disappeared from the top of my desk. I rarely needed to alphabetize my sections while my colleagues in other stores were constantly complaining of the mess their customers left behind.

"But aren't you supposed to leave cakes and cream out for them?" I found myself asking.

"You never leave a specific gift," Meran said. "Not unless you want him to leave. It's better simply to 'forget' a cake or a sweet treat on one of the shelves when you leave for the night."

"I haven't even done that. What could he be living on?"

Meran smiled as she looked around the store. "Maybe the books nourish him. Stranger things have been known to happen in Faerie."

"Faerie," I repeated slowly.

Bad enough I'd helped create a database on the Internet that had taken on a life of its own. Now my store was in Faerie. Or at least straddling the border, I supposed. Maybe the one had come about because of the other.

"Your hob will know what happened here last night," Meran said.

"But how would we even go about asking him?"

It seemed a logical question, since I'd never known I had one living with me in the first place. But Meran only smiled.

"Oh, I can usually get their attention," she told me.

She called out something in a foreign language, a handful of words that rang with great strength and appeared to linger and echo longer than they should. The poor little man who came sidling up from the basement in response looked absolutely terrified. He was all curly hair and raggedy clothes with a broad face that, I assumed from the laugh lines, normally didn't look so miserable. He was carrying a battered little leather carpetbag and held a brown cloth cap in his hand. He couldn't have been more than 2 feet tall.

All I could do was stare at him, though I did have the foresight to pick up Snippet before she could lunge in his direction. I could feel the growl rumbling in her chest more than hear it. I think she was as surprised as me to find that he'd been living in our basement all this time.

Meran sat on her haunches, bringing her head down to the general level of the hob's. To put him at ease, I supposed, so I did the same myself. The little man didn't appear to lose any of his nervousness. I could see his knees knocking against each other, his cheek twitching.

"B-begging your pardon, your ladyship," he said to Meran. His gaze slid to me and I gave him a quick smile. He blinked, swallowed hard, and returned his attention to my companion. "Dick Bobbins," he added, giving a quick nod of his head. "At your service, as it were. I'll just be on my way, then, no harm done."

"Why are you so frightened of me?" Meran asked.

He looked at the floor. "Well, you're a king's daughter, aren't you just, and I'm only me."

A king's daughter? I thought.

Meran smiled. "We're all only who we are, no one of more importance than the other."

"Easy for you to say," he began. Then his eyes grew wide and he put a hand to his mouth. "Oh, that was a bad thing to say to such a great and wise lady such as yourself."

Meran glanced at me. "They think we're like movie stars," she explained. "Just because we were born in a court instead of a hobhole."

I was getting a bit of a case of the celebrity nerves myself. Court? King's daughter? Who exactly *was* this woman?

"But you know," she went on, returning her attention to the little man, "my father's court was only a glade, our palace no more than a tree."

He nodded quickly, giving her a thin smile that never reached his eyes.

"Well, wonderful to meet you," he said. "Must be on my way now."

He picked up his carpetbag and started to sidle towards the other aisle that wasn't blocked by what he must see as two great big hulking women and a dog.

"But we need your help," Meran told him.

Whereupon he burst into tears.

The mothering instinct that makes me such a sap for Snippet kicked into gear and I wanted to hold him in my arms and comfort him. But I had Snippet to consider, straining in my grip, the growl in her chest quite audible now. And I wasn't sure how the little man would have taken my sympathies. After all, he might be child-sized, but for all his tears, he was obviously an adult, not a child. And if the stories were anything to go by, he was probably older than me – by a few hundred years.

Meran had no such compunction. She slipped up to him and put her arms around him, cradling his face against the crook of her shoulder.

It took a while before we coaxed the story out of him. I locked the front door and we went upstairs to my kitchen where I made tea for us all. Sitting at the table, raised up to the proper height by a stack of books, Dick told us about the pixies coming out of the computer screen, how they'd knocked down the bookcases and finally disappeared into the night. The small mug I'd given him looked enormous in his hands. He fell silent when he was done and stared glumly down at the steam rising from his tea.

"But none of what they did was your fault," I told him.

"Kind of you to say," he managed. He had to stop and sniff, wipe his nose on his sleeve. "But if I'd b-been braver—"

"They *would* have drowned you in a puddle," Meran said. "And I think you were brave, shouting at them the way you did and then rescuing your mistress from being pixy-led."

I remembered those dancing lights and shivered. I knew those stories as well. There weren't any swamps or marshes to be led into around here, but there were eighteen-wheelers out on the highway only a few blocks away. Entranced as I'd been, the pixies could easily have walked me right out in front of any one of them. I was lucky only to have a sore shoulder.

"Do you . . . really think so?" he asked, sitting up a little straighter.

We both nodded.

Snippet was lying under my chair, her curiosity having been satisfied that Dick was only one more visitor and therefore out-of-bounds in terms of biting and barking at. There'd been a nervous moment while she'd sniffed at his trembling hand and he'd looked as though he was ready to scurry up one of the bookcases, but they quickly made their peace. Now Snippet was only bored and had fallen asleep.

"Well," Meran said. "It's time we put our heads together and consider how we can put our unwanted visitors back where they came from and keep them there."

"Back on to the Internet?" I asked. "Do you really think we should?"

"Well, we could try to kill them . . ."

I shook my head. That seemed too extreme. I started to protest only to see that she'd been teasing me.

"We could take a thousand of them out of the Web," Meran said, "and still not have them all. Once tricksy folk like pixies have their foot in a place, you can't ever be completely rid of them." She smiled. "But if we can get them to go back in, there are measures we can take to stop them from troubling you again."

"And what about everybody else on-line?" I asked.

Meran shrugged. "They'll have to take their chances – just like they do when they go for a walk in the woods. The little people are everywhere."

I glanced across my kitchen table to where the hob was sitting and thought, no kidding.

"The trick, if you'll pardon my speaking out of turn," Dick said, "is to play on their curiosity."

Meran gave him an encouraging smile. "We want your help," she said. "Go on."

The little man sat up straighter still and put his shoulders back.

"We could use a book that's never been read," he said. "We could put it in the middle of the road, in front of the store. That would certainly make me curious."

"An excellent idea," Meran told him.

"And then we could use the old spell of bell, book and candle. The churchmen stole that one from us."

Even I'd heard of it. Bell, book and candle had once been another way of saying excommunication in the Catholic Church. After pronouncing the sentence, the officiating cleric would close his book, extinguish the candle, and toll the bell as if for someone who had died. The book symbolized the book of life, the candle a man's soul, removed from the sight of God as the candle had been from the sight of men.

But I didn't get the unread book bit.

"Do you mean a brand-new book?" I asked. "A particular copy that nobody might have opened yet, or one that's so bad that no one's actually made their way all the way through it?"

"Though someone would have had to," Dick said, "for it to have been published in the first place. I meant the way books were made in the old days, with the pages still sealed. You had to cut them apart as you read them."

"Oh, I remember those," Meran said.

Like she was there. I took another look at her and sighed. Maybe she had been.

"Do you have any like that?" she asked.

"Yes," I said slowly, unable to hide my reluctance.

I didn't particularly like the idea of putting a collector's item like that out in the middle of the road.

But in the end, that's what we did.

The only book I had that passed Dick's inspection was *The Trembling of the Veil* by William Butler Yeats, number seventy-one of a thousand-copy edition privately printed by T. Werner Laurie, Ltd in 1922. All the pages were still sealed at the top. It was currently listing on the Internet in the $450 to $500 range and I kept it safely stowed away in the glass-doored bookcase that held my first editions.

The other two items were easier to deal with. I had a lovely brass bell that my friend Tatiana had given me for Christmas last year and a whole box of fat white candles just because I liked to burn them. But it broke my heart to go out on to the street around two a.m., and place the Yeats on the pavement.

We left the front door to the store ajar, the computer on. I wasn't entirely sure how we were supposed to lure the pixies back into the store and then on to the Internet once more, but Meran took a flute out of her bag and fit the wooden pieces of it together. She spoke of a calling-on music and Dick nodded sagely, so I simply went along with their better experience. Mind you, I also wasn't all that sure that my Yeats would actually draw the pixies back in the first place, but what did I know?

We all hid in the alleyway running between my store and the futon shop, except for Snippet, who was locked up in my apartment. She hadn't been very pleased by that. After an hour of crouching in the cold in the alley, I wasn't feeling very pleased myself. What if the pixies didn't come? What if they did, but they approached from the fields behind the store and came traipsing up this very alleyway?

By three thirty we all had a terrible chill. Looking up at my apartment, I could see Snippet lying in the window of the dining-room, looking down at us. She didn't appear to have forgiven me yet and I would happily have changed places with her.

"Maybe we should just—"

I didn't get to finish with "call it a night". Meran put a finger to her lips and hugged the wall. I looked past her to the street.

At first I didn't see anything. There was just my Yeats, lying there on the pavement, waiting for a car to come and run over it. But then I saw the little man, not even half the size of Dick, come creeping up from the sewer grating. He was followed by two more. Another pair came down the brick wall of the temporary office help building across the street. Small dancing lights that I remembered too clearly from last night dipped and wove their way from the other end of the block, descending to the pavement and becoming more of the little men when they drew near to the book. One of them poked at it with his foot and I had visions of them tearing it apart.

Meran glanced at Dick and he nodded, mouthing the words, "That's the lot of them."

She nodded back and took her flute out from under her coat where she'd been keeping it warm.

At this point I wasn't really thinking of how the calling music would work. I'm sure my mouth hung agape as I stared at the pixies. I felt light-headed, a big grin tugging at my lips. Yes, they were pranksters, and mean-spirited ones at that. But they were also magical. The way they'd changed from little lights to little men . . . I'd never seen anything like it before. The hob who lived in my bookstore was magical, too, of course, but somehow it wasn't the same thing. He was already familiar, so down-to-earth. Sitting around during the afternoon and evening while we waited, I'd had a delightful time talking books with him, as though he were an old friend. I'd completely forgotten that he was a little magic man himself.

The pixies were truly puzzled by the book. I suppose it would be odd from any perspective, a book that old, never once having been opened or read. It defeated the whole purpose of why it had been made.

I'm not sure when Meran began to play her flute. The soft breathy sound of it seemed to come from nowhere and everywhere, all at once, a resonant wave of slow, stately notes, one falling after the other, rolling into a melody that was at once hauntingly strange and heartachingly familiar.

The pixies lifted their heads at the sound. I wasn't sure what I'd expected, but when they began to dance, I almost clapped my hands. They were so funny. Their bodies kept perfect time to the music, but their little eyes glared at Meran as she stepped out of the alley and Pied Pipered them into the store.

Dick fetched the Yeats and then he and I followed after, arriving in time to see the music make the little men dance up on to my chair, on to the desk, until they began to vanish, one by one, into the screen of my monitor, a fat candle sitting on top of it, its flame flickering with their movement. Dick opened the book and I took the bell out of my pocket.

Meran took the flute from her lips.

"Now," she said.

Dick slapped the book closed, she leaned forward and blew out the candle while I began to chime the bell, the clear brass notes ringing in the silence left behind by the flute. We saw a horde of little faces staring out at us from the screen, eyes glaring. One of the little men actually popped back through, but Dick caught him by the leg and tossed him back into the screen.

Meran laid her flute down on the desk and brought out a garland she'd made earlier of rowan twigs, green leaves and red berry sprigs still attached in places. When she laid it on top of the monitor, we heard the modem dial up my Internet service. When the connection was made, the little men vanished from the screen. The last turned his bum towards us and let out a loud fart before he, too, was gone.

The three of us couldn't help it. We all broke up.

"That went rather well," Meran said when we finally caught our breath. "My husband Cerin is usually the one to handle this sort of thing, but it's nice to know I haven't forgotten how to deal with such rascals myself. And that it's probably best he didn't come along this evening. He can seem rather fierce and I don't doubt poor Dick here would have thought him far too menacing."

I looked around the store.

"Where *is* Dick?" I asked.

But the little man was gone. I couldn't believe it. Surely he hadn't just up and left us like in the stories.

"Hobs and brownies," Meran said when I asked, her voice gentle, "they tend to take their leave rather abruptly when the tale is done."

"I thought you had to leave them a suit of clothes or something."

Meran shrugged. "Sometimes simply being identified is enough to make them go."

"Why does it have to be like that?"

"I'm not really sure. I suppose it's a rule or something, or a geas – a thing that has to happen. Or perhaps it's no more than a simple habit they've handed down from one generation to the next."

"But I *loved* the idea of him living here," I said. "I thought it would be so much fun. With all the work he's been doing. I'd have been happy to make him a partner."

Meran smiled. "Faerie and commerce don't usually go hand in hand."

"But you and your husband play music for money."

Her smile grew wider, her eyes enigmatic, but also amused. "What makes you think we're faerie?" she asked.

"Well, you . . . that is . . ."

"I'll tell you a secret," she said, relenting. "We're something else again, but what exactly that might be, even we have no idea any more. Mostly we're the same as you. Where we differ is that Cerin and I always live with half a foot in the otherworld that you've only visited these past few days."

"And only the borders of it, I'm sure."

She shrugged. "Faerie is everywhere. It just *seems* closer at certain times, in certain places."

She began to take her flute apart and stow the wooden pieces away in the instrument's carrying case.

"Your hob will be fine," she said. "The kindly ones such as he always find a good household to live in."

"I hope so," I said. "But all the same, I was really looking forward to getting to know him better."

Dick Bobbins got an odd feeling listening to the two of them talk, his mistress and the oak king's daughter. Neither was quite what he'd expected. Mistress Holly was far kinder and not at all the brusque, rather self-centred human that figured in so many old hob fireside tales. And her ladyship . . . well, who would have thought that one of the high-born would treat a simple hob as though they stood on equal footing? It was all very unexpected.

But it was time for him to go. He could feel it in his blood and in his bones.

He waited while they said their goodbyes. Waited while Mistress Holly took the dog out for a last quick pee before the pair of them retired to their apartment. Then he had the store completely to himself, with no chance of unexpected company. He fetched his little leather carpetbag from his hobhole behind the furnace and came back upstairs to say goodbye to the books, to the store, to his home.

Finally all there was left to do was to spell the door open, step outside and go. He hesitated on the welcoming carpet, thinking of what Mistress Holly had asked, what her ladyship had answered. Was the leaving song that ran in his blood and rumbled in his bones truly a geas, or only habit? How was a poor hob to know? If it was a rule, then who had made it and what would happen if he broke it?

He took a step away from the door, back into the store and paused, waiting for he didn't know what. Some force to propel him out the door. A flash of light to burn down from the sky and strike him where he stood. Instead all he felt was the heaviness in his heart and the funny tingling warmth he'd known when he'd heard the mistress say how she'd been looking forward to getting to know him. That she wanted him to be a partner in her store. Him. Dick Bobbins, of all things.

He looked at the stairs leading up to her apartment.

Just as an experiment, he made his way over to them, then up the risers, one by one, until he stood at her door.

Oh, did he dare, did he dare?

He took a deep breath and squared his shoulders. Then, setting down his carpetbag, he twisted his cloth cap in his hands for a long moment before he finally lifted an arm and rapped a knuckle against the wood panel of Mistress Holly's door.

The Moon Pool

A. Merritt

One vein of fantasy we have not yet explored is that of the lost world, the type popularized by H. Rider Haggard in King Solomon's Mines *(1885) and more significantly* She *(1887). For a while, during the first quarter of the twentieth century, the lost-world adventure was probably the most popular form of fantasy – or more appropriately science fantasy, as it was from the lost-race adventure that one strand of science fiction emerged. There were plenty of exponents of this story form but the two most influential, after Haggard, were Edgar Rice Burroughs, with his adventures of Tarzan, and Abraham Merritt. At one time Merritt (1884–1943), who became editor of Hearst's* American Weekly, *was one of the bestselling authors of fantasy, but in the last fifty years he has pretty much become forgotten. His early story, "The Moon Pool", was one of the most popular ever published in* All-Story Weekly, *where it first appeared in 1918. Unfortunately when the story was reworked into the novel* The Moon Pool *(1919) it lost most of its impact. The original story has hardly ever been reprinted since, and I don't think it has ever appeared in Britain before.*

1. The Throckmartin Mystery

I AM BREAKING A LONG SILENCE TO CLEAR the name of Dr David Throckmartin and to lift the shadow of scandal from his wife

and of Dr Charles Stanton, his assistant. That I have not found
the courage to do so before, all men who are jealous of their
scientific reputations will understand when they have read the
facts entrusted to me alone.

I shall first recapitulate what has actually been known of the
Throckmartin expedition to the island of Ponape in the Carolines
– the Throckmartin Mystery, as it is called.

Dr Throckmartin set forth, you will recall, to make some
observations of Nan-Matal, that extraordinary group of island
ruins, remains of a high and prehistoric civilization, that are
clustered along the vast shore of Ponape. With him went his wife
to whom he had been wedded less than half a year. The daughter
of Professor Frazier-Smith, she was as deeply interested and
almost as well informed as he upon these relics of a vanished race
that titanically strew certain islands of the Pacific and form the
basis for the theory of a submerged Pacific continent.

Mrs Throckmartin, it will be recalled, was much younger,
fifteen years at least, than her husband. Dr Charles Stanton, who
accompanied them as Dr Throckmartin's assistant, was about her
age. These three and a Swedish woman, Thora Helversen, who
had been Edith Throckmartin's nurse in babyhood and who was
entirely devoted to her, made up the expedition.

Dr Throckmartin planned to spend a year among the ruins, not
only of Ponape, but of Lele – the twin centres of that colossal
riddle of humanity whose answer has its roots in immeasurable
antiquity; a weird flower of man-made civilization that blossomed ages before the seeds of Egypt were sown; of whose arts we
know little and of whose science and secret knowledge of nature
nothing.

He carried with him complete equipment for his work and
gathered at Ponape a dozen or so natives for labourers. They went
straight to Metalanim harbour and set up their camp on the island
called Uschen-Tau in the group known as the Nan-Matal. You
will remember that these islands are entirely uninhabited and are
shunned by the people on the main island.

Three months later Dr Throckmartin appeared at Port Moresby, Papua. He came on a schooner manned by Solomon

Islanders and commanded by a Chinese half-breed captain. He reported that he was on his way to Melbourne for additional scientific equipment and whites to help him in his excavations, saying that the superstition of the natives made their aid negligible. He went immediately on board the steamer *Southern Queen* which was sailing that same morning. Three nights later he disappeared from the *Southern Queen* and it was officially reported that he had met death either by being swept overboard or by casting himself into the sea.

A relief boat sent with the news to Ponape found the Throckmartin camp on the island Uschen-Tau and a smaller camp on the island called Nan-Tanach. All the equipment, clothing, supplies were intact. But of Mrs Throckmartin, of Dr Stanton, or of Thora Helversen they could find not a single trace!

The natives who had been employed by the archaeologist were questioned. They said that the ruins were the abode of great spirits – *ani* – who were particularly powerful when the moon was at the full. On these nights all the islanders were doubly careful to give the ruins wide berth. Upon being employed, they had demanded leave from the day before full moon until it was on the wane and this had been granted them by Dr Throckmartin. Thrice they had left the expedition alone on these nights. On their third return they had found the four white people gone and they "knew that the *ani* had eaten them". They were afraid and had fled.

That was all.

The Chinese half-caste was found and reluctantly testified at last that he had picked Dr Throckmartin up from a small boat about 50 miles off Ponape. The scientist had seemed half mad, but he had given the seaman a large sum of money to bring him to Port Moresby and to say, if questioned, that he had boarded the boat at Ponape harbour.

That is all that has been known to anyone of the fate of the Throckmartin expedition.

Why, you will ask, do I break silence now; and how came I in possession of the facts I am about to set forth?

To the first I answer: I was at the Geographical Club recently and I overheard two members talking. They mentioned the name of Throckmartin and I became an eavesdropper.

One said: "Of course what probably happened was that Throckmartin killed them all. It's a dangerous thing for a man to marry a woman so much younger than himself and then throw her into the necessarily close company of exploration with a man as young and as agreeable as Stanton was. The inevitable happened, no doubt. Throckmartin discovered; avenged himself. Then followed remorse and suicide."

"Throckmartin didn't seem to be that kind," said the other thoughtfully.

"No, he didn't," agreed the first.

"Isn't there another story?" went on the second speaker. "Something about Mrs Throckmartin running away with Stanton and taking the woman, Thora, with her? Somebody told me they had been recognized in Singapore recently."

"You can take your pick of the two stories," replied the other man. "It's one or the other I suppose."

It was neither one nor the other of them. I know – and I will answer now the second question – because I was with Throckmartin when he – vanished. I know what he told me and I know what my own eyes saw. Incredible, abnormal, against all the known facts of our science as it was, I testify to it. And it is my intention, after this is published, to sail to Ponape, to go to the Nan-Matal and to the islet beneath whose frowning walls dwells the mystery that Throckmartin sought and found – and that at the last sought and found Throckmartin!

I will leave behind me a copy of the map of the islands that he gave me. Also his sketch of the great courtyard of Nan-Tanach, the location of the moon door, his indication of the probable location of the moon pool and the passage to it and his approximation of the position of the shining globes. If I do not return and there are any with enough belief, scientific curiosity and courage to follow, these will furnish a plain trail.

I will now proceed straightforwardly with my narrative.

For six months I had been on the d'Entrecasteaux Islands gathering data for the concluding chapters of my book upon

"Flora of the Volcanic Islands of the South Pacific". The day before, I had reached Port Moresby and had seen my specimens safely stored on board the *Southern Queen*. As I sat on the upper deck that morning I thought, with homesick mind, of the long leagues between me and Melbourne and the longer ones between Melbourne and New York.

It was one of Papua's yellow mornings, when she shows herself in her most sombre, most baleful mood. The sky was a smouldering ochre. Over the island brooded a spirit sullen, implacable and alien; filled with the threat of latent, malefic forces waiting to be unleashed. It seemed an emanation from the untamed, sinister heart of Papua herself – sinister even when she smiles. And now and then, on the wind, came a breath from unexplored jungles, filled with unfamiliar odours, mysterious, and menacing.

It is on such mornings that Papua speaks to you of her immemorial ancientness and of her power. I am not unduly imaginative but it is a mood that makes me shrink – I mention it because it bears directly upon Dr Throckmartin's fate. Nor is the mood Papua's alone. I have felt it in New Guinea, in Australia, in the Solomons and in the Carolines. But it is in Papua that it seems most articulate. It is as though she said: "I am the ancient of days; I have seen the earth in the throes of its shaping; I am the primeval; I have seen races born and die and, lo, in my breast are secrets that would blast you by the telling, you pale babes of a puling age. You and I ought not to be in the same world; yet I am and I shall be! Never will you fathom me and you I hate though I tolerate! I tolerate – but how long?"

And then I seem to see a giant paw that reaches from Papua towards the outer world, stretching and sheathing monstrous claws.

All feel this mood of hers. Her own people have it woven in them, part of their web and woof; flashing into light unexpectedly like a soul from another universe; masking itself as swiftly.

I fought against Papua as every white man must on one of her yellow mornings. And as I fought I saw a tall figure come striding down the pier. Behind him came a Kapa-Kapa boy swinging a new valise. There was something familiar about the tall man. As he reached the gangplank he looked up straight into my eyes, stared at me for a moment and waved his hand. It was Dr Throckmartin!

Coincident with my recognition of him there came a shock of surprise that was definitely – unpleasant. It was Throckmartin – but there was something disturbingly different about him and the man I had known so well and had bidden farewell less than a year before. He was then, as you know, just turned forty, lithe, erect, muscular; the face of a student and of a seeker. His controlling expression was one of enthusiasm, of intellectual keenness, of – what shall I say – expectant search. His ever eagerly questioning brain had stamped itself upon his face.

I sought in my mind for an explanation of that which I had felt on the flash of his greeting. Hurrying down to the lower deck I found him with the purser. As I spoke he turned and held out to me an eager hand – and then I saw what the change was that had come over him!

He knew, of course, by my face the uncontrollable shock that my closer look had given me. His eyes filled and he turned briskly to the purser; then hurried off to his stateroom, leaving me standing, half dazed.

At the stair he half turned.

"Oh, Goodwin," he said. "I'd like to see you later. Just now – there's something I must write before we start—"

He went up swiftly.

"'E looks rather queer, eh?" said the purser. "Know 'im well, sir? Seems to 'ave given you quite a start, sir."

I made some reply and went slowly to my chair. I tried to analyse what it was that had disturbed me so; what profound change in Throckmartin that had so shaken me. Now it came to me. It was as though the man had suffered some terrific soul-searing shock of rapture and horror combined; some soul cataclysm that in its climax had remoulded his face deep from within; setting on it the seal of wedded joy and fear. As though indeed ecstasy supernal and terror infernal had once come to him hand in hand, taken possession of him, looked out of his eyes and, departing, left behind upon him ineradicably their shadow.

Alternately I looked out over the port and paced about the deck, striving to read the riddle; to banish it from my mind. And all the time still over Papua brooded its baleful spirit of ancient evil, unfathomable, not to be understood; nor had it lifted when the *Southern Queen* lifted anchor and steamed out into the gulf.

2. Down the Moon Path

I watched with relief the shores sink down behind us; welcomed the touch of the free sea wind. We seemed to be drawing away from something malefic; something that lurked within the island spell I have described, and the thought crept into my mind, spoke – whispered rather – from Throckmartin's face.

I had hoped – and within the hope was an inexplicable shrinking, an unexpressed dread – that I would meet Throckmartin at lunch. He did not come down and I was sensible of a distinct relief within my disappointment. All that afternoon I lounged about uneasily but still he kept to his cabin. Nor did he appear at dinner.

Dusk and night fell swiftly. I was warm and went back to my deckchair. The *Southern Queen* was rolling to a disquieting swell and I had the place to myself.

Over the heavens was a canopy of cloud, glowing faintly and testifying to the moon riding behind it. There was much phosphorescence. Now and then, before the ship and at the sides, arose those strange little swirls of mist that steam up from the Southern Ocean like the breath of sea monsters, whirl for a moment and disappear. I lighted a cigarette and tried once more to banish Throckmartin's face from my mind.

Suddenly the deck door opened and through it came Throckmartin himself. He paused uncertainly, looked up at the sky with a curiously eager, intent gaze, hesitated, then closed the door behind him.

"Throckmartin," I called. "Come sit with me. It's Goodwin."

Immediately he made his way to me, sitting beside me with a gasp of relief that I noted curiously. His hand touched mine and gripped it with tenseness that hurt. His hand was icelike. I puffed up my cigarette and by its glow scanned him closely. He was watching a large swirl of the mist that was passing before the ship. The phosphorescence beneath it illumined it with a fitful opalescence. I saw fear in his eyes. The swirl passed; he sighed; his grip relaxed and he sank back.

"Throckmartin," I said, wasting no time in preliminaries. "What's wrong? Can I help you?"

He was silent.

"Is your wife all right and what are you doing here when I heard you had gone to the Carolines for a year?" I went on.

I felt his body grow tense again. He did not speak for a moment and then: "I'm going to Melbourne, Goodwin," he said. "I need a few things – need them urgently. And more men – white men."

His voice was low; preoccupied. It was as though the brain that dictated the words did so perfunctorily, half impatiently; aloof, watching, strained to catch the first hint of approach of something dreaded.

"You are making progress then?" I asked. It was a banal question, put forth in a blind effort to claim his attention.

"Progress?" he repeated. "Progress—"

He stopped abruptly; rose from his chair, gazed intently towards the north. I followed his gaze. Far, far away the moon had broken through the clouds. Almost on the horizon, you could see the faint luminescence of it upon the quiet sea. The distant patch of light quivered and shook. The clouds thickened again and it was gone. The ship raced southwards, swiftly.

Throckmartin dropped into his chair. He lighted a cigarette with a hand that trembled. The flash of the match fell on his face and I noted with a queer thrill of apprehension that its unfamiliar expression had deepened; become curiously intensified as though a faint acid had passed over it, etching its lines faintly deeper.

"It's the full moon tonight, isn't it?" he asked, palpably with studied inconsequence.

"The first night of full moon," I answered. He was silent again. I sat silent too, waiting for him to make up his mind to speak. He turned to me as though he had made a sudden resolution.

"Goodwin," he said. "I do need help. If ever man needed it, I do. Goodwin, can you imagine yourself in another world, alien, unfamiliar, a world of terror, whose unknown joy is its greatest terror of all; you all alone there; a stranger! As such a man would need help, so I need—"

He paused abruptly and arose to his feet stiffly; the cigarette dropped from his fingers. I saw that the moon had again broken through the clouds, and this time much nearer. Not a mile away was the patch of light that it threw upon the waves. Back of it, to the rim of the sea was a lane of moonlight; it was a gleaming gigantic serpent racing over the rim of the world straight and surely towards the ship.

Throckmartin gazed at it as though turned to stone. He stiffened to it as a pointer does to a hidden covey. To me from him pulsed a thrill of terror – but terror tinged with an unfamiliar, an infernal joy. It came to me and passed away – leaving me trembling with its shock of bitter sweet.

He bent forward, all his soul in his eyes. The moon path swept closer, closer still. It was now less than half a mile away. From it the ship fled; almost it came to me, as though pursued. Down upon it, swift and straight, a radiant torrent cleaving the waves, raced the moon stream. And then—

"Good God!" breathed Throckmartin, and if ever the words were a prayer and an invocation they were.

And then, for the first time I saw – *it*!

The moon path, as I have said, stretched to the horizon and was bordered by darkness. It was as though the clouds above had been parted to form a lane – drawn aside like curtains or as the waters of the Red Sea were held back to let the hosts of Israel through. On each side of the stream was the black shadow cast by the folds of the high canopies. And straight as a road between the opaque walls gleamed, shimmered and danced the shining, racing, rapids of moonlight.

Far, it seemed immeasurably far, along this stream of silver fire I sensed, rather than saw, something coming. It drew into sight as a deeper glow within the light. On and on it sped towards us – an opalescent mistiness that swept on with the suggestion of some winged creature in darting flight. Dimly there crept into my mind memory of the Dyak legend of the winged messenger of Buddha – the Akla bird whose feathers are woven of the moon rays, whose heart is a living opal, whose wings in flight echo the crystal clear music of the white stars, but whose beak is of frozen flame and shreds the souls of the unbelievers. Still it sped on, and now there came to me sweet, insistent tinklings – like a pizzicati on violins of glass, crystalline, as purest, clearest glass transformed to sound. And again the myth of the Akla bird came to me.

But now it was close to the end of the white path; close up to the barrier of darkness still between the ship and the sparkling head of the moon stream. And now it beat up against that barrier as a bird against the bars of its cage. And I knew that this was no mist born of sea and air. It whirled with shimmering plumes, with swirls of lacy light, with spirals of living vapour. It held within it odd, unfamiliar gleams as of shifting mother-of-pearl. Coruscations and glittering atoms drifted through it as though it drew them from the rays that bathed it.

Nearer and nearer it came, borne on the sparkling waves, and less and less grew the protecting wall of shadow between it and us. The crystalline sounds were louder – rhythmic as music from another planet.

Now I saw that within the mistiness was a core, a nucleus of intenser light – veined, opaline, effulgent, intensely alive. And above it, tangled in the plumes and spirals that throbbed and whirled, were seven glowing lights.

Through all the incessant but strangely ordered movement of the – *thing* – these lights held firm and steady. They were seven – like seven little moons. One was of a pearly pink, one of delicate nacreous blue, one of lambent saffron, one of the emerald you see in the shallow waters of tropic isles; a deathly white; a ghostly amethyst; and one of the silver that is seen only when the flying fish leap beneath the moon. There they shone – these seven little varicoloured orbs within the opaline mistiness of whatever it was that, poised and expectant, waited to be drawn to us on the light-filled waves.

The tinkling music was louder still. It pierced the ears with a shower of tiny lances; it made the heart beat jubilantly – and checked it dolorously. It closed your throat with a throb of rapture and gripped it tight like the hand of infinite sorrow!

Came to me now a murmuring cry, stilling the crystal-clear notes, it was articulate – but as though from something utterly foreign to this world. The ear took the cry and translated with conscious labour into the sounds of earth. And even as it compassed, the brain shrank from it irresistibly, and simultaneously it seemed, reached towards it with irresistible eagerness.

"Av-o-lo-ha! Av-o-lo-ha!" So the cry seemed to throb.

The grip of Throckmartin's hand relaxed. He walked stiffly towards the front of the deck, straight towards the vision, now but a few yards away from the bow. I ran towards him and gripped him – and fell back. For now his face had lost all human semblance. Utter agony and utter ecstasy – there they were side by side, not resisting each other; unholy inhuman companions blending into a look that none of God's creatures should wear – and deep, deep as his soul! A devil and a god dwelling harmoniously side by side! So must Satan, newly fallen, still divine, seeing heaven and contemplating hell, have looked.

And then – swiftly the moon path faded! The clouds swept over the sky as though a hand had drawn them together. Up from the south came a roaring squall. As the moon vanished what I had seen vanished with it, blotted out as an image on a magic lantern; the tinkling ceased abruptly, leaving a silence like that which follows an abrupt and stupendous thunder clap. There was nothing about us but silence and blackness!

Through me there passed a great trembling as one who had stood on the very verge of the gulf wherein the men of the Louisades say lurks the fisher of the souls of men, and has been plucked back by sheerest chance.

Throckmartin passed an arm around me.

"It is as I thought," he said. In his voice was a new note: of the calm certainty that has swept aside a waiting terror of the unknown. "Now I know! Come with me to my cabin, old friend. For now that you too have seen I can tell you" – he hesitated – "what it was you saw," he ended.

As we passed through the door we came face to face with the ship's first officer. Throckmartin turned quickly, but not soon enough for the mate not to see and stare with amazement. His eyes turned questioningly to me.

With a strong effort of will Throckmartin composed his face into at least a semblance of normality.

"Are we going to have much of a storm?" he asked.

"Yes," said the mate. Then the seaman, getting the better of his curiosity, added, profanely: "We'll probably have it all the way to Melbourne."

Throckmartin straightened as though with a new thought. He gripped the officer's sleeve eagerly.

"You mean at least cloudy weather for" – he hesitated – "for the next three nights, say?"

"And for three more," replied the mate.

"Thank God!" cried Throckmartin, and I think I never heard such relief and hope as was in his voice.

The sailor stood amazed. "Thank God?" he repeated. "Thank – what d'ye mean?"

But Throckmartin was moving onwards to his cabin. I started to follow. The first officer stopped me.

"Your friend," he said, "is he ill?"

"The sea!" I answered hurriedly. "He's not used to it. I am going to look after him."

I saw doubt and disbelief in the seaman's eyes but I hurried on. For I knew now that Throckmartin was ill indeed – but that it was a sickness neither the ship's doctor nor any other could heal.

3. "Dead! All Dead!"

Throckmartin was sitting on the side of his berth as I entered. He had taken off his coat. He was leaning over, face in hands.

"Lock the door," he said quietly, not raising his head. "Close the portholes and draw the curtains; and, have you an electric flash in your pocket – a good, strong one?"

He glanced at the small pocket flash I handed him and clicked it on. "Not big enough I'm afraid," he said. "And after all" – he hesitated – "it's only a theory."

"What's only a theory?" I asked in astonishment.

"Thinking of it as a weapon against – what you saw," he said, with a wry smile.

"Throckmartin," I cried. "What was it? Did I really see that thing – there in the moon path? Did I really hear—"

"This for instance," he interrupted.

Softly he whispered: "Av-o-lo-ha!" With the murmur I seemed to hear again the crystalline unearthly music; an echo of it, faint, sinister, mocking, jubilant.

"Throckmartin," I said. "What was it? What are you flying from, man? Where is your wife – and Stanton?"

"Dead!" he said monotonously. "Dead! All dead!" Then as I recoiled in horror: "All dead. Edith, Stanton, Thora – dead, or worse. And Edith in the moon pool – with them – drawn by what you saw on the moon path – and that wants me – and that has put its brand upon me, and pursues me."

With a vicious movement he ripped open his shirt.

"Look at this," he said. I gazed. Around his chest, an inch above his heart, the skin was white as pearl. The whiteness was sharply defined against the healthy tint of the body. He turned and I saw it ran around his back. It circled him. The band made a perfect cincture about 2 inches wide.

"Burn it!" he said, and offered me his cigarette. I drew back. He gestured – peremptorily. I pressed the glowing end of the cigarette into the ribbon of white flesh. He did not flinch nor was there odour of burning nor, as I drew the little cylinder away, any mark upon the whiteness.

"Feel it!" he commanded again. I placed my fingers upon the band. It was cold – like frozen marble.

He handed me a small penknife.

"Cut!" he ordered. This time, my scientific interest fully aroused, I did so without reluctance. The blade cut into flesh. I waited for the blood to come. None appeared. I drew out the knife and thrust it in again, fully a quarter of an inch deep. I might have been cutting paper so far as any evidence followed that what I was piercing was human skin and muscle.

Another thought came to me and I drew back, revolted.

"Throckmartin," I whispered. "Not leprosy!"

"Nothing so easy," he said. "Look again and find the places you cut."

I looked, as he bade me, and in the white ring there was not a single mark. Where I had pressed the blade there was no trace. It was as though the skin had parted to make way for the blade and closed.

Throckmartin arose and drew his shirt about him.

"Two things you have seen," he said. "*It*, and its mark – the seal it placed on me that gives it, I think, the power to follow me. Seeing, you must believe my story. Goodwin, I tell you again that my wife is dead – or worse, I do not know; the prey of – what you saw; so, too, is Stanton; so Thora. How –" He stopped for a moment.

Then continued: "And I am going to Melbourne for the things to empty its den and its shrine; for dynamite to destroy it and its lair – if anything made on earth will destroy it; and for white men with courage to use them. Perhaps – perhaps after you have heard, you will be one of these men?" He looked at me a bit wistfully. "And now, do not interrupt me, I beg of you, till I am through, for" – he smiled wanly – "the mate may be wrong. And if he is" – he arose and paced twice about the room – "if he is I may not have time to tell you."

"Throckmartin," I answered, "I have no closed mind. Tell me – and if I can I will help."

He took my hand and pressed it.

"Goodwin," he began, "if I have seemed to take the death of my wife lightly – or rather" – his face contorted – "or rather, if I have seemed to pass it by as something not of first importance to me – believe me it is not so. If the rope is long enough, if what the mate says is so – if there is cloudy weather until the moon begins to wane – I can conquer, that I know. But if it does not, if the dweller in the moon pool gets me, then must you or someone avenge my wife – and me – and Stanton. Yet I cannot believe that

God would let a thing like that conquer! But why did He then let it take my Edith? And why does He allow it to exist? Are there things stronger than God, do you think, Goodwin?"

He turned to me feverishly. I hesitated.

"I do not know just how you define God," I said. "If you mean the will to know, working through science—"

He waved me aside impatiently.

"Science," he said. "What is our science against that? Or against the science of whatever cursed, vanished race that made it – or made the way for it to enter this world of ours?"

With an effort he regained control of himself.

"Goodwin," he said, "do you know at all of the ruins on the Carolines; the cyclopean, megolithic cities and harbours of Ponape and Lele, of Kusaie, of Ruk and Hogolu, and a score of other islets there? Particularly, do you know of the Nan-Matal and Metalanim?"

"Of the Metalanim I have heard and seen photographs," I said. "They call it, don't they, the Lost Venice of the Pacific?"

"Look at this map," said Throckmartin. He handed me the map. "That," he went on, "is Christian's map of Metalanim harbour and the Nan-Matal. Do you see the rectangles marked Nan-Tanach?"

"Yes," I said.

"There," he said, "under those walls is the moon pool and the seven gleaming lights that raise the dweller in the pool and the altar and shrine of the dweller. And there in the moon pool with it lie Edith and Stanton and Thora."

"The dweller in the moon pool?" I repeated half incredulously.

"The thing you saw," said Throckmartin solemnly.

A solid sheet of rain swept the ports, and the *Southern Queen* began to roll on the rising swells. Throckmartin drew another deep breath of relief, and drawing aside a curtain peered out into the night. Its blackness seemed to reassure him. At any rate, when he sat again he was calm.

"There are no more wonderful ruins in the world than those of the island Venice of Metalanim on the east shore of Ponape," he said almost casually. "They take in some fifty islets and cover with their intersecting canals and lagoons about 12 square miles. Who built them? None knows! When were they built? Ages before the memory of present man, that is sure. Ten thousand, 20,000, 100,000 years ago – the last more likely.

"All these islets, Goodwin, are squared, and their shores are frowning sea walls of gigantic basalt blocks hewn and put in place by the hands of ancient man. Each inner waterfront is faced with a terrace of those basalt blocks which stand out 6 feet above the shallow canals that meander between them. On the islets behind these walls are cyclopean and time-shattered fortresses, palaces, terraces, pyramids; immense courtyards, strewn with ruins – and all so old that they seem to wither the eyes of those who look on them.

"There has been a great subsidence. You can stand out of Metalanim harbour for three miles and look down upon the tops of similar monolithic structures and walls 20 feet below you in the water.

"And all about, strung on their canals, are the bulwarked islets with their enigmatic giant walls peering through the dense growths of mangroves – dead, deserted for incalculable ages; shunned by those who live near.

"You as a botanist are familiar with the evidence that a vast shadowy continent existed in the Pacific – a continent that was not rent asunder by volcanic forces as was that legendary one of Atlantis in the Eastern Ocean. My work in Java, in Papua and in the Ladrones had set my mind upon this Pacific lost land. Just as the Azores are believed to be the last high peaks of Atlantis, so evidence came to me steadily that Ponape and Lele and their basalt bulwarked islets were the last points of the slowly sunken western land clinging still to the sunlight, and had been the last refuge and sacred places of the rulers of that race which had lost their immemorial home under the rising waters of the Pacific.

"I believed that under these ruins I might find the evidence of what I sought. Time and again I had encountered legends of subterranean networks beneath the Nan-Matal, of passages running back into the main island itself; basalt corridors that followed the lines of the shallow canals and ran under them to islet after islet, linking them in mysterious chains.

"My – my wife and I had talked before we were married of making this our great work. After the honeymoon we prepared for the expedition. It was to be my monument. Stanton was as enthusiastic as ourselves. We sailed, as you know, last May in fulfilment of our dreams.

"At Ponape we selected, not without difficulty, workmen to help us – diggers. I had to make extraordinary inducements before I could get together my force. Their beliefs are gloomy, these Ponapeans. They people their swamps, their forests, their mountains and shores with malignant spirits – *ani* they call them. And they are afraid, bitterly afraid of the isles of ruins and what they think the ruins hide. I do not wonder – now! For their fear has come down to them, through the ages, from the people 'before their fathers', as they call them, who, they say, made these mighty spirits their slaves and messengers.

"When they were told where they were to go, and how long we expected to stay, they murmured. Those who, at last, were tempted made what I thought then merely a superstitious proviso that they were to be allowed to go away on the three nights of the full moon. If only I had heeded them and gone, too!"

He stopped and again over his face the lines etched deep.

"We passed," he went on, "into Metalanim harbour. Off to our left – a mile away – arose a massive quadrangle. Its walls were all of 40 feet high and hundreds of feet on each side. As we passed it our natives grew very silent; watched it furtively, fearfully. I knew it for the ruins that are called Nan-Tanach, the 'place of frowning walls'. And at the silence of my men I recalled what Christian had written of this place; of how he had come upon its 'ancient platforms and tetragonal enclosures of stonework; its wonder of tortuous alleyways and labyrinth of shallow canals; grim masses of stonework peering out from behind verdant screens; cyclopean barricades'. And now, when we had turned into its ghostly shadows, straight away the merriment of our guides was hushed and conversation died down to whispers. For we were close to Nan-Tanach – the place of lofty walls, the most remarkable of all the Metalanim ruins." He arose and stood over me.

"Nan-Tanach, Goodwin," he said solemnly, "a place where merriment is hushed indeed and words are stifled; Nan-Tanach, where the moon pool lies hidden, lies hidden behind the moon rock, but sends its diabolic soul out – even through the prisoning stone." He raised clenched hands. "Oh, heaven," he breathed, "grant me that I may blast it from earth!"

He was silent for a little time.

"Of course I wanted to pitch our camp there," he began again quietly, "but I soon gave up that idea. The natives were panic-stricken – threatened to turn back. 'No,' they said, 'too great *ani* there. We go to any other place – but not there.' Although, even then, I felt that the secret of the place was in Nan-Tanach, I found it necessary to give in. The labourers were essential to the success of the expedition, and I told myself that after a little time had passed and I had persuaded them that there was nothing anywhere that could molest them, we would move our tents to it. We finally picked for our base the islet called Uschen-Tau – you see it here." He pointed to the map. "It was close to the isle of desire, but far enough away from it to satisfy our men. There was an excellent camping-place there and a spring of fresh water. It offered, besides, an excellent field for preliminary work before attacking the larger ruins. We pitched our tents, and in a couple of days the work was in full swing."

4. The Moon Rock

"I do not intend to tell you now," Throckmartin continued, "the results of the next two weeks, Goodwin, nor of what we found. Later, if I am allowed, I will lay all that before you. It is sufficient to say that at the end of those two weeks I had found confirmation of many of my theories, and we were well under way to solve a mystery of humanity's youth – so we thought. But enough. I must hurry on to the first stirrings of the inexplicable thing that was in store for us.

"The place, for all its decay and desolation, had not infected us with any touch of morbidity – that is not Edith, Stanton or myself. My wife was happy; never had she been happier. Stanton and she, while engrossed in the work as much as I, were of the same age, and they frankly enjoyed the companionship that only youth can give youth. I was glad – never jealous.

"But Thora was very unhappy. She was a Swede, as you know, and in her blood ran the beliefs and superstitions of the North-land, some of them so strangely akin to those of this far southern land; beliefs of spirits of mountain and forest and water – werewolves and beings malign. From the first she showed a curious sensitivity to what, I suppose, may be called the 'influences' of the place. She said it 'smelled' of ghosts and warlocks.

"I laughed at her then – but now I believe that this sensitivity of what we call primitive people is perhaps only a clearer perception of the unknown which we, who deny the unknown, have lost.

"A prey to these fears, Thora always followed my wife about like a shadow; carried with her always a little sharp hand-axe, and although we twitted her about the futility of chopping phantoms with such a weapon she would not relinquish it.

"Two weeks slipped by, and at their end the spokesman for our natives came to us. The next night was the full of the moon, he said. He reminded me of my promise. They would go back to their village next morning; they would return after the third night, as at that time the power of the *ani* would begin to wane with the moon. They left us sundry charms for our 'protection', and solemnly cautioned us to keep as far away as possible from Nan-Tanach during their absence – although their leader politely informed us that, no doubt, we were stronger than the spirits. Half exasperated, half amused, I watched them go.

"No work could be done without them, of course, so we decided to spend the days of their absence junketing about the southern islets of the group. Under the moon the ruins were inexpressibly weird and beautiful. We marked down several spots for subsequent exploration, and on the morning of the third day set forth along the east face of the breakwater for our camp on Uschen-Tau, planning to have everything in readiness for the return of our men the next day.

"We landed just before dusk, tired and ready for our cots. It was only a little after ten o'clock when Edith awakened me.

"'Listen!' she said. 'Lean over with your ear close to the ground!' I did so, and seemed to hear, far, far below, as though coming up from great distances, a faint chanting. It gathered strength, died down, ended; began, gathered volume, faded away into silence.

"'It's the waves rolling on rocks somewhere,' I said. 'We're probably over some ledge of rock that carries the sound.'

"'It's the first time I've heard it,' replied my wife doubtfully. We listened again. Then through the dim rhythms, deep beneath us, another sound came. It drifted across the lagoon that lay between us and Nan-Tanach in little tinkling waves. It was music – of a sort; I won't describe the strange effect it had upon me. You've felt it –"

"You mean on the deck?" I asked. Throckmartin nodded.

"I went to the flap of the tent," he continued, "and peered out. As I did so Stanton lifted his flap and walked out into the moonlight, looking over to the other islet and listening. I called to him.

"'That's the queerest sound!' he said. He listened again. 'Crystalline! Like little notes of translucent glass. Like the bells of crystal on the sistrums of Isis at Dendarah Temple,' he added half dreamily. We gazed intently at the island. Suddenly, on the gigantic sea wall, moving slowly, rhythmically, we saw a little group of lights. Stanton laughed.

"'The beggars!' he exclaimed. 'That's why they wanted to get away, is it? Don't you see, Dave, it's some sort of a festival – rites of some kind that they hold during the full moon! That's why they were so eager to have us keep away, too.'

"I felt a curious sense of relief, although I had not been sensible of any oppression. The explanation seemed good. It explained the tinkling music and also the chanting – worshippers, no doubt, in the ruins – their voices carried along passages I now knew honeycombed the whole Nan-Matal.

"'Let's slip over,' suggested Stanton – but I would not.

"'They're a difficult lot as it is,' I said. 'If we break into one of their religious ceremonies they'll probably never forgive us. Let's keep out of any family party where we haven't been invited.'

" 'That's so,' agreed Stanton.

"The strange tinkling music, if music it can be called, rose and fell, rose and fell, now laden with sorrow, now filled with joy.

" 'There's something – something very unsettling about it,' said Edith at last soberly. 'I wonder what they make those sounds with. They frighten me half to death, and, at the same time, they make me feel as though some enormous rapture was just around the corner.'

"I had noted this effect, too, although I had said nothing of it. And at the same time there came to me a clear perception that the chanting which had preceded it had seemed to come from a vast multitude – thousands more than the place we were contemplating could possibly have held. Of course, I thought, this might be due to some acoustic property of the basalt; an amplification of sound by some gigantic sounding-board of rock; still—

" 'It's devilish uncanny!' broke in Stanton, answering my thought.

"And as he spoke the flap of Thora's tent was raised and out into the moonlight strode the old Swede. She was the great Norse type – tall, deep-breasted, moulded on the old Viking lines. Her sixty years had slipped from her. She looked like some ancient priestess of Odin." He hesitated. "She knew," he said slowly, "something more far-seeing than my science had given her sight. She warned me – she warned me! Fools and mad that we are to pass such things by without heed!" He brushed a hand over his eyes.

"She stood there," he went on. "Her eyes were wide, brilliant, staring. She thrust her head forward towards Nan-Tanach, regarding the moving lights; she listened. Suddenly she raised her arms and made a curious gesture to the moon. It was an archaic movement; she seemed to drag it from remote antiquity – yet in it was a strange suggestion of power. Twice she repeated this gesture and – the tinkling died away! She turned to us.

" 'Go!' she said, and her voice seemed to come from far distances. 'Go from here – and quickly! Go while you may. They

have called.' She pointed to the islet. 'They know you are here.
They wait.' Her eyes widened further. 'It is there,' she wailed. 'It
beckons – the – the –'

"She fell at Edith's feet, and as she fell over the lagoon came
again the tinklings, now with a quicker note of jubilance – almost
of triumph.

"We ran to Thora, Stanton and I, and picked her up. Her head
rolled and her face, eyes closed, turned as though drawn full into
the moonlight. I felt in my heart a throb of unfamiliar fear – for
her face had changed again. Stamped upon it was a look of
mingled transport and horror; alien, terrifying, strangely revolt-
ing. It was" – he thrust his face close to my eyes – "what you see
in mine!"

For a dozen heartbeats I stared at him, fascinated; then he sank
back again into the half-shadow of the berth.

"I managed to hide her face from Edith," he went on. "I
thought she had suffered some sort of a nervous seizure. We
carried her into her tent. Once within the unholy mask dropped
from her, and she was again only the kindly, rugged old woman. I
watched her throughout the night. The sounds from Nan-Tanach continued until about an hour before moonset. In the
morning Thora awoke, none the worse, apparently. She had
had bad dreams, she said. She could not remember what they
were – except that they had warned her of danger. She was oddly
sullen, and I noted that throughout the morning her gaze returned again half fascinatedly, half wonderingly to the neighbouring isles.

"That afternoon the natives returned. They were so exuberant
in their apparent relief to find us well and intact that Stanton's
suspicions of them were confirmed. He slyly told their leader that
from the noise they had made on Nan-Tanach the night before
they must have thoroughly enjoyed themselves.

"I think I never saw such stark terror as the Ponapean manifested at the remark! Stanton himself was so plainly startled that
he tried to pass it over as a jest. He met poor success! The men
seemed panic-stricken, and for a time I thought they were about
to abandon us – but they did not. They pitched their camp at the

western side of the island, out of sight of Nan-Tanach. I noticed that they built large fires, and whenever I awoke that night I heard their voices in slow, minor chant – one of their song 'charms', I thought drowsily, against evil *ani*. I heard nothing else; the place of frowning walls was wrapped in silence – no lights showed. The next morning the men were quiet, a little depressed, but as the hours wore on they regained their spirits, and soon life at the camp was going on just as it had before.

"You will understand, Goodwin, how the occurrences I have related would excite the scientific curiosity. We rejected immediately, of course, any explanation admitting the supernatural. Why not? Except the curiously disquieting effects of the tinkling music and Thora's behaviour there was nothing to warrant any such fantastic theories – even if our minds had been the kind to harbour them.

"We came to the conclusion that there must be a passageway between Ponape and Nan-Tanach, known to the natives, and used by them during their rites. Ceremonies were probably held in great vaults or caverns beneath the ruins.

"We decided at last that on the next departure of our labourers we would set forth immediately to Nan-Tanach. We would investigate during the day, and at evening my wife and Thora would go back to camp, leaving Stanton and me to spend the night on the island, observing from some safe hiding-place what might occur.

"The moon waned; appeared crescent in the west; waxed slowly towards the full. Before the men left us they literally prayed us to accompany them. Their importunities only made us more eager to see what it was that, we were now convinced, they wanted to conceal from us. At least that was true of Stanton and myself. It was not true of Edith. She was thoughtful, abstracted, reluctant. Thora, on the other hand, showed an unusual restlessness, almost an eagerness to go. Goodwin" – he paused – "Goodwin, I know now that the poison was working in Thora, and that women have perceptions that we men lack – forebodings, sensings. I wish to heaven I had known it then. Edith!" he cried suddenly. "Edith, come back to me! Forgive me!"

I stretched the decanter out to him. He drank deeply. Soon he had regained control of himself.

"When the men were out of sight around the turn of the harbour," he went on, "we took our boat and made straight for Nan-Tanach. Soon its mighty sea wall towered above us. We passed through the water gate with its gigantic hewn prisms of basalt and landed beside a half-submerged pier. In front of us stretched a series of giant steps leading into a vast court strewn with fragments of fallen pillars. In the centre of the court, beyond the shattered pillars, rose another terrace of basalt blocks, concealing, I knew, still another enclosure.

"And now, Goodwin, for the better understanding of what follows and to guide you, should I – not be able to accompany you when you go there, listen carefully to my description of this place: Nan-Tanach is literally three rectangles. The first rectangle is the sea wall, built up of monoliths. Gigantic steps lead up from the landing of the sea gate through the entrance to the courtyard.

"This courtyard is surrounded by another, inner basalt wall.

"Within the courtyard is the second enclosure. Its terrace, of the same basalt as the outer walls, is about 20 feet high. Entrance is gained to it by many breaches which time has made in its stonework. This is the inner court, the heart of Nan-Tanach! There lies the great central vault with which is associated the one name of living being that has come to us out of the mists of the past. The natives say it was the treasure-house of Chau-te-leur, a mighty king who reigned long 'before their fathers'. As Chau is the ancient Ponapean word both for sun and king, the name means 'place of the sun king'.

"And opposite this place of the sun king is the moon rock that hides the moon pool.

"It was Stanton who first found what I call the moon rock. We had been inspecting the inner courtyard; Edith and Thora were getting together our lunch. I forgot to say that we had previously gone all over the islet and had found not a trace of living thing. I came out of the vault of Chau-te-leur to find Stanton before a part of the terrace studying it wonderingly.

"'What do you make of this?' he asked me as I came up. He

pointed to the wall. I followed his finger and saw a slab of stone about 15 feet high and 10 wide. At first all I noticed was the exquisite nicety with which its edges joined the blocks about it. Then I realized that its colour was subtly different – tinged with grey and of a smooth, peculiar deadness.

" 'Looks more like calcite than basalt,' I said. I touched it and withdrew my hand quickly, for at the contact every nerve in my arm tingled as though a shock of frozen electricity had passed through it. It was not cold as we know cold that I felt. It was a chill force; the phrase I have used – frozen electricity – describes it better than anything else. Stanton looked at me oddly.

" 'So you felt it, too,' he said. 'I was wondering whether I was developing hallucinations like Thora. Notice, by the way, that the blocks beside it are quite warm beneath the sun.'

"I felt them and touched the greyish stone again. The same faint shock ran through my hand – a tingling chill that had in it a suggestion of substance, of force. We examined the slab more closely. Its edges were cut as though by an engraver of jewels. They fitted against the neighbouring blocks in almost a hairline. Its base, we saw, was slightly curved, and fitted as closely as top and sides upon the huge stones on which it rested. And then we noted that these stones had been hollowed to follow the line of the grey stone's foot. There was a semicircular depression running from one side of the slab to the other. It was as though the grey rock stood in the centre of a shallow cup – revealing half, covering half. Something about this hollow attracted me. I reached down and felt it. Goodwin, although the balance of the stones that formed it, like all the stones of the courtyard, were rough and age-worn – this was as smooth, as even-surfaced as though it just left the hands of the polisher.

" 'It's a door!' exclaimed Stanton. 'It swings around in that little cup. That's what make the hollow so smooth.'

" 'Maybe you're right,' I replied. 'But how the devil can we open it?'

"We went over the slab again, pressing upon its edges, thrusting against its sides. During one of those efforts I happened to look up – and cried out. For a foot above and on each side of the corner of the grey rock's lintel I had seen a slight convexity, visible only from the angle at which my gaze struck it. These bosses on the basalt were circular, 18 inches in diameter, as we learned later, and at the centre extended 2 inches only beyond the face of the terrace. Unless one looked directly up at them while leaning against the moon rock – for this slab, Goodwin, *is* the moon rock – they were invisible. And none would dare stand there!

"We carried with us a small scaling-ladder, and up this I went. The bosses were apparently nothing more than chiselled curvatures in the stone. I laid my hand on the one I was examining, and drew it back so sharply I almost threw myself from the ladder. In my palm, at the base of my thumb, I had felt the same shock that I had in touching the slab below. I put my hand back. The impression came from a spot not more than an inch wide. I went carefully over the entire convexity, and six times more the chill ran through my arm. There were, Goodwin, seven circles an inch wide in the curved place, each of which communicated the precise sensation I have described. The convexity on the opposite side of the slab gave precisely the same results. But no amount of touching or of pressing these spots singly or in any combination gave the slightest promise of motion to the slab itself.

"'And yet – they're what open it,' said Stanton positively.

"'Why do you say that?' I asked.

"'I don't know,' he answered hesitatingly. 'But something tells me so. Throck,' he went on half earnestly, half laughingly, 'the purely scientific part of me is fighting the purely human part of me. The scientific part is urging me to find some way to get that slab either down or open. The human part is just as strongly urging me to do nothing of the sort and get away while I can!'

"He laughed again – shamefacedly.

"'Which will it be?' he asked; and I thought that in his tone the human side of him was ascendant.

"'It will probably stay as it is – unless we blow it to bits,' I said.

"'I thought of that,' he answered, 'and I wouldn't dare,' he added sombrely enough. And even as I had spoken there came to me the same feeling that he had expressed. It was as though something passed out of the grey rock that struck my heart as a hand strikes an impious lip. We turned away – uneasily, and faced Thora coming through a breach in the terrace.

" 'Miss Edith wants you quick,' she began – and stopped. I saw her eyes go past me and widen. She was looking at the grey rock. Her body grew suddenly rigid; she took a few stiff steps forward and ran straight to it. We saw her cast herself upon its breast, hands and face pressed against it; heard her scream as though her very soul was being drawn from her; and watched her fall at its foot. As we picked her up I saw steal from her face the look I had observed when I first heard the crystal music of Nan-Tanach – that unhuman mingling of opposites!"

5. Av-o-Lo-Ha

"We carried Thora back, down to where Edith was waiting. We told her what had happened and what we had found. She listened gravely, and as we finished Thora sighed and opened her eyes.

" 'I would like to see the stone,' she said. 'Charles, you stay here with Thora.' We passed through the outer court silently – and stood before the rock. She touched it, drew back her hand as I had; thrust it forward again resolutely and held it there. She seemed to be listening. Then she turned to me.

" 'David,' said my wife, and the wistfulness in her voice hurt me, 'David, would you be very, very disappointed if we went from here – without trying to find out any more about it – would you?'

"Goodwin, I never wanted anything so much in my life as I wanted to learn what that rock concealed. You will understand: the cumulative curiosity that all the happenings had caused; the certainty that before me was an entrance to a place that, while known to the natives – for I still clung to that theory – was utterly unknown to any man of my race; that within, ready for my finding, was the answer to the stupendous riddle of these islands and a lost chapter in the history of humanity. There before me – and was I asked to turn away, leaving it unread!

"Nevertheless, I tried to master my desire, and I answered: 'Edith, not a bit if you want us to do it.'

"She read my struggle in my eyes. She looked at me searchingly for a moment and then turned back towards the grey rock. I saw a shiver pass through her. I felt a tinge of remorse and pity!

" 'Edith,' I exclaimed, 'we'll go!'

"She looked at me hard. 'Science is a jealous mistress,' she quoted. 'No, after all it may be just fancy. At any rate, you can't run away. No! But, Dave, I'm going to stay too!'

" 'You are not!' I exclaimed. 'You're going back to the camp with Thora. Stanton and I will be all right.'

" 'I'm going to stay,' she repeated. And there was no changing her decision. As we neared the others she laid a hand on my arm.

" 'Dave,' she said, 'if there should be something – well – inexplicable tonight, something that seems too dangerous, will you promise to go back to our own islet tomorrow, or, while we can, and wait until the natives return?'

"I promised eagerly – for the desire to stay and see what came with the night was like a fire within me.

"And would to heaven I had not waited another moment, Goodwin; would to heaven I had gathered them all together then and sailed back on the instant through the mangroves to Uschen-Tau!

"We found Thora on her feet again and singularly composed. She claimed to have no more recollection of what had happened after she had spoken to Stanton and to me in front of the grey rock than she had after the seizure on Uschen-Tau. She grew sullen under our questioning, precisely as she had before. But to my astonishment, when she heard of our arrangements for the night, she betrayed a febrile excitement that had in it something of exultance.

"We had picked a place about 500 feet away from the steps leading into the outer court.

"We settled down just before dusk to wait for whatever might come. I was nearest the giant steps; next to me Edith; then Thora, and last Stanton. Each of us had with us automatic pistols, and all, except Thora, had rifles.

"Night fell. After a time the eastern sky began to lighten, and we knew that the moon was rising; grew lighter still, and the orb peeped over the sea; swam suddenly into full sight. Edith gripped my hand, for, as though the full emergence into the heavens had been a signal, we heard begin beneath us the deep chanting. It came from illimitable depths.

"The moon poured her rays down upon us, and I saw Stanton start. On the instant I caught the sound that had roused him. It came from the inner enclosure. It was like a long, soft sighing. It was not human; seemed in some way mechanical. I glanced at Edith and then at Thora. My wife was intently listening. Thora sat, as she had since we had placed ourselves, elbows on knees, her hands covering her face.

"And then suddenly from the moonlight flooding us there came to me a great drowsiness. Sleep seemed to drip from the rays and fall upon my eyes, closing them – closing them inexorably. I felt Edith's hand relax in mine, and under my own heavy lids saw her nodding. I saw Stanton's head fall upon his breast and his body sway drunkenly. I tried to rise – to fight against the profound desire for slumber that pressed in on me.

"And as I fought I saw Thora raise her head as though listening; saw her rise and turn her face towards the gateway. For a moment she gazed, and my drugged eyes seemed to perceive within it a deeper, stronger radiance. Thora looked at us. There was infinite despair in her face – and expectancy. I tried again to rise, and a surge of sleep rushed over me. Dimly, as I sank within it, I heard a crystalline chiming; raised my lids once more with a supreme effort, saw Thora, bathed in light, standing at the top of the stairs, and then – sleep took me for its very own, swept me into the very heart of oblivion!

"Dawn was breaking when I wakened. Recollection rushed back on me and I thrust a panic-stricken hand out towards Edith; touched her and felt my heart give a great leap of thankfulness. She stirred, sat up, rubbing dazed eyes. I glanced towards Stanton. He lay on his side, back towards us, head in arms.

"Edith looked at me laughingly. 'Heavens! What sleep!' she said. Memory came to her. Her face paled. 'What happened?' she whispered. 'What made us sleep like that?' She looked over to Stanton, sprang to her feet, ran to him, shook him. He turned over with a mighty yawn, and I saw relief lighten her face as it had lightened my heart.

"Stanton raised himself stiffly. He looked at us. 'What's the matter?' he exclaimed. 'You look as though you've seen ghosts!'

"Edith caught my hands. 'Where's Thora?' she cried. Before I could answer she ran out into the open calling: 'Thora! Thora!'

"Stanton stared at me. 'Taken!' was all I could say. Together we went to my wife, now standing beside the great stone steps, looking up fearfully at the gateway into the terraces. There I told them what I had seen before sleep had drowned me. And together then we ran up the stairs, through the court and up to the grey rock.

"The grey rock was closed as it had been the day before, nor was there trace of its having opened. No trace! Even as I thought this Edith dropped to her knees before it and reached towards something lying at its foot. It was a little piece of grey silk. I knew it for part of the kerchief Thora wore about her hair. Edith took the fragment; hesitated. I saw then that it had been *cut* from the kerchief as though by a razor-edge; I saw, too, that a few threads ran from it – down towards the base of the slab; ran to the base of the grey rock and under it! The grey rock was a door! And it had opened and Thora had passed through it!

"I think, Goodwin, that for the next few minutes we all were a little insane. We beat upon that diabolic entrance with our hands, with stones and clubs. At last reason came back to us. Stanton set forth for the camp to bring back blasting powder and tools. While he was gone Edith and I searched the whole islet for any other clue. We found not a trace of Thora nor any indication of any living being save ourselves. We went back to the gateway to find Stanton returned.

"Goodwin, during the next two hours we tried every way in our power to force entrance through the slab. The rock within effective blasting radius of the cursed door resisted our drills. We tried explosions at the base of the slab with charges covered by rock. They made not the slightest impression on the surface beneath, expending their force, of course, upon the slighter resistance of their coverings.

"Afternoon found us hopeless, so far as breaking through the rock was concerned. Night was coming on and before it came we would have to decide our course of action. I wanted to go to Ponape for help. But Edith objected that this would take hours and after we had reached there it would be impossible to persuade our men to return with us that night, if at all. What then was left? Clearly only one of two choices: to go back to our camp and wait for our men to return and on their return try to persuade them to go with us to Nan-Tanach. But this would mean the abandonment of Thora for at least two days. We could not do it; it would have been too cowardly.

"The other choice was to wait where we were for night to come; to wait for the rock to open as it had the night before, and to make a sortie through it for Thora before it could close again. With the sun had come confidence; at least a shattering of the mephitic mists of superstition with which the strangeness of the things that had befallen us had clouded for a time our minds. In that brilliant light there seemed no place for phantoms.

"The evidence that the slab had opened was unmistakable, but might not Thora simply have *found* it open through some mechanism, still working after ages, and dependent for its action upon laws of physics unknown to us upon the full light of the moon? The assertion of the natives that the *ani* had greatest power at this time might be a far-flung reflection of knowledge which had found ways to use forces contained in moonlight, as we have found ways to utilize the forces in the sun's rays. If so, Thora was probably behind the slab, sending out prayers to us for help.

"But how explain the sleep that had descended upon us? Might it not have been some emanation from plants or gaseous emanations from the island itself? Such things were far from uncommon, we agreed. In some way, the period of their greatest activity might coincide with the period of the moon, but if this were so why had not Thora also slept?

"As dusk fell we looked over our weapons. Edith was an excellent shot with both rifle and pistol. With the idea that the impulse towards sleep was the result either of emanations such as I have described or manmade, we constructed rough-and-ready but effective neutralizers, which we placed over our mouths and nostrils. We had decided that my wife was to remain in the hollow spot. Stanton would take up a station on the far side of the stairway and I would place myself opposite him on the side near Edith. The place I picked out was less than 500 feet from her, and I could reassure myself now as to her safety, as I looked down upon the hollow wherein she crouched. As the phenomena had previously synchronized with the rising of the moon, we had no reason to think they would occur any earlier this night.

"A faint glow in the sky heralded the moon. I kissed Edith, and Stanton and I took our places. The moon dawn increased rapidly; the disc swam up, and in a moment it seemed was shining in full radiance upon ruins and sea.

"As it rose there came as on the night before the curious little sighing sound from the inner terrace. I saw Stanton straighten up and stare intently through the gateway, rifle ready. Even at the distance he was from me, I discerned amazement in his eyes. The moonlight within the gateway thickened, grew stronger. I watched his amazement grow into sheer wonder.

"I arose.

" 'Stanton, what do you see?' I called cautiously. He waved a silencing hand. I turned my head to look at Edith. A shock ran through me. She lay upon her side. Her face was turned full towards the moon. She was in deepest sleep!

"As I turned again to call to Stanton, my eyes swept the head of the steps and stopped, fascinated. For the moonlight had thickened more. It seemed to be – curdled there; and through it ran little gleams and veins of shimmering white fire. A languor passed through me. It was not the ineffable drowsiness of the preceding night. It was a sapping of all will to move. I tore my eyes away and forced them upon Stanton. I tried to call out to him. I had not the will to make my lips move! I had struggled against this paralysis and as I did so I felt through me a sharp shock. It was like a blow. And with it came utter inability to make a single motion. Goodwin, I could not even move my eyes!

"I saw Stanton leap upon the steps and move towards the gateway. As he did so the light in the courtyard grew dazzlingly brilliant. Through it rained tiny tinklings that set the heart to racing with pure joy and stilled it with terror.

"And now for the first time I heard that cry, '*Av-o-lo-ha*! *Av-o-lo-ha*!' the cry you heard on deck. It murmured with the strange effect of a sound only partly in our own space – as though it were part of a fuller phrase passing through from another dimension and losing much as it came; infinitely caressing, infinitely cruel!

"On Stanton's face I saw come the look I dreaded – and yet knew would appear; that mingled expression of delight and fear. The two lay side by side as they had on Thora, but were intensified. He walked on up the stairs; disappeared beyond the range of my fixed gaze. Again I heard the murmur: '*Av-o-lo-ha*!' There was triumph in it now and triumph in the storm of tinklings that swept over it.

"For another heartbeat there was silence. Then a louder burst of sound and ringing through it Stanton's voice from the courtyard – a great cry, a scream – filled with ecstasy insupportable and horror unimaginable! And again there was silence. I strove to burst the invisible bonds that held me. I could not. Even my eyelids were fixed. Within them my eyes, dry and aching, burned.

"Then, Goodwin, I first saw the inexplicable! The crystalline music swelled. Where I sat I could take in the gateway and its basalt portals, rough and broken, rising to the top of the wall 40 feet above, shattered, ruined portals – unclimbable. From this gateway an intenser light began to flow. It grew, it gushed, and into it, into my sight, walked Stanton.

"Stanton! But – Goodwin! What a vision!" He ceased. I waited – waited.

6. Into the Moon Pool

"Goodwin," Throckmartin said at last, "I can describe him only as a thing of living light. He radiated light; was filled with light; overflowed with it. Around him was a shining cloud that whirled through and around him in radiant swirls, shimmering tentacles, luminescent, coruscating spirals.

"I saw his face. It shone with a rapture too great to be borne by living men, and was shadowed with insuperable misery. It was as though his face had been remoulded by the hand of God and the hand of Satan, working together and in harmony. You have seen it on my face. But you have never seen it in the degree that Stanton bore it. The eyes were wide open and fixed, as though upon some inward vision of hell and heaven! He walked like the corpse of a man damned who carried within him an angel of light.

"The music swelled again. I heard again the murmuring: '*Av-o-lo-ha!*' Stanton turned, facing the ragged side of the portal. And then I saw that the light that filled and surrounded him had a nucleus, a core – some thing shiftingly human-shaped – that dissolved and changed, gathered itself, whirled through and beyond him and back again. And as this shining nucleus passed through him Stanton's whole body pulsed with light. As the luminescence moved, there moved with it, still and serene always, seven tiny globes of light like seven little moons.

"So much I saw and then swiftly Stanton seemed to be lifted – levitated – up the unscalable wall and to its top. The glow faded from the moonlight, the tinkling music grew fainter. I tried again to move. The spell still held me fast. The tears were running down now from my rigid lids and brought relief to my tortured eyes.

"I have said my gaze was fixed. It was. But from the side, peripherally, it took in a part of the far wall of the outer enclosure. Ages seemed to pass and I saw a radiance stealing along it. Soon there came into sight the figure that was Stanton. Far away he was – on the gigantic wall. But still I could see the shining spirals whirling jubilantly around and through him; felt rather than saw his tranced face beneath the seven lights. A swirl of crystal notes, and he had passed. And all the time, as though from some opened well of light, the courtyard gleamed and sent out silver fires that dimmed the moon rays, yet seemed strangely to be a part of them.

"Ten times he passed before me so. The luminescence came

with the music; swam for a while along the man-made cliff of basalt and passed away. Between times eternities rolled and still I crouched there, a helpless thing of stone with eyes that would not close!

"At last the moon neared the horizon. There came a louder burst of sound; the second, and last, cry of Stanton, like an echo of the first! Again the soft sigh from the inner terrace. Then – utter silence. The light faded; the moon was setting and with a rush life and power to move returned to me, I made a leap for the steps, rushed up them, through the gateway and straight to the grey rock. It was closed – as I knew it would be. But did I dream it or did I hear, echoing through it as though from vast distances a triumphant shouting: '*Av-o-lo-ha! Av-o-lo-ha*!'?

"I remembered Edith. I ran back to her. At my touch she wakened; looked at me wonderingly; raised herself on a hand.

"'Dave!' she said. 'I slept – after all.' She saw the despair on my face and leaped to her feet. 'Dave!' she cried. 'What is it? Where's Charles?'

"I lighted a fire before I spoke. Then I told her. And for the balance of that night we sat before the flames, arms around each other like two frightened children."

Suddenly Throckmartin held his hands out to me appealingly.

"Goodwin, old friend!" he cried. "Don't look at me as though I were mad. It's truth, absolute truth. Wait."

I comforted him as well as I could. After a little time he took up his story.

"Never," he said, "did man welcome the sun as we did that morning. As soon as it was light we went back to the courtyard. The basalt walls whereon I had seen Stanton were black and silent. The terraces were as they had been. The grey slab was in its place. In the shallow hollow at its base was – nothing. Nothing – nothing was there anywhere on the islet of Stanton, not a trace, not a sign on Nan-Tanach to show that he had ever lived.

"What were we to do? Precisely the same arguments that had kept us there the night before held good now – and doubly good. We could not abandon these two; could not go as long as there was the faintest hope of finding them; and yet for love of each other how could we remain? I loved my wife, Goodwin – how much I never knew until that day; and she loved me as deeply.

" 'It takes only one each night,' she said. 'Beloved, let it take me.' "

"I wept, Goodwin. We both wept.

" 'We will meet it together,' she said. And it was thus at last that we arranged it."

"That took great courage indeed, Throckmartin," I interrupted. He looked at me eagerly.

"You do believe then?" he exclaimed.

"I believe," I said. He pressed my hand with a grip that nearly crushed it.

"Now," he told me, "I do not fear. If I fail, you will prepare and carry on the work."

I promised. And – heaven forgive me – that was three years ago.

"It did take courage," he went on, again quietly. "More than courage. For we knew it was renunciation. Each of us in our hearts felt that one of us would not be there to see the sun rise. And each of us prayed that the death, if death it was, would not come first to the other.

"We talked it all over carefully, bringing to bear all our power of analysis and habit of calm, scientific thought. We considered minutely the time element in the phenomena. Although the deep chanting began at the very moment of moonrise, fully five minutes had passed between its full lifting and the strange sighing sound from the inner terrace. I went back in memory over the happenings of the night before. At least fifteen minutes had intervened between the first heralding sigh and the intensification of the moonlight in the courtyard. And this glow grew for at least ten minutes more before the first burst of the crystal notes.

"The sighing sound – of what had it reminded me? Of course – of a door revolving and swishing softly along its base.

" 'Edith!' I cried. 'I think I have it! The grey rock opens five minutes after upon the moonrise. But whoever or whatever it is that comes through it must wait until the moon has risen higher, or else it must come from a distance. The thing to do is not to wait for it, but to surprise it before it passes out the door. We will go into the inner court early. You will take your rifle and pistol and hide yourself where you can command the opening – if the slab does open. The instant it moves I will enter. It's our best chance, Edith. I think it's our only one.'

"My wife demurred strongly. She wanted to go with me. But I convinced her that it was better for her to stand guard without, prepared to help me if I were forced from what lay behind the rock again into the open.

"The day passed too swiftly. In the face of what we feared our love seemed stronger than ever. Was it the flare of the spark before extinguishment? I wondered. We prepared and ate a good dinner. We tried to keep our minds from anything but scientific aspect of the phenomena. We agreed that whatever it was its cause must be human, and that we must keep that fact in mind every second. But what kind of men could create such prodigies? We thrilled at the thought of finding perhaps the remnants of a vanished race, living perhaps in cities over whose rocky skies the Pacific rolled; exercising there the lost wisdom of the half-gods of earth's youth.

"At the half-hour before moonrise we two went into the inner courtyard. I took my place at the side of the grey rock. Edith crouched behind a broken pillar 20 feet away, slipped her rifle-barrel over it so that it would cover the opening.

"The minutes crept by. The courtyard was very quiet. The darkness lessened and through the breaches of the terrace I watched the far sky softly lighten. With the first pale flush the stillness became intensified. It deepened, became unbearably expectant. The moon rose, showed the quarter, the half, then swam up into full sight like a great bubble.

"Its rays fell upon the wall before me and suddenly upon the convexities I have described seven little circles of light sprang out. They gleamed, glimmered, grew brighter, shone. The gigantic slab before me turned as though on a pivot, sighing softly as it moved.

"For a moment I gasped in amazement. It was like a conjurer's trick. And the moving slab I noticed was also glowing, becoming opalescent like the little shining circles above.

"Only for a second I gazed and then with a word to Edith flung myself through the opening which the slab had uncovered. Before me was a platform and from the platform steps led downward into a smooth corridor. This passage was not dark; it glowed with the same faint silvery radiance as the door. Down it I raced. As I ran, plainer than ever before, I heard the chanting. The passage turned abruptly, passed parallel to the walls of the outer court-yard and then once more led abruptly downward. Still I ran, and as I ran I looked at the watch on my wrist. Less than three minutes had elapsed.

"The passage ended. Before me was a high vaulted arch. For a moment I paused. It seemed to open into space; a space filled with lambent, coruscating, many-coloured mist whose brightness grew even as I watched. I passed through the arch and stopped in sheer awe!

"In front of me was a pool. It was circular, perhaps 20 feet wide. Around it ran a low, softly curved lip of glimmering silvery stone. Its water was palest blue. The pool with its silvery rim was like a great blue eye staring upward.

"Upon it streamed seven shafts of radiance. They poured down upon the blue eye like cylindrical torrents; they were like shining pillars of light rising from a sapphire floor.

"One was the tender pink of the pearl; one of the aurora's green; a third a deathly white; the fourth the blue in mother-of-pearl; a shimmering column of pale amber; a beam of amethyst; a shaft of molten silver. Such are the colours of the seven lights that stream upon the moon pool. I drew closer, awestricken. The shafts did not illumine the depths. They played upon the surface and seemed there to diffuse, to melt into it. The pool drank them!

"Through the water tiny gleams of phosphorescence began to dart, sparkles and coruscations of pale incandescence. And far, far below I sensed a movement, a shifting glow as of something slowly rising.

"I looked upwards, following the radiant pillars to their source. Far above were seven shining globes, and it was from these that the rays poured. Even as I watched their brightness grew. They were like seven moons set high in some caverned heaven. Slowly their splendour increased, and with it the splendour of the seven beams streaming from them. It came to me that they were crystals of some unknown kind set in the roof of the moon pool's vault and that their light was drawn from the moon shining high above them. They were wonderful, those lights – and what must have been the knowledge of those who set them there!

"Brighter and brighter they grew as the moon climbed higher, sending its full radiance down through them. I tore my gaze away and stared at the pool. It had grown milky, opalescent. The rays gushing into it seemed to be filling it; it was alive with sparklings, scintillations, glimmerings. And the luminescence I had seen rising from its depths was larger, nearer!

"A swirl of mist floated up from its surface. It drifted within the embrace of the rosy beam and hung there for a moment. The beam seemed to embrace it, sending through it little shining corpuscles, tiny rosy spirallings. The mist absorbed the rays, was strengthened by it, gained substance. Another swirl sprang into the amber shaft, clung and fed there, moved swiftly towards the first and mingled with it. And now other swirls arose, here and there, too fast to be counted, hung poised in the embrace of the light streams; flashed and pulsed into each other.

"Thicker and thicker still they arose until the surface of the pool was a pulsating pillar of opalescent mist; steadily growing stronger; drawing within it life from the seven beams falling upon it; drawing to it from below the darting, red atoms of the pool. Into its centre was passing the luminescence I had sensed rising from the far depths. And the centre glowed, throbbed, began to send out questing swirls and tendrils.

"There forming before me was *that* which had walked with Stanton, which had taken Thora – the thing I had come to find!

"With the shock of realization my brain sprang into action. My hand fell to my pistol and I fired shot after shot into its radiance. The place rang with the explosions and there came to me a sense of unforgivable profanation. Devilish as I knew it to be, that chamber of the moon pool seemed also – in some way – holy. As though a god and a demon dwelled there, inextricably commingled.

"As I shot the pillar wavered; the water grew more disturbed. The mist swayed and shook; gathered itself again. I slipped a second clip into the automatic and, another idea coming to me, took careful aim at one of the globes in the roof. From thence I knew came the force that shaped the dweller in the pool. From the pouring rays came its strength. If I could destroy them I could check its forming. I fired again and again. If I hit the globes I did no damage. The little motes in their beams danced with the motes in the mist, troubled. That was all.

"Up from the pool like little bells, like bubbles of crystal notes rose the tinklings. Their notes were higher, had lost their sweetness, were angry, as it were, with themselves.

"And then out from the inexplicable, hovering over the pool, swept a shining swirl. It caught me above the heart; wrapped itself around me. I felt an icy coldness and then there rushed over me a mingled ecstasy and horror. Every atom of me quivered with delight and at the same time shrank with despair. There was nothing loathsome in it. But it was as though the icy soul of evil and the fiery soul of good had stepped together within me. The pistol dropped from my hand.

"So I stood while the pool gleamed and sparkled; the streams of light grew more intense and the mist glowed and strengthened. I saw that its shining core had shape – but a shape that my eyes and brain could not define. It was as though a being of another sphere should assume what it might of human semblance, but was not able to conceal that what human eyes saw was but a part of it. It was neither man nor woman; it was unearthly and androgynous. Even as I found its human semblance it changed. And still the mingled rapture and terror held me. Only in a little corner of my brain dwelled something untouched; something that held itself apart and watched. Was it the soul? I have never believed – and yet—

"Over the head of the misty body there sprang suddenly out seven little lights. Each was the colour of the beam beneath which it rested. I knew now that the dweller was – complete!

"And then behind me I heard a scream. It was Edith's voice. It came to me that she had heard the shots and followed me. I felt every faculty concentrate into a mighty effort. I wrenched myself free from the gripping tentacle and it swept back. I turned to catch Edith, and as I did so slipped – fell. As I dropped I saw the radiant shape above the pool leap swiftly for me!

"There was the rush past me and as the dweller paused, straight into it raced Edith, arms outstretched to shield me from it!"

He trembled.

"She threw herself squarely within its diabolic splendour," he whispered. "She stopped and reeled as though she had encountered solidity. And as she faltered it wrapped its shining self around her. The crystal tinklings burst forth jubilantly. The light filled her, ran through and around her as it had with Stanton, and I saw drop upon her face – the look. From the pillar came the murmur: '*Av-o-lo-ha!*' The vault echoed it.

" 'Edith!' I cried. 'Edith!' I was in agony. She must have heard me, even through the – thing. I saw her try to free herself. Her rush had taken her to the very verge of the moon pool. She tottered; and in an instant she fell – with the radiance still holding her, still swirling and winding around and through her – into the moon pool! She sank, Goodwin, and with her went the dweller!

"I dragged myself to the brink. Far down I saw a shining, many-coloured nebulous cloud descending; caught a glimpse of Edith's face, disappearing; her eyes stared up to me filled with supernal ecstasy and horror. And – vanished!

"I looked about me stupidly. The seven globes still poured their radiance upon the pool. It was pale blue again. Its sparklings and coruscations were gone. From far below there came a muffled outburst of triumphant chanting!

" 'Edith!' I cried again. 'Edith, come back to me!' And then a darkness fell upon me. I remember running back through the shimmering corridors and out into the courtyard. Reason had left me. When it returned I was far out at sea in our boat wholly estranged from civilization. A day later I was picked up by the schooner in which I came to Port Moresby.

"I have formed a plan; you must hear it, Goodwin." He fell upon his berth. I bent over him. Exhaustion and the relief of telling his story had been too much for him. He slept like the dead.

7. The Dweller Comes

All that night I watched over him. When dawn broke I went to my room to get a little sleep myself. But my slumber was haunted.

The next day the storm was unabated. Throckmartin came to me at lunch. He looked better. His strange expression had waned. He had regained much of his old alertness.

"Come to my cabin," he said. There, he stripped his shirt from him. "Something is happening," he said. "The mark is smaller." It was as he said.

"I'm escaping," he whispered jubilantly. "Just let me get to Melbourne safely, and then we'll see who'll win! For, Goodwin, I'm not at all sure that Edith is dead – as we know death – nor that the others are. There was something outside experience there – some great mystery."

And all that day he talked to me of his plans.

"There's a natural explanation, of course," he said. "My theory is that the moon rock is of some composition sensitive to the action of moon rays; somewhat as the metal selenium is to sun rays. There is a powerful quality in moonlight, as both science and legends can attest. We know of its effect upon the mentality, the nervous system, even upon certain diseases.

"The moon slab is of some material that reacts to moonlight. The circles over the top are, without doubt, its operating agency. When the light strikes them they release the mechanism that opens the slab, just as you can open doors with sunlight by an ingenious arrangement of selenium cells. Apparently it takes the strength of the full moon to do this. We will first try a concentration of the rays of the *nearly* full moon upon these circles to see whether that will open the rock. If it does we will be able to investigate the pool without interruption from – from – what emanates.

"Look, here on the chart are their locations. I have made this in duplicate for you in the event of something happening to me."

He worked upon the chart a little more.

"Here," he said, "is where I believe the seven great globes to be. They are probably hidden somewhere in the ruins of the islet called Tau, where they can catch the first moon rays. I have calculated that when I entered I went so far this way – here is the turn; so far this way, took this other turn and ran down this long, curving corridor to the hall of the moon pool. That ought to make lights, at least approximately, here." He pointed.

"They are certainly cleverly concealed, but they must be open to the air to get the light. They should not be too hard to find. They must be found." He hesitated again. "I suppose it would be safer to destroy them, for it is clearly through them that the phenomenon of the pool is manifested; and yet, to destroy so wonderful a thing! Perhaps the better way would be to have some men up by them, and if it were necessary, to protect those below, to destroy them on signal. Or they might simply be covered. That would neutralize them. To destroy them –" He hesitated again. "No, the phenomenon is too important to be destroyed without fullest investigation." His face clouded again. "But it is *not* human; it can't be," he muttered. He turned to me and laughed. "The old conflict between science and too frail human credulity!" he said.

Again: "We need half a dozen diving-suits. The pool must be entered and searched to its depths. That will indeed take courage, yet in the time of the new moon it should be safe, or perhaps better after the dweller is destroyed or made safe."

We went over plans, accepted them, rejected them, and still the storm raged – and all that day and all that night.

I hurry to the end. That afternoon there came a steady lightening of the clouds which Throckmartin watched with deep uneasiness. Towards dusk they broke away suddenly and soon the sky was clear. The stars came twinkling out.

"It will be tonight," Throckmartin said to me. "Goodwin, friend, stand by me. Tonight it will come, and I must fight."

I could say nothing. About an hour before moonrise we went to his cabin. We fastened the portholes tightly and turned on the lights. Throckmartin had some queer theory that the electric rays

would be a bar to his pursuer. I don't know why. A little later he
complained of increasing sleepiness.

"But it's just weariness," he said. "Not at all like that other
drowsiness. It's an hour till moonrise still," he yawned at last.
"Wake me up a good fifteen minutes before."

He lay upon the berth. I sat thinking. I came to myself with a
start. What time was it? I looked at my watch and jumped to the
porthole. It was full moonlight; the orb had been up for fully half
an hour. I strode over to Throckmartin and shook him by the
shoulder.

"Up, quick, man!" I cried. He rose sleepily. His shirt fell open
at the neck and I looked, in amazement, at the white band around
his chest. Even under the electric light it shone softly, as though
little flecks of light were in it.

Throckmartin seemed only half awake. He looked down at his
breast, saw the glowing cincture, and smiled.

"Oh, yes," he said drowsily, "it's coming – to take me back to
Edith! Well, I'm glad."

"Throckmartin!" I cried. "Wake up! Fight."

"Fight!" he said. "No use; keep the maps; come after us."

He went to the port and drowsily drew aside the curtain. The
moon traced a broad path of light straight to the ship. Under its
rays the band around his chest gleamed brighter and brighter;
shot forth little rays; seemed to move.

He peered out intently and, suddenly, before I could stop him,
threw open the port. I saw a glimmering presence moving swiftly
along the moon path towards us, skimming over the waters.

And with it raced little crystal tinklings and far off I heard a
long-drawn murmuring cry.

On the instant the lights went out in the cabin, evidently
throughout the ship, for I heard shouting above. I sprang back
into a corner and crouched there. At the porthole was a radiance;
swirls and spirals of living white cold fire. It poured into the
cabin and it was filled with dancing motes of light, and over the
radiant core of it shone seven little lights like tiny moons. It
gathered Throckmartin to it. Light pulsed through and from
him. I saw his skin turn to a translucent, shimmering whiteness

like illumined porcelain. His face became unrecognizable, inhuman with the monstrous twin expressions. So he stood for a moment. The pillar of light seemed to hesitate and the seven lights to contemplate me. I shrank further down into the corner. I saw Throckmartin drawn to the port. The room filled with murmuring. I fainted.

When I awakened the lights were burning again.

But of Throckmartin there was no trace!

There are some things that we are bound to regret all our lives. I suppose I was unbalanced by what I had seen. I could not think clearly. But there came to me the sheer impossibility of telling the ship's officers what I had seen; what Throckmartin had told me. They would accuse me, I felt, of his murder. At neither appearance of the phenomenon had any save our two selves witnessed it. I was certain of this because they would surely have discussed it. Why none had seen it I do not know.

The next morning when Throckmartin's absence was noted, I merely said that I had left him early in the evening. It occurred to no one to doubt me, or to question me further. His strangeness had caused much comment; all had thought him half mad. And so it was officially reported that he had fallen or jumped from the ship during the failure of the lights, the cause of which was another mystery of that night.

Afterwards, the same inhibition held me back from making his and my story known to my fellow scientists.

But this inhibition is suddenly dead, and I am not sure that its death is not a summons from Throckmartin.

And now I am going to Nan-Tanach to make amends for my cowardice by seeking out the dweller. So sure am I that all I have written here is absolutely true.

The Man who Painted the Dragon Griaule

Lucius Shepard

Like Harlan Ellison, Lucius Shepard (b. 1947) is another of those writers who chews up traditional stories and spits them out as masterpieces. In fact it's hard to think of anything by Shepard that is remotely traditional, yet all the hallmarks of fantasy fiction are there. The following features a lost, remote valley, a dragon, a beautiful girl, magic – all the usual trappings – but it's far from a usual story. It's the type of story fantasy was made for. Shepard isn't a prolific writer but he has produced enough for several collections: The Jaguar Hunter *(1987),* Nantucket Slayrides *(1989) and* The Ends of the Earth *(1991).*

"Other than the Sichi Collection, Cattanay's only surviving works are to be found in the Municipal Gallery at Regensburg, a group of eight oils-on-canvas, most notable among them being *Woman With Oranges*. These paintings constitute his portion of a student exhibition hung some weeks after he had left the city of his birth and travelled south to Teocinte, there to present his proposal to the city fathers; it is unlikely he ever learned of the disposition of his work, and even more unlikely that he was aware of the general critical indifference with which it was received. Perhaps the most interesting of the group to modern scholars, the most indicative as to Cattanay's later preoccupations, is the *Self Portrait*, painted at the age of twenty-eight, a year before his departure.

"The majority of the canvas is a richly varnished black in which the vague shapes of floorboards are presented, barely visible. Two irregular slashes of gold cross the blackness, and within these we can see a section of the artist's thin features and the shoulder panel of his shirt. The perspective given is that we are looking down at the artist, perhaps through a tear in the roof, and that he is looking up at us, squinting into the light, his mouth distorted by a grimace born of intense concentration. On first viewing the painting, I was struck by the atmosphere of tension that radiated from it. It seemed I was spying upon a man imprisoned within a shadow having two golden bars, tormented by the possibilities of light beyond the walls. And though this may be the reaction of the art historian, not the less knowledge-able and therefore more trustworthy response of the gal-lery-goer, it also seemed that this imprisonment was self-imposed, that he could have easily escaped his confine; but that he had realized a feeling of stricture was an essential fuel to his ambition, and so had chained himself to this arduous and thoroughly unreasonable chore of perception . . ."

– from *Meric Cattany:*
The Politics of Conception by Reade Holland, Ph.D

1

IN 1853, IN A COUNTRY FAR TO THE SOUTH, in a world separated from this one by the thinnest margin of possibility, a dragon named Griaule dominated the region of the Carbonales Valley, a fertile area centring upon the town of Teocinte and renowned for its production of silver, mahogany and indigo. There were other dragons in those days, most dwelling on the rocky islands west of Patagonia – tiny, irascible creatures, the largest of them no bigger than a swallow. But Griaule was one of the great beasts who had ruled an age. Over the centuries he had grown to stand 750 feet high at the mid-back, and from the tip of his tail to his nose he was 6,000 feet long. (It should be noted here that the growth of dragons was due not to caloric intake, but to the absorption of energy derived from the passage of time.) Had it not been for a miscast spell, Griaule would have died millennia before. The wizard entrusted with the task of slaying him – knowing his own life would be forfeited as a result of the magical backwash – had experienced a last-second twinge of fear, and, diminished by this ounce of courage, the spell had flown a mortal inch awry. Though the wizard's whereabouts were unknown, Griaule had remained alive. His heart had stopped, his breath stilled, but his mind continued to seethe, to send forth the gloomy vibrations that enslaved all who stayed for long within range of his influence.

This dominance of Griaule's was an elusive thing. The people of the valley attributed their dour character to years of living under his mental shadow, yet there were other regional populations who maintained a harsh face to the world and had no dragon on which to blame the condition; they also attributed their frequent raids against the neighbouring states to Griaule's effect, claiming to be a peaceful folk at heart – but again, was this not human nature? Perhaps the most certifiable proof of Griaule's primacy was the fact that despite a standing offer of a fortune in silver to anyone who could kill him, no one had succeeded. Hundreds of plans had been put forward, and all had failed, either through inanition or impracticality. The archives of Teocinte were filled with schematics for enormous steam-powered swords and other such improbable devices, and the architects of these plans had every one stayed too long in the valley and become part of the disgruntled populace. And so they went on with their lives, coming and going, always returning, bound to the valley, until one spring day in 1853, Meric Cattanay arrived and proposed that the dragon be painted.

He was a lanky young man with a shock of black hair and a pinched look to his cheeks; he affected the loose trousers and shirt of a peasant, and waved his arms to make a point. His eyes grew wide when listening, as if his brain were bursting with illumination, and at times he talked incoherently about "the conceptual statement of death by art". And though the city fathers could not be sure, though they allowed for the possibility that he simply had an unfortunate manner, it seemed he was mocking them. All in all, he was not the sort they were inclined to trust. But, because he had come armed with such a wealth of diagrams and charts, they were forced to give him serious consideration.

"I don't believe Griaule will be able to perceive the menace in a process as subtle as art," Meric told them. "We'll proceed as if we were going to illustrate him, grace his side with a work of true vision, and all the while we'll be poisoning him with the paint."

The city fathers voiced their incredulity, and Meric waited impatiently until they quieted. He did not enjoy dealing with these worthies. Seated at their long table, sour-faced, a huge smudge of soot on the wall above their heads like an ugly thought they were sharing, they reminded him of the Wine Merchants Association in Regensburg, the time they had rejected his group portrait.

"Paint can be deadly stuff," he said after their muttering had died down. "Take vert Veronese, for example. It's derived from oxide of chrome and barium. Just a whiff would make you keel over. But we have to go about it seriously, create a real piece of art. If we just slap paint on his side, he might see through us."

The first step in the process, he told them, would be to build a tower of scaffolding, complete with hoists and ladders, that would brace against the supraocular plates above the dragon's eye; this would provide a direct route to a 700-foot-square loading platform and base station behind the eye. He estimated it would take 81,000 board feet of lumber, and a crew of ninety men should be able to finish construction within five months. Ground crews accompanied by chemists and geologists would search out limestone deposits (useful in priming the scales) and sources of pigments, whether organic or minerals such as azurite and hematite. Other teams would be set to scraping the dragon's side clean of algae, peeled skin, any decayed material, and afterwards would laminate the surface with resins.

"It would be easier to bleach him with quicklime," he said. "But that way we lose the discolourations and ridges generated by growth and age, and I think what we'll paint will be defined by those shapes. Anything else would look like a damn tattoo!"

There would be storage vats and mills: edge-runner mills to separate pigments from crude ores, ball mills to powder the pigments, pug mills to mix them with oil. There would be boiling vats and calciners – 15-foot-high furnaces used to produce caustic lime for sealant solutions.

"We'll build most of them atop the dragon's head for purposes of access," he said. "On the frontoparital plate." He checked some figures. "By my reckoning, the plate's about 350 feet wide. Does that sound accurate?"

Most of the city fathers were stunned by the prospect, but one managed a nod, and another asked, "How long will it take for him to die?"

"Hard to say," came the answer. "Who knows how much poison he's capable of absorbing. It might just take a few years. But in the worst instance, within forty or fifty years, enough chemicals will have seeped through the scales to have weakened the skeleton, and he'll fall in like an old barn."

"Forty years!" exclaimed someone. "Preposterous!"

"Or fifty." Meric smiled. "That way we'll have time to finish the painting." He turned and walked to the window and stood gazing out at the white stone houses of Teocinte. This was going to be the sticky part, but if he read them right, they would not believe in the plan if it seemed too easy. They needed to feel they were making a sacrifice, that they were nobly bound to a great labour. "If it does take forty or fifty years," he went on, "the project will drain your resources. Timber, animal life, minerals. Everything will be used up by the work. Your lives will be totally changed. But I guarantee you'll be rid of him."

The city fathers broke into an outraged babble.

"Do you really want to kill him?" cried Meric, stalking over to them and planting his fists on the table. "You've been waiting centuries for someone to come along and chop off his head or send him up in a puff of smoke. That's not going to happen!

There is no easy solution. But there is a practical one, an elegant one. To use the stuff of the land he dominates to destroy him. It will *not* be easy, but you *will* be rid of him. And that's what you want, isn't it?"

They were silent, exchanging glances, and he saw that they now believed he could do what he proposed and were wondering if the cost was too high.

"I'll need 500 ounces of silver to hire engineers and artisans," said Meric. "Think it over. I'll take a few days and go see this dragon of yours . . . inspect the scales and so forth. When I return, you can give me your answer."

The city fathers grumbled and scratched their heads, but at last they agreed to put the question before the body politic. They asked for a week in which to decide and appointed Jarcke, who was the mayoress of Hangtown, to guide Meric to Griaule.

The valley extended 70 miles from north to south, and was enclosed by jungled hills whose folded sides and spiny backs gave rise to the idea that beasts were sleeping beneath them. The valley floor was cultivated into fields of bananas and cane and melons, and where it was not cultivated there were stands of thistle palms and berry thickets and the occasional giant fig brooding sentinel over the rest. Jarcke and Meric tethered their horses a half-hour's ride from town and began to ascend a gentle incline that rose into the notch between two hills. Sweaty and short of breath, Meric stopped a third of the way up; but Jarcke kept plodding along, unaware he was no longer following. She was by nature as blunt as her name – a stump beer keg of a woman with a brown, weathered face. Though she appeared to be ten years older than Meric, she was nearly the same age. She wore a grey robe belted at the waist with a leather band that held four throwing knives, and a coil of rope was slung over her shoulder.

"How much further?" called Meric.

She turned and frowned. "You're standin' on his tail. Rest of him's around back of the hill."

A pinprick of chill bloomed in Meric's abdomen, and he stared down at the grass, expecting it to dissolve and reveal a mass of glittering scales.

"Why don't we take the horses?" he asked.

"Horses don't like it up here." She grunted with amusement. "Neither do most people, for that matter." She trudged off.

Another twenty minutes brought them to the other side of the hill high above the valley floor. The land continued to slope upwards, but more gently than before. Gnarled, stunted oaks pushed up from thickets of chokecherry, and insects sizzled in the weeds. They might have been walking on a natural shelf several hundred feet across; but ahead of them, where the ground rose abruptly, a number of thick, greenish-black columns broke from the earth. Leathery folds hung between them, and these were encrusted with clumps of earth and brocaded with mould. They had the look of a collapsed palisade and the ghosted feel of ancient ruins.

"Them's the wings," said Jarcke. "Mostly they's covered, but you can catch sight of 'em off the edge, and up near Hangtown there's places where you can walk in under 'em . . . but I wouldn't advise it."

"I'd like to take a look off the edge," said Meric, unable to tear his eyes away from the wings; though the surfaces of the leaves gleamed in the strong sun, the wings seemed to absorb the light, as if their age and strangeness were proof against reflection.

Jarcke led him to a glade in which tree ferns and oaks crowded together and cast a green gloom, and where the earth sloped sharply downwards. She lashed her rope to an oak and tied the other end around Meric's waist. "Give a yank when you want to stop, and another when you want to be hauled up," she said, and began paying out the rope, letting him walk backwards against her pull.

Ferns tickled Meric's neck as he pushed through the brush, and the oak leaves pricked his cheeks. Suddenly he emerged into bright sunlight. On looking down, he found his feet were braced against a fold of the dragon's wing, and on looking up, he saw that the wing vanished beneath a mantle of earth and vegetation. He let Jarcke lower him a dozen feet more, yanked, and gazed off northwards along the enormous swell of Griaule's side.

The swells were hexagonals 30 feet across and half that distance high; their basic colour was a pale greenish gold, but some were whitish, draped with peels of dead skin, and others were overgrown by viridian moss, and the rest were scrolled with patterns of lichen and algae that resembled the characters of a serpentine alphabet. Birds had nested in the cracks, and ferns plumed from the interstices, thousands of them lifting in the breeze. It was a great hanging garden whose scope took Meric's breath away – like looking around the curve of a fossil moon. The sense of all the centuries accreted in the scales made him dizzy, and he found he could not turn his head, but could only stare at the panorama, his soul shrivelling with a comprehension of the timelessness and bulk of this creature to which he clung like a fly. He lost perspective on the scene – Griaule's side was bigger than the sky, possessing its own potent gravity, and it seemed completely reasonable that he should be able to walk out along it and suffer no fall. He started to do so, and Jarcke, mistaking the strain on the rope for signal, hauled him up, dragging him across the wing, through the dirt and ferns, and back into the glade. He lay speechless and gasping at her feet.

"Big 'un, ain't he," she said, and grinned.

After Meric had got his legs under him, they set off towards Hangtown; but they had not gone 100 yards, following a trail that wound through the thickets, before Jarcke whipped out a knife and hurled it at a raccoon-sized creature that leaped out in front of them.

"Skizzer," she said, kneeling beside it and pulling the knife from its neck. "Calls 'em that 'cause they hisses when they runs. They eats snakes, but they'll go after children what ain't careful."

Meric dropped down next to her. The skizzer's body was covered with short black fur, but its head was hairless, corpse-pale, the skin wrinkled as if it had been immersed too long in water. Its face was squinty-eyed, flat-nosed, with a disproportionately large jaw that hinged open to expose a nasty set of teeth.

"They's the dragon's critters," said Jarcke. "Used to live in his bunghole." She pressed one of its paws, and claws curved like hooks slid forth. "They'd hang around the lip and drop on other

critters what wandered in. And if nothin' wandered in . . ." She
pried out the tongue with her knife – its surface was studded with
jagged points like the blade of a rasp. "Then they'd lick Griaule
clean for their supper."

Back in Teocinte, the dragon had seemed to Meric a simple
thing, a big lizard with a tick of life left inside, the residue of a dim
sensibility; but he was beginning to suspect that this tick of life
was more complex than any he had encountered.

"My gram used to say," Jarcke went on, "that the old dragons
could fling themselves up to the sun in a blink and travel back to
their own world, and when they come back, they'd bring the
skizzers and all the rest with 'em. They was immortal, she said.
Only the young ones came here 'cause later on they grew too big
to fly on earth." She made a sour face. "Don't know as I believe
it."

"Then you're a fool," said Meric.

Jarcke glanced up at him, her hand twitching towards her belt.

"How can you live here and *not* believe it!" he said, surprised
to hear himself so fervently defending a myth. "God! This—" He
broke off, noticing the flicker of a smile on her face.

She clucked her tongue, apparently satisfied by something.
"Come on," she said. "I want to be at the eye before sunset."

The peaks of Griaule's folded wings, completely overgrown by
grass and shrubs and dwarfish trees, formed two spiny hills that
cast a shadow over Hangtown and the narrow lake around which
it sprawled. Jarcke said the lake was a stream flowing off the hill
behind the dragon, and that it drained away through the mem-
branes of his wing and down on to his shoulder. It was beautiful
beneath the wing, she told him. Ferns and waterfalls. But it was
reckoned an evil place. From a distance the town looked pictur-
esque – rustic cabins, smoking chimneys. As they approached,
however, the cabins resolved into dilapidated shanties with
missing boards and broken windows; suds and garbage and offal
floated in the shallows of the lake. Aside from a few men idling on
the stoops, who squinted at Meric and nodded glumly at Jarcke,
no one was about. The grass blades stirred in the breeze, spiders

scuttled under the shanties, and there was an air of torpor and dissolution.

Jarcke seemed embarrassed by the town. She made no attempt at introductions, stopping only long enough to fetch another coil of rope from one of the shanties, and as they walked between the wings, down through the neck spines – a forest of greenish-gold spikes burnished by the lowering sun – she explained how the townsfolk grubbed a livelihood from Griaule. Herbs gathered on his back were valued as medicine and charms, as were the peels of dead skin; the artefacts left by previous Hangtown generations were of some worth to various collectors.

"Then there's scale hunters," she said with disgust. "Henry Sichi from Port Chantay'll pay good money for pieces of scale, and though it's bad luck to do it, some'll have a go at chippin' off the loose 'uns." She walked a few paces in silence. "But there's others who've got better reasons for livin' here."

The frontal spike above Griaule's eyes was whorled at the base like a narwhal's horn and curved back towards the wings. Jarcke attached the ropes to eyebolts drilled into the spike, tied one about her waist, the other about Meric's; she cautioned him to wait, and rappelled off the side. In a moment she called for him to come down. Once again he grew dizzy as he descended; he glimpsed a clawed foot far below, mossy fangs jutting from an impossibly long jaw; and then he began to spin and bash against the scales. Jarcke gathered him in and helped him sit on the lip of the socket.

"Damn!" she said, stamping her foot.

A 3-foot-long section of the adjoining scale shifted slowly away. Peering close, Meric saw that while in texture and hue it was indistinguishable from the scale, there was a hairline division between it and the surface. Jarcke, her face twisted in disgust, continued to harry the thing until it moved out of reach.

"Call 'em flakes," she said when he asked what it was. "Some kind of insect. Got a long tube that they pokes down between the scales and sucks the blood. See there?" She pointed off to where a flock of birds were wheeling close to Griaule's side; a chip of pale gold broke loose and went tumbling down to the valley. "Birds pry 'em off, let 'em bust open, and eats the innards." She hunkered down beside him and after a moment asked, "You really think you can do it?"

"What? You mean kill the dragon?"

She nodded.

"Certainly," he said, and then added, lying, "I've spent years devising the method."

"If all the paint's goin' to be atop his head, how're you goin' to get it to where the paintin's done?"

"That's no problem. We'll pipe it to wherever it's needed."

She nodded again. "You're a clever fellow," she said; and when Meric, pleased, made as if to thank her for the compliment, she cut in and said, "Don't mean nothin' by it. Bein' clever ain't an accomplishment. It's just somethin' you come by, like bein' tall." She turned away, ending the conversation.

Meric was weary of being awestruck, but even so he could not help marvelling at the eye. By his estimate it was 70 feet long and 50 feet high, and it was shuttered by an opaque membrane that was unusually clear of algae and lichen, glistening, with vague glints of colour visible behind it. As the westering sun reddened and sank between two distant hills, the membrane began to quiver and then split open down the centre. With the ponderous slowness of a theatre curtain opening, the halves slid apart to reveal the glowing humour. Terrified by the idea that Griaule could see him, Meric sprang to his feet, but Jarcke restrained him.

"Stay still and watch," she said.

He had no choice – the eye was mesmerizing. The pupil was slit and featureless black, but the humour . . . he had never seen such fiery blues and crimsons and golds. What had looked to be vague glints, odd refractions of the sunset, he now realized were photic reactions of some sort. Fairy rings of light developed deep within the eye, expanded into spoked shapes, flooded the humour, and faded – only to be replaced by another and another. He felt the pressure of Griaule's vision, his ancient mind, pouring through him, and as if in response to this pressure, memories bubbled up in his thoughts. Particularly sharp ones. The way a bowlful of brush water had looked after freezing over during a winter's night – a delicate, fractured flower of murky yellow. An archipelago of orange peels that his girl had left strewn across the floor of the studio. Sketching atop Jokenam Hill one sunrise, the snow-capped roofs of Regensburg below pitched at all angles like broken paving stones, and silver shafts of the sun striking down through a leaden overcast. It was as if these things were being drawn forth for his inspection. Then they were washed away by what also seemed a memory, though at the same time it was wholly unfamiliar. Essentially, it was a landscape of light, and he was plunging through it, up and up. Prisms and lattices of iridescent fire bloomed around him, and everything was a roaring fall into brightness, and finally he was clear into its white furnace heart, his own heart swelling with the joy of his strength and dominion.

It was dusk before Meric realized the eye had closed. His mouth hung open, his eyes ached from straining to see, and his tongue was glued to his palate. Jarcke sat motionless, buried in shadow.

"Th . . ." He had to swallow to clear his throat of mucus. "This is the reason you live here, isn't it?"

"Part of the reason," she said. "I can see things comin' way up here. Things to watch out for, things to study on."

She stood and walked to the lip of the socket and spat off the edge; the valley stretched out grey and unreal behind her, the folds of the hills barely visible in the gathering dusk.

"I seen you comin'," she said.

A week later, after much exploration, much talk, they went down into Teocinte. The town was a shambles – shattered windows, slogans painted on the walls, glass and torn banners and spoiled food littering the streets – as if there had been both a celebration and a battle. Which there had. The city fathers met with Meric in the town hall and informed him that his plan had been approved. They presented him a chest containing 500 ounces of silver and said that the entire resources of the community were at his disposal. They offered a wagon and a team to transport him and the chest to Regensburg and asked if any of the preliminary work could be begun during his absence.

Meric hefted one of the silver bars. In its cold gleam he saw the object of his desire; two, perhaps three years of freedom, of doing the work he wanted and not having to accept commissions. But all that had been confused. He glanced at Jarcke; she was staring out the window, leaving it to him. He set the bar back in the chest and shut the lid.

"You'll have to send someone else," he said. And then, as the city fathers looked at each other askance, he laughed and laughed at how easily he had discarded all his dreams and expectations.

It had been eleven years since I had been to the valley, twelve since work had begun on the painting, and I was appalled by the changes that had taken place. Many of the hills were scraped brown and treeless, and there was a general dearth of wildlife. Griaule, of course, was most changed. Scaffolding hung from his back; artisans, suspended by webworks of ropes, crawled over his side; and all the scales to be worked had either been painted or primed. The tower rising to his eye was swarmed by labourers, and at night the calciners and vats atop his head belched flame into the sky, making it seem there was a mill town in the heavens. At his feet was a brawling shantytown populated by prostitutes, workers, gamblers, ne'er-do-wells of every sort, and soldiers: the burdensome cost of the project had encouraged the city fathers of Teocinte to form a regular militia, which regularly plundered the adjoining states and had posted occupation forces to some areas. Herds of frightened animals milled in the slaughtering pens, waiting to be rendered into oils and pigments. Wagons filled with ores and vegetable products rattled in the streets. I myself had brought a cargo of madder roots from which a rose tint would be derived.

It was not easy to arrange a meeting with Cattanay. While he did none of the actual painting, he was always busy in his office consulting with engineers and artisans, or involved in some other part of the logistical process. When at last I did meet with him, I found he had changed as drastically as Griaule. His hair had gone grey, deep lines scored his features, and his right shoulder had a peculiar bulge at its mid-point – the product of a fall. He was amused by the fact that I wanted to buy the painting, to collect the scales after Griaule's death, and I do not believe he took me at all seriously. But the woman Jarcke, his constant companion, informed him that I was a responsible businessman, that I had already bought the bones, the teeth, even the dirt beneath Griaule's belly (this I eventually sold as having magical properties).

"Well," said Cattanay, "I suppose someone has to own them."

He led me outside, and we stood looking at the painting.

"You'll keep them together?" he asked.

I said, "Yes."

"If you'll put that in writing," he said, "then they're yours."

Having expected to haggle long and hard over the price, I was flabbergasted; but I was even more flabbergasted by what he said next.

"Do you think it's any good?" he asked.

Cattanay did not consider the painting to be the work of *his* imagination; he felt he was simply illuminating the shapes that appeared on Griaule's side and was convinced that once the paint was applied, new shapes were produced beneath it, causing him to make constant changes. He saw himself as an artisan more than a creative artist. But to put his question into perspective, people were beginning to flock from all over the world and marvel at the painting. Some claimed they saw intimations of the future in its gleaming surface; others underwent transfiguring experiences; still others – artists themselves – attempted to capture something of the work on canvas, hopeful of establishing reputations merely by being competent copyists of Cattanay's art. The painting was nonrepresentational in character, essentially a wash of pale gold spread across the dragon's side; but buried beneath the laminated surface were a myriad tints of iridescent colour that, as the sun passed through the heavens and the light bloomed and faded, solidified into innumerable forms and figures that seemed to flow back and forth. I will not try to categorize these forms, because there was no end to them; they were as varied as the conditions under which they were viewed. But I will say that on the morning I met with Cattanay, I – who was the soul of the practical man, without a visionary bone in my body – felt as though I were being whirled away into the painting, up through geometries of light, latticeworks of rainbow colour that built the way the edges of a cloud build, past orbs, spirals, wheels of flame . . .

– from *This Business of Griaule*
by Henry Sichi

2

There had been several women in Meric's life since he arrived in the valley; most had been attracted by his growing fame and his association with the mystery of the dragon, and most had left him for the same reasons, feeling daunted and unappreciated. But Lise was different in two respects. First, because she loved Meric truly and well; and second, because she was married – albeit unhappily – to a man named Pardiel, the foreman of the calciner crew. She did not love him as she did Meric, yet she respected him and felt obliged to consider carefully before ending the relationship. Meric had never known such as introspective soul. She was twelve years younger than he, tall and lovely, with sun-streaked hair and brown eyes that went dark and seemed to turn inward whenever she was pensive. She was in the habit of analysing everything that affected her, drawing back from her emotions and inspecting them as if they were a clutch of strange insects she had discovered crawling on her skirt. Though her penchant for self-examination kept her from him, Meric viewed it as a kind of baffling virtue. He had the classic malady and could find no fault with her. For almost a year they were as happy as could be expected; they talked long hours and walked together, and on those occasions when Pardiel worked double shifts and was forced to bed down by his furnaces, they spent the nights making love in the cavernous spaces beneath the dragon's wing.

It was still reckoned an evil place. Something far worse than skizzers or flakes was rumoured to live there, and the ravages of this creature were blamed for every disappearance, even that of the most malcontented labourer. But Meric did not give credence to the rumours. He half believed Griaule had chosen him to be his executioner and that the dragon would never let him be harmed; and besides, it was the only place where they could be assured of privacy.

A crude stair led under the wing, handholds and steps hacked from the scales – doubtless the work of scale hunters. It was a treacherous passage, 600 feet above the valley floor; but Lise and Meric were secured by ropes, and over the months, driven by the urgency of passion, they adapted to it. Their favourite spot lay 50 feet in (Lise would go no further; she was afraid even if he was not), near a waterfall that trickled over the leathery folds, causing them to glisten with a mineral brilliance. It was eerily beautiful, a haunted gallery. Peels of dead skin hung down from the shadows like torn veils of ectoplasm; ferns sprouted from the vanes, which were thicker than cathedral columns; swallows curved through the black air. Sometimes, lying with her hidden by a tuck of the wing, Meric would think the beating of their hearts was what really animated the place, that the instant they left, the water ceased flowing and the swallows vanished. He had an unshakable faith in the transforming power of their affections, and one morning as they dressed, preparing to return to Hangtown, he asked her to leave with him.

"To another part of the valley?" She laughed sadly. "What good would that do? Pardiel would follow us."

"No," he said. "To another country. Anywhere far from here."

"We can't," she said, kicking at the wing. "Not until Griaule dies. Have you forgotten?"

"We haven't tried."

"Others have."

"But we'd be strong enough. I know it!"

"You're a romantic," she said gloomily, and stared out over the slope of Griaule's back at the valley. Sunrise had washed the hills to crimson, and even the tips of the wings were glowing a dull red.

"Of course I'm a romantic!" He stood, angry. "What the hell's wrong with that?"

She sighed with exasperation. "You wouldn't leave your work," she said. "And if we did leave, what work would you do? Would—"

"Why must everything be a problem in advance!" he shouted. "I'll tattoo elephants! I'll paint murals on the chests of giants, I'll illuminate whales! Who else is better qualified?"

She smiled, and his anger evaporated.

"I didn't mean it that way," she said. "I just wondered if you could be satisfied with anything else."

She reached out her hand to be pulled up, and he drew her into an embrace. As he held her, inhaling the scent of vanilla water from her hair, he saw a diminutive figure silhouetted against the backdrop of the valley. It did not seem real – a black homunculus – and even when it began to come forward, growing larger and larger, it looked less a man than a magical keyhole opening in a crimson set hillside. But Meric knew from the man's rolling walk and the hulking set of his shoulders that it was Pardiel; he was carrying a long-handled hook, one of those used by artisans to manoeuvre along the scales.

Meric tensed, and Lise looked back to see what had alarmed him. "Oh, my God!" she said, moving out of the embrace.

Pardiel stopped a dozen feet away. He said nothing. His face was in shadow, and the hook swung lazily from his hand. Lise took a step towards him, then stepped back and stood in front of Meric as if to shield him. Seeing this, Pardiel let out an inarticulate yell and charged, slashing with the hook. Meric pushed Lise aside and ducked. He caught a brimstone whiff of the calciners as Pardiel rushed past and went sprawling, tripped by some irregularity in the scale. Deathly afraid, knowing he was no match for the foreman, Meric seized Lise's hand and ran deeper under the wing. He hoped Pardiel would be too frightened to follow, leery of the creature that was rumoured to live there; but he was not. He came after them at a measured pace, tapping the hook against his leg.

Higher on Griaule's back, the wing was dimpled downwards by hundreds of bulges, and this created a maze of small chambers and tunnels so low that they had to crouch to pass along them. The sound of their breathing and the scrape of their feet were amplified by the enclosed spaces, and Meric could no longer hear Pardiel. He had never been this deep before. He had thought it would be pitch-dark; but the lichen and algae adhering to the wing were luminescent and patterned every surface, even the scales beneath them, with whorls of blue and green fire that shed a sickly radiance. It was as if they were giants crawling through a universe whose starry matter had not yet congealed into galaxies and nebulas. In the wan light, Lise's face – turned back to him now and again – was teary and frantic; and then, as she straightened, passing into still another chamber, she drew in breath with a shriek.

At first Meric thought Pardiel had somehow managed to get ahead of them; but on entering he saw that the cause of her fright was a man propped in a sitting position against the far wall. He looked mummified. Wisps of brittle hair poked up from his scalp, the shapes of his bones were visible through his skin, and his eyes were empty holes. Between his legs was a scatter of dust where his genitals had been. Meric pushed Lise towards the next tunnel, but she resisted and pointed at the man.

"His eyes," she said, horror-struck.

Though the eyes were mostly a negative black, Meric now realized they were shot through by opalescent flickers. He felt compelled to kneel beside the man; it was a sudden, motiveless urge that gripped him, bent him to its will, and released him a second later. As he rested his hand on the scale, he brushed a massive ring that was lying beneath the shrunken fingers. Its stone was black, shot through by flickers identical to those within the eyes, and incised with the letter *S*. He found his gaze was deflected away from both the stone and the eyes, as if they contained charges repellent to the senses. He touched the man's withered arm; the flesh was rock-hard, petrified. But alive. From that brief touch he gained an impression of the man's life, of gazing for centuries at the same patch of unearthly fire, of a mind gone beyond mere madness into a perverse rapture, a meditation upon some foul principle. He snatched back his hand in revulsion.

There was a noise behind them, and Meric jumped up, pushing Lise into the next tunnel. "Go right," he whispered. "We'll circle back towards the stair." But Pardiel was too close to confuse with such tactics, and their flight became a wild chase, scrambling, falling, catching glimpses of Pardiel's smoke-stained face, until finally – as Meric came to a large chamber – he felt the hook bite into his thigh. He went down, clutching at the wound, pulling the hook loose. The next moment Pardiel was atop him; Lise appeared over his shoulder, but he knocked her away and locked his fingers in Meric's hair and smashed his head against the scale. Lise screamed, and white lights fired through Meric's skull. Again his head was smashed down. And again. Dimly, he saw Lise struggling with Pardiel, saw her shoved away, saw the hook raised high and the foreman's mouth distorted by a grimace. Then the grimace vanished. His jaw dropped open and he reached behind him as if to scratch his shoulder blade. A line of dark blood eeled from his mouth and he collapsed, smothering Meric beneath his chest. Meric heard voices. He tried to dislodge the body, and the effects drained the last of his strength. He whirled down through a blackness that seemed as negative and inexhaustible as the petrified man's eyes.

Someone had propped his head on their lap and was bathing his brow with a damp cloth. He assumed it was Lise, but when he asked what had happened, it was Jarcke who answered, saying, "Had to kill him." His head throbbed, his leg throbbed even worse, and his eyes would not focus. The peels of dead skin hanging overhead appeared to be writhing. He realized they were out near the edge of the wing.

"Where's Lise?"

"Don't worry," said Jarcke. "You'll see her again." She made it sound like an indictment.

"Where is she?"

"Sent her back to Hangtown. Won't do you two bein' seen hand in hand the same day Pardiel's missin'."

"She wouldn't have left . . ." He blinked, trying to see her face; the lines around her mouth were etched deep and reminded him of the patterns of lichen on the dragon's scale. "What did you do?"

"Convinced her it was best," said Jarcke. "Don' you know she's just foolin' with you?"

"I've got to talk with her." He was full of remorse, and it was unthinkable that Lise should be bearing her grief alone; but when he struggled to rise, pain lanced through his leg.

"You wouldn't get 10 feet," she said. "Soon as your head's clear, I'll help you with the stairs."

He closed his eyes, resolving to find Lise the instant he got back to Hangtown; together they would decide what to do. The scale beneath him was cool, and that coolness was transmitted to his skin, his flesh, as if he were merging with it, becoming one of its ridges.

"What was the wizard's name?" he asked after a while, recalling the petrified man, the ring and its incised letter. "The one who tried to kill Griaule . . ."

"Don't know as I ever heard it," said Jarcke. "But I reckon it's him back there."

"You saw him?"

"I was chasin' a scale hunter once what stole some rope, and I found him instead. Pretty miserable sort, whoever he is."

Her fingers trailed over his shoulder – a gentle, treasuring touch. He did not understand what it signalled, being too concerned with Lise, with the terrifying potentials of all that had happened; but years later, after things had passed beyond remedy, he cursed himself for not having understood.

At length Jarcke helped him to his feet, and they climbed up to Hangtown, to bitter realizations and regrets, leaving Pardiel to the birds or the weather or worse.

It seems it is considered irreligious for a woman in love to hesitate or examine the situation, to do anything other than blindly follow the impulse of her emotions. I felt the brunt of such an attitude – people judged it my fault for not having acted quickly and decisively one way or another. Perhaps I was overcautious. I do not claim to be free of blame, only innocent of sacrilege. I believe I might have eventually left Pardiel – there was not enough in the relationship to sustain happiness for either of us. But I had good reason for cautious examination. My husband was not an evil man, and there were matters of loyalty between us.

I could not face Meric after Pardiel's death, and I moved to another part of the valley. He tried to see me on many occasions, but I always refused. Though I was greatly tempted, my guilt was greater. Four years later, after Jarcke died – crushed by a runaway wagon – one of her associates wrote and told me Jarcke had been in love with Meric, that it had been she who had informed Pardiel of the affair, and that she may well have staged the murder. The letter acted somewhat to expiate my guilt, and I weighed the possibility of seeing Meric again. But too much time had passed, and we had both assumed other lives. I decided against it. Six years later, when Griaule's influence had weakened sufficiently to allow emigration, I moved to Port Chantay. I did not hear from Meric for almost twenty years after that, and then one day I received a letter, which I will reproduce in part.

"My old friend from Regensburg, Louis Dardano, has been living here for the past few years, engaged in writing my biography. The narrative has a breezy feel, like a tale being told in a tavern, which – if you recall my telling you how this all began – is quite appropriate. But on reading it, I am amazed my life has had such a simple shape. One task, one passion. God, Lise! Seventy years old, and I still dream of you. And I still think of what happened that morning under the wing. Strange, that it has taken me all this time to realize it was not Jarcke, not you or I who were culpable, but Griaule. How obvious it seems now. I was leaving, and he needed me to complete the expression on his side, his dream of flying, of escape, to grant him the death of his desire. I am certain you will think I have leaped to this assumption, but I remind you that it has been a leap of forty years' duration. I know Griaule, know his monstrous subtlety. I can see it at work in every action that has taken place in the valley since my arrival. I was a fool not to understand that his powers were at the heart of our sad conclusion.

"The army now runs everything here, as no doubt you are aware. It is rumoured they are planning a winter campaign against Regensburg. Can you believe it! Their fathers were ignorant, but this generation is brutally stupid. Otherwise, the work goes well and things are as usual with me. My shoulder aches, children stare at me on the street, and it is whispered I am mad . . ."

– from *Under Griaule's Wing*
by Lise Claverie

3

Acne-scarred, lean, arrogant, Major Hauk was a very young major with a limp. When Meric had entered, the major had been practising his signature; it was a thing of elegant loops and flourishes, obviously intended to have a place in posterity. As he strode back and forth during their conversation, he paused frequently to admire himself in the window glass, settling the hang of his red jacket or running his fingers along the crease of his white trousers. It was the new style of uniform, the first Meric had seen at close range, and he noted with amusement the dragons embossed on the epaulets. He wondered if Griaule was capable of such an irony, if his influence was sufficiently discreet to have planted the idea for this comic opera apparel in the brain of some general's wife.

". . . not a question of manpower," the major was saying, "but of —" He broke off, and after a moment cleared his throat.

Meric, who had been studying the blotches on the backs of his hands, glanced up; the cane that had been resting against his knee slipped and clattered to the floor.

"A question of *matériel*," said the major firmly. "The price of antimony, for example . . ."

"Hardly use it any more," said Meric. "I'm almost done with the mineral reds."

A look of impatience crossed the major's face. "Very well," he said; he stooped to his desk and shuffled through some papers. "Ah! Here's a bill for a shipment of cuttlefish from which you derive . . ." He shuffled more papers.

"Syrian brown," said Meric gruffly. "I'm done with that, too. Golds and violets are all I need any more. A little blue and rose." He wished the man would stop badgering him; he wanted to be at the eye before sunset.

As the major continued his accounting, Meric's gaze wandered out the window. The shantytown surrounding Griaule had swelled into a city and now sprawled across the hills. Most of the buildings were permanent, wood and stone, and the cant of the roofs, the smoke from the factories around the perimeter, put him in mind of Regensburg. All the natural beauty of the land had been drained into the painting. Blackish grey rain clouds were muscling up from the east, but the afternoon sun shone clear and shed a heavy gold radiance on Griaule's side. It looked as if the sunlight were an extension of the gleaming resins, as if the thickness of the paint were becoming infinite. He let the major's voice recede to a buzz and followed the scatter and dazzle of the images; and then, with a start, he realized the major was sounding him out about stopping the work.

The idea panicked him at first. He tried to interrupt, to raise objections; but the major talked through him, and as Meric thought it over, he grew less and less opposed. The painting would never be finished, and he was tired. Perhaps it was time to have done with it, to accept a university post somewhere and enjoy life for a while.

"We've been thinking about a temporary stoppage," said Major Hauk. "Then if the winter campaign goes well . . ." He smiled. "If we're not visited by plague and pestilence, we'll assume things are in hand. Of course we'd like your opinion."

Meric felt a surge of anger towards this smug little monster. "In my opinion, you people are idiots," he said. "You wear Griaule's image on your shoulders, weave him on your flags, and yet you don't have the least comprehension of what that means. You think it's just a useful symbol . . ."

"Excuse me," said the major stiffly.

"The hell I will!" Meric groped for his cane and heaved up to his feet. "You see yourselves as conquerors. Shapers of destiny. But all your rapes and slaughters are Griaule's expressions. *His* will. You're every bit as much his parasites as the skizzers."

The major sat, picked up a pen, and began to write.

"It astounds me," Meric went on, "that you can live next to a miracle, a source of mystery, and treat him as if he were an oddly shaped rock."

The major kept writing.

"What are you doing?" asked Meric.

"My recommendation," said the major without looking up.

"Which is?"

"That we initiate stoppage at once."

They exchanged hostile stares, and Meric turned to leave; but as he took hold of the doorknob, the major spoke again.

"We owe you so much," he said; he wore an expression of mingled pity and respect that further irritated Meric.

"How many men have you killed, Major?" he asked, opening the door.

"I'm not sure. I was in the artillery. We were never able to be sure."

"Well, I'm sure of my tally," said Meric. "It's taken me forty years to amass it. Fifteen hundred and ninety-three men and women. Poisoned, scalded, broken by falls, savaged by animals. Murdered. Why don't we – you and I – just call it even."

Though it was a sultry afternoon, he felt cold as he walked towards the tower – an internal cold that left him light-headed and weak. He tried to think what he would do. The idea of a university post seemed less appealing away from the major's office; he would soon grow weary of worshipful students and in-depth dissections of his work by jealous academics. A man hailed him as he turned into the market. Meric waved but did not stop, and heard another man say, *"That's* Cattanay?" (That ragged old ruin?)

The colours of the market were too bright, the smells of charcoal cookery too cloying, the crowds too thick, and he made for the side streets, hobbling past one-room stucco houses and tiny stores where they sold cooking oil by the ounce and cut cigars in half if you could not afford a whole one. Garbage, tornados of dust and flies, drunks with bloody mouths. Somebody had tied wires around a pariah dog – a bitch with slack teats; the wires had sliced into her flesh, and she lay panting in an alley mouth, gaunt ribs flecked with pink lather, gazing into nowhere. She, thought Meric, and not Griaule, should be the symbol of their flag.

As he rode the hoist up the side of the tower, he fell into his old habit of jotting down notes for the next day. *What's that cord of wood doing on level five? Slow leak of chrome yellow from pipes on level twelve.* Only when he saw a man dismantling some scaffolding did he recall Major Hauk's recommendation and understand that the order must already have been given. The loss of his work struck home to him then, and he leaned against the railing, his chest constricted and his eyes brimming. He straightened, ashamed of himself. The sun hung in a haze of iron-coloured light low above the western hills, looking red and bloated and vile as a vulture's ruff. That polluted sky was his creation as much as was the painting, and it would be good to leave it behind. Once away from the valley, from all the influences of the place, he would be able to consider the future.

A young girl was sitting on the twentieth level just beneath the eye. Years before, the ritual of viewing the eye had grown to cultish proportions; there had been group chanting and praying and discussions of the experience. But these were more practical times, and no doubt the young men and women who had congregated here were now manning administrative desks somewhere in the burgeoning empire. They were the ones about whom Dardano should write; they, and all the eccentric characters who had played roles in this slow pageant. The gypsy woman who had danced every night by the eye, hoping to charm Griaule into killing her faithless lover – she had gone away satisfied. The man who had tried to extract one of the fangs – nobody knew what had become of him. The scale hunters, the artisans. A history of Hangtown would be a volume in itself.

The walk had left Meric weak and breathless; he sat down clumsily beside the girl, who smiled. He could not remember her name, but she came often to the eye. Small and dark, with an inner reserve that reminded him of Lise. He laughed inwardly – most women reminded him of Lise in some way.

"Are you all right?" she asked, her brow wrinkled with concern.

"Oh, yes," he said; he felt a need for conversation to take his mind off things, but he could think of nothing more to say. She was so young! All freshness and gleam and nerves.

"This will be my last time," she said. "At least for a while. I'll miss it." And then, before he could ask why, she added, "I'm getting married tomorrow, and we're moving away."

He offered congratulations and asked her who was the lucky fellow.

"Just a boy." She tossed her hair, as if to dismiss the boy's importance; she gazed up at the shuttered membrane. "What's it like for you when the eye opens?" she asked.

"Like everyone else," he said. "I remember . . . memories of my life. Other lives, too." He did not tell her about Griaule's memory of flight; he had never told anyone except Lise about that.

"All those bits of souls trapped in there," she said, gesturing at the eye. "What do they mean to him? Why does he show them to us?"

"I imagine he has his purposes, but I can't explain them."

"Once I remembered being with you," said the girl, peeking at him shyly through a dark curl. "We were under the wing."

He glanced at her sharply. "Tell me."

"We were . . . together," she said, blushing. "Intimate, you know. I was very afraid of the place, of the sounds and shadows. But I loved you so much, it didn't matter. We made love all night, and I was surprised because I thought that kind of passion was just in stories, something people had invented to make up for how ordinary it really was. And in the morning even that dreadful place had become beautiful, with the wing tips glowing red and the waterfall echoing . . ." She lowered her eyes. "Ever since I had that memory, I've been a little in love with you."

"Lise," he said, feeling helpless before her.

"Was that her name?"

He nodded and put a hand to his brow, trying to pinch back the emotions that flooded him.

"I'm sorry." Her lips grazed his cheek, and just that slight touch seemed to weaken him further. "I wanted to tell you how she felt in case she hadn't told you herself. She was very troubled by something, and I wasn't sure she had."

She shifted away from him, made uncomfortable by the intensity of his reaction, and they sat without speaking. Meric became lost in watching how the sun glazed the scales to reddish gold, how the light was channelled along the ridges in molten streams that paled as the day wound down. He was startled when the girl jumped to her feet and backed towards the hoist.

"He's dead," she said wonderingly.

Meric looked at her, uncomprehending.

"See?" She pointed at the sun, which showed a crimson sliver above the hill. "He's dead," she repeated, and the expression on her face flowed between fear and exultation.

The idea of Griaule's death was too large for Meric's mind to encompass, and he turned to the eye to find a counterproof – no glints of colour flickered beneath the membrane. He heard the hoist creak as the girl headed down, but he continued to wait. Perhaps only the dragon's vision had failed. No. It was likely not a coincidence that work had been officially terminated today. Stunned, he sat staring at the lifeless membrane until the sun sank below the hills; then he stood and went over to the hoist. Before he could throw the switch, the cables thrummed – somebody heading up. Of course. The girl would have spread the news, and all the Major Hauks and their underlings would be hurrying to test Griaule's reflexes. He did not want to be here when they arrived, to watch them pose with their trophy like successful fishermen.

It was hard work climbing up to the frontoparietal plate. The ladder swayed, the wind buffeted him, and by the time he clambered on to the plate, he was giddy, his chest full of twinges. He hobbled forward and leaned against the rust-caked side of a boiling vat. Shadowy in the twilight, the great furnaces and vats towered around him, and it seemed this system of fiery devices reeking of cooked flesh and minerals was the actual machinery of Griaule's thought materialized above his skull. Energyless, abandoned. They had been replaced by more efficient equipment down below, and it had been – what was it? – almost five years since they were last used. Cobwebs veiled a pyramid of firewood; the stairs leading to the rims of the vats were crumbling. The plate itself was scarred and coated with sludge.

"Cattanay!"

Someone shouted from below, and the top of the ladder trembled. God, they were coming after him! Bubbling over with congratulations and plans for testimonial dinners, memorial plaques, specially struck medals. They would have him draped in bunting and bronzed and covered with pigeon shit before they were done. All these years he had been among them, both their slave and their master, yet he had never felt at home. Leaning heavily on his cane, he made his way past the frontal spike – blackened by years of oily smoke – and down between the wings to Hangtown. It was a ghost town, now. Weeds overgrowing the collapsed shanties; the lake a stinking pit, drained after some children had drowned in the summer of '91. Where Jarcke's home had stood was a huge pile of animal bones, taking a pale shine from the half-light. Wind keened through the tattered shrubs.

"Meric!" "Cattanay."

The voices were closer.

Well, there was one place where they would not follow.

The leaves of the thickets were speckled with mould and

brittle, flaking away as he brushed them. He hesitated at the top
of the scale hunters' stair. He had no rope. Though he had done
the climb unaided many times, it had been quite a few years. The
gusts of wind, the shouts, the sweep of the valley and the lights
scattered across it like diamonds on grey velvet – it all seemed a
single inconstant medium. He heard the brush crunch behind
him, more voices. To hell with it! Gritting his teeth against a
twinge of pain in his shoulder, hooking his cane over his belt, he
inched on to the stair and locked his fingers in the handholds.
The wind whipped his clothes and threatened to pry him loose
and send him pinwheeling off. Once he slipped; once he froze,
unable to move backward or forward. But at last he reached the
bottom and edged upslope until he found a spot flat enough to
stand.

The mystery of the place suddenly bore in upon him, and he
was afraid. He half turned to the stair, thinking he would go back
to Hangtown and accept the hurly-burly. But a moment later he
realized how foolish a thought that was. Waves of weakness
poured through him, his heart hammered, and white dazzles
flared in his vision. His chest felt heavy as iron. Rattled, he went a
few steps forward, the cane pocking the silence. It was too dark to
see more than outlines, but up ahead was the fold of wing where
he and Lise had sheltered. He walked towards it, intent on
revisiting it; then he remembered the girl beneath the eye and
understood that he had already said that good-bye. And it *was*
good-bye – that he understood vividly. He kept walking. Blackness looked to be welling from the wing joint, from the entrances
to the maze of luminous tunnels where they had stumbled on to
the petrified man. Had it really been the old wizard, doomed by
magical justice to moulder and live on and on? It made sense. At
least it accorded with what happened to wizards who slew their
dragons.

"Griaule?" he whispered to the darkness, and cocked his head,
half expecting an answer. The sound of his voice pointed up the
immensity of the great gallery under the wing, the emptiness, and
he recalled how vital a habitat it had once been. Flakes shifting
over the surface, skizzers, peculiar insects fuming in the thickets,

the glum populace of Hangtown, waterfalls. He had never been able to picture Griaule fully alive – that kind of vitality was beyond the powers of the imagination. Yet he wondered if by some miracle the dragon were alive now, flying up through his golden night to the sun's core. Or had that merely been a dream, a bit of tissue glittering deep in the cold tons of his brain? He laughed. Ask the stars for their first names, and you'd be more likely to receive a reply.

He decided not to walk any further; it was really no decision. Pain was spreading through his shoulder, so intense he imagined it must be glowing inside. Carefully, carefully, he lowered himself and lay propped on an elbow, hanging on to the cane. Good, magical wood. Cut from a hawthorn atop Griaule's haunch. A man had once offered him a small fortune for it. Who would claim it now? Probably old Henry Sichi would snatch it for his museum, stick it in a glass case next to his boots. What a joke! He decided to lie flat on his stomach, resting his chin on an arm – the stony coolness beneath acted to muffle the pain. Amusing, how the range of one's decision dwindled. You decided to paint a dragon, to send hundreds of men searching for malachite and cochineal beetles, to love a woman, to heighten an undertone here and there, and finally to position your body a certain way. He seemed to have reached the end of the process. What next? He tried to regulate his breathing, to ease the pressure on his chest. Then, as something rustled out near the wing joint, he turned on his side. He thought he detected movement, a gleaming blackness flowing towards him . . . or else it was only the haphazard firing of his nerves playing tricks with his vision. More surprised than afraid, wanting to see, he peered into the darkness and felt his heart beating erratically against the dragon's scale.

It's foolish to draw simple conclusions from complex events, but I suppose there must be both moral and truth to this life, these events. I'll leave that to the gadflies. The historians, the social scientists, the expert apologists for reality. All I know is that he had a fight with his girlfriend over money and walked out. He sent her a letter saying he had gone south and would be back in a few months with more money than she could ever spend. I had no idea what he'd done. The whole thing about Griaule had just been a bunch of us sitting around the Red Bear, drinking up my pay – I'd sold an article – and somebody said, "Wouldn't it be great if Dardano didn't have to write articles, if we didn't have to paint pictures that colour-co-ordinated with people's furniture or slave at getting the gooey smiles of little nieces and nephews just right?" All sorts of improbable moneymaking schemes were put forward. Robberies, kidnappings. Then the idea of swindling the city fathers of Teocinte came up, and the entire plan was fleshed out in minutes. Scribbled on napkins, scrawled on sketchpads. A group effort. I keep trying to remember if anyone got a glassy look in their eye, if I felt a cold tendril of Griaule's thought stirring my brains. But I can't. It was a half-hour's sensation, nothing more. A drunken whimsy, an art-school metaphor. Shortly thereafter, we ran out of money and staggered into the streets. It was snowing – big wet flakes that melted down our collars. God, we were drunk! Laughing, balancing on the icy railing of the University Bridge. Making faces at the bundled-up burghers and their fat ladies who huffed and puffed past, spouting steam and never giving us a glance, and none of us – not even the burghers – knowing that we were living our happy ending in advance . . .

> – from *The Man Who Painted
> The Dragon Griaule* by Louis Dardano

Nets of Silver and Gold

James P. Blaylock

The work of James P. Blaylock (b. 1950) might at first seem conventional, before you realize that he is parodying convention. Works such as his early The Elfin Ship *(1982) and its sequel* The Disappearing Dwarf *(1983) might at first appear to be clones of* The Hobbit, *but Blaylock leads you down the garden path and into the woods. Over the years his fantasies have become more surreal, trespassing into the steampunk territory on the borders of science fiction (as in* The Digging Leviathan, *1984) or luring you into an apparent but unusual children's fantasy,* The Magic Spectacles *(1991). In Blaylock's stories the barriers between the real and the unreal are constantly moving and you never quite know where you are, as the following beautifully demonstrates.*

MY WIFE AND I WERE TRAVELLING ALONG THE Normandy coast when we met John Kendal in St Malo. It was in a hotel café – the name of the place escapes me. He sat before a tremendous plate of periwinkles, all heaped into a little seashell monument. With a long needle he poked at the things, removing the grey lump inside each and piling it neatly on the opposite side of the plate. He worked at it for the space of half an hour, and in that time I had no idea it was my old childhood friend Kendal who sat there.

So intent and delicate were his movements that he gave the

impression of someone suspicious that one of the periwinkles held a tremendous pearl, which would, at any moment, come rolling out of the mouth of a dark little shell on to his plate.

It wasn't until he paused for a moment to sip his wine that I looked at his face and knew who he was. People change a great deal over the years, but Kendal, somehow, hadn't. His hair was longer and wilder, and he was twenty years older than I remembered him, but that's all. His antics with the periwinkles made perfect sense.

Seeing him there labouring over the shells reminded me of our first meeting, forty years earlier when we were both boys. On the day after I'd moved into the neighbourhood I came across him lying on the street, peering down through one of the nickel-sized holes in an iron manhole cover, watching the rippling water that ran along below the street and reflected a long cylinder of sunlight that shone through the opposite hole. He told me right off that he did most of his water gazing on partly cloudy and windy days when the passing shadows would suddenly darken and obscure the water below and he could see nothing at all. He'd wait there, gazing down into utter darkness, until without any warning the clouds would pass and the diamond glint of sunlight would reappear, sparkling on the running water.

It was all a very romantic notion, and I took to practising the art myself, although not nearly as often as did Kendal, and always vaguely fearful that I'd be run down in the road by a passing car. He had no such fears. The sunlit waters implied vague and wonderful promise to him that I sometimes felt but never fully understood.

And here he was eating periwinkles in St Malo. He was living there. I haven't any idea how he paid his rent or bought his periwinkles and wine. It didn't seem to matter. Nor did it surprise him that we'd met by wild coincidence, twenty years and 6,000 miles distant from our last meeting in California. We hadn't even communicated in the intervening years.

As we sat into the evening and talked, I was struck by the idea that he'd become eccentric. Then it occurred to me that he'd been eccentric at eight years old when he'd spent his free time peering through manhole covers. What he'd become, I can't for the life of me say. My wife, who sees things more clearly than I do, understood immediately, even as she watched him manipulate his periwinkles, that he was slightly off-centre. Not the sort who goes raging about the streets with an axe, but the sort who doesn't even acknowledge the street, who looks right through it, who inhabits some distant shifting world.

That isn't to say that my wife disliked him. He won her sympathies at once by carrying on about the sunsets at St Malo, sunsets which, for two days running, we had missed because I hadn't had the energy to walk from the railway hotel to the old city. He could see them, he said, from his window, which overlooked the sea wall and the scores of rocky little islands and light towers that stretched out into the ocean along the coast there. It was spectacular, the sun sinking like a ball of wet fire into a sea turned orange. It seemed to set purely for the amusement of the city of St Malo. He had the notion that if he could find just the right sort of rowboat – the wooden shoe of Winken, Blinken and Nod or the pea-green boat of the Owl and the Pussycat – he could catch the sun as it set and follow it into the depths of the sea.

The next afternoon my wife and I drank a beer at a café above that same sea wall and watched the sunset ourselves. I'll admit that Kendal was right – not a half-mile of green sea rolled between the rocky shore and the sun when it set. There are legends, or so we were told, that when the old gods fished from the rocks off St Malo, one of them cast his golden net with such force that it encircled the sun. Thinking that he'd ensnared a great glowing fish, he hauled it almost into shore before realizing his error and setting it free. The sun had been so taken with the beauty of the coastline thereabouts that it has since followed that same path every evening when it sails from the sky.

It's quite possible that Kendal had heard the same tale and that his nautical pursuit of the setting sun was suggested by it. All in all it doesn't matter much, for it's just as likely that if he had heard the myth, he half believed it. He had the uncanny ability to make others believe such tales too, just as he'd imbued me with a sense of the importance of watching that sunlit water beneath the street, for reasons that I can't at all remember, reasons that have never been defined.

So we talked that first evening over wine and food, and I discovered that he'd never given up the business of watching, of peering through holes. He told us that he had taken for the summer the most amazing rooms, directly above the sea wall. They were in the oldest part of the city, all stone and hand-hewn timber. He'd been told by the landlady that at one time, hundreds of years ago perhaps, his room had attached to it a stone balcony, thrusting out over the ocean beyond a heavy, studded oak door. The stones had long since broken loose and fallen into the sea, and the old door had been nailed shut against the possibility of someone stumbling through it drunk or while sleepwalking, and dropping the 30-odd feet into the tide pools below.

There was a keyhole in the door, however, encrusted with verdigris, through which one could peer out over the sea. Kendal, it seemed, spent a good deal of time doing just that. He could as easily have watched the sunsets through either of two long, mullioned windows in the same wall, but that, he quickly insisted, wouldn't have been the same thing. There was something about keyholes – about this particular keyhole – something he couldn't quite fathom.

My wife, not knowing him as I did, insisted that he explain himself, and his story, I'm afraid, went a ways towards overturning the romantic notion she'd formed of him after his eloquent description of the sunsets.

He had been in the rooms a week before he even saw the keyhole. He was engaged, he said, in certain studies. The view from the windows was such that his eyes were inevitably drawn to and through them towards the sea so that he paid little attention to the old door. One afternoon, however, he'd been sitting at his desk working at something – I haven't the foggiest idea what – when he noticed through the corner of his eye that a thin ray of sunlight slanted in through the keyhole and illuminated a little patch of carpet, evoking, he said, old memories and fresh anticipation. There was nothing for him to do but peer through the keyhole.

Shimmering beyond was an expanse of pale green ocean which joined, at the abrupt line of the horizon, an almost equal expanse of blue sky. It wasn't at all an odd thing to find, quite what he'd expected, but the simple symmetry of the sea and sky with their delicate Easter egg colours kept him at the keyhole for a bit, waiting, perhaps for a gust of wind to toss the surface of the sea or for a cloud to drift into view. As it happened, a sailing ship appeared, just spars and rigging at first, then the tossing bowsprit as the ship arched up over the horizon. He hadn't any idea what sort of ship it was; he knew nothing, he told us, of ships. But it was altogether a wonderful thing as it appeared there with its billowing sails and complexity of rigging and looking for all the world as if it had sailed in from another age.

He leaped up and dug about in his wardrobe for a pair of opera glasses, then returned to the window to have a closer look at the antique ship. But there was, he insisted, no ship there. It must have swung around and sailed back out to sea – curious and unlikely behaviour, it seemed to him.

Out of sudden curiosity he peered once again through the keyhole, but there was only the sea and the sky lying placidly, one atop the other.

He had suspicions, he said, about the keyhole, suspicions that had been fostered years before. He half felt as if the keyhole had been waiting there for him, impossible as that sounds on the face of it, and he determined, quite literally, to keep an eye on it.

His determination faded, however, as he became once again involved in his studies. He was standing at the window late the following afternoon, thinking about the sunset and toying with the idea of going down to the café for a cup of coffee. He felt a bit of a fool, he said, for his suspicions about the keyhole, and he decided that it was time to lay them to rest. So he crouched before it and peered through, seeing, to his wild surprise, not ocean and sky and sailing boats, but a study, his own study: the littered desk between cases of books, the rose-coloured armchair beside a tobacco stand, the ungainly pole lamp standing like an impossible stiltlegged flamingo with a hat on. He determined to keep watch, not to look away and so lose it like he had lost the incredible ship. He'd wait, he said, until something happened, anything.

But then he began to wonder at the odds and ends heaped on the desk. They were all familiar; nothing was there that shouldn't have been. But he couldn't be sure – he couldn't swear that the millefiori paperweight, an old French globe that was the only thing of real value he owned, wasn't in the wrong spot. There it was on the left of the desk, sitting atop a copy of *Mr Brittling Sees it Through*. Yet he was almost sure that behind him it lay next to a bowl of oranges on the right. He could picture it in his mind. It sat opposite *Mr Brittling*, not atop it.

It began to irritate him, like an itch that he couldn't quite reach. He had to know about the paperweight, and yet he was sure that if he turned, even for an instant, his mysterious keyhole study would sail off in the wake of the disappearing galleon. When he finally gave up and looked away, it seemed to him that he saw, just out of the corner of his eye, the study door begin to swing open as if someone were pushing in through it. But the momentum of rising carried him off, and when he peered through again, after just the slip of an instant, there was the tranquil sea, broken just a bit by little wind waves, and the blue expanse of sky interrupted by the rag-tag end of a fleeing cloud.

He'd been right about the paperweight. He was possessed thereafter with wonder at the nature of that keyhole. You and I would have been concerned with the nature of our minds, with our sanity, but not John Kendal. Just the opposite was the case. For a week he crouched there, spending long hours, squinting until he got a headache, seeing nothing but sea and sky and, in the evening, the setting sun. He'd sneak up on it. He'd act nonchalant, as if he were bending over before it to pick up a dropped pencil or a bit of lint from the carpet. But the keyhole, he said, couldn't be fooled. He even tried whistling in a cheerful and foolish manner to add credence to his air of unconcern. At night there was nothing but darkness beyond, darkness and a little cluster of stars. Later yet a glint of moonlight shone through maddeningly, only perceptible if the room were dark and if he stood just so, somewhere near the north-east corner of the study.

Bits of fleeting doubt began to surface towards the end of the week, the suspicion, perhaps, that he'd been the victim of a particularly vivid dream brought on by an overabundance of periwinkles, which, apparently, he ate by the bushel basketful. It occurred to him that his compulsion was very much like that of a peeping tom, and that his studies were woefully neglected. Finally he simply grew tired of it. He resolved late one Saturday night that he'd had enough, that he'd made a fool of himself and that he'd quite simply put the matter to rest by having nothing more to do with it. He'd shove a wad of chewing gum into the thing if he had to, buy a key and leave it in the hole so as to block the little cylinder of sunlight that filtered in. It was the sunlight, after all, that set him off. It was all very clear to him. Psychology could explain it. He was searching for that same sunlight he'd become so familiar with as a child. Well, he'd have no more of it.

So he sat there, pretending to be reading in his chair, but thinking, of course, of the keyhole – knowing that he was thinking about it and denying it at the same time. He wondered suddenly, irrationally, if the keyhole knew he was thinking about it, and if he hadn't ought to lazy along over towards it and have one last peek – just to put the issue to rest, to dash it to bits. He could see just the faintest silver thread of watery moonbeam slanting in, vaguely illuminating that bit of carpet.

He rushed at the door, casting his book down on to the armchair, pulling his pipe out of his mouth. He'd been tormented long enough. He'd have one last look, just to satisfy himself once and for all; then he'd stuff it full of something, anything – wet paper, perhaps, or a wad of sticky tape.

Through the keyhole once again was his study. His book lay on the armchair. The telltale paperweight wasn't on the desk at all. It was in the hand of a woman with whom he was utterly unfamiliar. She had the complexion of a gypsy, he said, and the most amazing black hair and dark eyes. She was watching someone, that much was certain, smiling at someone – at him? – in a pouty sort of way. It was maddening. He shouted through the keyhole at her, something which must have sounded amazing and lunatic to his neighbours. A moment later there was a shuffling outside

his study door, as if someone had come to investigate and was
working up the courage to knock. He looked up quickly, cursing,
fearing the disturbance that didn't come. And when he returned
to his keyhole a moment later, there was, of course, nothing but
the dark sea and sky and a few cold stars around a gibbous moon.
The study and the gypsy were gone.

He was quite convinced that they weren't in any true sense
gone; that they were real couldn't be argued. He became possessed by the idea that if the contents of his study existed on both
sides of that door, then the dark woman with her pouty smile did
also. It was merely a matter of time, he was sure of it, before he'd
turn a corner on his way to the café or the railway station and
catch sight of her. It wouldn't surprise him if he bumped into her
at the market. He could picture it very plainly; her packages
scattering, he apologizing, scooping them up, she with a look of
vague recognition on her face, wondering at him, at their chance
meeting. Dinner, perhaps, would follow. Or more likely she'd go
along on her way. Then, a week later, a month later, he'd board
the bus for Mont St Michel and there she'd be, beside an empty
seat. It would be fate and nothing less.

At the time of our chance meeting over periwinkles, of course,
fate hadn't yet played its hand. She never re-entered either of
the two studies. Kendal, however, spent more time than ever at
his keyhole. He had no more misgivings. And he was rewarded
for his faith, mostly by the sight of an empty, book-scattered
room.

Once, early one morning, he peeped through and, with a thrill
of strange apprehension, saw himself at work at his desk, writing
madly, scribbling things down. Papers lay on the floor. His hair
was tousled. He wore his salmon-coloured smoking jacket, the
one with Peking dragons on the lapels, and it appeared as if he'd
been up all night – assuming, of course, that the world of the
keyhole operated according to the same clock time as our world.
But then who could say that it wasn't our world? Kendal wondered at first what in the devil he was working on with such wild
abandon. It seemed to be going very well indeed, if the thirty or
forty pages on the floor weren't scrap.

He watched himself write for a time, hoping, he said, for the return of the dark woman. He was possessed by the idea that she was his lover. His manic writing paused and he sat back in his chair and tamped a bit wearily at his pipe, blowing first through the stem to clear it out. He swivelled round, bent over, closed one eye, and peered, to Kendal's sudden horror, at the keyhole. In a fit of determination he slammed his pipe into an ashtray, rose, and strode across towards the old door, bending and peering, his eye hovering not 3 inches from the eye of his shellfish-loving counterpart. For one strange moment, said Kendal, he didn't know absolutely who he was, or which study he occupied. He pinched himself, trite as it sounds, and convinced himself that he, at least, was no figment. "Hello!" he shouted. "There *is* someone here! You're not imagining things!" It felt good to reassure himself. "You're perfectly sane!" he shouted a bit louder. The eye disappeared. There was a knocking at his study door which nearly tumbled him over backwards. For one sudden moment he'd been certain that the knocking had come from the door into the other study. But it hadn't. There was another knock, and when he opened the door and looked out into the hallway, there was his landlady, giving him the glad eye. She looked past him into the empty room, nodding to him, asking him some contrived question about the rent. He shook his head and was brusque with her, he said, which was unfortunate, because in truth she was a friendly sort. Her concern was justifiable. He hurried her away and bent back across to his keyhole.

The study beyond was empty. The papers on the floor had been gathered into a heap that lay beside the desk. Obviously they weren't trash. It had been a productive night, the sort that gave him a great deal of satisfaction, a sense of wellbeing. He watched the empty study for an hour, waiting there, and was surprised to see, suddenly, a widening patch of sunlight playing out quickly across the floor, as if someone were opening a door and a quick rush of daylight were flooding in. Just as suddenly it was cut off. It wasn't the study door that had opened in the room beyond; he could see the edge of it quite clearly off to the left of the desk. And it wasn't curtains being drawn; he hadn't any curtains. No, a door had been opened, that much was sure, and there could be no doubt which door it was.

He paused in the telling of his story and filled his glass. He'd worked himself into a state. His hand trembled. My wife raised her eyebrows at me, but Kendal didn't see it. He was lost in his tale. He ordered coffee and heaped sugar into it, begging us not to assume that he'd gone mad.

"Of course not," said my wife. "Of course not."

"What I saw," he continued, gazing into his coffee, "were little men."

My wife choked on her wine. It wasn't hard to guess why, but she made a grand effort to make it seem otherwise. Kendal held up a knowing hand and shook his head quickly, as if he were satisfied with her disbelief. I put on a serious face. "Little men?" I said. "Midgets, do you mean?"

He shrugged.

What he had seen at first were the shadows of whoever had come through the old door. He wondered, straight off, where they had come from. After all, he had been peering through a keyhole in the door in question. There was, it seemed, a door beyond the door, and perhaps others beyond that – countless others – a veritable mirrored hallway of reflected doors with little men creeping about down the corridors, and dark women stealing out of one door and through another, and doors creaking open to reveal the wave-tossed galleon slanting in towards a rocky shore. Kendal saw endless possibility, but he hadn't enough time right then to be anything but mystified by it.

One of the little men, as he insisted on calling them, began to haul volumes out of the bookcases, tossing them around on to the floor. Another picked up the piled papers, rummaged in the desk drawer for scissors, and began cutting paper dolls – strings and strings of them. Another wrestled several pages away, found a pencil, and set out to doctor up the manuscript, chewing the end of his pencil, laughing and scribbling away. Yet another appeared, to Kendal's horror, opening the liquor cabinet and yanking out bottles, examining labels, nodding over them with a satisfied air. Pieces of clothing flew into sight, tossed, no doubt, from the closet by a fifth and unseen vandal. His favourite tweed coat shot out, folding over the shade of the pole lamp and hanging there sadly as the liquor cabinet elf squirted at it with the soda water siphon. It was a sad state of affairs. Any possible humour in the scene was dashed by the certain fact that it was *his* rooms being ransacked, that it was his tweed jacket that lay now in a sodden heap on the floor beside the overturned lamp. One of the devils juggled the paperweight along with two oranges. He was wonderfully dexterous. Kendal held his breath. The one who had been at his clothes wandered in with a hammer. He snatched one of the oranges from the juggler, set it atop *Mr Brittling*, and smashed it to pulp. Then he made a grab for the paperweight. Kendal was stupefied. The juggler dropped both the weight and the orange and they rolled out of sight behind the armchair. A struggle ensued, one elf poking the other in the eye and yanking at his hair, the other threatening with his hammer, fending the first off. They collapsed on to the carpet and went scrambling out of view. Kendal watched in futile horror the head and upper handle of the hammer rise and fall three times above the back of the chair. He shouted into the keyhole, screamed into it, whacked his fist against the door. There was a general pause within. He'd been heard. He was quite sure of it. The elf with the soda water bottle hunched over, squinting towards him, stepping across on tiptoe as if he were the soul of secrecy, and with a mad grin he aimed the siphon at the keyhole.

Kendal leaped to his feet. He wouldn't, he said, stand the indignity of it. He felt as if he were a character in a foolish play, as if a crowd of people were watching, laughing at his expense. (My wife pinched me under the table.) He waited for a moment, fully expecting soda water to splatter through the keyhole. Nothing happened. He was sure, he said, that they were hovering there, that when he looked again they'd all be waiting, laughing, would squirt him in the eye. But when he could stand it no longer, he peeked through and saw no little men, no study, no gypsy temptress – only the sea and the sky and, to his amazement, the old galleon, sails reefed, riding on the calm water a half-mile offshore.

He sat most of the rest of the day in the café above the sea wall, watching the sun fall. He could see, from where he sat, the old studded door that opened into empty air, and he tried to convince himself that if he squinted sharply enough or turned his head just so, he could make out phantom shapes, figments, ghosts perhaps, fumbling around outside that door, carrying on.

He knew, he said, that he should be recording all this business about the keyhole – writing it down. In print, perhaps, the pieces would fall into order. He could look at it with an objective eye, get his bearings. The more he thought about it, the more necessary the task became, and late that evening he returned to his rooms, sat at his desk, and began to write. He scribbled feverishly, casting finished pages over his shoulder, littering the floor. He speculated and philosophized. As it grew later his ideas and the events that prompted them seemed to deepen in importance, as if the night was salting the affair with mystery. Some of it, he insisted, was shamefully maudlin – the sort of thing you write late at night and pitch into the trash in the light of day.

Early the next morning he found himself empty of ideas, seated at his desk, dressed in his smoking jacket with the Peking dragons on the lapels. It was only then that the thought struck him – the idea that he was being watched through the keyhole, that he was watching himself.

"What does all this mean?" he cried, facing the studded door. There was, of course, no response. He snatched up a clean sheet of paper and a pen. "Write a message," he wrote. "Roll it up and poke it through the keyhole." He stood before the desk holding it up so that if indeed he were watching just then he'd get a good look at it. It was a brilliant idea. He waited for a bit but nothing happened. He stepped across and peeked through the keyhole and was rewarded with the sight of the ruined study. The little men had gone and had quite apparently taken his liquor with them. He tore off excess paper from around his note and rolled what was left into a tight little tube. Then he twisted it even tighter and threaded it through the keyhole, shoving it past the far side with the end of a coat hanger. When he peered into the keyhole again the study had vanished.

He was exhausted, he told us, from the ordeal. He decided at first to sleep, not so much out of the need for it, as to be on hand if the little men appeared. But then he vowed that they wouldn't hold him in thrall. He'd go about his business. Let them play their pranks! If he caught them at it he'd make it warm for them. They'd sing a sorry tune. He'd force them, he said, to take him along aboard the galleon. Just to play devil's advocate he drank two quick fingers of his best Scotch – they wouldn't have all of it – and he went out on to the street, locking the door behind him, and spent the better part of the day walking, one eye out for the gypsy girl with the pouty lips.

Some time around two in the afternoon he began to grow anxious. He remembered, suddenly, the sight of the hammer rising and falling beyond the armchair, and he cursed himself for not having slipped the paperweight into his pocket. There was nothing for it but to return at once – to make sure. His wandering about town had accomplished nothing anyway. If he was fated to find the dark woman, then he'd find her, or she him. He might as well be anywhere. He hurried along, and as he drew closer to home he became more certain of what he'd find. As it turned out, he was half correct.

His study was a mess. The tweed coat was a ruin, sprayed with soda water and crushed orange. His papers were reduced to snippings and his books littered the floor. *Mr Brittling Sees it Through* was the sorriest of the lot. The liquor cabinet was empty but for a half-bottle of crème de menthe from which the cap had been removed. He was furious. He stormed back and forth, nearly stumbling over the remains of the broken paperweight that had somehow been knocked under the sleeve of his soaked coat. It lay in two neat halves, the edges of several glass canes protruding through the broken sides like little pieces of Christmas candy. The hammer from the shelf in his closet lay beside it.

Kendal raged about, trying to think, waving the hammer over his head. He strode towards the door, understanding what it was he had to do. And it was then that he saw what he hadn't expected to see: a little rolled and twisted bit of paper lying right at the edge of the carpet. He unrolled it, shaking. "Write a message," it read. "Roll it up and poke it through the keyhole."

"By God!" he shouted. "We'll see!" And he began to pry out the nails that held the door shut. It wasn't an easy thing. Not by a long sight. He had to rather beat the door up to get at them. But he was determined – he'd come to the end of his rope. One by one they squeaked loose. He paused after the fourth to peer through the keyhole, and there was the sun, the sky, a cloud. Below lay the sea, calm and glistening and dappled with sunlight, broken by a long rowboat in which sat five little men, one at the tiller and four more pulling on the oars, making away towards the setting sun and the galleon anchored offshore, heaving on the groundswell.

He wrenched at the nails. He tore at them. He knew it would do him no good to go to the windows. He couldn't get at them through the windows. He peered through the keyhole again. The rowboat was a speck on the water. Finally the last of the nails pulled loose, and, shouting, he pushed the door outward on its hinges with such a rush of relief and anticipation that he nearly pitched out into the open air. He caught himself on the old jamb and hung on, searching the horizon for the galleon. There was nothing there. At the café below him, a dozen idlers gawked up, puzzled, wondering at his antics. He couldn't be sure, he said, which world they occupied, so he searched for himself on the veranda, but didn't seem to be there. Slamming the door shut, he hurried down and asked them about the elves in the rowboat, but the lot of them denied having seen anything. They winked at each other. A fat man with ruined shoes laughed out loud. Kendal raged at them. He knew their kind. Did they want to see what those filthy devils had done to his rooms? None of them did.

Kendal poked idly at his seashells, stirring them around on their plate. He had calmed down a bit later, he told us, regretting his folly. The people in the café would think him a wildman, a lunatic. My wife shook her head at that. "Not at all," she said, hoping to cheer him. He shrugged in resignation and emptied his coffee cup. From the pocket of his coat he pulled a crystal hemisphere, his antique paperweight, and he showed it to us very sadly, pointing out certain identifying marks; a peculiar pink rose, a glass rod with a date in it – 1846 I believe it was. The top of the thing was spider-webbed with cracks where it had been struck with the hammer. It seemed to us that Kendal could hardly bear looking at it, but that he had it with him as a bit of circumstantial evidence.

After the shouted accusations in the café, he'd walked about town again, searching, and had ended up at the restaurant in our hotel, eating periwinkles. It was there that we found him.

He'd been fairly buoyant, wrestling with his shellfish and sipping wine, and, as I said, his discussion of the sunsets was engaging. By the time he'd come to the end of his tale, however, he was as deflated as a sprung balloon. He looked very much like a man who hadn't slept in two days. We started in on another bottle of wine, and he toyed with the idea of eating more shellfish and spoke desultorily about his mystery, now and then breaking into rage or rapture. He seemed particularly enthralled by the possibility that the little men had heard him shout at them, could quite possibly have squirted soda water into his eye through the keyhole. It seemed to hint at connections, real connections. He had pretty well run himself down when on the sidewalk outside, in the glow of the arc lamps, a little knot of people hurried past. One was an olive-complected woman with long black hair and deep, dark, round eyes and full lips. She looked in briefly (as did several of the others) as she walked past, disappearing quickly into the night.

Kendal sat for a moment, frozen, with a wild look in his eye. He jumped up. I wanted to protest. My wife clutched my arm, encouraging me, I suppose, to dissuade him. Enough was enough, after all. But I wasn't at all sure that he hadn't every reason to leap up as he did. He shouted his address to us as he raced out of the restaurant, forgetting entirely to pay his bill, which had amounted by then to about thirty-five francs. We settled it for him and rose to leave. There on the table, shoving out from beneath the cloth napkin, was the broken crystal paperweight with its little garden of glass flowers. I dropped it into the pocket of my coat.

I revealed to my wife, as we walked down the road towards the sea, Kendal's youthful predilection for gazing down manhole covers. There had been other habits and peculiarities – rhinestone and marble treasures that he buried roundabout in his childhood, drawing up elaborate maps, hiding them away and stumbling upon them years later with wild excitement and anticipation. I recalled that he'd once got hold of an old telescope and spent hours each evening gazing at the stars, not for the sake of any sort of study, mind you, but just for the beauty and the wonder of it.

My wife, of course, began to develop suspicions about poor Kendal. I produced the broken paperweight and shrugged, but she pointed out, no doubt wisely, that a broken paperweight was hardly evidence of a magical keyhole and of little men coming and going across the sea in an old galleon that no one but John Kendal could see. I put the paperweight away.

Next day we were both in agreement about one thing – that we'd look Kendal up in his rooms. My wife affected the attitude of someone whose duty it was to visit a sick friend, but I still suspect that there was more to it than that; there certainly was for me. We decided, however, to wait until evening so as to give him a chance to sleep.

We found ourselves eating supper at the café that had figured so prominently in his story. We sat outdoors in a far corner of the terrace where we could see, quite clearly, Kendal's studded door. I admit that I could perceive no evidence of any ruined balcony – no broken corbels, no cracked stone, no rusty holes in the wall where a railing might have been secured.

We finished our meal, left the café, and followed cobbled streets up the hill. Quite truthfully, I felt a little foolish, like a Boy Scout off on a snipe hunt or a person who suspects that the man he's about to shake hands with is wearing a concealed buzzer on his palm. Part of me, however, not only believed Kendal's story, but very much wanted it to be true.

We found his rooms quite easily, but we didn't find Kendal. He wasn't in. The door was ajar about an inch, and when I knocked against it, it creaked open even further. "Hello!" I shouted past it. There was no response. "I'll just tiptoe in to see if he's asleep," I told my wife. She said I was presuming a great deal to be sneaking into a man's rooms when he was out, but I reminded her that at one time Kendal and I had been the closest of friends. And besides, he'd quite obviously been despondent that previous evening; it would be criminal to go off without investigating. That last bit touched her. But as I say, there was no Kendal inside, asleep or otherwise. There was quite simply a mess, just as he had promised.

He'd made some effort at straightening things away. Half the books had found their way haphazardly on to the shelves; the rest were stacked on the floor. The tweed coat lay in its heap, and I'll admit that the first thing I did when I entered the room was to feel it. The top had dried in the air, but it was still wet beneath, and stiff with the juice and pulp of squashed orange. On the desk lay the copy of Wells's *Mr Brittling Sees it Through*, covered with the remains of a second orange. His liquor cabinet sat empty but for the uncapped bottle of crème de menthe. The old half of the broken paperweight lay canted over atop the desk. Clothing littered the floor about the door of the closet. All of it bore out Kendal's tale.

Protruding from the keyhole in the old door was a twisted bit of paper. My wife, as curious by then as I was, pulled the thing out and unrolled it. Written on it in block letters were the words, "I must speak to you." In what time or space they'd come to be written, I can't for the life of me say. It was impossible to know whether the message was coming or going.

My wife pushed open one of the big mullioned casement windows and I looked out at the setting sun. She called me over and pointed towards the tidepools below. There, among anemones and chitons and crabs, floated a half-dozen bits of paper, some still twisted up, some relaxed and drifting like leaves. In another hour the tide would wash in and carry them away.

On impulse I bent over to have a look through that keyhole, a thrill of anticipation surging within me along with vague feelings of dread, as if I were about to tear open the lid of Pandora's box or of the merchant Abudah's chest. I certainly had no desire to have *my* tweed coat pulped with oranges, and yet if there were little men afoot, coming and going through magical doors . . . Well, suffice it to say that I understood Kendal's quest in quite the same ethereal and instinctive way that I understood his peering down holes in the street forty years earlier.

So I had a look. Just touching the dark sea was a vast and red sun. Silhouetted against it were the spars and masts of a wonderful ship, looping up over the horizon, driving towards shore. And rowing out towards the ship, long oars dipping rhythmically, was a tiny rowboat carrying a man with dark, wild hair. On a thwart opposite sat the olive-skinned woman. I'm certain of it. That they were hurrying to meet the galleon there can be no doubt. They were already a long way from shore.

"Do you see it?" I cried.

"Yes," said my wife, supposing that I was referring to the sunset. "Beautiful isn't it?"

"The ship!" I shouted, leaping up. "Do you see the ship?" But of course she didn't. Through the windows there was no ship to be seen. Nor was there any rowboat. "Through the keyhole!" I cried. "Quickly."

To humour me, I suppose, she had a go at it. But there was nothing in the keyhole but the tip of the sun, just a tiny arched slice now; disappearing beneath the swell. She stood up, raised her eyebrows, and gestured towards the keyhole as if inviting me to have another look for myself. Nothing but cold green sea lay beyond, tinted with dying fire.

We left a note atop his desk, but either he never returned, or he hadn't the time or desire to visit us at our hotel. I suspect that the former was the case. Our train left for Cherbourg next morning.

We haven't seen him since. It's possible, of course, that we will, that his travels will lead him home again to California and that he'll look us up. He has our address. But as for myself, I rather believe that we won't, that his course is set and that his travels have led him in some other direction entirely.

The Phantasma of Q——

Lisa Goldstein

Lisa Goldstein (b. 1953) creates worlds just slightly removed from our own. The Red Magician *(1982) is set in a recogniz-able Eastern Europe just before the Second World War where a magician tries to keep his world separate from what is happening around him.* Tourists *(1989) is set in a variable world, called Amaz, where a family are seeking an ancient treasure which may or may not be part of the world.* Strange Devices of the Sun and Moon *(1993) is set in an Elizabethan world of faerie. Like Blaylock's work, the shift between fantasy and reality is not always apparent. Just as in the following story.*

I THINK I'VE SEEN HER AGAIN.

It was on one of my rare forays into London, rare, perforce, because my old bones cannot stand the continuous jarring motion of the train into town and the even worse jostling of the people packed into the underground. It is galling to me that I, who have ventured into nearly every continent and seen sights most men can only dream of, should be confined to a little village, that I should have to plan for a trip to the capital with all the care and precision of a voyage to the interior of Africa. However, it cannot be helped.

I went to London to deliver to my publishers the latest instalment of my memoirs – and to be treated to a rich dinner at my editor's club, one of my few indulgences nowadays. Over a glass of very good port I hinted at the marvels I would reveal in later episodes: the hippogriff, the centaur, the phoenix I had tracked down in Arabia.

My editor listened, as engrossed as a child, and when I had finished he remarked that the first volume of my memoirs had done very well. "People love to read about these journeys to exotic places," he said. "Especially now that civilization is making inroads nearly everywhere. In another ten years, I wager, most of these wonderful creatures will be extinct, or will have hidden themselves so well they'll never be found."

"Ten years, is it?" I said. "Fortunately I'll probably be dead by then."

He laughed, uncertain whether I had made a joke or not.

After dinner I left him and walked, a little unsteadily, to the nearest underground station. The train I wanted was just closing its doors, and I knew that I would not be able to run for it. *She* ran, however, flying past me, and slipped into the car just before the train pulled out.

It was she, I was almost certain of it. She looked exactly the same. Forty years had not changed her in the slightest. Well, they wouldn't, would they?

Now the question is, do I tell Wallis? He has less reason to love her than I do.

I have just telephoned Wallis. I had no idea whether or not he still lived in London; for all I knew he had returned to the States. And yet the operator I spoke to found him after a wait of only a few minutes, which seemed nearly as marvellous as anything I have encountered on my travels. Perhaps the wonder has not died out of the world after all.

He sounded, like myself, years older and years more tired. "Hello," I said. "Is this Samuel Wallis?"

"Yes," he said. "Who is this?"

"James Arbuthnot," I said.

There was a long silence. "Arbuthnot," he said finally. "What brings you to phone me?"

"I think I've seen her. She's in London, Wallis."

There was another silence. I thought he was going to ask me who "she" was, but he of course remembered her as vividly as I did. "Is she?" he said.

"Yes. I saw her on the underground."

"And what do you expect me to do about it? Scour London for her? I don't want to see her again – you of all people should know that. And you know why."

"I thought you might keep your eyes peeled. I don't live in London—"

"Yes, I know. I've read the first volume of your memoirs. Are you going to mention her, mention that episode, in the next volume?"

"I don't know. I hadn't thought to."

"Good. Leave it alone, Arbuthnot. It won't do either of us any good."

"But perhaps I will now," I said, moved by an impulse I didn't entirely understand. "Perhaps I'll find her, and ask her—"

"Leave it alone," Wallis said again, and put the phone down.

Over the next few days I couldn't settle down to continue my memoirs. Was I going to mention her? I hadn't planned to, but now I found that I could think of nothing else.

There was no help for it. I would have to get that incident out of the way, get it clear in my mind, before I could go on.

It started as so many of my journeys did, with the chance word spoken at the Royal Explorers Club. The club itself unfortunately no longer exists, though the building still stands, a massive pillared structure once filled with animals and plants, statuary and stelae, jewels and mummies, urns and reliquaries, all our marvels collected from all over the world.

I went there in the autumn of 1885, to give a talk about my unsuccessful voyage to Crete to seek out the Minotaur. Afterwards a few of the members, some known to me and some not, settled back in the club's plush leather chairs to reminisce. "Do you know," one of the fellows said, "a friend of mine claims to have sighted a phantasma in the north," and he named a forest near the village of Q————.

I was interested, of course. More than a little interested, if the truth be known, because a friend of mine, a man named Witherspoon, had told me a few months earlier that he had invented a device that made it possible to identify a phantasma. (Witherspoon, you may remember from the first volume of my memoirs, is the man who invented the oneiroscope, a device for capturing dreams.) They look like us, like ordinary people, though the consensus among explorers is that there are more females than males among them. The ancient Greeks called them Muses, and had distinguished nine of them, all women. Sightings by members of the Explorers Club seem to suggest that there are more than nine, though perhaps not many more; they are very elusive. A man who had captured one, or who was even in the presence of one, would be filled with ideas that would seem to burst from him; he would never lack for inspiration and creative force. I paid a visit to Witherspoon and arranged to borrow the device he had invented, which he called a musopticon.

The musopticon proved to be a bulky, boxlike structure about two feet on each side. Witherspoon had constructed it of mahogany, and the levers, dials and gears of brass; it was also bound with decorations of brass along the sides, so that the whole thing was extraordinarily heavy. I brought it to a craftsman who had done work for me before and had him make me a knapsack of canvas so that I could carry it on my back; he also made pockets in the knapsack for my other instruments.

I took a train to Q——— and a cab to my lodgings. I would be staying with Mrs Jones, a woman who rented out rooms in her house. It was late afternoon by the time I finished unpacking, and I went downstairs to see if Mrs Jones had made tea. I was very displeased to discover that she had other guests, a young man and woman. More people than I had heard the rumours about the phantasma, and I hoped that these other guests were not here for the purpose of finding her. Surely, I thought, an explorer would not bring his wife along on an expedition. And yet what other reason was there to travel to this remote village?

We made our introductions. The man was Samuel Wallis and his wife was Adele; from their accents I judged they were Americans. Wallis was lean and fit, with long glossy hair parted in the middle. Mrs Wallis was as young as he and rather beautiful, with hair the same mahogany as my musopticon and wide slate-grey eyes. We settled down to our tea.

"Are you Arbuthnot the explorer?" Wallis asked me.

I admitted that I was.

"And does that fantastical instrument I saw being carried upstairs belong to you?" he asked. I hesitated, and he went on. "You don't have to admit anything if you don't want to. I should warn you, though, that we may both be after the same thing. Have you heard there may be a phantasma in the area?"

I confess that my heart sank at his words. "Yes," I said. "That's why I'm here."

"Good man," he said. "It's best to get these things out in the open, don't you think?" He held up his teacup, and I saw that he intended to propose a toast, as though we were drinking spirits. "May the best man win."

I could not argue with that. We clicked our cups together and drank. Mrs Jones bustled out from the kitchen. "Can I get you more tea?" she asked. "Or sandwiches?"

Wallis's eyes were shining eagerly. And I, too, felt a sudden strong urge to be off, to implement some ideas I was beginning to have, to start combing the woods for the phantasma. "Have you made any discoveries I might be familiar with?" I asked him.

"This is my first expedition," he said. Mrs Jones began to clear away the tea things. "But one has to start somewhere, don't you think? And I believe I have some rather original ideas about where to look."

"And what does your wife intend to do while you are away?"

"Oh, I'm going with him," Mrs Wallis said. I said nothing. It is commonplace knowledge that women lack the stamina and initiative needed for the long, arduous journeys of exploration. I was starting to feel more optimistic; Wallis was a rank beginner and clearly posed no threat to me.

*   *   *

We left early the next day. We ate the hearty breakfast Mrs Jones prepared for us, and then I bade farewell to Wallis and his wife in the chill dawn light and set off towards the forest, carrying the musopticon and my other instruments on my back.

The forest was ancient, perhaps a remnant of the huge wood that had once covered much of England. I had taken only a few steps in when the light around me grew dim; the trees began to arch towards each other, their leaves and branches plaiting overhead to form a living canopy. Oak and ash, alder and thorn, they grew thickly around me and their leaves underfoot muted my steps. I stopped, took the compass from my pack and got my bearings, then headed north.

The forest was terribly silent; I heard no birds, no small animals scurrying in the undergrowth. When it came time for me to take my bearings again, the gloom was so intense that I could not see the face of the compass or the brass dials of the musopticon, and had to light a lucifer match to be able to read them.

I shouldered the musopticon and continued on. As I tramped through the woods I wondered how Wallis and his wife were faring in this strange place, whether Mrs Wallis, or even her husband, had grown oppressed by the gloom and turned back. We were all amateurs in the literal sense, all of us adventuring for love and not for money, but a sort of professional ethic had arisen among the members of the Explorers Club, and Wallis did not seem one of our sort.

Around midday I felt the first stirrings of hunger. I took out my pocket watch and lit another match to check the time, then ate the bread and cheese Mrs Jones had prepared. Shortly after that I deemed it best to start back. I took another reading with the musopticon, recorded no activity once again, and began to head south, towards the village of Q————.

The forest seemed even darker as I walked back; oppressively so. I began to go faster, as fast as my various instruments would allow; they made a wild chiming noise together in my pack as I ran. I was eager to see people again, eager even to see Mr and Mrs Wallis. I reached the end of the forest at four in the afternoon and

came to Q—— and Mrs Jones's homely house shortly thereafter.

To my chagrin I found that the Wallises were still out. Mrs
Jones fluttered around me (if so stout a woman can be said to
flutter), helping me off with my pack, bringing me tea and
sandwiches. "Are you certain they haven't returned?" I asked
as I settled down with a chipped plate of sandwiches on my knee.

"I've been here all day," Mrs Jones said. "I'd have seen them if
they'd come back."

The stresses of the day were beginning to take their toll. I
settled back in an overstuffed chair and watched as Mrs Jones
turned up the gas lights and lit the fire. Her tea towel, I noticed,
was a souvenir from the Great Exhibition at the Crystal Palace,
over thirty years ago – probably the last time the poor dear had
been away from home. I must have been in hundreds of parlours
just like this one, I reflected, and the familiarity of my surroundings worked a strange kind of magic on me. I grew certain that I
would find the phantasma, if not tomorrow, then some time
during my stay at Q——; in my tired state I even thought I
knew which paths within the forest to pursue. At that moment
Mr and Mrs Wallis came into the parlour, talking to one another
and laughing. Mrs Jones hurried into the kitchen for more
sandwiches.

"Arbuthnot, good afternoon," Wallis said. He caught sight of
the bulky pack near my chair and laughed louder. "Good Lord,
Adele, look at all this equipment. Come, sir, who are you really –
the White Knight in Carroll's *Through the Looking Glass*?"

"And where's Alice?" Mrs Wallis asked.

"Why, you must be Alice, my dear," Wallis said. "But then
who am I?"

Their banter annoyed me. "How was your day in the forest?" I
asked, as politely as I could.

"Oh, very good, very good," Wallis said. "Well, we haven't
discovered anything yet, but we have some ideas where to look.
And you?"

"The same," I said shortly. My annoyance with them grew. To
me, and to my fellows at the club, exploration was almost a sacred

task; certainly we felt that it should not be approached in such a light-hearted, frivolous spirit. And what were these ideas they claimed to have had?

"Dark in there, though, isn't it?" Wallis said.

"A bit."

"A bit! Listen to him, Adele! I suppose you have gas lamps in that pack of yours? Along with a full set of Dickens?"

"I have matches, certainly. Don't you?"

"Matches!" he said, smiting his forehead in what was intended to be a comical manner. "I knew we forgot something."

Mrs Jones returned with more sandwiches. I stood and shouldered my pack. "I'm afraid I'll have to leave you," I said. "I must write my journal entry for today." And in truth I was anxious to return to my room; I wanted to record the insights I had had while relaxing and taking tea.

"Good afternoon," Wallis said. His manner seemed to soften. "I hope we haven't offended you – we were only joking."

"Oh, no," I said, abstracted. I nodded to the couple and began to climb the stairs.

I set off eagerly the next morning, so early that I did not encounter the Wallises. The night before I had started a map of the forest, sketching in the areas I had already explored. It seemed to me I had found a spot the phantasma might frequent, a lonely place about a mile away that was halfway between Q———— and the nearest village. Some of the writers I had consulted before I set out thought that these creatures preferred places of solitude and quiet.

Now I skirted the forest, holding the compass in one hand and my rough map in the other. The sun rose higher in the sky. As I walked, though, I began to wonder what had made me so certain I would find the phantasma in this area. It looked the same as any other part of the forest, as deserted and as far from civilization as anything I had already seen. If you could count the Wallis couple as civilization, I thought, and laughed bitterly to myself.

My thoughts turned to the encounter I had had with them the evening before. What had they discovered? What were the ideas they said they had? How galling it would be, I thought, if these utter beginners were to find the phantasma before I did.

When I had judged that I had walked a mile from Q————, I entered the forest. The great trees clustered around me, dark and silent, as I passed. I performed all the same actions as before, lighting matches, getting my bearings from the compass, checking the various dials and gauges on the musopticon. By the time I was ready for my midday meal I had grown tired and irritated, certain I was wasting my time.

My evil mood grew worse as I turned back, and continued to plague me as I walked towards my lodgings. I opened the door to Mrs Jones's house and heard Wallis laughing. His wife said something I couldn't hear and Wallis laughed harder.

It is strange to relate, I know, but I felt happy and carefree just at hearing their voices. Gone were the fears that they would find the phantasma before I did, the annoyance I had felt the day before at their light-hearted banter. I was eager to see people, I suppose, and I hurried forward as though they were old friends.

Mr and Mrs Wallis were sitting in the parlour, Mrs Jones setting out the tea things. "Look, it's the White Knight!" Mr Wallis called out cheerfully. "How goes it, old chap?"

I slung my knapsack from my shoulders and settled into one of the overstuffed chairs. For some reason, perhaps to check on my equipment, I thought to open my pack and look inside. Every one of the musopticon's dials was vibrating madly.

I excused myself as soon as I could and went up to my room to think. The phantasma was here, in this very house. It was Adele Wallis, I was almost certain of it. Or could it be Samuel? No – the creatures were mostly women, and my intuitive feeling, the one that every good explorer learns to trust, was urging me towards the wife.

This revelation created almost more problems than it solved, however. Did her husband know? If he did, why had he come all this way, and why did he claim to be searching for a phantasma? And if he didn't, why hadn't she told him?

But so many other things seemed to make sense now. The

clarity I had felt in her presence, the way I had seemed to generate one fresh idea after another about where to explore next. Even the happiness that surrounded the couple, that they seemed to bring with them wherever they went: surely the act of creation is accompanied by exactly that sort of joy.

What should I do now? There were rooms and rooms upstairs at the Explorers Club containing the strange things that I and other members had found, the salamanders and rocs and mermaids. If I could bring Adele Wallis to London, the club would never lack for ideas; we would explore for ever; we would move from triumph to triumph. And I would get the credit; all of this would be due to me.

I vowed to talk to Adele Wallis, to get her away from her husband somehow.

I had my opportunity a few days later. The wait was irksome, as I had to pretend to be searching for the phantasma lest her husband become suspicious. I would leave the house and trek towards the forest, then turn back and spend the day in the village, drinking tea and talking to the inhabitants. It seemed to me that even these rude villagers had more than their share of creativity, that, for example, their speech was full of unexpected poetic conceits. Could this blossoming be the result of Adele Wallis's visit?

Then Mrs Wallis fell ill. I feigned illness myself and spent the day in Mrs Jones's parlour, covered in a shawl and drinking tea. Mrs Jones moved around me, wearing her everlasting apron, dusting her fusty knick-knacks and sweeping.

As the hours passed I began to grow impatient, and wildly excited; it became more and more difficult to sustain my pretence of illness. I saw myself travelling the world, Mrs Wallis at my side, making the kinds of discoveries most explorers only dream of. I would return to England, speak at conferences and meetings around the country. Perhaps there would even be a knighthood.

At last, around teatime, Adele Wallis made her way down the stairs. I had set the musopticon down near my chair, and as she came into the room I opened the pack and took a look at it. As I had hoped, all the pointers in all the dials were vibrating as one. Mrs Wallis accepted a cup of tea and settled in her chair.

"Oh, dear, are you ill too?" she asked me.

"I wanted to talk to you, Mrs Wallis," I said.

She looked up quickly at that. I saw plain fear in her eyes, and she glanced at Mrs Jones to make sure we wouldn't be left alone together. "What about, Mr Arbuthnot?"

"I know what you are," I said.

Now she looked puzzled. "Do you, Mr Arbuthnot?" she said. "And what am I?"

"You're the phantasma. You're what I've come all this way to find, I and your husband as well."

She threw back her head and laughed. "I am, am I?" she said. "And what brings you to this extraordinary conclusion?"

"Look here." I showed her the musopticon, the rapid agitation of the dials. "This device says that that is what you are."

"Does it? Well, then, one of us is mistaken, either me or that device. I am not the phantasma, Mr Arbuthnot. I'm not what you think I am."

"Come back with me to London," I said urgently. "Let me present you to the Explorers Club, show them what you are."

"And then what? My husband's told me all about your club. Will you lock me in a cage, along with all the other unfortunates you've picked up on your travels? No, thank you."

"No, of course not," I said, though in truth I hadn't worked out all the logistics of the thing. How would I keep her at the club during those times when we weren't travelling? Well, I would solve that problem when we got there. "Just come with me. Travel with me back to London."

It was at this point, unfortunately, that Mr Wallis came into the parlour.

What followed was like something from a bad French farce. Mr Wallis accused me of trying to steal his wife, I tried to explain that I wanted his wife for a higher, more scientific, purpose, and Mrs Wallis, for some reason, kept referring to me as "that horrible man". Finally, after I had repeated the word "phantasma" at least a dozen times, the anger appeared to drain out of him.

"You're saying that Adele is – Adele is the phantasma?" he said.

"Yes," I said.

He looked at his wife. "No, of course I'm not, Sam," Mrs Wallis said with some asperity. "Don't you think you would know it if I was?"

"I don't know," Wallis said, bemused. "How would I know? You might be."

"Don't be ridiculous," Mrs Wallis said.

"Look at this," I said. "It's a musopticon, made by the inventor Witherspoon. Look at these dials. They're recording the presence of a phantasma right here, right in this room."

"I have had plenty of ideas lately," Wallis said. "It seems as if I've been full of ideas, more than one man can possibly follow up in one lifetime. My dear, if you are—"

"I'm not. I'm Adele Ambrose Wallis, of Boston. You've known my family for years, for God's sake."

"Don't swear, dear," Wallis said.

"And if I were the phantasma, what did you plan to do with me? This horrible man here wants to bring me to London, to put me in a cage along with the dragons and werewolves and God knows what else. And you? What would you do?"

"Why, nothing, dear. You'd still be my wife, my beloved wife. I'd keep you close to me—"

"So you could take advantage of all the ideas you'd have?"

"You would of course be a help with my explorations. My muse and inspiration, as well as my wife. I would make the most amazing discoveries – there would be no stopping me. Why, I might even be eligible for membership in the Explorers Club."

"And here I thought I was your companion!"

"You are that as well, of course—"

"But you wouldn't mind using me for your own ends—"

"For our ends, dear. Your talent would benefit both of us."

"For the very last time, I'm not the phantasma."

"Then how do you explain those dials?" Wallis said.

"I don't know," Mrs Wallis said angrily. "Ask Mr Arbuthnot – it's his machine."

With that she left the room. A moment later we heard the front door slam.

"Adele!" Wallis said, following her. "Adele, dearest . . ."

I sat where I was, too astonished by this recent turn of events to do anything else. I happened to glance down at that moment; the dials of the musopticon were, if anything, more violent in their action than before.

The only other person in the room was Mrs Jones. I looked up at her, too startled to speak.

"Yes," she said.

"Would you – would you come back with me to London?"

"No, of course not. Not after what Mrs Wallis said. Is it true you put your discoveries in cages?"

"Some – some of them." I felt paralysed before her. Her face was ancient, calm, wise. She seemed to have wings – or were those just the ties on her apron?

"I'll have to leave you now, Mr Arbuthnot," the phantasma said.

She spoke a few words. The room and everything in it vanished; I stood out in the open, with the village of Q———— all around me. The sun was setting. Far away, on the high street, I could see labourers walking home. Adele Wallis was marching towards the train station; her husband ran at her side, gesturing frantically.

I have thought about that incident nearly every day in the forty years since then. I heard through the Explorers Club that Samuel Wallis and his wife got a divorce; Adele Wallis went back to her family in Boston. Samuel made a few discoveries, nothing of importance, and then seemed to give up exploring, or at least his name was never mentioned again at the club.

What I wondered about most of all, though, was why I had failed to recognize the phantasma. I had prided myself on having the intuition of a true explorer, an intuition that had stood me in good stead on many of my voyages of discovery. Seldom have I been so terribly wrong.

It is only now, writing this, that I think I begin to understand. I am – I was – an explorer; I thought I could solve the mysteries that beset our lives by chasing after the exotic, the unique, the rare. But Mrs Jones showed me another aspect of our condition, what I could only call the mystery of the commonplace. The mystery that exists in aprons, and tea towels, and knick-knacks, the inspiration that can come from all these things. I am sorry now that I never settled down long enough to know any of this.

I am preparing to undertake my last expedition. I will go to London, to the underground stations, and search for her there. And if I find her I will not attempt to capture her, but will tell her – tell her what? – tell her that at long last I understand.

Audience

Jack Womack

*Jack Womack (b. 1956) is probably better known as a writer of
dark and baroque science fiction such as* Ambient *(1987) and*
Heathern *(1990), but once in a while he turns his hand to a
more subtle canvas. Long ago H. G. Wells wrote "The Magic
Shop" (1903), about a place that sells genuine magic tricks.
Since then there has been a steady trickle – of stories about such
magical places. Check out Avram Davidson's anthology* Magic for Sale *(1983) for plenty of examples. Here's one of the
latest and certainly more unusual.*

MALL MUSEUMS IN LARGE CITIES INEVITABLY ATTRACT me
whenever I travel. Their haphazard assemblages – ran-
domly displayed in no evident pattern, fitfully identified by
yellowing cards – on occasion contain items so memorably unsettling as thereafter to blot from the mind the holdings of the
Smithsonian, or Hermitage, or Louvre. I happened upon such a
place one afternoon while strolling in the Low City, near the
Margarethestrasse, down an alley branching off St Jermyn's
Close. The surrounding rows of soot-shrouded houses leaned
into their dank passageway; their roofs caressed rather than
touched, and their shadows shut away their inhabitants from
notions of time or season. Overlooking all was the close's six-
spired cathedral, which itself served, until the recent political
upheavals, as the Museum of Atheistic Belief. The cathedral's

carillons proclaimed the fifteenth hour as I knocked at the door of the Hall of Lost Sounds, and for a moment I feared that, in their din, my own would go unheard.

"Thank you for seeing me," the curator said as I entered. I would have guessed him to be no older than seventy. His voice held the measured resonance of a cello, and he declaimed his notes almost in the manner of a *Sprechstimmer*.

"How much?" I asked. He shook his head. "You don't charge admission?"

"Who would come?"

A wholly unrecognizable accent misted his words. Much about his place appeared medieval, but then, so did its district – while wandering its byways, I'd thought I could as well have come armed with halberd rather than backpack, ducking the splash of chamber pots and not the offers of touts. The curator lingered in his museum's antechamber as if awaiting some necessary cue before our tour could begin, and we listened to the cathedral bells clanging out their last.

"It must hearten," I offered, "hearing them again after so long."

"No other noise assaults my walls," he said. "Lost sounds are sometimes better left lost. I keep only those which tickle your ear like a lover's tongue."

The curator gestured that we should begin, and we entered the museum proper. Wooden planks attached at floor and ceiling, aligned along the left wall, partitioned half of the first room into alcoves. "Each space possesses its own eigentone," he said.

"Pardon?" I said.

"Excuse me. The reflections within are accurate, and in accordance with acoustic principles. If the audience can be satisfied, it will be."

An iron bouquet was affixed to the door frame. The curator tugged at one of its sprigs, and fire leaped hissing from the cardinal blossom. The creamy light revealed a coiled, valveless horn resembling a golden snake. Retrieving it from its cubicle, he cradled the instrument in his arms as if it were his sister's baby.

"A posthorn," he said. "The mail came four times daily, the

nature of each delivery denoted by unvarying leitmotifs." Pressing its mouthpiece against his lips, the curator blew three clear, ascending notes, each possessing an oddly pitched, yet not unattractive tone. "Such music, heard across miles, foretold of letters from your lover." Lifting the horn again, he played another short series, in a sharper key. "That prepared you to receive unforeseen gifts." He coughed until his lungs rattled; then replaced the horn within its enclosure. "Every signal, continually heard from childhood into age, was as familiar as a mother's voice. Once the deliveries ended, it was decreed that the posthorn should never again be played by anyone."

"You just played it," I said.

He nodded. "In a different country. Let us go on." The next cubicle held a black telephone, its sleek skin unblemished by touchpads, screen, or dial. Two short, tintinnabulate bursts shattered the moment's stillness as unexpectedly as a mandrake's cry. "It's for you," the curator said.

When I lifted the receiver to my ear I heard a woman, speaking with a voice infused with a semblance of life. "Rhinelander Exchange," she said, pronouncing each syllable with equal emphasis. "Number, please."

"Cities were divided into Exchanges," the curator said as I hung up. "While the operator made your connection, you'd hear a musical passage chosen to best represent the Exchange dialled. My wife lived in Endicott before we married, and whenever I'd call, I'd hear passages from Messiaen, awaiting her hello."

"That's remarkable."

He smiled. "After we married we lived in Hansa, and friends listened to Webern until we answered. I should now make a point concerning historical accuracy. Your immediate experience notwithstanding, the telephone would of course have rung only if someone called you. My exhibits merely approximate a sound's original context."

"The operator's accent was the same as yours," I said. "What is your native language?"

"Lost," he said. "I should say, it's been years since I've had need to speak it."

"I've never heard such an accent before."

"And now you have," said the curator, passing through a doorway into another dim room. I followed. Though I didn't see precisely where tile supplanted the flooring's wood, I felt, before I heard, the transformation underfoot. In the centre of the room was a small round table; on the table's marble top, an antique coffee grinder and porcelain candelabra holding a single, slender candle. He pulled one of two wrought-iron chairs away from the table, scraping the legs across the tile with the sound of many fingernails drawn along a blackboard.

"Sit," he said, lighting the candle; its wax crackled and snapped as the wick caught fire. As I sat, raking the other chair's iron over that ceramic floor, the curator shut his eyes, sealing himself against all distractions, and listened as if to a wombed heartbeat, his look assuring that, by dint of concentration, he would suck the sound dry of vibration before it could decay.

"Before they closed them all, my wife and I went to the cafés every evening, along with everyone else. We were quite social, once," he said, spinning the grinder's crank. "The waiter ground the beans at your table before preparing your coffee. We sat for hours, eating and talking and listening to music. Most establishments employed musicians, that their harmonics might lend melody to the crowd's drone. None of the songs was ever recorded. Transcriptions were on occasion made, but afterwards, all were effaced."

"Why?"

"Because we loved them," he said. "As the evening drew on, the older patrons went along their way, leaving behind only younger couples still uncertain whether each best suited the other. At midnight, at the hour conversation settles into the whispers of those making love with words, the oublovium player came forward to take her solo."

From a bag hidden beneath the table, the curator withdrew a wooden cylinder, turned with the symmetries of an hourglass. Leaning the blunt upper end of the instrument against his collarbone, crooking one arm around its mid-section, he placed the lower, open end in his lap. Then he lifted from his bag the

oublovium's apparent bow, a thin rod no longer than the oublovium itself, its form reminiscent of a dandelion, tipped not
with seeds but with a ball of fine wire. Inserting its tuft into the
opening, the curator slid the pole along unseen strings within the
instrument, rolling the rod's length between his fingers as he
drew it in and out. The notes produced bore the closest affinity to
those of a harp, played at impossible tempo with a multitude of
hands.

"I could as well sit at a piano and strike at the keyboard with
my elbows," he said. "Anyone could make such trifling motions
as these, but there were few virtuosi. Women, solely, mastered
the oublovium. No one plays it today. I doubt that anyone would
recognize it if they saw one."

"But who closed the cafés?"

If the curator knew, perhaps he no longer had reason to tell. He
shook his head, and returned his instrument to his bag. "One day
they were there, and the next, they weren't."

He redirected his attentions, undoubtedly anticipating that he
would be aware of the subsequent attraction before I would. The
room in which we sat seemed smaller than it was, and felt ever
more so the longer we sat there, but before my vague discomfort
hardened into claustrophobia, I took notice of a bright, pellucid
sound overhead; a faint tinkling, a clatter of miniature cymbals.
Staring up I saw a mobile attached to the ceiling, made up of
shiny glass shards hanging by threads, clinking together as they
twirled in the candle-warmed air.

"Trams ran throughout the cities," he continued. "A staff
protruded from the prow of each car, above the engine driver's
window. Chimes such as those were tied to the end of each staff,
and as the cars raced down the tracks, the wind signalled to those
waiting at the next stop ahead, promising that their patience
would be shortly rewarded. On maps, the tramlines were identified by the spectral colours, and each car's hue matched its line.

"Upon boarding, you dropped your gold token into a black fare
box. When it issued your receipt, the box thanked you, not in
words but with a sound truly lost. All I can offer is a description,
bearing less relation to its actuality than a dead lover's lock of hair

bears to the head from which it grew." The curator stood, motioning that I should do the same. "The mechanism's three notes comprised an ascending diatonic triad, impressing itself into the ear as a chirp rather than a chord, in intonation closer to a cricket's than to a bird's, yet louder, as if the insect nestled unseen within your clothing while it sang." He paused. "Can you hear it?" Before I might answer, he went on. "I've saved what could be saved, but so much was lost. If no one knows a tree falls in the forest, the question shouldn't be did it fall? but, was it there before it fell?"

We moved into another room as he spoke. There were three tiny windows on our right, admitting no purer light than might have eked through at sunset, in winter, on a cloudy day. Once more my shoes slid across a surface of altered texture; the clack of my heels reverberated against the walls with hollow echoes, and when I glanced down I saw what appeared, in the gloom, as bleached cobblestones, or the small skulls of babies.

"We rode the Blue Line, going to the seashore. At the beach-front was the spa, which was built of plum-coloured bricks and had 900 rooms. People came from all around to enjoy the waters. A promenade encircled the spa, and ran as well down to the dockside. Seashells were used to pave their walkways, and those of the quays. Travellers inevitably remarked on our city's sound-less sea, thinking the breakers pounded silently against the sand. Throughout the day and into the night the surf went unheard beneath the footsteps of thousands strolling over the shells. It's curious to realize that the only one of our sounds visitors recalled, afterwards, was one they never heard.

"Every summer night when the Guildhall's clock struck ten, the Ensemble Pyrotechnique undertook their most elaborate works on the strand. We'd sit on the public terraces overlooking the ocean and watch them fire their flowers into heaven. It was on one such night I proposed to my wife. Each year, on our anniversary, we'd ride the Blue Line to the seashore, each time remembering where we'd been, each time giving thanks for where we had come, blessing that moment from that time on until there was no time left."

I'd only imagined the cry of the fare box; now, enveloping myself within the curator's descriptions, feeling seashells beneath my feet, allowing his recollections to mingle with my own, I heard the fireworks bursting with the wet pop of flashbulbs exploding in the lamps of old cameras. That a memory of sound could so intrude into the physical world wasn't surprising in itself; who hasn't heard a fragment of a hated song and, hours later, still found it there, as impacted as a bean in the ear of a child? What was not so much unexpected as unnatural was the perceived immediacy of fireworks; of the bitter tang of gunpowder, of peripheral flashes glimpsed between my horizon and the beamed ceiling's azimuth. Shutting my eyes, I heard an unseen sea's unheard heartbeat.

"The shells were removed concurrently with the tramlines," the curator said, tapping the floor with the toe of his shoe. "The Guildhall was demolished. The spa was burned to the ground."

"Why?" I asked. "What happened?" As my words bounced from the walls back into my ears, I discerned an unaccountable lowering of the timbre of my voice, and a seeming dislocation of the direction from which it came. Some acoustic anomaly, or eigentonic flaw – perhaps accidental, perhaps not – was likely responsible; yet the unsettling impression that my voice no longer came from within me, but from somewhere without, heightened my awareness of how it might feel to have my own sound taken away. I hadn't experience enough then, nor do I now, to estimate how much I would thereafter miss it. "I don't understand."

"Nor did we," he said. "Unfortunately, but unavoidably, the remainder of the museum is quite dark. Take care, hereout."

"Where is your country?" I asked; receiving no reply, I rephrased my question. "Where was it?"

He answered only by guiding me towards another room. Stepping into its twilight, I heard our shoes crunching against the floor as if, having drifted without warning into another world's stronger gravity, our bodies increased in mass, compressing all underfoot. The resulting sound was identical to one included in my own collection, but I knew of no method by which the curator could have carpeted this chamber with snow.

"In this country, the image of winter bears faint relation to its verity," he said. "In the country I knew, each season was distinguished as much by its sounds as by its climate. Most of those were not so much lost as misplaced, and so I leave their acquisition to others. In my country, the seasons so differed from one to the next that, in some years, we might have been living successively on four dissimilar planets."

The curator stopped, and together we stood in the dark. At first I thought the continuing sound of our footsteps to be nothing more than sustained echoes. "Our weather changed before we did. One year snow fell in September. We foresaw a hard winter ahead. It was, but not because of the weather, for it never snowed again."

The rhythm of the ongoing footsteps quickened, increasing in volume as well as number until it seemed we were encroached upon by multitudes. If their stamp was but a recorded beat, as I thought it must be, its verisimilitude was nonetheless so perfect that only a single taping could have separated sound from source. The curator's face was obscured by shadow, and I was unable to gather from his reaction how I should respond to the perfection of his masters.

"Our national bird flocked in such numbers as to block out the afternoon sun."

An abrupt fluttering rose and roared around us. I instinctively braced myself, to keep from being blown over by that avian hurricane, but then realized that this room's sonic properties misled me once again; even my hair remained unruffled in the feathery gale. The swift bombardment from above served as an appropriate counterpoint to the unremitting ground attack.

"Their popular name was the pococurante," said the curator. "The populace favoured Voltaire. The birds nested in our birch forests every spring, arriving in clouds, snapping off tree limbs beneath their cumulative weight. Pococurantes were greyish blue, and the males had yellow heads and scarlet bellies. Their mottled eggs had a fishy flavour, though the birds themselves tasted something like chicken. The call of the pococurante was inoffensive, and familiar to all."

He mimed its song, whistling two notes; the first higher, and allegro, the second lower, and largo, an onomatopoeic *uh-oh* in the key of E flat.

"Pococurantes coupled for life. If one died, the survivor mourned its mate, refusing to fly away until it, too, was killed. Their numbers declined rapidly after the trees were chopped down. When the remaining birds set off upon their last migration, they were blasted from the sky until their blood fell like rain. The last time I heard a pococurante, I was half the age I am now." Though his face remained cloaked, through the darkness I perceived his smile, and its ambiguity. "That was also the first time I heard one."

"Would you repeat their call for me?" I asked.

"Certainly."

Attuning my ear to the chords of extinction, I knew an illuminatory moment. An unlikely admixture of sorrow, fear, and nostalgia for another's memories irrupted through my spirit, and as I considered the criteria by which donations might be judged worthy of a Hall of Lost Sounds, I pictured seventeenth-century explorers lying sleepless during their first night on Mauritius, kept awake by the squawk of dodos; imagined Manhattanites, in the thirties, grabbing instinctively for their glassware as the El rumbled up Sixth Avenue; tried to recall the intonation of my prepubescent voice. Some sounds one surely expected always to hear, and so never listened at the time they were made; perhaps inevitably those noises thought most unendurable when initially heard only later proved the most precious, and most irrecoverable.

"You like that one?" Before I could state my affirmation, his thoughts wandered elsewhere; I doubt that he cared. "I hear it now as you hear me."

The curator led me to the far side of the room. Cries of pococurante and drum of quickstep waned, overwhelmed by a thunderous fusillade, so loud that I guessed the rest of the tour would be delivered with gestures. Still, over sharp reports of creaking wood, against an unceasing advance of caissons bumping across stone, I heard him plainly, as if he stood in a lecture hall, addressing an audience of one.

"Long before the disruptions began, delivery carts were used in our cities to conserve fuel," the curator said. "They were pressed into general service to speed our own migration. Much of what a house contained that was important could be hauled by the largest carriages. Whatever their size, the wagons never held enough. When I left, I carried my belongings with me."

However chimerical its nature, the crash of a thousand inessential wagons hurtling towards us so unnerved me that with each pass I flinched, attempting to avoid an onslaught I knew was evanescent. Without benefit of imagination, I heard horses neighing when whips cracked against their withers; drivers shouting out curses over the groan of their loads. I pretend no understanding of sonology, but I thought it impossible that any phonographic agency could so truly reproduce such pandemonium; I felt that through some subtle technique I heard those sounds exactly as he did when they ricocheted off the walls of his skull. Possibly that was his trick, or what he wished me to believe was his trick, that he drew from his mind at command recollections so assiduously cherished as to have developed an alternate existence, nearly independent of his own. A suitable audience could be therefore gratified, assured that not only had there been a tree which fell, but that the sound it made upon falling would echo through its forest unto eternity.

"Why did you have to leave your country?" I asked.

"She left me," he said. "I should have preferred to stay. Come along, now."

Grateful to be removed from the earsplitting tumult, I followed the curator and we entered a brighter, quieter hall. In the ceiling's elliptical dome was an oculus, threaded with a strand of light. Two doors faced us, one open, one closed. Gazing into the visible threshold's abyss, I saw neither exhibits nor even room beyond. The curator stopped, and we went no further.

"My wife and I were awakened one night by sirens," he said. "We opened our windows and watched the spa burn down. In keeping with the season we tried to reimagine what we saw as a Hallowe'en spectacle, and shuddered at the vision of black skeletons silhouetted against an orange field. But sorrow overwhelmed our disregard of what we knew to be real, and we returned to bed, unsuccessful in our attempts to transform a funeral into a holiday. It was only the week before that we'd sat on the beachfront terraces, enjoying the fireworks, leaving before we'd intended with every expectation of returning when we wished.

"The next morning we rode our bicycles to the beach, anxious to look at ruins other than our own. On the way we passed the avenue's empty shops, where haberdashers and tobacconists, watchmakers and smiths, joiners and cobblers and ostlers plied their trades long before our grandparents were born. The cafés were shuttered. Gilt and neon signs were covered over by billboards telling of unfamiliar people and places. So crowded with those departing was the Central Station that the passengers' clamour muted that of their trains. We reached the seashore. The ashes had mixed with the sand, and as we walked over them we listened to the ocean, hearing it anew, if not for the first time. Its swell terrified my wife, and we walked our cycles home, bereft of emotion, feeling too drained to race back uphill. That morning, all anyone knew was rumours and lies, and what wasn't said didn't matter as much as what wasn't done. My country was taken from us, though if not with our wishes, then undoubtedly with dutiful acquiescence.

"Couples living in such circumstances so often find their challenges insurmountable. We talked of what we might do. All we could do was talk, and try to make the other listen. We drifted apart, all the while wanting to stay together. One day, sooner than expected, I came home to find her gone."

His expression remained unchanged as he weaved his words around me. A softer sound, its origin as enigmatic as the rest, insinuated itself into my ears, a steady uninflected jingling, heard as if it came from far beneath the floor.

"You can always speak to one who isn't there, of course, as long as you don't expect answers," the curator said. "We planted pinwheels in our gardens in memory of the dead. Miniature sleigh bells were attached to their vanes, so that when the wind spun the wheels around, the souls they honoured would ascend with a soothing accompaniment."

Though his face evinced no untoward emotion – nor, in fact, any emotion at all – I perceived that he felt he should cry, even if he no longer could. The sound of his sorrow was evidently one he had been unable, or unwilling, to preserve. "Though the past survives only through its artefacts," he said, "every museum must limit its acquisitions."

"Your country," I said. "Your wife. Where are they?" Taking my arm, he walked the short distance across the hall with me, and pointed to the open door.

"Listen."

Craning my head towards its darkness, I heard not silence, but the absence of sound. Staring into that void, straining to catch noises that simply weren't there, I better comprehended the true worth of his collection and how irreplaceable it would be, once it was lost. He'd deliberately left vague the magnitude of his tragedy; what else of his world was he unable to save? Did I miss what he had retained all the more? Could any public loss be greater than any private one, or did one inescapably serve as no more than grace note to the other, if they happened to coincide?

The curator began singing a tune of unsettling pitch, his notes wobbling in and out of key. The words were, I suppose, in his original tongue, a speech engorged with glottal phrasings, surprising syllabic leaps and discordant cadences, bearing no relation to any language I've heard before, or since. After a single verse and chorus, he stopped. "Our song," he told me. "The last exhibit of my museum."

As he concluded his sentence, the cathedral bells rang out the sixteenth hour, shaking the walls with sonorous peals. The curator grimaced, showing even less appreciation of their auditory terrorism. Once the toll concluded he directed me to the other door. "Now I hear my wife's voice," he said, unlatching the lock, easing me forward. "Thank you for hearing mine."

Before I could reply, he closed the door behind me. I found

myself in afternoon sunlight, some distance from the alley, deaf-
ened by Gaon Prospect's cacophony – the roars of its buses and
taxis and trucks, the chants of its hawkers.

Children screamed at one another, police blew whistles, car
alarms blared, and a thousand radios bleated across the encom-
passing dissonance of Montrouge.

There were numerous cafés on the Prospect and, selecting one
of more subdued ambience than the rest, I took a seat and ordered
currant genever. Late into the evening I rifled the accessions of
my own museum, replaying sounds as I came upon them. Too
many of its holdings were unavailable, however diligent the
search, but the sole surprise was that they'd been stolen with
such ease; if I hadn't looked, I'd have never missed them. A
friend of mine, a composer, once spoke to me of Webern: how in
his music the rests contribute as much, if not more, as the notes;
that having a sense of what was missing made all the clearer what
remained. Until that afternoon I'd preferred tunes more easily
mastered. The curator's songs stuck closer to me than I thought
desirable, and only with some effort did I erase them from my
mind.

The Edge of the World

Michael Swanwick

We end, in a way, almost like we started, but instead of a wall around the world, here we have simply the edge of the world, and nothing else. Michael Swanwick (b. 1950) was inspired into writing fiction through his love for The Lord of the Rings, *but like all good writers he did not slavishly imitate but created anew. The* Iron Dragon's Daughter *(1993) is the closest to a harsh and savage anti-fantasy as you are ever likely to get. Better known as a writer of science fiction, with such powerful novels as* In the Drift *(1984),* Griffin's Egg *(1991) and* Stations of the Tide *(1991), Swanwick has written a number of fantasy stories yet just about every one treats the fantastic as if it were real, with a logical scientific basis. Except the following, which defies logic. And where else can our voyage through fantasy end but at the very edge of the world.*

THE DAY THAT DONNA AND PIGGY AND RUSS WENT TO see the Edge of the World was a hot one. They were sitting on the kerb by the gas station that noontime, sharing a Coke and watching the big Starlifters lumber up into the air, one by one, out of Toldenarba AFB. The sky rumbled with their passing. There'd been an incident in the Persian Gulf, and half the American forces in the Twilight Emirates were on alert.

"My old man says when the Big One goes up, the base will be the first to go," Piggy said speculatively. "Treaties won't allow us to defend it. One bomber comes in high and *whaboom*" – he made soft nuclear explosion noises – "it's all gone." He was wearing camouflage pants and a khaki T-shirt with an iron-on reading: KILL 'EM ALL AND LET GOD SORT 'EM OUT. Donna watched as he took off his glasses to polish them on his shirt. His face went slack and vacant, then livened as he put them back on again, as if he were playing with a mask.

"You should be so lucky," Donna said. "Mrs Khashoggi is still going to want that paper done on Monday morning, Armageddon or not."

"Yeah, can you believe her?" Piggy said. "That weird accent! And all that memorization! Cut me some slack. I mean, who cares whether Ackronnion was part of the Mezentian Dynasty?"

"You ought to care, dipshit," Russ said. "Local history's the only decent class the school's got." Russ was the smartest boy Donna had ever met, never mind the fact that he was flunking out. He had soulful eyes and a radical haircut, short on the sides with a dyed-blond punklock down the back of his neck. "Man, I opened the *Excerpts from Epics* text that first night, thinking it was going to be the same old bullshit, and I stayed up till dawn. Got to school without a wink of sleep, but I'd managed to read every last word. This is one weird part of the world; its history is full of dragons and magic and all kinds of weird monsters. Do you realize that in the eighteenth century three members of the British legation were eaten by demons? That's in the historical record!"

Russ was an enigma to Donna. The first time they'd met, hanging with the misfits at an American School dance, he'd tried to put a hand down her pants, and she'd slugged him good, almost breaking his nose. She could still hear his surprised laughter as blood ran down his chin. They'd been friends ever since. Only there were limits to friendship, and now she was waiting for him to make his move and hoping he'd get down to it before her father was rotated out.

In Japan she'd known a girl who had taken a razor blade and carved her boyfriend's name in the palm of her hand. How could she do that, Donna had wanted to know? Her friend had shrugged, said, "As long as it gets me noticed." It wasn't until Russ that Donna understood.

"Strange country," Russ said dreamily. "The sky beyond the Edge is supposed to be full of demons and serpents and shit. They say that if you stare into it long enough, you'll go mad."

They all three looked at one another.

"Well, hell," Piggy said. "What are we waiting for?"

The Edge of the World lay beyond the railroad tracks. They bicycled through the American enclave into the old native quarter. The streets were narrow here, the sideyards crammed with broken trucks, rusted-out buses, even yachts up in cradles with staved-in sides. Garage doors were black mouths hissing and spitting welding sparks, throbbing to the hammered sound of worked metal. They hid their bikes in a patch of scrub apricot trees where the railroad crossed the industrial canal and hiked across.

Time had altered the character of the city where it bordered the Edge. Gone were the archers in their towers, vigilant against a threat that never came. Gone were the rose quartz palaces with their thousand windows, not a one of which overlooked the Edge. The battlements where blind musicians once piped up the dawn now survived only in Mrs Khashoggi's texts. Where they had been was now a drear line of weary factory buildings, their lower windows cinderblocked or bricked up and those beyond reach of vandals' stones painted over in patchwork squares of grey and faded blue.

A steam whistle sounded and lines of factory workers shambled back inside, brown men in chinos and white shirts, Syrian and Lebanese labourers imported to do work no native Toldenarban would touch. A shredded net waved forlornly from a basketball hoop set up by the loading dock.

There was a section of hurricane fence down. They scrambled through.

As they cut across the grounds, a loud whine arose from within the factory building. Down the way another plant lifted its voice in a solid wham-wham-wham as rhythmic and unrelenting as a headache. One by one the factories shook themselves from their midday drowse and went back to work. "Why do they locate these things along the Edge?" Donna asked.

"It's so they can dump their chemical waste over the Edge," Russ explained. "These were all erected before the emir nationalized the culverts that the Russian Protectorate built."

Behind the factory was a chest-high concrete wall, rough-edged and pebbly with the slow erosion of cement. Weeds grew in clumps at its foot. Beyond was nothing but sky.

Piggy ran ahead and spat over the Edge. "Hey, remember what Nixon said when he came here? *It is indeed a long way down.* What a guy!"

Donna leaned against the wall. A film of haze tinted the sky grey, intensifying at the focal point to dirty brown, as if a dead spot were burned into the centre of her vision. When she looked down, her eyes kept grabbing for ground and finding more sky. There were a few wispy clouds in the distance and nothing more. No serpents coiled in the air. She should have felt disappointed but, really, she hadn't expected better. This was of a piece with all the natural wonders she had ever seen, the waterfalls, geysers and scenic vistas that inevitably included power lines, railings and parking lots absent from the postcards. Russ was staring intently ahead, hawklike, frowning. His jaw worked slightly, and she wondered what he saw.

"Hey, look what I found!" Piggy whooped. "It's a stairway!"

They joined him at the top of an institutional-looking concrete and iron stairway. It zigzagged down the cliff towards an infinitely distant and non-existent Below, dwindling into hazy blue. Quietly, as if he'd impressed himself, Piggy said, "What do you suppose is down there?"

"Only one way to find out, isn't there?" Russ said.

Russ went first, then Piggy, then Donna, the steps ringing dully under their feet. Graffiti covered the rocks, worn spraypaint letters in yellow and black and red scrawled one over the other and faded by time and weather into mutual unreadability, and on the iron railings, words and arrows and triangles had been markered on to or dug into the paint with knife or nail: JURGEN BIN SHEISSKOPF. MOTLEY CRUE. DEATH TO SATAN AMERICA IMPERIALIST. Seventeen steps down, the first landing was filthy with broken brown glass, bits of crumbled concrete, cigarette butts, soggy, half-melted cardboard. The stairway folded back on itself and they followed it down.

"You ever had *fugu*?" Piggy asked. Without waiting for an answer, he said, "It's Japanese poisonous blowfish. It has to be prepared very carefully – they license the chefs – and even so, several people die every year. It's considered a great delicacy."

"Nothing tastes that good," Russ said.

"It's not the flavour," Piggy said enthusiastically. "It's the poison. Properly prepared, see, there's a very small amount left in the sashimi and you get a threshold dose. Your lips and the tips of your fingers turn cold. Numb. That's how you know you're having the real thing. That's how you know you're living right on the edge."

"I'm already living on the edge," Russ said. He looked startled when Piggy laughed.

A fat moon floated in the sky, pale as a disc of ice melting in blue water. It bounced after them as they descended, kicking aside loose soda bottles in styrofoam sleeves, crushed Marlboro boxes, a scattering of carbonized spark plugs. On one landing they found a crumpled shopping cart, and Piggy had to muscle it over the railing and watch it fall. "Sure is a lot of crap here," he observed. The landing smelled faintly of urine.

"It'll get better further down," Russ said. "We're still near the top, where people can come to get drunk after work." He pushed on down. Far to one side they could see the brown flow from the industrial canal where it spilled into space, widening and then slowly dispersing into rainbowed mist, distance glamouring its beauty.

"How far are we planning to go?" Donna asked apprehensively.

"Don't be a weak sister," Piggy sneered. Russ said nothing.

The deeper they went, the shabbier the stairway grew, and the spottier its maintenance. Pipes were missing from the railing.

Where patches of paint had fallen away the bolts anchoring the stair to the rock were walnut-sized lumps of rust.

Needle-clawed marsupials chittered warningly from niches in the rock as they passed. Tufts of grass and moth-white gentians grew in the loess-filled cracks.

Hours passed. Donna's feet and calves and the small of her back grew increasingly sore, but she refused to be the one to complain. By degrees she stopped looking over the side and out into the sky, and stared instead at her feet flashing in and out of sight while one hand went slap-grab-tug on the rail. She felt sweaty and miserable.

Back home she had a half-finished paper on the Three Days' Incident of March 1810, when the French Occupation, by order of Napoleon himself, had fired cannonade after cannonade over the Edge into nothingness. They had hoped to make rainstorms of devastating force that would lash and destroy their enemies, and created instead only a gunpowder haze, history's first great failure in weather control. This descent was equally futile, Donna thought, an endless and wearying exercise in nothing. Just the same as the rest of her life. Every time her father was re-posted, she had resolved to change, to be somebody different this time around, whatever the price, even if – no, especially if – it meant playacting something she was not. Last year in Germany when she'd gone out with that local boy with the Alfa Romeo and instead of jerking him off had used her mouth, she had thought: Everything's going to be different now. But no.

Nothing ever changed.

"Heads up!" Russ said. "There's some steps missing here!" He leaped, and the landing gonged hollowly under his sneakers. Then again as Piggy jumped after.

Donna hesitated. There were five steps gone and a drop of 20 feet before the stairway cut back beneath itself. The cliff bulged outwards here, and if she slipped she'd probably miss the stairs altogether.

She felt the rock draw away from her to either side, and was suddenly aware that she was connected to the world by the merest speck of matter, barely enough to anchor her feet. The sky wrapped itself about her, extending to infinity, depthless and absolute. She could extend her arms and fall into it for ever. What would happen to her then? she wondered. Would she die of thirst and starvation, or would the speed of her fall grow so great that the oxygen would be sucked from her lungs, leaving her to strangle in a sea of air? "Come on, Donna!" Piggy shouted up at her. "Don't be a pussy!"

"Russ—" she said quaveringly.

But Russ wasn't looking her way. He was frowning downwards, anxious to be going. "Don't push the lady," he said. "We can go on by ourselves."

Donna choked with anger and hurt and desperation all at once. She took a deep breath and, heart scudding, leaped. Sky and rock wheeled over her head. For an instant she was floating, falling totally lost and filled with a panicky awareness that she was about to die. Then she crashed on to the landing. It hurt like hell, and at first she feared she'd pulled an ankle. Piggy grabbed her shoulders and rubbed the side of her head with his knuckles. "I knew you could do it, you wimp."

Donna knocked away his arm. "Okay, wise-ass. How are you expecting to get us back up?"

The smile disappeared from Piggy's face. His mouth opened, closed. His head jerked fearfully upwards. An acrobat could leap across, grab the step and flip up without any trouble at all. "I – I mean, I—"

"Don't worry about it," Russ said impatiently. "We'll think of something." He started down again.

It wasn't natural, Donna realized, his attitude. There was something obsessive about his desire to descend the stairway. It was like the time he'd brought his father's revolver to school along with a story about playing Russian roulette that morning before breakfast. "Three times!" he'd said proudly.

He'd had that same crazy look on him, and she hadn't the slightest notion then or now how she could help him.

Russ walked like an automaton, wordlessly, tirelessly, never hurrying up or slowing down. Donna followed in concerned silence, while Piggy scurried between them, chattering like somebody's pet Pekingese. This struck Donna as so apt as to be almost allegorical: the two of them together yet alone, the distance between filled with noise. She thought of this distance, this silence, as the sun passed behind the cliff and the afternoon heat lost its edge.

The stairs changed to cement-jacketed brick with small buttresses cut into the rock. There was a pile of stems and cherry pits on one landing, and the railing above them was white with bird droppings. Piggy leaned over the rail and said, "Hey, I can see seagulls down there. Flying around."

"Where?" Russ leaned over the railing, then said scornfully, "Those are pigeons. The Ghazoddis used to release them for rifle practice."

As Piggy turned to follow Russ down again, Donna caught a glimpse into his eyes, liquid and trembling with helplessness and despair. She'd seen that fear in him only once before, months ago when she'd stopped by his house on the way to school, just after the emir's assassination.

The living-room windows were draped and the room seemed unnaturally gloomy after being out in the morning sun. Blue television light flickered over shelves of shadowy ceramic figurines: Dresden milkmaids, Chantilly Chinamen, Meissen pug-dogs connected by a gold chain held in their champed jaws, naked Delft nymphs dancing.

Piggy's mother sat in a limp dressing-gown, hair unbrushed, watching the funeral. She held a cup of oily-looking coffee in one hand. Donna was surprised to see her up so early. Everyone said that she had a bad problem with alcohol, that even by service wife standards she was out of control.

"Look at them," Piggy's mother said. On the screen were solemn processions of camels and Cadillacs, sheikhs in jellaba, keffigeh and mirrorshades, European dignitaries with wives in tasteful grey Parisian fashions. "They've got their nerve."

"Where did you put my lunch?" Piggy said loudly from the kitchen.

"Making fun of the Kennedys like that!" The emir's youngest

son, no more than four years old, salaamed his father's casket as it passed before him. "That kid's bad enough, but you should see the mother, crying as if her heart were broken. It's enough to turn your stomach. If I were Jackie, I'd . . ."

Donna and Piggy and Russ had gone bowling the night the emir was shot. This was out in the ruck of cheap joints that surrounded the base, catering almost exclusively to servicemen. When the muzak piped through overhead speakers was interrupted for the news bulletin, everyone had stood up and cheered. *Up we go*, someone had begun singing, and the rest had joined in, *into the wild blue yonder* . . . Donna had felt so sick with fear and disgust she had thrown up in the parking lot. "I don't think they're making fun of anyone," Donna said. "They're just—"

"Don't talk to her!" The refrigerator door slammed shut. A cupboard door slammed open.

Piggy's mother smiled bitterly. "This is exactly what you'd expect from these ragheads. Pretending they're white people, deliberately mocking their betters. Filthy brown animals."

"*Mother*! Where is my fucking lunch?"

She looked at him then, jaw tightening. "Don't you use that kind of language on me, young man."

"All right!" Piggy shouted. "All right, I'm going to school without lunch! Shows how much you care!"

He turned to Donna and in the instant before he grabbed her wrist and dragged her out of the house, Donna could no longer hear the words, could only see that universe of baffled futility haunting Piggy's eyes. That same look she glimpsed today.

The railings were wooden now, half the posts rotting at their bases, with an occasional plank missing, wrenched off and thrown over the side by previous visitors. Donna's knees buckled and she stumbled, almost lurching into the rock. "I have to stop," she said, hating herself for it. "I cannot go one more step."

Piggy immediately collapsed on the landing. Russ hesitated, then climbed up to join them. They three sat staring out into nothing, legs over the Edge, arms clutching the rail.

Piggy found a Pepsi can, logo in flowing Arabic, among the

rubble. He held it in his left hand and began sticking holes in it with his butterfly knife, again and again, cackling like a demented sex criminal. "Exterminate the brutes!" he said happily. Then, with absolutely no transition he asked, "How are we ever going to get back up?" so dolorously Donna had to bite back her laughter.

"Look, I just want to go on down a little bit more," Russ said.

"Why?" Piggy sounded petulant.

"So I can get down enough to get away from this garbage." He gestured at the cigarette butts, the broken brown glass, sparser than above but still there. "Just a little further, okay, guys?" There was an edge to his voice, and under that the faintest hint of a plea. Donna felt helpless before those eyes. She wished they were alone, so she could ask him what was wrong.

Donna doubted that Russ himself knew what he expected to find down below. Did he think that if he went down far enough, he'd never have to climb back? She remembered the time in Mr Herriman's algebra class when a sudden tension in the air had made her glance across the room at Russ, and he was, with great concentration, tearing the pages out of his maths text and dropping them one by one on the floor. He'd taken a five-day suspension for that, and Donna had never found out what it was all about. But there was a kind of glorious arrogance to the act; Russ had been born out of time. He really should have been a medieval prince, a Medici or one of the Sabakan pretenders.

"Okay," Donna said, and Piggy of course had to go along.

Seven flights further down the modern stairs came to an end. The wooden railing of the last short, septambic flight had been torn off entire, and laid across the steps. They had to step carefully between the uprights and the rails. But when they stood at the absolute bottom, they saw that there were stairs beyond the final landing, steps that had been cut into the stone itself. They were curving swaybacked things that millennia of rain and foot traffic had worn so uneven they were almost unpassable.

Piggy groaned. "Man, you *can't* expect us to go down that thing."

"Nobody's asking you," Russ said.

*   *   *

They descended the old stairway backwards and on all fours. The wind breezed up, hitting them with the force of an expected shove first to one side and then the other. There were times when Donna was so frightened she thought she was going to freeze up and never move again. But at last the stone broadened and became a wide, even ledge, with caves leading back into the rock.

The cliff face here was green-white with lichen, and had in ancient times been laboriously smoothed and carved. Between each cave (their mouths alone left in a natural state, unaltered) were heavy-thighed women – goddesses, perhaps, or demons or sacred dancers – their breasts and faces chipped away by the image-hating followers of the Prophet at a time when Mohammed yet lived. Their hands held loops of vines in which were entangled moons, cycling from new through waxing quarter and gibbous to full and then back through gibbous and waning quarter to dark. Piggy was gasping, his face bright with sweat, but he kept up his blustery front. "What the fuck is all this shit, man?"

"It was a monastery," Russ said. He walked along the ledge dazedly, a wondering half-smile on his lips. "I read about this." He stopped at a turquoise automobile door someone had flung over the Edge to be caught and tossed by fluke winds, the only piece of trash that had made it down this far. "Give me a hand."

He and Piggy lifted the door, swung it back and forth three times to build up momentum, then lofted it over the lip of the rock. They all three lay down on their stomachs to watch it fall away, turning end over end and seeming finally to flicker as it dwindled smaller and smaller, still falling. At last it shrank below the threshold of visibility and became one of a number of shifting motes in the downbelow, part of the slow, mazy movement of dead blood cells in the eyes' vitreous humours. Donna turned over on her back, drew her head back from the rim, stared upwards. The cliff seemed to be slowly tumbling forward, all the world inexorably, dizzyingly leaning down to crush her.

"Let's go explore the caves," Piggy suggested.

They were empty. The interiors of the caves extended no more than 30 feet into the rock, but they had all been elaborately worked, arched ceiling carved with thousands of *faux tesserae*, walls adorned with bas-relief pillars. Between the pillars the walls were taken up with long shelves carved into the stone. No artefacts remained, not so much as a potsherd or a splinter of bone. Piggy shone his pocket flash into every shadowy niche. "Somebody's been here before us and taken everything." he said.

"The Historic Registry people, probably." Russ ran a hand over one shelf. It was the perfect depth and height for a line of 3-pound coffee cans. "This is where they stowed the skulls. When a monk grew so spiritually developed he no longer needed the crutch of physical existence, his fellows would render the flesh from his bones and enshrine his skull. They poured wax in the sockets, then pushed in opals while it was still warm. They slept beneath the faintly gleaming eyes of their superiors."

When they emerged it was twilight, the first stars appearing from behind a sky fading from blue to purple. Donna looked down on the moon. It was as big as a plate, full and bright. The rilles, dry seas and mountain chains were preternaturally distinct. Somewhere in the middle was Tranquility Base, where Neil Armstrong had planted the American flag.

"Jeez, it's late," Donna said. "If we don't start home soon, my mom is going to have a cow."

"We still haven't figured a way to get back up," Piggy reminded her. Then, "We'll probably have to stay here. Learn to eat owls and grow crops sideways on the cliff face. Start our own civilization. Our only serious problem is the imbalance of sexes, but even that's not insurmountable." He put an arm around Donna's shoulders, grabbed at her breast. "You'd pull the train for us, wouldn't you, Donna?"

Angrily she pushed him away and said, "You keep a clean mouth! I'm so tired of your juvenile talk and behaviour."

"Hey, calm down, it's cool." That panicky look was back in his eyes, the forced knowledge that he was not in control, could never be in control, that there was no such thing as control. He smiled weakly, placatingly.

"No, it is not. It is most emphatically not 'cool'." Suddenly she was white and shaking with fury. Piggy was a spoiler. His simple presence ruined any chance she might have had to talk with Russ, find out just what was bugging him, get him to finally, really notice her. "I am sick of having to deal with your immaturity, your filthy language and your crude behaviour."

Piggy turned pink and began stuttering.

Russ reached a hand into his pocket, pulled out a chunk of foil-wrapped hash, and a native tin pipe with a carved coral bowl. The kind of thing the local beggar kids sold for twenty-nine cents. "Anybody want to get stoned?" he asked suavely.

"You bastard!" Piggy laughed. "You told me you were out!"

Russ shrugged. "I lied." He lit the pipe carefully, drew in, passed it to Donna. She took it from his fingers, felt how cold they were to her touch, looked up over the pipe and saw his face, thin and ascetic, eyelids closed, pale and Christlike through the blue smoke. She loved him intensely in that instant and wished she could sacrifice herself for his happiness. The pipe's stem was overwarm, almost hot, between her lips. She drew in deep.

The smoke was raspy in her throat, then tight and swirling in her lungs. It shot up into her head, filled it with buzzing harmonics: the air, the sky, the rock behind her back all buzzing, ballooning her skull outwards in a visionary rush that forced wide open first her eyes and then her mouth. She choked and spasmodically coughed. More smoke than she could imagine possibly holding in her lungs gushed out into the universe.

"Hey, watch that pipe!" Piggy snatched it from her distant fingers. They tingled with pinpricks of pain like tiny stars in the darkness of her flesh. "You were spilling the hash!" The evening light was abuzz with energy, the sky swarming up into her eyes. Staring out into the darkening air, the moon rising below her and the stars as close and friendly as those in a children's book illustration, she felt at peace, detached from worldly cares. "Tell us about the monastery, Russ," she said, in the same voice she might have used a decade before to ask her father for a story.

"Yeah, tell us about the monastery, Unca Russ," Piggy said, but with jeering undertones. Piggy was always sucking up to Russ, but there was tension there too, and his sarcastic little

challenges were far from rare. It was classic beta male jealousy, straight out of Primate Psychology 101.

"It's very old," Russ said. "Before the Sufis, before Mohammed, even before the Zoroastrians crossed the gulf, the native mystics would renounce the world and go to live in cliffs on the Edge of the World. They cut the steps down, and once down, they never went back up again."

"How did they eat then?" Piggy asked sceptically.

"They wished their food into existence. No, really! It was all in their creation myth: in the beginning all was Chaos and Desire. The world was brought out of Chaos – by which they meant unformed matter – by Desire, or Will. It gets a little inconsistent after that, because it wasn't really a religion, but more like a system of magic. They believed that the world wasn't complete yet, that for some complicated reason it could never be complete. So there's still traces of the old Chaos lingering just beyond the Edge, and it can be tapped by those who desire it strongly enough, if they have distanced themselves from the things of the world. These mystics used to come down here to meditate against the moon and work miracles.

"This wasn't sophisticated stuff like the Tantric monks in Tibet or anything, remember. It was like a primitive form of animism, a way to force the universe to give you what you wanted. So the holy men would come down here and they'd wish for . . . like riches, you know? Filigreed silver goblets with rubies, mounds of moonstones, elfinbone daggers sharper than Damascene steel. Only once they got them they weren't supposed to want them. They'd just throw them over the Edge. There were these monasteries all along the cliffs. The further from the world they were, the more spiritually advanced."

"So what happened to the monks?"

"There was a king – Althazar? I forget his name. He was this real greedhead, started sending his tax collectors down to gather up everything the monks brought into existence. Must've figured, hey, the monks weren't using them. Which as it turned out was like a real major blasphemy, and the monks got pissed. The boss mystics, all the real spiritual heavies, got together for this big

confab. Nobody knows how. There's one of the classics claims they could run sideways on the cliff just like it was the ground, but I don't know. Doesn't matter. So one night they all of them, every monk in the world, meditated at the same time. They chanted together, saying, It is not enough that Althazar should die, for he has blasphemed. He must suffer a doom such as has been visited on no man before. He must be unmade, uncreated, reduced to less than has ever been. And they prayed that there be no such king as Althazar, that his life and history be unmade, so that there never had been such king as Althazar.

"And he was no more.

"But so great was their yearning for oblivion that when Althazar ceased to be, his history and family as well, they were left feeling embittered and did not know why. And not knowing why, their hatred turned upon themselves, and their wish for destruction, and they too all of a single night, ceased to be." He fell silent.

At last Piggy said, "You believe that crap?" Then, when there was no answer, "It's none of it true, man! Got that? There's no magic, and there never was." Donna could see that he was really angry, threatened on some primal level by the possibility that someone he respected could even begin to believe in magic. His face got pink, the way it always did when he lost control.

"No, it's all bullshit," Russ said bitterly. "Like everything else."

They passed the pipe around again. Then Donna leaned back, stared straight out, and said, "If I could wish for anything, you know what I'd wish for?"

"Bigger tits?"

She was so weary now, so pleasantly washed out, that it was easy to ignore Piggy. "I'd wish I knew what the situation was."

"What situation?" Piggy asked. Donna was feeling languorous, not at all eager to explain herself, and she waved away the question. But he persisted. "What situation?"

"Any situation. I mean, all the time, I find myself talking with people and I don't know what's really going on. What games they're playing. Why they're acting the way they are. I wish I knew what the situation was."

The moon floated before her, big and fat and round as a griffin's egg, shining with power. She could feel that power washing through her, the background radiation of decayed chaos spread across the sky at a uniform three degrees Kelvin. Even now, spent and respent, a coin fingered and thinned to the worn edge of non-existence, there was power out there, enough to flatten planets.

Staring out at that great fat boojum snark of a moon, she felt the flow of potential worlds, and within the cold silver disc of that jester's skull, rank with magic, sensed the invisible presence of Russ's primitive monks, men whose minds were nowhere near comprehensible to her, yet vibrated with power, existing as matrices of patterned stress, no more actual than Donald Duck, but no less powerful either. She was caught in a waking fantasy, in which the sky was full of power and all of it accessible to her. Monks sat empty-handed over their wishing bowls, separated from her by the least fictions of time and reality. For an eternal instant all possibilities fanned out to either side, equally valid, no one more real than any other. Then the world turned under her, and her brain shifted back to real time.

"Me," Piggy said, "I just wish I knew how to get back up the stairs."

They were silent for a moment. Then it occurred to Donna that here was the perfect opportunity to find out what was bugging Russ. If she asked cautiously enough, if the question hit him just right, if she were just plain lucky, he might tell her everything. She cleared her throat. "Russ? What do you wish?"

In the bleakest voice imaginable, Russ said, "I wish I'd never been born."

She turned to ask him why, and he wasn't there.

"Hey," Donna said. "Where'd Russ go?"

Piggy looked at her oddly. "Who's Russ?"

It was a long trip back up. They carried the length of wooden railing between them, and every now and then Piggy said, "Hey, wasn't this a great idea of mine? This'll make a swell ladder."

"Yeah, great," Donna would say, because he got mad when she

didn't respond. He got mad, too, whenever she started to cry, but there wasn't anything she could do about that. She couldn't even explain why she was crying, because in all the world – of all his friends, acquaintances, teachers, even his parents – she was the only one who remembered that Russ had ever existed.

The horrible thing was that she had no specific memories of him, only a vague feeling of what his presence had been like, and a lingering sense of longing and frustration.

She no longer even remembered his face.

"Do you want to go first or last?" Piggy had asked her.

When she'd replied, "Last. If I go first, you'll stare at my ass all the way up," he'd actually blushed. Without Russ to show off in front of, Piggy was a completely different person, quiet and not at all abusive. He even kept his language clean. But that didn't help, for just being in his presence was enough to force understanding on her: that his bravado was fuelled by his insecurities and aspirations, that he masturbated nightly and with self-loathing, that he despised his parents and longed in vain for the least sign of love from them. That the way he treated her was the sum and total of all of this and more.

She knew exactly what the situation was.

Dear God, she prayed, let it be that I won't have this kind of understanding when I reach the top. Or else make it so that situations won't be so painful up there, that knowledge won't hurt like this, that horrible secrets won't lie under the most innocent word.

They carried their wooden burden upwards, back towards the world.